GlitterStrip

It's All Smoke and Mirrors

P G Robertson

Contents

Dedication   1

Prologue   2

1. The Gloss Fades   4

2. Mullumbimby Revival   11

3. SACC   18

4. Sydney   21

5. The Hearing   25

6. Major Crimes   31

7. Leaving Town   35

8. Gold Coast   40

9. Briefing   44

10. Backwater   50

11. Unpacking   55

12. First Surf   59

13. A Tidy Sum   64

14. Goon Squad   72

15. The Tempest   78

16. Super Sunday   84

17. The Chairman   90

18. Seaview 97

19. Odds and Ends 103

20. Brett Tompkins 109

21. Shadows 115

22. In the Job 120

23. Triangles 125

24. GlitterStrip 131

25. Supply 136

26. Click & Collect 141

27. BBQ 145

28. Sprung 149

29. What Next? 155

30. Dealing 160

31. Reunion 166

32. Patterns 170

33. Imports 176

34. High Profile 180

35. Party Time 186

36. Morning After 193

37. Surveillance 197

38. Easy 200

39. Wet Wednesday 205

40. Quarantine 210

41. Compartments 216

42. Briggs 221

43. Cronin   226

44. Mount Nathan   231

45. Collapse   235

Epilogue   239

Author's Note   248

So Many to Thank   249

Surfing Terminology & Australian-isms   250

I dedicate this book to my mother, a woman of considerable talents and achievements. Some small fraction of her formidable artistic abilities must have rubbed off somehow!

Prologue

I t was a beautiful place—if that was your thing. The dusty crushed-granite road wound its way between large eucalypt trees that stretched across the road. It was approaching midday, and the shadows cast by the trees made it difficult to spot the worst of the relentless corrugations. The car vainly ducked and weaved before it shuddered to a sudden stop.

The two men had driven from Sydney and it was almost disturbing, the quiet that greeted them as they exited their car—depressing, even. As soon as the dust settled, a squadron of flies descended, seemingly onto them in an instant, vying to enter every available orifice. A more desperate and godforsaken place the men had never visited.

One of the men looked down at his phone before speaking. 'This is the spot—according to the GPS coordinates we've been given. I wish we knew what we're looking for.' The loose plan, it seemed, going by the hand gestures, was best summarised as 'you look over that way and I'll look over this way'. This was a solid plan, considering the broad nature of the job they were tasked with.

Less than ten minutes had passed before one of them shouted out that he had found something. 'Bring the shovel,' he yelled to his mate, signalling that digging was involved, although who would do the digging was not clear. The tone of the man doing the yelling inferred that this would not be him, seeing as he'd done the finding.

It wasn't as big a job as feared. The digging man didn't want to get all sweaty. It was hot, being the middle of the day, even though summer was some way away. There had been no rain for months now and the soil was dry and dusty. He only needed to make a few digs before he hit something solid. 'It could be anything,' said the man holding the shovel before he carefully scraped away some of the loosely packed soil. Finding some purchase, he pressed down on the handle and levered up what he'd found.

It's quite a good preserver; dry, dusty soil in the bush. The tattooed arm that emerged from the ground was in remarkably good shape, all things considered. Male, most likely. The two men looked at each other, not particularly surprised by this development. This was part of the job, after all.

The man with the shovel scraped back the disturbed soil and returned the ground to normal—if by normal you meant ground that had an unnamed body buried in it. The man not wielding a shovel pulled out his mobile phone, pleased to find that he had mobile reception. There weren't many places so godforsaken that one couldn't make a phone call.

'It's me. It's a body. Looks male to me. You'd better get a team out to do it properly.'

Which was a rather offhanded way of saying that this was now a murder site.

Chapter 1

The Gloss Fades

I n one deep recess of her mind or another, Detective Angela Watson, Ange to everyone she knew, could feel the seeds of discontent taking hold. Sort of like when you feel a faint tickle niggling the back of your throat, hoping that you might be thirsty, knowing that a cold or flu is taking hold. She still loved Byron Bay, with its relaxed morning vibe as people sought their coffee fix, the smattering of indie-cool shops and edgy restaurants that persisted against a mainstream incursion, the energy that would pulse though the town on Friday and Saturday nights as people came together to find music or each other. Not to mention the fantastic waves—the region being a genuine surfing mecca.

However, little things were grating on her. Things like the increasingly common traffic jams that prevented her from getting to work on time, or that finding a convenient parking spot in the main street had become almost impossible. Her landlord had put up the rent, citing a strong demand for rental properties. She knew this would be true, as the region had been experiencing rapid growth on account of the Covid exodus from the big cities.

Byron Bay was bursting at the seams and tension-infused incidents belched to the surface daily. Road rage in Byron Bay was now a thing—who would have thought. A parochial disdain for outsiders and otherworldly views was also annoying, to say the least. Vaccination mandates and concerns over human rights had been keeping Ange busy, where divergent beliefs were flashpoints for aggression and violence. Frankly, Ange struggled to fathom which side was impinging on the rights of the other. It was hard to tell sometimes.

The town had changed more in the past two years than almost any time in history, trying to absorb an unprecedented influx of people seeking a different lifestyle. In Ange's eyes, their decisions to move to Byron were often fuelled by a glossy magazine perception of how the perfect life might be. Perhaps a move to Byron would magically transform them into relaxed bohemians, or that surrounding themselves with frangipanis and sandalwood candles might succeed where the cosmetic industry had depressingly failed. Sadly, discovering that they were still the same people beneath proved a rude shock, obviously the failure of something or someone else.

Late leaving the office one day, Ange had offered to attend to a nuisance complaint, seeing as it was close to where she lived. The station normally sent her colleague, Constable Billy Bassett, to deal with these sorts of complaints. Billy had a way of disarming people and diffusing any tension, but he was off on training down in Sydney, and Ange wasn't the type to pull rank and avoid chipping in with the daily grind around the office. She arrived at the address noted on the report, knocking on the door to find a fifty-something woman, her resort wear somehow failing to stretch in all the right places, the stretched look on her face signalling a similar inflexibility.

'What seems to be the trouble, Mrs Taylor-Smith?' asked Ange.

'It's Taylor-Smythe,' came the terse reply.

'OK, Mrs Taylor-Smythe, what seems to be the trouble?' Ange said, putting on her most patient and understanding voice.

'It's my neighbours. They're noisy and annoying. It drives me crazy,' she retorted sharply.

'OK, can you elaborate on the noise a touch? When, where, how loud?' Ange enquired.

'Well, it's the kids, actually. They come home from school, and their *mother* lets them play in the backyard. Every afternoon. They even bring their friends over, and they make quite a racket playing in the pool. That Marco Polo game is driving me insane,' Mrs Taylor-Smythe explained, certain that she was firmly within her rights to waste Ange's time expounding the depths of her arrogance.

She then delivered the coup de grâce. 'It sends Jellybean into quite a state.'

'And who or what, may I ask, is Jellybean?' Ange asked, as calmly as she dared, lest she either laugh or cry on the spot.

'My dog, Jellybean. He's quite highly strung, and those noisy children send him into a barking frenzy,' came the sad reply.

Ange, on the other hand, could think of nothing more heart-warming and adorable than the sound of children playing happily in the backyard. It made her Saturday afternoons to hear the cheerful voices of her neighbours' kids playing in the park across the road.

'Well, Mrs Taylor-Smythe, the kids are quite within their rights, and there are no laws that I know of to prevent children from playing in their own backyard. If they start playing loudly after eleven p.m., then I can probably help you,' Ange explained, struggling to keep her annoyance at bay.

Met with a sour pinched look, Ange quickly elaborated, lest Mrs Taylor-Smythe start barking. 'However, the law around incessant barking of dogs is quite clear. You had best keep Jellybean under control, Mrs Taylor-Smythe.'

As she drove away, Ange knew that a 'let me speak to the manager' complaint would be forthcoming, one that would force Ange to waste even more time writing a report in reply.

'Where do these people get off?' she had thought at the time, flabbergasted at some people's sense of entitlement, assured as they were of their own importance. Ange could have sworn that she recognised Mrs Taylor-Smythe from when she was out exercising a few days back. Three middle-aged women, walking abreast, resplendent in designer exercise gear, had refused to budge as they'd marched towards Ange, forcing her to abandon the walking track and veer into a garden bed. It was times like this that Ange wished she could whisk out her badge and give them what for, and perhaps even charge them for being a self-entitled you-know-what. She daydreamed about this fantasy all too frequently lately.

Ange spilled her frustration out on Billy over a beer. She was forming a view on the source of this trend, where our obsession with individual rights was creating a monster, a situation where the rights of society as a collective were being held hostage to those of noisy entitled individuals. Ange was on fire, stimulated by a podcast she had recently listened to. Apparently, a woman had moved to a lovely Swiss village and immediately started a campaign to silence the church bells that resonated in the mountains, convinced that her peace and quiet was more important than those of the villagers and centuries of tradition.

Nonetheless, it was the surf that kept these niggles at bay, combined, of course, with the natural beauty of Byron Bay and the surrounding region. Since her major case in Namba Heads, Ange had been a regular visitor to the small seaside village, securing a regular's discount at the picturesque caravan park. She loved the various surf spots and was learning their nuances—when they performed best and how to ride the waves they produced. Ange often caught up with Councillor Terry Scott and his wife, Jenny, for dinner on their deck. She had developed a genuine affection for the Scotts, and they perhaps treated Ange like a long-lost daughter, their shared country roots creating a simpatico as it did.

A paddle in the surf and a couple of waves always seemed the perfect salve for the niggles and concerns of her demanding job. Her new Bell board was beautiful. The CEO, Gus Bell, son of Bobby Bell, the legendary surfer and board shaper, had recently made Ange a magnificent custom-made six-foot-one-inch JayTee swallowtail fish design. Bobby Bell himself had signed her new board, and it sported an eye-catching mural painted by a local artist. She loved riding her new pride and joy in beach breaks and punchy point waves like First Point at Namba Heads. Gus had cut her a break on the retail price, but it had still put quite a hole in her limited police salary. 'Worth every penny,' Ange would think whenever she proudly walked down into the water, protectively clutching the surfboard under her arm amidst the envious looks of her fellow surfers.

Joe Kramer had barely drawn breath after his brush with the law and the difficulties surrounding his son following the case in Namba Heads. Ange and Billy had uncovered a major drug importation ring, one that had resulted in Joe's son, Ted Kramer, being squirrelled away in witness protection. This was not something that Joe Kramer seemed to lose any sleep over. His environmental activist group, the Byron Bay Coastal Protection Society, appeared to go from strength to strength.

Ange was sitting at her desk the following week when her boss, Sergeant Jim Grady, came over, battling to suppress a mischievous smile. Ange had given him the nickname of Bosley, a private and affectionate throwback to her childhood, when she'd played Charlie's Angels with her girlfriends, racing around the family farm and fighting imaginary master criminals.

'There's a guy in at the counter who wants to make a complaint about corruption. Can you handle it, Ange?' said Bosley, his smile blossoming with each word.

The words 'hospital pass' sprang to mind. Ange replied with an overly breezy tone. 'Sure, boss, happy to,' the trailing tone of the last two words letting her boss know she was well aware of the setup. He just smiled even more—if that was possible.

She went out to the front counter and introduced herself. Well-dressed forty-something man, fashionably unshaven, longish hair, his designer glasses adding a studious touch to his carefully curated sea-change image.

'Hello, Detective. Is there somewhere we can talk in private?' he asked, failing to give his name.

'Sure. Let me see if we have a room spare,' Ange replied. She quickly checked with the duty officer, securing a room before ushering in her visitor.

'OK, what seems to be the problem, Mr...?'

'Bruce Jackman. Pleased to meet you, Detective Watson. I'm the victim of official corruption.'

Ange's ears pricked up. 'OK, give me a summary, and we can decide where to go after that.'

'I'm doing a development in Belongil Beach. It's just a small duplex project on a site that I picked up recently. Probably paid too much, but time will tell on that. Anyway, I figured it would be a straightforward little deal, in and out. Before I purchased the property, I had a pre-lodgement meeting with the Council and explained what I wanted to do. There were absolutely no red flags on their side, so I went ahead with the purchase and lodged my development application. A few weeks later, I got a call from one of the planning officers saying that they had some fresh concerns about impacts on the environment, and I would need to submit a further report advising how the proposed development addresses their issues. This news floored me, but things became worse when a group called the Byron Bay Coastal Protection Society approached me and suggested that they could assist with dealing with the Council,' explained an increasingly agitated Bruce Jackman.

'Joe Kramer,' was all Ange said, her curt reply instantly sending Mr Jackman into a frenzy.

'That's the guy. He wants to charge me six thousand dollars for a report. Do you know him?'

'On an unrelated matter,' replied Ange, hiding behind a half-truth. 'What have you done about it?'

'Well, seeing how expensive the site is, I can't afford any lengthy delays. So, I'll probably have to pay the fee.'

'Do you wish to make an official complaint?' asked Ange, not really needing any more detail. She was aware of Joe Kramer's crafty shakedown. It surprised Ange just how brazen Kramer was, given how close he had flown to the sun at Namba Heads. Brett Tompkins, someone Ange had gotten to know in Namba

Heads—gotten to know in the biblical sense, actually—had become entangled with Joe Kramer's little sting operation.

'Well,' stammered Mr Jackman. 'Not really. I was hoping you could take over and leave me out of it. This development is one of several that I have planned. I can't afford to be blackballed by the Council.'

Ange knew just how clever Joe Kramer was. His report would be somewhat legitimate and he wouldn't leave any obvious tracks. 'That makes it hard, Mr Jackman. We really need a formal complaint and a full statement from you before we can dedicate any resources to your matter.' Ange didn't wish to disclose what she already knew about Joe Kramer, given the sensitive nature of the wider on-going investigation involving Major Crimes and the narcotics importation ring.

If Ange were honest, she doubted that Bruce Jackman could have gotten out of the room any more quickly, the realities of dealing with that level of pain over $6,000 now clear to him.

As they parted company, Ange handed over her card, saying, 'If you change your mind, please make contact again.'

Back at her desk, her boss came over to see what was going on.

'Joe Kramer up to his tricks again, boss. The guy doesn't want to take it any further. Let's call it a for-your-information visit,' Ange explained, her resigned look exaggerated for her boss's benefit.

Ange had to admit that Kramer's scam was ingenious. When he could smell a moneyed developer, he would reach out and offer to help them deal with the 'environmental aspects' of their application—for a fee, of course. If the developer refused Kramer's kind offer, they could find the council suddenly turning hostile towards their project. Whether Kramer had council officers in his pocket, or whether he was living off his reputation as a feared environmental activist, or whether he was actually providing some level of legitimate service, was hard to say. There was no love lost between Ange and Kramer.

Not that Ange was always on the side of developers. The police were often called out to matters involving developers and chainsaws. 'It's better to beg forgiveness rather than ask permission' was a common excuse. In her mind, environmental activism certainly had its place in raising awareness and balancing the development juggernaut. It was the zealots that she despised, the types who believed that the end justified the means, often harnessing cancel culture to bludgeon their myopic way of thinking onto the rest of society.

The lifestyle property market was going crazy. Covid-19 seemed to have brought about a regional revolution of sorts, and there were few more glamorous and desirable regional locations than Byron Bay. Ange reasoned that Joe Kramer must be making a killing.

Chapter 2

Mullumbimby Revival

'Billy. Billy. Snap out of it. We'll be late for class,' urged the young man sitting opposite Constable Billy Bassett. 'Where have you been? Do you always daydream like this?'

'Sorry to be rude. I was off with the fairies,' replied Billy, looking up from his half-eaten sandwich.

'I hope everything is OK?' kindly asked Billy's lunchtime companion.

The fact was that things could hardly be better in Billy's life. Not only was he loving his course on cybercrime, he genuinely loved his job. He had certainly won the lottery being posted to Byron Bay, considered the most glamorous of postings by his mates from the police force academy. His workmate, Detective Ange Watson, was the colleague that everybody dreamed about. If Billy were honest with himself, he was more than a little in love with Ange, not in a dating sort of way, but in a general awe and respect way—plus, he genuinely enjoyed her company. He would never say this out loud, seeing how touchy the police service was about these sorts of things nowadays, but Billy also found Ange very attractive, in an older woman sort of way. There was no chance that Billy would allow these feelings to affect their rapport, so he imagined Ange as his favourite older sister.

Billy looked younger than he really was, which proved a challenge for maintaining a steady partner, seeing how attracted he was to intelligent and worldly women—older women like his boss. His current squeeze was a graphic designer from Melbourne, distributions from her trust fund just enough to stifle any genuine attempts to find a job. There were plenty of start-up fashion and artistic ventures in and around Byron. Many of these fledgling enterprises seemed more about finding a purpose, following one's dreams, or perhaps indulging a long-time fantasy. That was what everyone was told nowadays—'just follow your dreams'. Anyhow, most people were passing through Byron Bay on one timescale or another. Billy fully expected his designer girlfriend would flitter away in a few months, quickly replaced by a facsimile or two.

It was Ange who pushed for him to attend a month-long course in Sydney about cybercrime. The course opened Billy's eyes to a whole new world, one which operated around and underneath society. It would shock the public to learn what was going on. Many would likely switch off all their devices for fear that their lives were being stolen online. Billy learned that they probably already had been stolen, perhaps used to facilitate a scam or misdirection of some sort. The course was teaching Billy the skills needed to infiltrate these nefarious networks and fight fire with fire, cloaked by a toolbox filled with clever software, shadow VPNs, viruses and spyware. Billy and his student colleagues argued vehemently over tech stuff. There were the usual Windows versus Apple debates, which security software was the most effective, and who had the best computer setup at home. Most were avid gamers, and much of the discussion over evening drinks was about the latest and greatest game, along with strategies to best any online adversaries. This was an area where Billy felt out of place. He preferred proper games to those online. A talented tennis player, Billy had once considered pursuing a college scholarship in the USA, perhaps even turning pro after that. That was before he'd fallen in love with IT and tech. That was his actual dream—to be the maestro behind a unicorn tech start-up. Despite his deficiencies as a gamer, Billy found his course intoxicating.

One point on which his fellow cybercrime colleagues agreed was that cryptocurrency sat at the centre of a new era in criminal activity. The crazy rise in the cryptocurrency market seemed to support this new world order. In fact, much of Billy's course involved getting under the hood of how cryptocurrency and blockchain technology worked. Of course, with such a bull market, Billy had taken the plunge and invested some of his hard-earned cash. This was proving a boon. His investment had risen over twenty percent while he was on the course. It sure seemed easy money. What could go wrong?

'No, everything couldn't be better. I hope you're loving this course as much as I am,' Billy replied to the concerned question of his cybercrime colleague. 'Let's get going. I'm really looking forward to this class on the Dark Web.'

The pair stood and cleaned up the table before dropping their food scraps into a nearby rubbish bin.

'I must say, this course is making me paranoid about what's going on out there in cyberspace,' commented Billy between mouthfuls, gulping down the last of his sandwich.

'I know, but it's certainly good for our career prospects,' suggested Billy's colleague with a mischievous smile.

With Billy away on his cybercrime course in Sydney, Ange felt as if her left arm had been removed. She hadn't realised how much she relied on him during their investigations. It was like swimming in treacle, struggling to work through a case involving dodgy services being sold online, headquartered in the Byron Bay industrial estate.

It wasn't like her, but Ange was dragging her feet around the station, waiting for her erstwhile colleague to return and help deal with the technical nature of her cases. The surf had been terrible over the last couple of weeks too, which wasn't helping her mood.

Her friend Lisa had a scrumptious cake bakery, selling her products through the market circuit that operated in the region. Lisa had asked Ange to help her out at the Mullumbimby markets for a few hours, seeing as she had some family sporting duties to deal with one Saturday morning. Ange always enjoyed lending Lisa a hand, often stopping by during her weekly fruit and veg shop to facilitate a welcome comfort or coffee break. Lisa's products were amazing, selling themselves in the main to a loyal and regular clientele.

They met at 5 a.m. in Mullumbimby, where Ange and Lisa erected their modest pop-up gazebo and arranged a delicious assortment of cakes, slices, and biscuits before Lisa departed on her errands. This was torture, as Ange's stomach growled incessantly. Lisa had told her to eat as much as she wanted. Fat chance of that, seeing as Ange was having to work increasingly harder to stay trim and fit, having reached an age where this seemed an unfair burden and more effort than it should.

The drive to Mullumbimby had put Ange into a dim place for a while, seeing as this was where Joe Kramer lived, along with his Byron Bay Coastal Protection Society. Joe Kramer was proving a bit of a nemesis for Ange. She found it galling that he could continue on his merry way, shaking down property developers in plain sight.

Another developer had alleged Kramer that had certain councillors and council planning officers in his pocket. This time, Ange and her boss felt Kramer might have bitten off more than he could chew and had thrown some resources at the allegation. Andrew Harkness from Flagstone Developments was planning to build a large high-end apartment complex in a prominent location on the beach. Ange had seen the billboard erected on the site and knew that the proposed apartments would be top shelf, with a price to match. According to Andrew Harkness, Kramer was asking $50,000 for his services. The developer had told Kramer to take a running jump in the proverbial, but was now finding Council against him, a complete about-face from a few months earlier.

Kramer was one wily customer. Building any semblance of a case was proving difficult with the limited resources and powers of a local police station. Ange called Andrew Harkness into the station to meet with her and her boss.

'Mr Harkness, we've dug as much as we can, but without some sort of concrete lead, we can't really take this much further,' Ange explained.

'That's really frustrating. It really upsets me that Kramer can get away with this. He must have support in the Council. What would you have me do, pay the fifty thousand dollars and let Kramer go on to the next sucker? That's certainly the most prudent business decision, but someone must stand up to this guy,' exclaimed the exasperated Andrew Harkness.

'I know this is annoying, but no magistrate is going to sign off on a warrant needed for us to take this any further. Also, Joe Kramer's reputation precedes him, which makes it even more difficult,' said Grady, jumping in and attempting to stamp some authority on the discussion.

'Do you believe me?' asked Andrew Harkness pointedly.

'Yes, we believe you, and we realise how frustrating this is,' replied Ange before looking towards her boss, securing his nod before continuing. She explained the idea that the two of them had workshopped earlier. 'We think you should make a complaint to the Standing Anti-Corruption Commission. SACC has far greater powers than we do. You'll need to convince them of your situation, and I don't think it's a process for the faint-hearted. We feel that this may be the only viable pathway forward if you want to see this through.'

That pulled up Andrew Harkness in his tracks. He said that he would think about it and left the station with the creased brow of someone unsure of what to do, whether he wanted to pull that trigger and expose himself to all manner of unintended consequences.

The fact was that a SACC investigation reversed the onus of proof, something that Ange had mixed feelings about. On one hand, she would love those sorts of powers for investigations where she was being stonewalled by procedural realities. On the other hand, she appreciated how this could easily result in a massive overreach of powers and infringements on individual freedoms, a privilege that was often taken for granted by citizens of a free country. SACC had a reputation as a ruthless and secretive body, a law unto themselves and nobody else.

Her day at the markets had not started particularly well when an unexpected shower came across the market site, drenching the stallholders, who rushed around like jackrabbits, pulling plastic sheeting over their wares and trying to keep the windborne rain from spoiling their day. Fortunately, the squall was fleeting, and Ange saved anything from being spoiled. A couple of regulars came by, asking about Lisa, disappointed that she wasn't on duty. Lisa was a card, and the success of her flourishing business was much about her personality and ability to connect with people—not to belittle her amazing culinary talents.

A woman came by, sporting her best cat's-bum face, asking if Ange had anything that was organic.

'Everything in this stall is based on organic products and fresh ingredients where possible,' Ange replied, putting on her best and most subservient smile.

'Well, why don't you say so?' came the terse reply, the cat's bum accentuated by slitted eyes.

Ange calmly walked around to the front of the stall and pointed out the large banner that ran across the front of the display table.

ALL OUR PRODUCTS ARE PREPARED USING FRESH
& ORGANIC PRODUCE

Not a word was said as Ange walked back around behind the counter. The woman seemed completely oblivious to her own ignorance. 'Well, I'll have an orange and poppy seed cupcake, then,' she demanded.

'That will be four dollars and fifty cents, thanks,' offered Ange as she placed the cake carefully in a recycled paper bag.

'That's ridiculous,' the woman remonstrated, no doubt vying for a discount.

'Do you still want it, then?' enquired Ange, not willing to budge an inch.

'Oh, well, I suppose so. It's disgraceful. Charging that price for a tiny cupcake,' ranted the woman before she handed over her money and marched away. Ange was certain that she was heading off to meet up with Mrs Taylor-Smythe and Jellybean at the organic coffee booth.

Less than fifteen minutes later, the same woman came back.

'I didn't like your cake. I want my money back,' she demanded.

'That's not how it works. I presume that you've already eaten your cake,' Ange replied, standing her ground.

The woman hissed her number one favourite phrase towards Ange. 'That's ridiculous. This is highway robbery. If you don't give me my money back, I'll post a bad review on Facebook. Then you'll be sorry.'

Ange took a deep breath, calmly stopping herself from saying something stupid. Knowing that it was probably wrong but feeling like the woman's behaviour had crossed the line, Ange reached into her back pocket to retrieve her wallet. She flipped it open. You should have seen the woman's face as she peered into the wallet and recognised the badge for what it was, before abruptly scurrying off. Ange hoped that this might stop the woman from scamming the next stallholder. She knew this wouldn't be any permanent fix, but at least they might be safe for today.

Lisa finally returned to relieve Ange, asking her how the morning had gone.

'Do you often have trouble with people asking for their money back?' Ange asked.

'Sometimes. There's one woman who tries on all sorts of stuff. I could get annoyed, but I almost find it amusing. How some people behave makes for some great dinner conversation,' Lisa replied.

'Short, blond bob, cat's-bum face?' Ange enquired of her friend, receiving a nod of affirmation. 'I don't think you'll see much of her again.' Lisa's questioning stares went unanswered.

No sooner had they settled behind the counter than Joe Kramer swung by, ambling along with his self-assured swagger.

'Is this a change of career, Detective? The job getting too much for you?' Kramer asked, his smug smile infuriating Ange. She knew better than to bite back and went about serving an actual customer.

Kramer pressed on. 'The society has a stand here as well. If you're looking for something to do, perhaps you could come over and give us a hand? We're always looking for new members and donors.'

Ange summoned up her most withering stare, something she was quite skilled at, and saw Kramer off without saying a word. His self-righteous smirk sent Ange into a dark place, where she imagined that pesky squall reappearing and a random bolt of lightning striking Kramer down, wiping that smug smile well and truly off his face. Ange smiled briefly at that pleasant daydream, retrieving her good humour courtesy of her wacky and vivid imagination.

Despite this imagined godsend, Ange had a sinking feeling that Joe Kramer would keep up with his hustle, something that left a nasty taste in her mouth, one that even Lisa's masterful creations would not shift.

Lisa and Ange enjoyed some genuine belly laughs over lunch at the pub, embellishing the day's experiences and the behaviours of their difficult customers. Ange had spent the morning playing her favourite mind game, imagining back-stories to sit behind the faces of their sweet-toothed patrons. She had Lisa in stitches with her comical recreations. What fun!

Chapter 3

SACC

Over six months had passed since her meeting with Andrew Harkness, and nothing else had come across her desk regarding Kramer's shakedown gig. That all changed when Ange arrived at her desk to find a very official envelope addressed to her. Emblazoned across the top, in government-issue bold crimson type, were the words 'STRICTLY PRIVATE AND CONFIDENTIAL'.

The enclosed letter requested—more accurately, demanded—that Ange appear in Sydney before SACC in just on two weeks. She was being called before the Commission in relation to official corruption investigations. The letter was scant on detail, other than a list of demands and an appearance date. Apparently, even disclosing the fact that she had been called before SACC was a criminal offence, which presumably included her boss. SACC had presumably crafted the letter to intimidate the reader, and it was doing an excellent job. Ange suddenly felt guilty of some transgression or other. 'Welcome to the Star Chamber,' was her immediate thought.

She rang the contact number listed on the letter and spoke to a very officious officer.

'I presume you can read, Detective. When it says non-disclosure, that is exactly what it means—*no disclosure*,' the unnamed officer demanded in a clipped tone.

'I can't just not turn up to work to attend your hearing. How do I manage that?' asked Ange.

'You should take holiday leave if necessary. I also recommend paying your own expenses. We don't want idle office gossip leaking our investigation.'

This was freaking Ange out. 'Will I be told what this is about? Do I need a solicitor?'

'Whether you need a solicitor is a matter for yourself. And, no, you will not be told in advance as to the thrust of our enquiries. You are required to answer any question that is put to you. Any failure to do so will be an offence,' insisted the voice with no name.

Ange hung up feeling very uncomfortable. She knew that this was in relation to Joe Kramer, but exactly how she was involved was unclear. The non-disclosure put her in a tricky spot. Ange had given her commitment to Senior Detective Sally Anders from Major Crimes to remain strictly tight-lipped about the ongoing narcotics investigation. Even more difficult was that her requested leave would coincide with Billy being away competing at his beloved Country Week tennis carnival.

Her boss was not happy with her request, particularly at such short notice. He probed and pushed, trying to get Ange to change the date. Ultimately, she prevailed, citing important personal reasons and promising to keep her absence as short as possible. It was hard not being able to disclose what this was all about to someone she trusted and respected. If nothing else, she needed some reassurance and support.

As things turned out, she didn't have to worry about that. The next morning, she was called into her boss's office as soon as she arrived. He had the Sydney Morning Herald open on his desk, the smiling face of Joe Kramer just below the headline, which he read out aloud for effect. 'Byron Bay Council under fire. SACC launches corruption investigation into developer payments. Is this why you need some leave?'

'I can't comment, boss,' replied Ange, knowing that this was an answer in itself. 'Mind if I borrow your paper for a bit?'

'Leaky Boat' were another two words often associated with a SACC investigation, where the mere mention of their involvement came with assumptions of guilt.

'Sure. Just remember, I have your back if it comes to that,' he commented reassuringly, handing over his newspaper.

Ange took a walk downtown to read the article over coffee, finding a corner seat at her favourite espresso bar away from any prying eyes. Ange had to hand it to Joe Kramer. He was in his element, despite the gravity of the situation.

'This is another case of big developers and a complicit government conspiring to stifle the voice of the Byron Bay Coastal Protection Society. The environment sure needs someone to stick up for it. I'm sorry, but I'm forbidden from making any further comment,' the article read.

Joe Kramer hadn't missed the opportunity to promote his society and the prospect of the government stifling free speech. The reality was that SACC was ostensibly independent of government, but Kramer knew full well that the public wouldn't see it that way.

The next two weeks were unsettling. She almost wished that she had let sleeping dogs lie and not suggested that Andrew Harkness take his complaint to SACC. Harkness might also regret his strategy, seeing as developers were always on the wrong side of public sentiment. Joe Kramer riled Ange more than she could stomach. He needed to be stopped.

Chapter 4

Sydney

O ne thing Ange had learnt with her chosen vocation was to make some time to have fun along the way. Her job could be physically and emotionally demanding, and she knew it was important to smell the roses and embrace the good things in life. Unfortunately, she often saw the very worst of human nature, and she could see how this could easily eat away at one's mental state.

Her impending SACC appearance aside, Ange was determined that the trip would not just be about that, perhaps adversely affecting her love of Sydney. Deciding to make a long weekend of it, she caught an early Saturday flight from Ballina to Sydney. Ange hadn't been to Sydney for six months or more, and she booked a nice studio apartment in Edgecliff, just near Rushcutters Bay. As soon as she had checked into her digs, she donned her walking gear and went exploring. Ange had forgotten just how spectacular Sydney Harbour was, and it was relaxing to wander along the foreshore, through the undulating streets of Woollahra, coming across hidden pubs and shops. She stumbled across the eclectic Oxford Street markets and picked up some funky new pyjamas, not that anyone interesting ever saw her in pyjamas anymore.

That evening, she caught up with some girlfriends from university, all married with children and workaholic husbands, straining to keep up with the pace of Sydney. They met at Amy's stylish townhouse in Bronte, a premium suburb within Sydney's Eastern Suburbs, and a relatively short stroll from the beach. Ange arrived to a scene of curated madness, rambunctious kids running around the house, dodging their parents' teetering champagne flutes, a culture shock on many fronts.

As things do at Sydney dinner parties, the conversation inevitably turned to real estate and house prices. The cost of a small two-bedroom townhouse like Amy's shocked Ange, so wildly out of reach for someone on a paltry detective's salary. Given the disconcerting reason for her being in Sydney, the evening left her with pangs of regret, wondering if she had made the right decision to become a police officer instead of securing a high-paying job and going down the same road as Amy and her friends.

Despite the general sense of mayhem, she found something cosy and appealing about the life that Amy and her husband, Robbie, had carved out for their two children. This was another regret that niggled, and Ange sometimes worried that she might have missed the boat on her own chance of having a family and some version of domestic bliss. No doubt her facsimile would be more like *Malcolm in the Middle* than *Happy Days*.

She slept badly that evening, not the problem of a comfortable bed, more one of an uncomfortable mind. Waking early, Ange put on her walking gear and caught the train to Bondi Junction, the next stop east from Edgecliff. The wintry morning was keeping beachgoers in bed, tucked under their duvets, snug and insulated from their hectic weekday lives. It was a crisp, cloudless day and Ange knew the beach would fill up soon enough. There were a few surfers out, trying to catch some small waves that the ocean was offering. At one end of the beach, she could see a surf school, like the one that she had taken after moving to Byron Bay. She silently said a small prayer for them, hoping that their surfing experiences would be as wonderful as hers.

Bondi Beach was truly one of the world's iconic and spectacular beaches. After taking some coffee at one of the many cafes and espresso bars, Ange headed south along the Bondi–Bronte coastal walk, towards Bronte Beach. She walked behind the Bondi Icebergs club, where she could see the stalwarts stroking the sea-filled swimming pool. It must have been freezing cold, but that was the idea—brace yourself for the shock and get on with it, feeling like a million dollars once you stepped from the pool after your laps. Ange found it difficult to imagine that anyone could feel like a million dollars without a wetsuit on, but the outlook north from the pool was certainly a million, if not a billion-dollar view.

Heading further south, rounding Mark's Park, she came to the delightful Tamarama Beach. This pocket-sized refuge of sand housed an appropriately sized surf club, cowering against the rocks and protected from the worst the sea could offer when in its foulest moods. In summer, the golden beach would overflow with kids, all running around frenetically in their brightly coloured sun tops. Today, in the cool westerly breeze, there were only a few brave swimmers, in for a quick dip after their own walk.

She loved seeing the kids at the Byron Bay Surf Club, dashing around on summer Sunday mornings, learning about the sea. 'Nippers' seemed the cutest of names for this institution, a cute play on the ghost crabs that scuttled around in the sand. A large percentage of Australia lives pressed against the coastline, and a trip to the surf is as Australian as Vegemite. Like all surfers, Ange had huge respect for the power of the ocean and the danger of the Australian surf. Unfortunately, many visitors to the beach did not share this respect. Hopefully, what the kids learned at Nippers would prevent them from being another of the yearly drowning tragedies, where the ocean would so readily claim the unwary.

Before reaching Bronte Beach, Ange sat on the rocks to watch some anglers trying to spin up dinner, tempting gullible fish onto their bright, flashy lures. There was a large school chopping up the water just offshore, feeding on some pilchards or the like. One angler hooked a nice tailor, unmistakable as it leaped and shook, flashing silver in the sunlight and attempting to disgorge the lure, or whatever it thought was tormenting it. These gyrations proved successful, and the angler loudly and expressively berated himself for leaving too much slack line. The fish, now free of its torment, darted off to pursue another pilchard or two. Pity, it would have made a tasty meal. Tailor wasn't Ange's favourite—she preferred whiting or flathead. However, most fresh fish was nice to eat, and tailor was no exception. The angler was still mumbling and grumbling as Ange picked herself up to continue her walk.

Arriving at Bronte Beach, she could see a large group of young men and women playing touch football in the expansive park that sat just behind the beach. It looked like fun, certainly strenuous enough. Some guys already had their shirts off, presumably more for the benefit of passing girls than due to heat exhaustion.

She came to the massive Waverley Cemetery, positioned on what surely ranked as one of the most expensive cemetery sites in the world. It seemed such a waste of valuable resources to have such a parcel of land dedicated to the dead, a clunky solution to the endless cycle of life and death. More ancient cultures tended towards a philosophy that we are born from the land and returned to it upon our death, certainly not to stake a personal claim on a plot of precious land in perpetuity, but to join it again. As she skirted around the rows and rows of monuments and headstones, Ange vowed she would never become a resident of any cemetery. She stopped and gazed out to sea, deciding on the spot that her ashes, when that time came, would be scattered across the ocean to merge forever with her beloved surf.

The rest of the walk was a blur, despite the spectacular scenery around her. By the time she arrived at Coogee Beach, the beach was full of living people, all seeking to harvest the insipid winter sun. Some beach volleyballers scrambled around in the sand, cheered on by a small crowd. Parents sat on the soft yellow sand as children raced around, chasing seagulls or each other. The odd, crazy person was swimming in defiance of the season. The scene had a certain softness, peaceful and gentle, perhaps not the vibrancy and energy of summer, but still an extraordinary sight.

With more day to while away, an easy bus and train journey deposited Ange to Circular Quay, where she wandered happily around The Rocks, the Sydney Opera House, and the Botanical Garden. By the end of the day, Ange realised she hadn't spent a single moment contemplating Joe Kramer and SACC. Mission accomplished. That respite was soon to come crashing down.

Chapter 5

The Hearing

Monday, the date of her appearance, finally came around. Ange was grabbing some coffee at a cosy place she had found on New South Head Road when her eye caught a newspaper left open on a bench. She spied her name in the lead article on page five.

> *Byron Bay Detective Angela Watson called to give evidence before SACC and answer questions relating to developer payments in a corruption enquiry into the Byron Bay Council.*

She was furious. The article made it look as if she was on the take. 'The enquiry was supposed to be secret, so how did the press even know that I'm appearing before the Commission?' she thought, steam coming out of her ears.

Reading further down the article, she saw the affair had also roped in Terry Scott.

> *Councillor Terry Scott has also been called before the Commission over his relationship with environmental groups dating back to the failed Tea Trees development in Namba Heads.*

Ange had gotten to like and respect Terry Scott during her time in Namba Heads, and they had become personal friends since her investigation. Terry was no shrinking violet, so Ange knew he would be apoplectic at the insinuation that he was in the pocket of environmentalists. In fact, Terry was firmly on the side of appropriate development, and eager to stimulate sensible economic growth in his small seaside town. The failed Tea Trees residential housing development in Namba Heads was the scene of Kramer's greatest victory, one that had taken Council and the developer to court and ultimately stopped the almost-completed project in its tracks, abandoned to the sandflies and the tea trees themselves. It remained a thorn in Terry's side.

Kramer was not about to miss a media opportunity, and it was Ange's strong suspicion that he had thrown her and Terry under the bus. It was a brazen move, considering that Kramer was ostensibly at the centre of the enquiry. She caught the train into Town Hall and walked over to the SACC offices in Elizabeth Street with plenty of time to dwell over her annoyance at being portrayed in the media that way. What would her friends think, those that she had just shared a meal with whilst their children played around them?

Having discharged the formalities at the front desk, Ange was ushered into a small anteroom by a stony-faced SACC officer. She waited pensively. It was a grim affair, a perfect match for Ange's grim mood. Nothing to read, not a single picture, like the prison cell that ultimately awaited some interviewees. She couldn't even do any work, as she had been required to hand over her phone on the way in.

Time dragged by interminably, well past the appearance time demanded of her. This was perhaps a ploy of intimidation, letting the victim stew in their own juices, allowing their doubts and misgivings to eat away at their self-assurance. If Ange was honest, it was a game she had played herself many times.

Finally, a suited and bespectacled man came through the door. 'Are you Detective Angela Watson?'

Ange remained silent, delivering the man a short sharp nod in reply.

'Follow me,' said the blank-faced man, evidently having failed Secrets of Being a Good Host 101.

The room contained fewer people than Ange had imagined. Two women and one man sat behind a long desk at the front of the room, opposite the door where Ange entered. There were a few administrative staff scatted around the perimeter, and what looked to Ange like a couple of prosecutors off to one side, heads down in their papers, not bothering to look up as Ange walked in. The expressionless man motioned her towards a single chair behind a small desk. She sat down.

Ange was first informed, in no uncertain terms, that she was compelled to answer any question asked of her, truthfully and to the best of her ability. A failure to do so would result in criminal charges being laid. There were no pleasantries offered, and certainly no 'thank you for taking the time to attend our happy gathering' acknowledgements.

One prosecutor looked up from his papers. 'Detective Watson, the purpose of today is to find out what you know about the actions of a Mr Joseph Kramer, the Byron Bay Coastal Protection Society, and the Byron Shire Council. I understand from prior testimony that you handled a complaint from Mr Andrew Harkness of Flagstone Projects, levelled against Mr Kramer. Is that correct?'

'Yes,' answered Ange, the first truthful answer under her belt. That modest success did absolutely nothing to calm her nerves.

'Can you tell us what transpired as a result of that complaint?' asked the prosecutor, looking over his glasses imperiously.

'Not much, really,' replied Ange. 'We interviewed Mr Harkness and promised to look into his matter.'

'Did you? Look into the matter, that is.'

'Yes, we made some preliminary enquiries, but we couldn't uncover anything to substantiate the complaint. Mr Harkness also could not provide us with any concrete evidence to support his claim,' replied Ange.

'But surely you were suspicious? After all, fifty thousand dollars is a lot of money for a simple report,' the prosecutor shot back.

'Yes, I was suspicious, but I don't know what sort of fees consultants charge for a large and prestigious development like Mr Harkness was proposing. I'm sure that the legal fees on the project would be many times that,' countered Ange, developing a smidgen of confidence with each question.

'You see, Detective, I'm trying to work out why you didn't fully investigate this complaint.'

'There was nowhere to go. There was certainly no evidence sufficient to secure a court order from a magistrate, something that would have allowed us to obtain copies of phone records or bank accounts. Police officers like us need to show some hard evidence to cause a magistrate to sign such a request. That's why I suggested he contact SACC if he wanted to pursue the matter, as I understand that you're not bound by such procedural annoyances,' answered Ange, her hackles rising.

'OK, Detective. Was this the only time you had fielded a complaint about Mr

Kramer in relation to development matters and the Council?'

This was the line of questioning that Ange had feared. She didn't wish to jeopardise the covert investigation underway with Major Crimes, nor get Brett Tompkins involved. Unfortunately, she was bound to answer any question levelled at her, and she had no intention of being charged on account of Joe Kramer and his activities.

'No,' she answered truthfully. 'A few months before, a small developer had come in with a similar complaint. He had even less to go on than Mr Harkness. Plus, he didn't want to be identified or take the matter further.'

'Why was that, Detective?'

'He was afraid of repercussions from Council and further delays on future projects. I asked him to think it over and come back if he wanted to pursue the matter, but I never heard from him again,' answered Ange, trying to look the prosecutor in the eyes, despite him not bothering to look up from his papers.

'Convenient,' said the prosecutor in a supercilious tone of voice, as if Ange's reply had confirmed some secret suspicion. He suddenly changed tack. 'Did you see today's paper, Detective?'

Ange nodded her response.

'Any ideas on how that story made it in the news, by any chance? You know that you're required to keep your appearance today secret.'

Ange was furious at being so flatly accused. 'That's absurd. What conceivable motive would I have to leak your investigation to the press? I assumed that this was Mr Kramer playing games and garnering publicity, or the rumours are true and SACC leaks like a sieve.'

Ange regretted those words as soon as they escaped her mouth, upset at herself for being so easily baited. She stared at the prosecutor, willing him to look her in the eyes. An uneasy moment of silence ensued, save for one woman at the head table coughing self-consciously into her elbow.

Not at all put off by Ange's brazen accusation, the prosecutor pushed on. 'I put it to you, Detective, that you were running interference for Mr Kramer, making sure nothing came of any complaints levelled against him,' said the persecutor, now fixing Ange in a penetrating stare.

'What nonsense. I have absolutely no love for Mr Kramer, and I would dearly love for SACC, with all your expansive investigative powers, to bring a stop to his little games. However, I gather that the reason that I'm here wasting my time is that you've assembled no more evidence than I did. Am I correct?'

'Please leave the questions to me, Detective,' replied the prosecutor quickly, shifting his gaze back down towards his desk and shuffling those damned papers, giving Ange the distinct impression that she was spot on. He looked at his colleagues.

'Are there any further questions for the witness?'

Ange was relieved when this question met a stony silence. She was sweating profusely about the prospect of a follow-up question and whether she had been involved in any other matters involving Joe Kramer. She was also worried that her brain snap might elicit a reprisal of some sort from the prosecutor.

'That will be all, Detective. We will be in contact if we need anything further from you. May I remind you that you must keep today's discussion strictly confidential,' said the woman sitting in the centre of the table in front of her, blithely ignoring Ange's indictment of a few moments ago. Ange's hackles rose, but she held herself in check this time. Evidently, the prosecutor had far more important matters amongst his papers than to acknowledge her.

She excused herself from the chamber, trembling with part relief and part indignation. Had she not wanted to escape that circus, she would have taken the woman to task over the thinly veiled accusation that Ange had acted indiscreetly. However, by far the most disturbing part of her appearance was the realisation that Joe Kramer would soon be off scot-free.

She couldn't shake the lingering impression that she was still somehow under suspicion, furious that Joe Kramer had pulled her into his clutches, as he had done to Brett Tompkins. A glass of wine was in order, so she rang one of her friends who worked in the city and arranged to meet for a drink at 5 p.m. In the meantime, some retail therapy might take her mind off things—and what better place than Sydney?

Ange was just into her second purchase along Pitt Street when her phone rang. It was one of those annoying Unidentified Caller types. Billy had filled her in on how to handle these.

'Once you answer, if there's silence on the other end of the call, quickly hang up. The scammers and telemarketers are using computer dialling from contacts lists they've purchased. Once the computer detects a human voice, it quickly transfers to a bank of waiting telephonists, their sales spiel at the ready. You need to hang up straight away. If the caller is legitimate, then they'll ring back. If not, the computer will have already moved on from you to the next victim,' Billy had explained. 'Also, never answer with your name. Scammers record your voice and use it for identity theft.' Billy loved all that stuff.

However, of late, Ange had noticed that the spammers and scammers were hijacking legitimate numbers to counter the many potential victims who were ignoring Unidentified Callers.

'Hello,' answered Ange tentatively, finger hovering near the hang-up icon on her phone and ready to ditch the call in a second.

'Hello, Detective Watson. It's Sally Anders here,' came the surprising reply.

'Oh. Hello, Detective Anders. How can I help you?' answered Ange.

It surprised Ange that Detective Sally Anders from Major Crimes would contact her out of the blue like this, and at such an inopportune moment. They hadn't spoken since their discussion at the Bangalow markets, where Anders had strongly advised Ange to leave the investigation involving a narcotics importation ring well and truly alone. That was hard, seeing as Ange had broken the case wide open during her investigation into the disappearance of Jake Thompson, the missing surfer. Ange had given her assurances to Anders and been true to her word ever since.

'I gather that you've had some fun and games today. I presume Joe Kramer may not be on this year's Christmas card list,' answered Sally Anders.

Ange didn't reply to this statement of fact.

'I'm pleased that you didn't disclose any information regarding the investigation today. That was well done,' continued Sally Anders.

'How on earth did you know that? I thought they held these interviews in the utmost secrecy,' queried Ange.

'We cross paths with SACC often enough,' offered Anders, not really any answer to Ange's question. 'Anyhow, do you have time to pop around to our office for a chat this afternoon? I'm sure you know where we're located, just off Bathurst Street. Come to the eleventh floor and ask for me,' asked Anders, more of a demand than a question.

'OK, see you soon. My credit card will thank you,' laughed Ange. She liked Sally Anders, despite her being such an intimidating woman. She picked up her shopping bags and headed towards Bathurst Street, curious about what Sally Anders might wish to see her about.

Chapter 6

Major Crimes

Arriving twenty minutes later at the Bathurst Street building, Ange eventually worked out how the newfangled lifts worked, and 'Carriage G' deposited her directly to the eleventh floor. Her confidence had taken a battering and she felt like a country hick.

Senior Detective Sally Anders came out to greet her. After dispensing with the pleasantries, the pair walked to a small meeting room directly off the foyer.

'Once again, well done with your discretion over our operation,' said Anders.

'I sure was sweating on a dreaded follow-up question, which might have put me in a terrible position. I get the feeling that they don't have much to go on. I hope I wasn't too harsh. I lost my cool at one point,' replied Ange, still upset with herself for that brain snap.

'I think you're right about the evidence, but I think the occasional strategically placed tantrum can work wonders. Your friend Councillor Terry Scott sure lost his cool. He straight out accused SACC of leaking his name to the press and throwing him to the dogs just because their investigation was failing. Apparently, he even accused them of bureaucratic incompetence, likening SACC to the KGB,' commented Anders, unable to suppress the small smile that crept into the side of her mouth.

Ange also smiled at the mental image of Terry Scott in full flight and knew that his fuse was short in such matters.

'It is a pity. I would have liked to see Joe Kramer stopped in his tracks,' commented Ange with a resigned look.

'SACC does plenty of good work, but they're also often used as an expedient attack dog, whose mere presence serves its own purpose. They can be a bit of a blunt instrument. I presume it was your suggestion for the aggrieved developer to approach SACC?'

'And look where that got me,' replied Ange, sarcastically confirming the allegation that Sally Anders had levelled at her. With the benefit of 20/20 hindsight, Ange silently reproached herself for stooping to that level. It had been an error of judgement that she was unlikely to make again.

'Personally, I don't think that they'll get anywhere with Joe Kramer, but perhaps I can make a call to one of my contacts over at the Taxation Office. We often work with them on financial crimes and they aren't above taking on a crusade or two. They might keep Kramer occupied for a while,' offered Anders.

'That cheers me up. Being called out to justify the tax-free status of his society might force Kramer to pull his head in. He's a smart guy and I guess he does some good work, but he's also righteous and arrogant, so he surely must have slipped up somewhere or other,' replied Ange, happy that Joe Kramer's troubles might not yet be over.

'Anyway, I wanted to ask if you would be interested in working with Major Crimes for a while?' asked Anders, finally getting to the point of their meeting. 'It would be on secondment from Byron Bay. I have already spoken to your boss, and he was very supportive.'

Ange thought that this was typical of Bosley, always pushing his staff forward in their careers.

'Sounds interesting. Would I need to move to Sydney?' she asked, the earnest look in her eyes betraying her intrigue at this prospect.

'Well, no. You might remember that we have a joint operation underway involving the New South Wales, Queensland and Federal Police services. We've been pursuing the narcotics syndicate you stumbled across. One trail that we've been following has led us to the Gold Coast, and it would be good to have someone on the ground who's not mixed up with the local police. Also, the recent press you've received may even be used to our advantage if we play our cards correctly,' explained Anders.

'So, would I be undercover or what?'

'Not really undercover, more off-grid. I think we can take advantage of the SACC publicity to build a story that you might be a police officer on the fringe. Internally, we could pass off your move as taking some time off for *personal reasons*, which people will interpret however they want. The syndicate seems to be one step ahead, and I'm concerned that we have a leak somewhere in the service, perhaps even here at Major Crimes. My plan is to keep you off the radar and operating independently. It also won't hurt that you're a surfer, as this should help you fit in with the Gold Coast scene. You'll have to play your part and resist any temptation to disclose to friends and colleagues that you're working for me. One never knows who has eyes and ears,' said Anders. She looked Ange squarely in the eyes and realised that she was close to having Ange on the hook.

'How long would I be working on the Gold Coast? What would I do with my apartment and all my gear?' asked Ange, thinking through some of the mundane practicalities of life.

'I expect you'll be there for at least six months. We'd put you up somewhere suitable. You can keep your apartment in Byron if you must, but it would be better if you moved out properly. The sooner, the better, really.'

'I'll need administrative support. What about Billy, my colleague at the Byron Bay station? He is a whizz with IT, and he just completed a course on cybercrime. We work really well together,' asked Ange, wondering how Anders knew about her love of surfing. Perhaps Bosley had told her.

'I like that idea. I'll speak to your boss about that as well,' replied Anders. 'What do you say? Do you need time to think about it?'

Ange looked directly at Anders whilst she quickly thought through the implications. Anders was not someone to trifle with, and Ange suspected that this was a one-time offer. Her heart was racing at the prospect of getting deep into an investigation, perhaps finally being able to wrap up the Namba Heads case.

It would be difficult letting some of her colleagues think she might be a dodgy cop. At least Billy and her boss, the people at the station whose opinions she valued the most, would know the actual story. She would have to disengage from her Byron friends, for a while at least. What about her Sydney friends, those who'd read this morning's paper? Some would think the worst. Others, the friends who knew her best, would probably think that she was an innocent victim, bludgeoned by bureaucracy. SACC investigations commonly blazed a wide path of destruction, after all.

These thoughts raced frenetically around Ange's mind whilst Anders waited for an answer, not breaking gaze for a second. Fresh doubts started knocking loudly at the door, trying to be heard. The faces of Gus Bell and Terry Scott flashed through her mind's eye. The longer she hesitated, the more these doubts would eat away at the excitement and self-assurance she felt in her heart.

'I'm in,' replied Ange decisively. 'When do you want me to start?'

'Excellent. I'll get the process rolling and start work developing your backstory. We can begin planning for you to move to the Gold Coast. Let's work towards a start date in two weeks' time. That should give you time to transfer any active cases and pack up your things?'

'OK, I should be able to manage all of that,' replied Ange. Anders had grossly overestimated the extent of Ange's 'things'. She wasn't much of a hoarder, other than surfboards and old wetsuits, of course.

'Great. I'll be in touch,' said Anders, signalling the end of their meeting. The woman was all business, something that gave Ange confidence in the proposed arrangements. Sally Anders didn't strike her as someone who left any loose ends.

Ange walked from the office in a daze, amazed at how her life had changed in an instant. She knew Anders had gifted her a massive opportunity. Her heightened sense of worth and excitement about where her life was going was certainly a far cry from her morning's distress.

Even the next day's newspaper couldn't dampen her spirits. Never one to miss an opportunity, Joe Kramer had taken full advantage of the free press, courtesy of SACC.

'It is critical that organisations like the Byron Bay Coastal Protection Society are here to keep developers, big business, and complicit government in check.'

A large colour photo of a resolute Joe Kramer sat beneath his damning quote. Donations would be forthcoming.

Chapter 7

Leaving Town

A rriving back at the office was a bittersweet moment for Ange. Although she was excited by the prospects ahead, leaving the station and Byron Bay would be tough. Technically on secondment, Ange knew deep down that she was unlikely to return. There were lots of significant memories associated with her time at Byron Bay.

Although she arrived quite early, the station was abuzz with action. Some of her colleagues were on their phones, others were staring intently at their computer screens. There was always something going on in a busy station like Byron Bay; drama and energy impregnated the walls, a tinge of misery and despair infused into the skirting boards. She had no sooner sat down at her desk when her boss called her and Billy into his office.

'I'm supposed to appear unhappy with you, but congratulations on your new job with Major Crimes. We will miss you here at the station, but it seems like a terrific opportunity,' said Grady, keeping a grim face despite his smiling eyes.

'Thanks, boss,' replied Ange. 'I understand that I'm to leave the office under a cloud, but how do you plan to handle Billy's exit?'

'Anders and I felt we don't need to make Billy out as being mixed up in your fracas with SACC, so we thought he could ostensibly be doing further training. Billy, Sally Anders wants you to start in Sydney and learn your way around the office. I looked over your caseload and I can't see any reason not to start on Monday. That will leave the weekend for you to pack up and get down to Sydney.'

'Suits me,' replied Billy. 'Happy to start as soon as possible.'

'Major Crimes will organise accommodation in Sydney, so you can leave your flat as is, for the time being at least. I'll let Anders know and they can organise your travel arrangements directly,' said Grady, waiting to secure nods from Billy and Ange before continuing.

'OK. I'll let everyone know at tomorrow's staff meeting that you aced your last course, and that you're off to undertake advanced training in Sydney. How about you head back to your desk now, Billy, but just leave the door slightly ajar on your way out? Ange, you and I can make a bit of a show today and work towards a final dust-up at the end of the week.'

Ange nodded in agreement and Billy walked from the office, making a sloppy job of shutting the door. He looked around the office, noting how interested everyone was in these proceedings. One officer looked up from his computer screen and glanced at Billy, then looked at the partly open door, wondering if Billy had intentionally left this ajar for their benefit.

Raising his voice, Grady kicked off their prearranged charade, his authoritative voice now reverberating about the station. 'I cannot tell you how disappointed I am in you, Detective Watson. I trusted you. You should have disclosed what was going on. I think it's time you reconsidered your future as a police officer, but it certainly won't be here in Byron Bay if I have anything to say about it. Get out of here!'

Ange tried to look defiant as she walked back to her desk. She could feel the eyes of her colleagues, pondering the implications of their pantomime. Oddly, she felt pangs of guilt, which was ridiculous in the circumstances. She had never considered herself worried or needy about the opinion of others. It surprised and alarmed her to feel this way.

Ange made a show of stacking the files on her desk before walking out of the station, looking dejected. That wasn't difficult, as the ruse was proving harder to pull off than she had imagined; now she was worried about her ability to maintain the persona of a cop with a questionable history.

She went for a walk along her beloved foreshore, trying to rid herself of these doubts and misgivings. The surf was a mere ripple, and the bay was at its spectacular best. The last of the morning's ocean swimmers were just finishing up and towelling off on the beach, chatting about their swim and their plans for the day ahead. Uncharacteristically, the scene was doing nothing to calm her nerves. She needed to stay active and started packing up.

The office supplies company was over in the industrial park, so she walked back to the station to retrieve her car and make the short drive. She swung into the car park at Bell Surfboards for some coffee and to drool over their beautiful creations. Not so much a diamonds girl, Ange had a weakness for surfboards instead.

As she sat down to drink her coffee, Gus Bell came down from his office on the mezzanine level.

'Hi, Ange. Seems like you had a tough time in Sydney over the matter with Joe Kramer. Are you OK?' asked Gus.

They had become firm friends after the Namba Heads case, and Ange had even wondered if something more might develop. This was going to be hard.

'Yes, it wasn't good, Gus. Actually, I'm leaving Byron Bay,' came Ange's clipped reply. She didn't trust herself to get into any great detail. Gus looked at her strangely and Ange immediately felt her stomach churn. She liked Gus and felt terrible that he might think less of her.

'Oh,' said Gus Bell. 'When do you leave? We'll miss you around here.'

'In the next couple of days,' replied Ange offhandedly, trying hard to act nonchalant but feeling anything but.

An uncomfortable couple of moments crawled by. Caught flat-footed, Ange was unsure of what else to say. Gus Bell eventually broke the strained silence to put them both out of their misery. 'Well, pop in and say goodbye before you leave.'

It was excruciating, not knowing whether to enact their usual peck on the cheek. Shaking hands would have been even weirder. Gus turned awkwardly and walked back towards his office. At one point he turned, as if to say something, but abandoned the move, plainly perplexed by what the heck was going on. Ange quickly finished her coffee and left, feeling dreadful, her mind filled with misgivings and regret about her decision. She also doubted her aptitude for clandestine work, pretending to be someone she wasn't.

She drove over to the office supplies outlet in a daze, picking out half a dozen large packing cartons, some bubble wrap, and packing tape. She added one of those ubiquitous filing boxes, one like the ill-fated Lehman Brothers employees used during the GFC as the company collapsed around them. Ange spent the rest of the day packing up her flat.

Sally Anders called late that afternoon, getting straight down to business. 'I hear that you've already made arrangements to leave the station,' commented her new boss.

'Yes, I can't bear to hang around, so I guess I'll pack up my desk tomorrow after we complete our little office pantomime. I've almost finished packing up my flat and already given notice, but I still have the flat for two weeks. Will you organise to have my gear collected and moved?' enquired Ange.

'That's all good. You'll need to leave your work car at the station. We'll organise a replacement when you get to the Gold Coast. How about I get someone to swing around your flat at 2 p.m. tomorrow and pick you up? You can give them the key. Pack enough gear for a couple of days and I'll arrange for a removal truck to pick up the rest of your things. We can catch up for a briefing as soon as you arrive at the Gold Coast. See you then, Detective,' replied Anders as she hung up from their call, small talk clearly not her strong suit.

Ange wandered down to her Vietnamese hole-in-the-wall for some comfort food before swinging by the pub for a glass of wine. As she sat there on her own, she felt a deep sense of loneliness and detachment, suddenly an interloper in her hometown. She gulped down her drink, eager to get out of there. It proved a restless night, the last in her cosy flat, nestled at the back of the town that she had grown to love so much. Memories swam in endless circles as she stared up at the ceiling.

She awoke early, hoping that the surf might have improved. Unfortunately, it was even smaller than yesterday if that were possible, rippled by an early-morning north-easterly that promised to strengthen during the day. She drove around all the most likely surf spots, walking hopefully down to the beach, only to be met by the resigned faces of other disappointed surfers as they passed. The best she could manage was a swim at Wategos Beach. As Ange walked down to the water's edge, she looked north across the bay, taking in the magnificent view, the sun glistening off the textured ocean. This breathtaking sight only added to her sense of melancholy.

Wanting to get her last performance over and done with, she arrived at the office mid-morning, discreetly placing her now-folded filing box under her desk before walking over to Grady's office. They put on quite a show, pointing at each other and putting on their best angry faces. After only a couple of minutes, Ange marched from her boss's office, slamming the door shut behind her. She could see everyone in the station looking at her as she filled the filing box with her personal items. Leaving her car keys prominently displayed in the centre of her empty desk, she walked from the station without so much as a goodbye. It felt like a scene from a UK crime series, herself a B-grade actor, the telltale filing box a conspicuous badge of disgrace.

She endured a sombre walk of imagined shame through town, before arriving at her flat. Opening the door, she placed the filing box on the living room floor, joining the packing cartons to complete the picture of abandonment. She simply could not get the mournful melody of the Beatles hit 'She's Leaving Home' out of her head. Her flat was indeed no longer her home. Ange could feel herself sliding into a deep depression.

She was about to head back to town for some sushi when there was a knock at the door. It was Jim Grady. He quickly closed the door and gave Ange a big hug. 'I know it was all a show, but I didn't want you to leave like that. I wanted to tell you how proud I am of you and to give you a proper goodbye,' he said.

Ange broke down, a sudden outpouring of all her doubts and fears as she cried on his shoulder. 'I'm not sure I'm up for this, boss,' she sobbed.

'Ange, you just don't realise how good you really are at this job. Give yourself some time and I'm sure you'll be fine,' he said in his most soothing voice. 'Keep in touch when all this is done. You're always welcome here at Byron Bay, but I know that you're off to bigger and brighter things. Good luck.'

With that, he left her flat, not knowing just how much the gesture had meant to Ange. Her sense of self-worth was rekindled and she walked back through town with her head held high, excited about the next chapter in her life.

Chapter 8

Gold Coast

B ang on 2 p.m., Ange responded to the knock at her door. Her chauffeur waited outside while she threw her favourite handbag over one shoulder and a duffel bag containing some clothes over the other. She reflexively searched for her detective's badge before walking out the door, realising with a start that it was back at the station—for good. To this point, Ange hadn't considered how integral that shiny metal badge had become to her character, and she felt almost naked without it.

Her driver was hardly a barrel of laughs, impassively opening the car door for Ange without so much as a peep, suggesting that the trip north to the Gold Coast would not come with any commentary or tourist info. The hour-and-a-half drive was a blur, a daze of doubts and regrets. Underneath these fears, Ange still felt excitement bubbling, particularly when she had no clue about her destination.

As the pair drove across the Tweed River, the level of development intensified. To the right, Ange could see the high-rises of Coolangatta and Kirra, home to two of Australia's most iconic surf breaks. Ange had surfed them a few times, but never at their best. Both breaks became absurdly busy when they were on, surfers coming from everywhere to snag a piece of the action.

Her ride kept to the highway, before taking the Broadbeach exit and heading east towards the cluster of skyscrapers that defined Surfers Paradise. This incredible density seemed incongruous to Ange, seeing as 'Surfers' was perched on the edge of the ocean and a spectacular stretch of beach. Turning west before they reached the beach, the car wound its way through the back streets, before coming to rest outside a seventies-looking low-set home, its bland double carport imitating any number of suburban houses in any number of suburban cul-de-sacs.

The ride apparently over, Ange retrieved her bags and was met by a smiling Sally Anders. The Gold Coast even had its effect on Anders, and she was wearing some stylish linen slacks under a loose-fitting blouse, looking almost touristy.

'Bang on time,' greeted Anders. 'Let me show you your new digs.'

Anders opened the door and led Ange into the house. 'Wow!' was all Ange could muster.

The boring and nondescript street frontage gave no clue what lay beyond. It was spectacular. It was as if Ange had walked into a scene from *Miami Vice*. The house looked straight across a wide stretch of the Nerang River towards Surfers Paradise, the sparking waterway alive with speedboats, jet skis, and tourist barges.

Before Ange could pick her jaw up off the floor, Anders explained. 'The house was confiscated under the proceeds of crime legislation. Some guy had an investment company that was really a pyramid scheme. Our Queensland colleagues caught up with him before he skipped town—heading for a tax haven somewhere, I understand. I convinced them we should make use of it for a while. What do you think?'

'What do you reckon?' replied Ange. 'My normal life will seem pretty drab after this place.'

'We didn't think that it would hurt your new persona to be so obviously living beyond the means of a former police officer,' Anders said as she turned and led Ange into the garage, handing over a set of keys to a relatively new VW Tiguan SUV along the way. 'This should be able to hold your surfboards.'

Ange felt she should be able to manage, still reeling from the view from her new kitchen.

'How about I leave you to get settled and find your way around? I'll brief you tomorrow. Your things should be delivered in the morning sometime. I have a spare key and I'll make sure someone is here to take delivery. How about you come to my apartment over in Surfers tomorrow around 10 a.m.? It's not bad either—another proceeds of crime special.'

'Seems like a lot of that going around,' observed Ange as Anders handed over a slip of paper containing the address of said apartment.

'OK, then,' concluded Anders. 'See you tomorrow.'

Ange walked her to the door before heading back to that view again. The house must have been at the pinnacle of style back in the day, a perennial bachelor pad, updated and modernised by a series of owners, each in the fast lane and speeding through on the way to somewhere else. Tucked off to the right, the kitchen overlooked a rectangular pool and a covered outdoor patio, complete with tables and chairs. To the left sat a large lounge room that was adorned with a massive flat-screen TV, ironically competing for attention with the expansive view over to Surfers, a view that Australians had been watching on television for years. The bedrooms were all tucked to the rear of the house, the master bedroom the only one with any sort of aspect to the river.

As she walked around, Ange imagined all the parties that the house must have seen over the years. She couldn't help but picture these soirees as 70s-style events, with headbands, tie-dye shirts and kaftans. She doubted that alcohol was the only thing consumed along the way.

Anyhow, Ange needed to do some shopping and check out the town. After putting on some exercise gear, she worked out how her new wheels performed. 'Very nice,' she thought, following the very English accented voice on the GPS navigation towards the nearest Aldi. Ange raced around the store, picking up enough provisions for the next few days.

After dropping her groceries back at the house, she drove over to survey the coastline. Finding a parking spot along the foreshore, somewhere on the north side of Surfers Paradise itself, she saw it was low tide. Ange marvelled at the impressively wide golden sandy beach that stretched a hundred metres or more before it met the ocean. This was in stark contrast to Byron Bay, where the sand had been scoured off the beach in an incident of headland bypassing, a natural phenomenon that occurred from time to time. 'Byron Bay could do with some of this sand,' Ange thought as she marvelled at the expanse in front of her. Perhaps it had once been their sand, anyway? Exactly how and when sand moved up and down the coast was still a mystery.

A stiff north-easterly breeze had whipped up a sea of whitecaps, drowning out whatever minuscule swell lay beneath. Ange walked down onto the beach and gazed back towards the high-rise apartment buildings. She looked up at the thousands of apartments, each worth a small fortune. Many were vacant, partly because of ongoing Covid-19 border restrictions, and partly because many would be second or holiday homes. Several large cranes dotted the sky, like giant versions of their namesakes, perched on whatever spare ground remained, helping deliver yet another skyscraper.

Nearing 4:30 p.m., there were lots of people pounding the pavement. Ange felt somewhat dowdy, as there was certainly no shortage of beautiful people on the wide walking track that hugged the coastline. The shadows from the skyscrapers grew into the water as she continued to walk south, each triggering a small shiver. She reflected just how different this was to Byron Bay, without a high-rise in sight, where afternoon sunsets were a favourite, a soft light infusing the ocean with a sense of calm.

The midwinter darkness came quickly, and the haloed light from the street-lamps created a very different perspective to the relaxed coastal scene that she had enjoyed only an hour ago. Ange knew that the Gold Coast maintained a Jekyll and Hyde personality. The relaxed beachy lifestyle of the day, with its wide sunny beach dotted with sunscreen and surfboard hire booths, juxtaposed with the night-time party reputation, complete with seedy nightclubs and dingy 'massage' parlours.

Suddenly feeling cold, Ange was pleased to arrive back at her car.

Chapter 9

Briefing

Ange had trouble adjusting to her new digs and endured a restless night's sleep. She checked her personal emails on her phone first up. There were several 'missing you' missives, but also a couple of 'I can't believe that you tricked me' rants. She would need to discuss these with Anders later that day, how best to navigate the many personal relationships that she had developed in Byron over the years.

She checked the address that Anders had provided on Google Maps. Realising that it was only a short walk, she dressed comfortably and wandered that way. She needed to find a decent café, and walking always proved the best way to scope out the streets. Byron had lots of character-filled cafes and espresso bars, some tucked away in the most unlikely places. Ange had assembled a hit list of favourites, her daily choice subject to her mood and company. She was pleased to find a nice enough cafe by the waterway at the end of her new street, just beside the Chevron Island bridge. Fortunately, the coffee was also good. Ange felt that there was no excuse for serving terrible coffee, and there were no second chances given.

Feeling human again after her poor night's sleep, Ange made her way towards the beach. The swell was small, but the light wind was now out of the west, smoothing the sea into a spectacular blue-green canvas, one that stretched a full 180 degrees. The air was crystal clear, and she could see the sand-pumping station to the north and Burleigh Heads to the south, the first headland to puncture almost twenty kilometres of uninterrupted sand. There were loads of people enjoying a walk along the beach. A few anglers dotted the water's edge, holding vigil over their chosen gutter, patiently awaiting their dinner to flash by. A surf school was having a tough time finding waves, but the students still seemed to have fun.

Given that her beloved surfboards were in transit, seeing the complete absence of swell was a relief to Ange. Hopefully, her boards would arrive safely and the sea would sense her presence and lift the swell. Surfers were always hungry for waves, and there was nothing more frustrating than to watch tasty waves roll in but be unable to feast. Happy that she was not missing out, Ange wandered along the esplanade until she came to Elkhorn Avenue, turned right, and then left up Orchid Avenue, filled with an eclectic mix of restaurants, real estate agencies, nightclubs, tattoo parlours, and tee shirt and gift shops. The local police station was on the left, strategically positioned right in the thick of things.

She approached Cavill Avenue, running perpendicular to the beach and a major pedestrian thoroughfare. To this point, Ange had only ever seen Cavill Avenue in a documentary on the ABC, but it was perhaps one of the best-known avenues in the country. Gold Coast Meter Maids had once made the area famous, teetering around in their gold bikinis and high heels, coming to the aid of coin-strapped motorists. It was all a giant publicity stunt introduced by the mayor in 1967 after a cyclone had devastated tourism. The Gold Coast had always pushed boundaries.

Ange saw the apartment block Anders had noted and made her way up to the eleventh floor, apartment 119. A guy dressed in jeans and a tee shirt answered the door.

'You must be Detective Watson. Peter Fredericks, nice to meet you.'

Ange held out her hand, delivering a firm handshake, country-style. 'Call me Ange, please.'

The pair walked down the corridor to a large, expansive room filled with desks and computer screens.

'Welcome to our Gold Coast nerve centre,' said Sally Anders. 'Nice view, huh?'

Ange walked over to the balcony, enthusiastically agreeing with her new boss. This was the first time she had experienced a Gold Coast high-rise, and she could now see the appeal. It was mesmerising, watching the comings and goings of the beach. She could see a concentration of swimmers and beachgoers corralled between the red-and-yellow flags marked out by lifesavers, doing the right thing despite the benign conditions. The students from the surf school floundered, conspicuous against the turquoise splendour.

Anders snapped Ange from her reverie. 'OK, so let's get down to it. You've already met Peter—he's our operations manager, and you'll get to know each other soon enough. Peter has set you up with a new laptop with access to our intranet. Does your phone have a dual SIM?'

'I'm pretty sure it does, but I've never used that option,' answered Ange, knowing that a call to Billy would be forthcoming.

'Good. You can still use your old number, but Peter has a new SIM card for you with a new number that you can use if need be. I'll also get some identification organised for you, but it'll be best if you use that sparingly. I don't need to tell you the importance of keeping a low profile.'

'Funny, my phone suddenly stopped ringing after the SACC fiasco,' Ange commented with a grimace. She was quickly getting to learn who her real friends were.

Anders looked her squarely in the eye. 'You know you can still pull out of this. I need to know that you're committed to your new job.'

'Don't worry, I'm all in,' answered Ange with more bravado than was honestly the case.

'Great. On that point, if anyone probes what you're doing up here, I suggest you say something evasive, like corporate investigations. People will make their own assessment of whatever that means.'

'Makes sense. Any ideas on how I deal with my friends? I'm getting some tough messages after the recent press.'

'Just blame sensational journalism, creating something from nothing as they do. Your real friends will know that to be true, and hangers-on will detach and drift away.'

Ange sensed the reality of this advice. Perhaps this SACC nonsense would be a spring-clean of sorts, a convenient way to identify those friends who were keepers, and those that needed to be thrown in the trash can and discarded.

'I suggest we schedule a regular catch-up, at least until we make some serious progress. How about we meet here every Tuesday at 10 a.m., at least for the near term? Peter, could you brief Ange about what's happened since Namba Heads?'

Sally Anders had posed no genuine questions in all of that. She was undoubtedly the boss of this outfit. Peter looked up from his screen, obviously having been listening all along. 'By the way, the password on your laptop is flathead, with a capital F, a capital H, and an exclamation mark tacked onto the end. I trust you'll remember that.'

A wide smile blossomed on Ange's face. 'That's easy to remember. Also tasty.

Speaking of flathead, what happened to Darren Billings, that goose of a sergeant from Namba Heads?'

'Billings remains on a tight leash. It's clear that he was a sideshow to this operation. We've been monitoring his phone and emails, but the criminal syndicate seems to have jettisoned him. He's still gambling like crazy, clearly having learnt no lessons. He's tying up valuable resources, so we'll probably wind back our surveillance soon,' answered Anders.

'I presume you haven't charged him in case it alerts the narcotics ring?' enquired Ange

'Correct. Plus, we don't really have any concrete evidence until we get a witness. This shouldn't be hard, as criminals normally take great delight in dumping on police. However, without some hard evidence, the police service union will probably get him off with a warning.'

'The poor people of Namba Heads, having to endure Billings as their local sergeant, at least for the time being. What about Ted Kramer? Isn't he cooperating?'

'Yes, but the syndicate was operating in silos. Ted Kramer knew nothing of the help that Billings had given them. Ted Kramer is also small fry and has proven of little or no use. We have him squirrelled away in an off-grid location for the indefinite future. His girlfriend, Amy Lightfoot, was supposed to lie low, but she's a party girl, that one. Face all over social media. That nothing seems to have happened to her makes me think she's also of no interest to the syndicate.'

Ange felt a brief sting of betrayal over the mention of Amy Lightfoot. Her social media profile seemed consistent with someone who might have an affair on the side with Brett Tompkins. The shadow cast by these thoughts was not lost on Sally Anders, who waited for it to flitter by before continuing her briefing.

'The two thugs that had acted as go-between to both Kramer and Billings are here on the Gold Coast. Both have New Zealand passports, and we've made sure they won't get any exit visas. Once international borders open up, we might have more trouble keeping them here. Our theory is that the syndicate will probably give them a job to do at some stage,' explained Anders.

Fredericks chimed in, having been ostensibly working on his laptop but obviously listening the whole time. 'We identified several outfits similar to what you uncovered in Namba Heads, but the syndicate abruptly put operations on ice a few months ago.'

'Why do you think that was? Did we slip up and expose our surveillance?' questioned Ange, thinking that this was curious. She caught herself for a moment, reflecting that she was now using 'we' instead of 'you' to describe Major Crimes.

'We don't believe we slipped up, but that's always possible. However, we need to consider the real possibility that we have an informant in our midst. Hence the tight team and the whole act about you being a cop with a questionable past,' replied Anders.

'How do you know that the operation had suspended and not just moved?'

'Well, our informants on the street are telling us that the supply of cocaine has dried up over the past few months. This lines up perfectly with when the trawler operation was shelved. Fresh supply has started to trickle through, but not at any scale that would show a systemised approach. Probably more a case of market demand bringing in backyard and opportunistic operators. I'm confident that we'll know when they get their next importation and distribution system operational.'

'How long do you think the syndicate has been around?' asked Ange.

'Who knows? Maybe as much as a decade. This mob is smart and highly organised. We simply do not know who's ultimately pulling the strings,' replied Anders with a resigned look on her face.

'Has supply been interrupted like this before?'

'Great question. Yes, it has. We saw a similar situation in 2019, which we feel led to the trawler operation. We had only just started our task force then, so we figure some external event must have caused that supply disruption. Either that or internal strife. Maybe even a turf war. We have no leads on any of that.'

'OK, so what do you want me to do?' asked Ange.

'Get to know the area and keep your eyes and ears open. We really need to wait for supply to come back onto the streets before we can do all that much,' replied Anders.

'There must be something useful I can do in the meantime. I'll go crazy up here on my own.'

Anders and Fredericks looked at each other as if something was bugging them. 'Well, there is an unrelated matter that's been shoved our way. It's somewhat of a distraction from what we're trying to do. Perhaps you could have a crack at it?'

'Sure,' replied Ange, happy to have something to take her mind off the SACC matter.

No time-waster, Anders was already back on her phone, typing a message of some sort. Peter Fredericks took the cue. 'OK, how about we call it quits for now? You get your laptop set up and get settled in, while I put together a brief. I'll email it to you in the next day or so.' Fredericks paused and wrote something down on a slip of paper. 'Here's your new email address. It has the same password as your laptop. The email address and password will also get you access to our intranet. Click on the shark icon on the home screen. You'll need to change your password the first time you log in.'

Ange looked at what Fredericks had written. *AWatson@carcharias.com.au*. 'Thanks. Nice to see that you kept the name Carcharias.' Ange thought this was a clever play on words, being the Greek word for shark and a good way to describe the syndicate.

'OK, then. Catch you later.'

With that, Peter Fredericks dived back into whatever was amusing him on his laptop. Anders dismissed Ange with a weak, offhanded smile before continuing with her phone messaging. Ange was fast learning that she was not about to be mollycoddled in her new role.

Chapter 10

Backwater

Ted Kramer was not loving his new life. Being sequestered away in Nolon, somewhere in the middle of nowhere, was definitely not his style. The place was boring him stupid. Due to start work as a labourer on one of the large, irrigated farms nearby, Ted felt was certain all the chemicals that they used would poison him. 'Organic' was a swear word in Nolon, unlike his hometown of Mullumbimby, where it was sacred. Plus, Ted was also allergic to routine, and the thought of legitimate hard labour made his skin crawl.

Nolon was as dreary a town as Ted had ever visited, which was the point, he supposed. Highway running straight down the middle, also serving as the main street, the town represented little more than a three-gear-change annoyance for the truckies that barrelled through 24/7. A withered creek snaked its way around the 'premium' houses to make up the northern boundary and to the south sat a scrubby rise that the locals called Nolon Hill. Apparently, the creek flooded often—badly, by all accounts. Ted had wondered whose hare-brained idea it had been to build a town there in the first place. A smudge on a smudge on a map nobody read.

At first, Ted enjoyed the security of knowing he was away from that mess in Namba Heads. Some of his old man's cunning had been passed down the line, and Ted had been careful about what he had told those naïve idiots from Major Crimes. His ruse about being worried for his girlfriend, Amy Lightfoot, had worked a treat. That was another thing he desperately needed, some female company. Not that he was ever going to find anyone as hot as Amy Lightfoot in this godforsaken dump. Anyway, his role in the trawler operation had been minor, so he didn't consider himself to be in actual danger.

The dowdy cafe-cum-milk-bar in the main street had a pay-as-you-go internet service, chugging away through an ancient desktop PC. Ted didn't realise such a service existed anymore, other than in B-grade movie reruns. And then there were the squadrons of flies that found their way into every orifice, buzzing their way through the useless curtain of multicoloured plastic strips each time someone passed through the doorway. Ted would never get used to those flies. It was all so squalid. He shouldn't complain; at least the milk bar offered a small but glacially slow window to the real world. His own computer had been confiscated, and his police-issue mobile phone was anything but smart.

Ted had been relieved to see that Amy had been active on social media again. Given strict instructions not to contact anyone, Ted always browsed incognito. Amy Lightfoot was smoking, and she clearly wasn't missing Ted. It made his incarceration even more painful to see Amy out enjoying herself like that while Ted was rotting away in a hell called Nolon. His dad's name showed up regularly in the news. There was always some controversy surrounding his father. Joe loved publicity for his blessed Byron Bay Coastal Protection Society, whichever way it came. Nothing on his mother—she had dropped out of Ted's world the moment she'd married that smug investment banker in Brisbane.

Ted always took a moment to check out the latest cryptocurrency prices. At least that was one thing that made him feel good. Those prices were going through the roof. He had accumulated quite a nice stash of Bitcoin and Ethereum over the past couple of years. Even though Major Crimes had hoovered up everything Ted owned and pulled it apart looking for leads, they could never steal his crypto.

The seed phrase needed to access his crypto wallet was a mouthful, certainly not something even Ted could remember. Engraving it on Bluey's tag had been the idea of a genius. Squeezing all those words onto that tiny metal tag had proven an exercise in frustration. It was worth it, though. Nobody but nobody would steal his seed phrase while Bluey was on the case. He could bite.

That Bluey and the complicated seed phrase were home in Mullumbimby removed any temptation for Ted to spend his new-found wealth. At the rate his crypto was appreciating, he would soon be a rich man. Not to mention that nice collection of NFTs that his mate Tyler from Mullumbimby had recommended that Ted invest in. That stuff was weird. Some of his NFTs had quadrupled in value, yet others were going nowhere.

Tyler was his supplier and the one who had set him up in the Namba Heads operation. He had promised Ted that the job was a 'sure thing'.

'The mob I'm working for has people inserted in the police force, really high up. They'll cover your tracks. It's a sweet deal,' Tyler had told Ted when he was recruiting him. Ted should have known that a sure thing rarely is.

How Tyler knew that there were cops on the payroll wasn't something that Ted had ever dwelled upon, but it all sounded exciting, very cloak-and-dagger; not to mention how good the money on offer was, all paid in crypto, of course. Ted was one of those guys who always found himself just on the wrong side of the tracks, and those temptations easily captured his attention. A permanent job as his father's minion wasn't a long-term option. He wasn't invested in the society like his old man was.

He would have started labouring on the farm already if that bloody cattle dog hadn't bitten him. The tinpot town didn't even have a decent gym, forcing Ted to jog on the streets. He wasn't going to let his buff body go down the toilet like his life had. There he was, minding his own business, jogging quietly along one of the back streets, when the mangy mutt had rushed out of someone's yard and bitten him badly on the leg. Ted liked dogs, but the mutt had caught him by surprise. He reasoned the mongrel must have still been able to smell Bluey on him.

By the next morning, his leg had blown up and looked infected. He rang an emergency number, stored in that pathetic excuse for a phone, and was told to drive across to Griffith to visit a certain doctor. He was to use the name Gerry, Gerry with a 'G'. The voice on the other end of the call would make the appointment and text him the details. A few minutes later, his phone pinged with a time and address.

Ted went straight away, arriving in Griffith well before the time of his appointment. Despite its shady history as a key centre of the illegal drug trade and the focus of a royal commission, Griffith was now a prosperous and thoroughly legitimate town, having been transformed by modern irrigation farming technology. All the major shops were there, so Ted whiled away some time by wandering around the town centre. The Optus shop was simply too tempting. He purchased a basic burner phone with $50 prepaid call credit.

He offered the name Gerry, with a 'G', to the receptionist at the surgery. No need to show ID or produce any Medicare card; the receptionist ushered Ted straight in to see the doctor. The wound dressed and a packet of antibiotics in his pocket, Ted was soon driving back to his hole in the ground. The burner phone was literally burning a hole in his pocket. Ted wasn't back at his digs for more than thirty minutes before it was activated and ready to rumble.

He knew Tyler's number off by heart, never daring to save that sucker on his phone. Lucky for Tyler.

'Hi, Tyler. It's Ted here.'

'Where you been, mate? You just vanished. The word is that you turned witness.'

'I had a few problems with the job in Namba Heads you put me in. I'm lying low for a while. They lost interest in me because I never told them anything they didn't already know. I figure the dust has settled. You still in business? Got anything for me?' said Ted, lying through his teeth.

'Might have. Where you at? Business is pretty messed up at the moment.'

'I'm holed up in a backwater out west near Griffith. Place called Nolon. Rhymes with colon, a genuine shithole. Let me know if you think of anything. I need to get out of here. Ring me on this number. It's a burner I picked up today.'

'Will do, brother. Catch you later.'

After a few days, the antibiotics had worked their magic, and his leg was feeling good. It was time to start some light jogging. Not wanting to risk getting bitten again, he drove out of town and parked on a dirt road, one that led to a place even more out of the way than Nolon. He had to admit that it was a beautiful place to jog, so peaceful and quiet, large eucalypt trees creating a mottled canvas on the dusty track, the odd animal disturbed from its solitude—hypnotic.

Ted lost himself on that track, recalling memories of happier times, before realising that he had been jogging for over thirty minutes. By the time he had turned around and was back near the car, his leg was hurting and he was feeling average. As he limped around that last corner, he could see two guys standing beside his car. A shiver of fear ran through him. They looked strangely familiar.

'Heh, Ted. Tyler told us to come and see you. We might have a job for you,' called out the tallest of the two.

'Phew,' thought Ted, relaxing as he joined the dots of the happenstance meeting. 'Good old Tyler.'

He plodded through those last hundred metres, trying vainly to remember why the two guys looked so familiar. As the smaller man shook his hand, a debilitating pain exploded in Ted's left kidney. It was as if someone had knocked the breath from his entire body, rendering him momentarily stunned and incapacitated.

Someone grasped his forehead from behind and pulled it back in an expert move. As he reeled from the pain emanating from his abdomen, a knife slashed across Ted's neck, quickly severing his trachea and carotid arteries.

The catastrophic loss of blood flow to Ted's brain caused a rapid loss of consciousness. In those last few moments before his brain stopped functioning, he raged against the injustice of what was happening. He was on their side. Why couldn't they see that? He was one of the good guys, so to speak.

Chapter 11

Unpacking

Ange arrived back from her briefing to find that all her stuff had been delivered, piled up in the middle of the lounge room of her new home in Surfers. Suddenly keen to get settled, Ange launched into the unpacking exercise.

The house seemed well appointed, so she kept all her kitchen stuff boxed up and stacked in the garage. She pulled a few special pieces from the memorabilia box and scattered them around: a picture of her parents down on the farm near Tamworth; a surfing photo taken by her friend Kerrie at The Pass in Byron Bay; a photo of her girlfriends out on the town at The Rocks in Sydney; a cute photo that her father had taken of her and her childhood girlfriends fashioning a disco in the shearing shed, bopping to the Beatles and ABBA, making do with her father's old scratched CDs. The rest of her memories remained in the box, deposited in the garage beside the kitchen paraphernalia.

Having her life piled up on the floor like this made Ange realise just how small a footprint she left. A feeling of concern that work was too big a part of her life washed over. This was something which had been pestering her of late, that she was being consumed by her career. It was unsettling how much trouble she had in maintaining any serious relationships. Ange loved her job as a detective and it was easy to blame this as the reason. Deep down, she knew the problem was her own, but she couldn't fathom any straightforward solutions.

At one point, she had consulted a therapist in Byron Bay. Ange should have known this would be a total waste of time and money the moment she walked into the room, assaulted by what she euphemistically called Byron Bay Whale Music. Being told to 'follow your heart' simply didn't cut it when she had to deal with criminals and malcontents daily. At least she came out of those sessions smelling of some nice incense.

Worse still was her propensity for always picking the wrong guys. 'Male fails', she called them. Perhaps she subconsciously made these bad choices as a protective mechanism. Whatever was going on, Ange had trouble letting go and opening up, which wasn't a great foundation on which to build a worthwhile relationship if she was honest with herself.

Her last fling, with Brett Tompkins whilst she was on the Namba Heads case, was a good example. It was ill-considered for sure, but the thrill of that dalliance kept her awake at night, reliving their steamy night together. She was disappointed just how easily Brett had duped her, finding out by accident that he had suddenly and mysteriously skipped town without so much as a goodbye. And then there was his secret affair with Ted Kramer's girlfriend, Amy Lightfoot. What a mess.

Her new house in order, Ange pulled herself together and fired up her new laptop, spending the balance of the day finding her way around the intranet. She had access to a global email list, which was much smaller than Ange had imagined. She saw Billy included in this list, so she made him a test case for her new email address.

Hi, Billy. Hope you're settled down in Sydney. Ciao! Ange.

Within seconds, the sound of an inbound email pinged on her laptop.

Great to hear from you. You should see all the gear they have here. It's another world—like Men in Black. *This is going to be fun.*

Ange smiled at the thought of Billy ensconced in front of a stack of monitors, all alive with moving images and data feeds. The fact was that crime was increasingly moving online, and people like Billy were essential to investigations. Delving into another's virtual life and communications treads a fine line of a person's right to confidentiality and privacy, a conundrum of priorities, whether to protect an individual or the community. Whenever Ange wished for ready access to sensitive information on a case, she knew that there were good reasons to justify herself and follow due process. A new world order shaped by the fear of Covid-19 would undoubtedly test the boundaries of these competing interests.

It was Friday, so Ange reluctantly pulled herself from such serious thoughts and hatched a plan to check out the famed Gold Coast nightlife just across the river. She didn't feel like cooking and had a sudden hankering for some Japanese food. She felt certain to find remnants of the 1990s Japanese obsession with Surfers Paradise. Wearing a cotton shirt and warm jacket over jeans and sneakers, she set off just before dark, heading east towards the beach. The canvas of high-rise apartments was coming alive with pinpricks of light, scattered like fireflies amongst the towered backdrop. It was an impressive sight, building a sense of energy that radiated and reflected in the Nerang River. Crossing over the bridge into Surfers itself, she was pleased to have dressed warmly, as the cool westerly wind was being funnelled and concentrated, whipping down Elkhorn Avenue and causing Ange to wrap her jacket tightly around.

She wandered over to the esplanade. The ability to gaze over the wide-open sea was a relief from the claustrophobic forest of sorts. The buildings, now behind, were creating some respite from the westerly breeze, so she took advantage of a park bench to enjoy the last light. It was easy to miss this spectacular moment and let the cares and pressures of the day get in the way. Gazing over a calm sea, amidst clear skies and a setting sun, is one of life's most pleasurable moments, when the blues and violets gradually merge into black. To her surprise, no starry night emerged. The man-made stars on the canvas behind were simply too much for their faraway twinkles.

Ange found a nice laid-back teppanyaki bar nearby, seating herself around the square cooking station beside four rambunctious men on a golfing trip, talking loudly about their missed putts. They couldn't believe their luck when Ange sat down beside. She had fun with their teasing banter, graciously fending off their requests to head out clubbing later. She guessed she would be the subject of discussion on the first tee tomorrow. The food was delicious.

Her Japanese chef, having concluded an impressive cooking school, cleaned his hotplate and wrote '*Thank You*' upside down in salt, signalling that it was time to pay the bill. Ange clapped her hands and laughed at this cute example of Japanese politeness, the chef bowing and smiling his way to the next customer. As she found her way back onto the streets, Ange pondered the dichotomy of the Japanese, knowing the hard side to their culture that was hidden amongst such politeness.

An image of herself set in a manga comic suddenly sprang into her wacky imagination, resplendent with golden meter maids and plaid-wearing Japanese golfers, herself as a whip-wielding dominatrix. It never ceased to amaze how such absurd thoughts ever came into her being. Once a daydreamer, always a daydreamer, and Ange knew this was a habit that was unlikely to change.

The crowd thickened as she approached the heart of Surfers. It was still mid-winter, and this was a mere smidgen of the partying throng that would fill the streets come spring and into summer. It would all come to a head during Schoolies Week, where over ten thousand teenagers would spill from their overpriced apartments and overtake the streets, revelling in their freedom after the confines of school. Schoolies on the Goldie was a rite of passage for Queensland and New South Wales kids once they finished secondary school, and this annual influx of cash was big business.

Despite the chilling wind, there were still lots of people about, checking out the many bars and nightclubs, each with its own intimidating bouncers and Covid check-in police. There were some big guys on the door, not unlike those she had seen when she was a uniformed policewoman in the Western Suburbs of Sydney. The menacing frown of these bouncers seemed an incongruous statement to Ange—'Come in here and have some fun. If not, we might beat you up.'

Back at university, one of her good friends had been hospitalised by a partic-ularly aggressive goon-cum-bouncer. He had the temerity to wish to meet with his already-inside girlfriend, as they had agreed. Truth be known, he had probably had too much to drink, but he certainly hadn't deserved the beating he'd suffered. From then on, Ange made sure never to let herself go over the edge of intoxication, particularly when in such a charged environment. These streets would surely host more than their fair share of beatings come the heat of summer.

Ange didn't feel like going solo in the many bars, so she picked up a bottle of wine on her walk home. She dearly hoped to make a few friends and find someone to socialise with. Anders and Fredericks didn't seem the type to waste time on social trivialities, so Ange reasoned she would be on her own in that regard. Fortuitously, the view from her house looking back over the Nerang River at the Gold Coast light show was probably one of the best seats in town.

Chapter 12

First Surf

Ange spent Saturday giving her new home a thorough clean before visiting the ginormous Pacific Fair Shopping Centre to pick up some essentials. The surf was pitiful. She wandered over to Broadbeach and sought a restaurant for a late lunch. Unfortunately for them, none were busy, and the border situation appeared to be visibly hurting.

By the time darkness fell, Ange had her new life in some sort of order. The last job was to log the TV into her Netflix account, and she settled in to watch *Marcella*, a gritty UK crime show that she was enjoying. There was more than one similarity between Ange and Marcella, a truth of which Ange was well aware.

The knowledge that the surf was tiny and her chores were complete saw Ange sleep in longer than usual on Sunday morning. To make matters worse, the high tide was at 6 a.m., so there would be no rush even if the swell had jumped. Ever the optimist, she threw her surfboards and a 3mm full-length steamer into the VW. Covering all bases, she pulled some walking gear over her bathers and drove over to the beach. Finding a parking spot someway north of Main Beach, she made the surfer's scurry of anticipation to the top of the sand dunes, ever hopeful that the surfing gods were on her side.

There was some groundswell showing, but the westerly wind was knocking it down to nothing more than an ankle snapper, crashing almost onto the beach itself. Every so often, a larger swell would try to break out wide, but there was nothing rideable that Ange could see. The point breaks would be even worse. Resigned to a pleasant stroll, Ange headed north along the Spit, an accurate description of the 800m wide isthmus of sand that separated the surf from the Gold Coast waterways. Finding the walking track, Ange picked up the pace to get some exercise. She hit the beach at one point and continued past the sand-pumping station until the beach abruptly ended at the large rock wall which defined the Gold Coast Seaway.

She climbed up onto the wall and looked north over the wide Seaway. It surprised Ange to see a few surfers paddling across the deep blue channel to the other side, dodging speedboats and jet skis as they zipped past. The Seaway looked about 150 metres wide, but distances over water were always deceiving, so Ange knew the paddle would be at least double that. She stood and watched the paddlers for a moment, before a super-interesting boat raced by—one filled with eight surfers and their surfboards. As it reached the open sea, the boat rounded the northern rock wall and disappeared. Ten minutes later, the same boat powered back, this time empty. Something interesting was going on.

Ange pulled up a map on her phone to see that the other side of the Seaway was technically South Stradbroke Island. A quick search revealed that South Straddie was one of those mystical swell magnets, where the topography of the sea bottom, combined with things like break walls and headlands, amplified whatever swell was around. Within minutes, another boatful of surfers whizzed over to the island.

This was something that Ange needed to check out, so she jogged back to her car and drove back to the Seaway as fast as she could. Parking her car, she saw that there was a small queue of surfers lined up, all in their wetsuits and clutching their boards. Shortboards seemed preferred, and Ange was itching to get wet. After a comfort stop, she quickly wrestled on her wetsuit and waxed her board, ready to go in no time. She figured the boat ride wouldn't be a freebie, so she tucked a few notes into the zipper on her wetsuit before making a show of stretching on the grassy verge while she discretely located a suitable place to hide her keys.

Ange wandered over to join the queue behind some forty-something-year-old guys, seemingly a group of three going by the banter that she overheard. As Ange stood waiting patiently in the line, the guy immediately in front turned and spoke to her.

'Wow. That's a spectacular-looking board. Where did you get it from?'

'It's a Bell Jay Tee from Byron. The mural is from a local artist from down that way,' Ange replied.

'I haven't seen you around before. I would certainly have remembered the board.'

'Yeah, I moved here this week from Byron Bay. This is actually my first surf since arriving. I never even knew about South Straddie until this morning. I did a quick search on my phone after I saw some guys paddling across the Seaway.'

The guy glanced over at the Seaway before replying. 'You won't find me doing that. Too many bull sharks for my liking.'

'Yes, and I guess they've gotten to know that breakfast is being delivered daily,' replied Ange.

The guy grimaced at that thought. 'I've surfed all my life but never worried about sharks until a handful of few years ago. I'm not sure if there are more aggressive sharks around these days, or whether it's our obsession with negative news.'

Ange had had a similar conversation with Terry Scott when she was working on the Namba Heads case. She leaned towards Terry's point of view. 'I'm of the view that sharks are habitual and benefit from learned behaviour, and I'm not keen that they learn at my expense. They're not as cunning as crocs, but I'm certain that they learn patterns. What has been happening at Cid Harbour in the Whitsundays lately is disturbing.'

'Feel free to stick with us and we can show you the ropes. It will be small today, but South Straddie can be a real ball-breaker when there's any decent swell around,' said the guy with a broad smile, his eyes suggesting an appealing openness.

'Does it break off the rock wall?' asked Ange, thinking that the surf spot might be a tightly packed point break.

'Yes and no. The surf drops in size the closer you go to the rock wall. The real action is the beach breaks further north, which are always larger and more power-ful. There's something about this spot that breaks up the swell and concentrates it into a series of A-frame peaks. It's a tube-riding paradise when it gets overhead. South Straddie munches plenty of surfboards, so I would leave your flash board at home on those days.'

The boat came back, and it was their turn. As quickly as possible, they all jumped in the water and the driver and a deckhand helped them on board, stack-ing their surfboards on top of the bimini in a specially made rack. He admired Ange's board, glancing over at her and stating the obvious. 'That's a cool-looking board.'

Ange smiled, looking up at her prized possession. 'Unfortunately, its owner is a big disappointment.'

Once everyone was on board, the boat whizzed off as the deckie started collecting a ten-dollar note from each joyrider. Ange bent down and retrieved hers from a zippered pocket, discreetly hidden near her right ankle and once reserved for car keys before they all became so high-tech and allergic to seawater.

'It's a return ticket,' explained her new surfing buddy, the oldest of the trio of mates. 'When you're ready to go, just paddle over to a pickup stop that will form out wide.'

The boat rounded the break wall and stopped just beyond the breaking waves. As the boat glided to a stop, the deckhand scattered the boards in the water, whilst their owners jumped in and swam to collect their rides. It was then only a short paddle over to the take-off zone. The surf was barely chest-high but breaking well on the sharp banks amidst a dropping tide. Ange jumped straight onto a wave, handling herself well and smiling as she paddled back out to her new friends.

'How about we drift slowly north and see if there's a bit more size up that way?' said one of her three new mates.

'I'm Ange, by the way. Thanks for showing me the ropes.'

The guy looked around and pointed out his mates in the line-up. 'My name's Brian. That's Gav, and the old dude who's been chatting you up goes by Higgsy.'

Ange had great fun, an unexpected pleasure seeing as she hadn't considered a decent surf was possible. After a good couple of hours, Higgsy called out to say that he was pulling the pin, and the three paddled over to a gaggle of surfers sitting out wide. Ange joined them, suddenly feeling weary, exacerbated by her longish walk/jog of earlier.

As they sat waiting for their ride, Ange expressed her amazement at how punchy the waves were. Brian explained that there was another similar spot called Duranbah on the northern wall of the Tweed River. 'You can drive right up to a car park in front of the beach, so the place is crazy busy most of the time. With all the closures, I guess it's a lot quieter than usual just now, seeing as Duranbah sits just on the New South Wales side of the border. If I'm honest, I don't miss the hassling when Duranbah is working.'

Once they were safely back on the shore, Higgsy asked Ange if she wanted to join them for a late brunch. There was a spot that they always went to on Tedder Avenue that made a mean scrambled eggs and bacon wrap. It was nice, having some company to share her day with. The three guys had to dash off before long, citing pressures from wives and children. 'Our wives tolerate our Sunday surf. Saturdays are all about kids' sport, but they know how grumpy we get without our weekly fix,' said Brian with a huge grin.

'We normally have another woman in our ranks, Jen, but her husband is off on a golfing trip, so she's minding their kids today. Jen would enjoy having another woman around. She's always harping on about the lack of women surfers. Would you like me to include you in the loop?' offered Higgsy.

Ange had taken an instant liking to her new surfing buddies. Plus, it would be great to find another woman to surf with, something that she'd never enjoyed back in Byron. 'OK, sounds great,' replied Ange.

The pair traded texts, and with that, Ange became part of the crew.

'Higgsy is a wizard at analysing when the surf will be good and where. You're in the hands of an expert,' commented Gav, the more reserved of the three, openly appreciative of Higgsy's expertise.

'With five of us, we'll make our own crowd,' said Brian, his way of welcoming Ange.

'Two women in the group. I hope none of you have jealous wives,' joked Ange.

'Look at us,' laughed Higgsy. 'I reckon they're safe.'

Chapter 13

A Tidy Sum

A sudden and deep lethargy washed over Ange the moment she extracted herself from a long and relaxing warm shower, restoring her core body temperature and relaxing her tired muscles. Ignoring the soft ping on her phone, she collapsed onto her bed and immediately fell into a deep slumber. When she finally awoke, feeling groggy and disorientated, she realised she must have been asleep for over an hour.

Everyone knows that twenty minutes is the ideal time for a catnap to deliver a burst of energy, anything longer a problem. Ange was annoyed with herself, knowing that her body clock might now be disrupted. She stumbled over to her laptop to check whatever mail had arrived, finding a short and to-the-point email from Peter Fredericks. She clicked on the PDF attachment and started reading.

The document was quite short, scant on any real detail. A report of suspected fraud had come through to Major Crimes. An accountant by the name of Pat Crowley, principal of Crowley's Forensic Accountants, had raised the alert. He'd had been called in to help restructure the Queensland operations of a large construction company and found something untoward.

Headquartered in Sydney, Jack's Constructions held a Queensland building licence and boasted a large local operation. Despite appearing busy and successful, the Queensland division was struggling to make any real profit. The chairman had called in Mr Crowley to dig into the books. Ange's jaw dropped when she read the estimated scale of the suspected fraud. Five-plus million dollars was a large enough sum to make anyone suspicious; it might even be money laundering. Ange resolved to pop up to Brisbane and interview Mr Crowley as soon as possible.

She shot an email back to Fredericks.

Wow, that is a large sum of money to go missing. Are you happy for me to contact Crowley and get the ball rolling?

His reply was short and sharp.

Go for it.

Ange decided she would contact Mr Crowley first thing on Monday and settled in to do some research on Jack's Constructions. The company had been around for over fifty years and had an impressive website. The project list on the 'About Us' tab contained loads of buildings around the country, some of which Ange recognised and had even visited over the years. There were a few projects on the Gold Coast, and a couple in Surfers Paradise. Ange typed a few addresses into Google Maps and jumped in the car to make a lap of inspection.

The company certainly appeared to be one of substance, and the completed projects featured on their website were even more impressive in the flesh, towering behemoths that took their place comfortably amongst the crowded skyline. It struck her as odd that an established construction company would engage in money laundering and risk their business that way. Ange hoped that Pat Crowley could answer that question.

She was still reeling at the scale of the alleged fraud, so she spent the rest of the day brushing up on the world of financial crimes. Her searching revealed that white-collar crime was big business, and she read about other similar situations where employers had had their pockets fleeced from within. An interesting podcast series caught her eye, published by one of the financial papers, which she downloaded for her own education.

The next morning Ange woke early to a stiff southerly breeze. The surf report confirmed her suspicions that trying to catch a wave would be a waste of time. She went for a brisk walk instead, grabbing coffee and a pastry at the nearby cafe. On the way home, she saw an elderly woman tending to her garden. Her house was on a corner block and boasted a huge frontage to the river. Ange smiled at the woman as she walked by.

'I see that you've recently moved in?' said the woman, slim and of average height, short grey hair under a wide-brimmed hat, the demeanour of an inquisitive willie wagtail, all fidgety and alert. 'I saw a truck dropping off your things,' she explained to Ange's look of surprise. 'I'm Ada, by the way, and that's Frank,' she added, gesturing towards a large Labrador that waddled over for a pat. 'Franky's an excellent judge of character.'

Ange walked over to the woman and shook her hand before giving Frank a long rough-and-tumble scratch of the head. Ange had grown up with dogs on the farm, so she knew how to handle them. 'Ange. Pleased to meet you.'

'So, I see you've moved into the pyramid man's house.' Ange gave another of her surprised looks, to which Ada elaborated, 'That's what we called him around here. He scammed some of my friends. I wish that they'd spoken to me before they invested their savings with that man. I saw all the parties, the flash cars and even flashier women. He wasn't someone that I would trust my savings with, that's for sure.'

Ange acted coy. 'I didn't know that. I just rented the house through an agency. It's a glorious spot you have here.'

'My husband and I moved here almost fifty years ago, when the Gold Coast was nothing,' said the woman. She answered Ange's reflexive glance around the garden. 'He passed away quite a few years back. I couldn't bear to leave my garden, so it's just me and Franky rattling around the house now. Of course, part of the appeal of keeping this place is that I get lots of visitors, grandchildren and even a few great-grandchildren now. The parents are always worried about the river, of course, but I successfully raised my family here. Once I tell the kids about the bull sharks, they tend to stay clear,' Ada said with a big mischievous smile. 'The neighbourhood has changed a lot, in more ways than one. We never worried about bull sharks when my children were growing up, but you wouldn't catch me swimming in the river nowadays. Even Franky, who normally loves the water, stays clear of the canal. I swear he knows what lurks beneath. Anyhow, it's nice to see a friendly face move in.'

Ange smiled, a kind smile that came naturally across her face. She wasn't ready to get too deep in a conversation, so she said her goodbyes, excusing herself politely and wandering back to her house. Along the way, she contemplated this encounter. Ada was just the sort of person any neighbourhood should wish as a resident. Not much would pass by this woman unnoticed.

Ange soon sat at the former kitchen table of the pyramid man, the clever name for the previous resident that Ada had provided. Feeling ready for the day, she opened the report that Fredericks had sent her the day before and rang the number for Pat Crowley.

'Hello, Mr Crowley, my name is Angela Watson, and I've been asked to investigate a report that you lodged with the New South Wales police. A suspected fraud concerning Jack's Constructions?'

'Yes, that's correct. The chairman asked me to find out why the division hadn't been performing. I've been doing some more work on the issue and made some progress since I lodged that report,' replied Crowley.

'I would prefer to discuss this in person. I'm based on the Gold Coast, but I could be in Brisbane by 11 a.m. Can you make time today?'

'Actually, 11 a.m. is good. You should miss the worst of the commuter traffic. It can be horrific,' replied Crowley.

Ange noted the realities of travelling between Brisbane and the Gold Coast. 'See you then, and thanks for the tip about the traffic. I just moved to the Gold Coast, so I guess managing the traffic is something I need to get my head around.'

Ange left her house just after 9 a.m., figuring she could kill some time in Brisbane if she arrived early. It was fortunate that she left early—the traffic was bumper-to-bumper all the way. It was hard to stay calm, as there were plenty of idiots on the road. At one point, a tradie tailgated her in a 4WD ute, convinced that his work was more important than hers, entitling him to jump the queue and endanger everyone. If she had still had one, she would have been sorely tempted to flash her badge and pull that jerk over. However, she had bigger fish to fry, five-plus million of them, in fact.

After almost two maddening hours avoiding duelling 4WD twin cabs and impatient SUVs, Ange was forced into a mad rush from the parking station, arriving at the accountant's Anne Street office just in time, flustered and frustrated. The shiny lift deposited Ange on the twenty-seventh floor, directly into an ultra-modern reception area. After identifying herself, Ange walked over to the window to admire the impressive panorama over the Brisbane River as it snaked its way through the CBD. The languid river scene below helped slow her heart rate and calm the morning's aggravation. An expensive view, no doubt. Crowley's Forensic Accountants seemed to do OK.

Pat Crowley came out to greet Ange, ushering her into a meeting room that was perched at the south-eastern corner of the floor. Handsome despite his rapidly approaching middle age, Crowley was tall and athletic and moved with the easy confidence of a sportsman. Ange's first impression was one of competence and intelligence, sentiments bolstered by his firm and direct handshake.

Ange opened the conversation. 'Mr Crowley, I'm an investigator with Major Crimes in Sydney. Your alert came through to us, partly because Jack's Constructions is domiciled in Sydney, and party because of the sum of money involved.'

'Call me Pat, please. How come you're based on the Gold Coast?'

'We run many cases, and one that I'm involved with is a joint task force involving the Queensland and New South Wales Police,' explained Ange.

A wry smile crept across Pat's face. 'Well, the Gold Coast is the perfect place. It seems a magnet for shady deals and dodgy operators. I actually like the Goldie, but it has its seedy side.'

'That's not the first time I've heard that sentiment. Anyhow, you said that you've been looking further into the anomalies that you discovered. How is that all going?'

'Well, at first, I thought that this was a money laundering scheme. The sums of money were so massive. However, Jack's Constructions is an old, established, and reputable company, one with an impressive track record. On reflection, I can't see why they would risk all of that. When you turn over many hundreds of millions per annum, five or even ten million dollars isn't worth crossing the tracks for.'

Ange nodded her agreement with that logic. 'I drove around some of their projects yesterday, which are all very impressive.'

'I now believe that this is a case of fraud and embezzlement. There is a pattern of fake suppliers and invoices that go back several years. Based on some of the rough analysis I've done, the fraud could be as much as ten million dollars, but I really can't say exactly how much money has been siphoned off this way. At this point, I can verify over three million, but I've only just scratched the surface.'

The sum of money involved staggered Ange. 'How does one hoover up that amount of money?'

'It's actually quite easy and is something that happens more than you think. Basically, someone with connections inside the company sets up dummy suppliers and then raises invoices against those suppliers. These get allocated to certain jobs and paid in the normal course of events.'

Ange's brow furrowed as she asked the obvious question. 'It still seems like a lot of money. Why wasn't this picked up by someone?'

'Well, a construction company of this size processes thousands of invoices each month. Over time, people become complacent. The company is private and isn't required by law to be audited, which would presumably have picked this up. Personally, I think any company the size of Jack's should undertake a proper annual audit. Audits are a pain in the proverbial, but worth the effort, in my humble opinion. When I raised the subject with the chairman, he said that there had been a lot of resistance to engaging an auditor, citing extra unnecessary work and distraction.'

'I'll bet the board will rue that oversight,' Ange thought to herself before continuing her questioning. 'What are your thoughts on who might be behind this?'

'I'm not sure, but it needs to be someone high up and with some level of authority. It's a family company, with the usual tension and jealousies amongst the next generation. There's a limit to how far I can go on this before it becomes a criminal investigation and I need to step out. That assumes that the board presses charges, which they might not wish to do if this is internal and something that might risk their reputation. As it is, they won't be happy that I've reported this to the police,' he implored, looking across the table at Ange for validation.

'I agree with that logic. So, what are the chances of money laundering given your clearer insight into the matter?' probed Ange, knowing that she would be bound to report this to AUSTRAC should that be the case. AUSTRAC was Australia's anti-money laundering agency and there was a big crackdown underway following on from high-profile cases involving banks and casinos.

'Unlikely. My bet is good old-fashioned embezzlement. To pull this off over a sustained period, there definitely needed to be someone on the inside or with access to the accounts. I'm due to meet with the chairman on Friday. Obviously, it will ultimately be a decision of the entire board to take this further, and I'll need to disclose my report to the police. Can you give us a week to run all that to ground?'

'Are there any risks in waiting?' asked Ange.

'No, not in my opinion. I've set up some alerts when invoices come in from any of the suspicious suppliers that I've identified. One came in on Friday, which shows that they don't realise I'm poking around. The matter is strictly between the chairman and me. It'll be his call when to involve the board. Of course, if it is actual money laundering, then I presume that you guys will take the matter out of our hands.'

'OK,' concluded Ange, keeping vague about what she might or might not do. 'I'll keep quiet until then, but how about we agree to meet here again next Monday at 11 a.m.? By the way, are there any current projects under construction on the Gold Coast? I'd like to discreetly swing by sometime to familiarise myself.'

'They have a large apartment project in Broadbeach. Given that I don't know how long the fraud has been going on, I worked backwards, starting at the latest project. The latest suspicious invoice submitted relates to this project. I'll text you the address when I get back to my desk.'

'OK, thanks. See you then,' said Ange as she wrote her number and tore a page out of her ever-present notebook. With that, Crowley escorted Ange to the lift, waiting with her for the car to arrive before the pair parted.

Crowley's text came in whilst Ange was enjoying a sushi lunch in the city, sustenance to brave the drive back to the Gold Coast. She assumed that the traffic would be better than this morning. It wasn't. Ange's head was spinning faster than her wheels for much of the tedious journey, wondering how someone could have pulled off such a colossal scam right under everyone's noses.

She invested the balance of the afternoon in learning about Jack's Constructions and the family members who might be the beneficiaries of any financial windfall. Enjoying top billing on a Google search were the many stories about the death of the company's founder, Thomas Jack, and his wife, Alison. Ange remembered that incident herself, as it had been big news. Apparently, the Jacks had been travelling to a game park in Kenya when their light plane had crashed in bad weather, killing everyone on board. There were lots of accusations of the pilot being bullied to make the flight against his better judgement, essentially blaming Tom Jack for the tragedy. The *Sydney Morning Herald* had run a lengthy obituary for the man, describing him as a 'tough and shrewd businessman', obituary-speak suggesting that the man had made more than a few enemies during his career.

The family had largely gone to ground after the tragedy, and her search identified only a smattering of images in the social pages, mostly the CEO, the eldest of the siblings, accompanied by his glamorous-looking wife. Bob Turnbull, the independent chairman, had been a long-time friend and business associate of Tom Jack. The only family member who wasn't on the board of directors was the youngest sibling, Alison Jack, who seemed to do well for herself as a finance executive in Hong Kong.

The one incident where the company had not stayed under the radar related to their involvement in the Aluminium Composite Panel scandal, ACP for short. It seemed like a big deal for Sam Jack and the company, as the matter turned into a witch-hunt. Ange spent some time reading about the whole sorry affair and learning what the fuss was all about.

In 2017, a fire had broken out in Grenfell Tower in West London, killing seventy-two people. The building had all but exploded in a fireball after the panels, supposed to be non-combustible, had caught alight. Essentially just two sheets of aluminium bonded together over a foam core, ACP sheets seemed like the perfect building product. Not only were they quick to erect, they were light and durable and never needed painting, also providing terrific insulation.

They'd once been prohibitively expensive for all but high-end projects, but cheap imports had been flooding the market and were being widely used all over the world. Australia was no exception, and the Jacks had gotten in on the game, both as a user but also as an importer and wholesaler, selling their products to other construction companies as a business-to-business supplier. When a Melbourne apartment block had caught fire in 2019, ACP cladding had been blamed and the authorities had launched an investigation. Any panels imported into Australia required stringent fire ratings. Unfortunately, new testing revealed that most panels failed, rendering them essentially illegal. Ange could only imagine the legal minefield that was created in all that. Jack's Constructions became embroiled in the ensuing firestorm, so to speak.

Ange was intrigued and fully engaged, the SACC matter now an increasingly distant memory. She could see how tricky it might be for Pat Crowley and Bob Turnbull, should any of the family members be involved in fraud.

Chapter 14

Goon Squad

Ange awoke Tuesday morning to dull skies and driving rain, blown in by a stiff south-easterly wind. Seeing as she was due to meet Anders and Fredericks at 10 a.m., she put some washing on and took in a leisurely breakfast. The washing machine maybe wasn't the loudest that Ange had experienced, but it was definitely amongst the top three. Whilst it whizzed and clunked away in the background, Ange erupted an espresso from her trusty, well worn Bialetti stovetop coffee maker. The pyramid man had enjoyed a flash-looking espresso machine, prominently parked on the kitchen bench, however, Ange found the ritual of making her coffee old-school, just as she had in Byron most mornings, helped centre her mind on the day ahead.

Sustenance in hand, she jumped on her laptop and checked out the address of the construction site that Pat Crowley had texted her, which was just south of Anders' apartment. Not wanting to deal with the hassles of parking, Ange decided to brave the weather and walk, thereby killing two birds with one stone and knocking off her daily exercise.

A few months back, Ange had splashed out on some expensive Lululemon exercise gear that her friend Kerrie had convinced her to purchase. Kerrie was a successful lifestyle influencer in Byron Bay and knew her stuff. It impressed Ange how the gear she had purchased kept all the right things in all the right places, something her usual bargain-bin gear failed to emulate after a couple of washes. She had found it challenging to feel comfortable during the first few wears, decked out so glamorously and praying that she wouldn't morph into one of her nemeses from the Cape Byron walking track. Stretchy exercise gear was so damned comfortable that she had swiftly dispensed with those concerns.

Clothes extracted from one noisy appliance and whirring dry in another, Ange pulled on her flash exercise kit and tentatively poked her head out the back door. The rain had abated somewhat, but it was windy and bleak, far beyond her flimsy folding umbrella. After a brief rumble through her storage boxes, she finally made the street around 8:30 a.m., wearing her trusty khaki Driza-Bone, a three-quarter weatherproof jacket which was a 'relaxed-fit' remnant from her days on the farm. As Ange's self-appointed stylist, Kerrie would have had kittens, rolling her eyes expressively at such a fashion disaster, then dragging Ange on another expensive shopping trip.

She wandered past Ada's house. Even Franky, Ada's water-loving Labrador, was too wise to be caught outside. She imagined Franky curled up at the feet of his mistress as she read the paper over tea. Ada seemed the type that needed her daily fix of news, debated, and opinionated later that day over the bridge table. Ange surmised that Ada's poison would be English breakfast, loose-leaf no less.

These mind games came unbidden to Ange, a trait she had developed as a young girl on the farm, where loneliness could be flailed away by a healthy imagination. As she rolled these musings around in her mind, she formed images and ideas, arranging them into patterns, then pulling them apart when they didn't quite fit, remaking them until they sat comfortably. An unconscious diversion perhaps, but these secret ruminations would often spring back into action when triggered by real-world conditions. The pig-tailed version of herself never realised that these mind games were training her for a career as a detective, which hadn't once been a daydreamed future state. She had imagined becoming a happily married doctor or vet back then, or perhaps the gritty lawyer her father harped on about, someone to give him free legal advice on which to assail the irrigation regulator.

Once Ange emerged from her daydream and the protection of her street, she turned east onto Thomas Drive and the full force of the wind and rain assailed her. Forced to pull down the brim of her cap and draw over the hood of her Driza-Bone, she quickly concluded that walking was not such a good idea after all. The shop assistant at Lululemon had been silent on how her leggings would perform in driving rain. It wasn't their strong point, but Ange pushed on, wondering how Sally Anders might feel as she dripped through their weekly meeting.

Things were better once she reached the relative protection of Surfers and its skyscrapers, but the wind tugged frantically at her clothes at each intersection, hell-bent on removing her cap. The bleak windswept streets painted a very different picture of Surfers. There were only a few locals around, those compelled by some chore or another to brave the tempest. At one point the weather worsened, if that was possible, and she sought refuge in a cafe in Broadbeach. Shaking herself off to order a coffee and check directions on her phone, Ange saw that her destination was four blocks south and to the left.

Full of caffeine and ready to do battle again, Ange put her head down and marched along Surf Parade towards the building site, exposed to the gale's full force. She counted the blocks on her fingers as she went, risking her cap at the fourth to look up and check the street sign. Britannia Avenue, that was it. A partially completed high-rise sat a hundred or so metres down to her left.

Given the driving rain, the construction site was subdued, but there was still some activity and she could hear the occasional squeal of machinery, the only sound capable of piercing through the howling wind. The tower crane was stationary, at least from lifting things. Once more risking her cap to the gale, Ange could see it swaying and shuddering as the wind whistled through the massive gantry. She imagined how confronting it would be to sit up in the cabin on such a day, normally the most spectacular seat in town.

Ange peered through the hoarding where possible, but there wasn't much to see, other than that this was a legitimate project of some magnitude. As she walked along the site frontage, a white SUV edged out of the driveway access and cut her off. Ange glanced unconsciously at the two stubbled occupants as they crossed her path, annoyed that they hadn't bothered to check for pedestrians, the demented type that might be out walking in such weather. Both driver and passenger peered around the hoarding to check for any oncoming traffic, first left and then right. The pair glanced at Ange when they saw her patiently waiting beside the driveway but made no apologies and continued blithely onto the street, accelerating rapidly as they drove away.

Ange couldn't believe her eyes. She was certain that these were the same two characters she had seen last summer, skulking around with Sergeant Darren Billings at the Bangalow markets.

Having caught a good look, Ange quickly ducked her head and pulled down the hood of her Driza-Bone, ostensibly to avoid the rain. She didn't need to take any chances of being identified. Ange texted herself the registration number of the departing car, worried that the surge of adrenaline might erode her memory. Her head was spinning all the way to Anders' apartment, wondering if her overactive imagination was playing tricks. She hardly noticed the weather.

Safely inside the apartment, Ange removed her jacket and draped it over the bathroom door. Peter Fredericks looked up from his computer and took in her apparel. He looked Ange up and down and then motioned to her not-so-Driza-Bone as it dripped away happily. 'Interesting outfit. Have you been at Pilates or out droving sheep?' He seemed quite impressed by his own humour.

Ange had other things on her mind. 'Do you have some pictures of those two thugs who I saw with Darren Billings? You know, the ones that were involved in the Namba Heads operation?'

Anders looked up from her computer screen, not having acknowledged Ange until that point. 'Lomax and Smith? The two Kiwis? Why do you ask?'

Ange left that question hang as she waited for Fredericks to dig up some surveillance shots of the two thugs and display them on his screen. 'That's them. I was sure it was. Phew, I thought I must be going bonkers, my imagination playing tricks again,' she blurted out.

'What do you mean?' asked Anders.

'Let me start at the beginning,' replied Ange. 'Yesterday, I drove up to Brisbane and met with that accountant.' Met with confused stares, she elaborated. 'You know—the suspected multimillion-dollar money laundering case involving that family-owned construction company.' Once understanding flashed across her colleagues' eyes, she pushed on. 'Well, the accountant felt that this might be a case of fraud and embezzlement rather than money laundering. He uncovered a series of fake suppliers and invoices going back several years and feels that it must be someone internal, perhaps even a family member.'

'What has that got to do with those guys?' chimed in Fredericks, pointing to his screen.

'Well, I checked out one of the firm's construction sites on my way over. They have a large high-rise project on Britannia Avenue, just south of here. As I was walking by, a car came out of the site containing two guys. I thought I must be seeing things at first, but I'm now certain it was them. It seems a bit Scooby Doo-ish now that I'm retelling the story,' said Ange, suddenly doubting herself.

'Where there's smoke, there's usually fire,' commented Anders. 'Peter, can you have a look to see if we have access to any surveillance cameras in that area?'

As Peter Fredericks dived back into his laptop, Anders turned to Ange. 'Did you get the number plate of the car?'

Ange looked down at her phone, pleased that she had taken the precaution of texting the number to herself. 'The vehicle's number plate is 286 VNK, a white SUV. I was too intent on the number plate as it drove away to catch the model, but it was a Mitsubishi of some sort.'

Fredericks looked up from his laptop. 'We have two, one on the corner of Broadbeach Avenue and the other out at the Gold Coast highway intersection. I'll get a feed into our system and set up an alert for the number plate.' He paused for a minute, typing on his laptop. 'A 2015 Mitsubishi Outlander. Registered to a company based out of a PO box in Nerang. CVU Pty Ltd. A generic cutesy company name like that would suggest a ready-made company structure which was purchased off the shelf.'

Ange wandered over to the big glass door to the balcony, where the shrieking wind was prying and trying to find a way through. The sea was a complete mess. At this height, Ange could see the outline of the many wind squalls as they whistled by and ruffled the sea. To the southeast, she could see a large rain shower bearing down, perhaps thirty minutes away. This inspiring vista helped calm her racing mind, slowing it down to a more productive pace, churning through permutations and combinations of her discovery. She could sense that they had been gifted a lucky break and were on to something.

'OK, what should we do now? Pat Crowley, the accountant, is speaking to the chairman of Jack's Constructions on Friday. He promised to come back to me next week with the outcome of that discussion. This changes everything, doesn't it?' Ange enquired, looking back at Anders.

'Yes and no,' replied Anders. 'It could be a coincidence. Perhaps they were visiting someone unrelated at the building site. Hopefully, the surveillance cameras will help answer that question. Also, we don't need to alert the company in case there is something illegal going on. It wouldn't help if they cover up their tracks before we can take any action. I think we need to wait and see if those goons come back. We should try to find out if they've ever had any relationship with Jack's Constructions.'

'How about we get Billy onto that? He can also start poking around and build a profile on Jack's Constructions,' suggested Ange.

'Agreed. He can also dig into that company the vehicle is registered to. Peter, can you send Ange the dossiers on those two goons and let her know if they visit the construction site again? Also, get onto our colleagues in the Queensland Police and tag the number plate with the motorway cameras and any mobile patrols. Don't make a big deal of it, just a vehicle of moderate interest. We don't want any patrol vehicles giving chase.'

'What should I do?' asked Ange, suddenly feeling left out.

'What you do best, Ange—hanging around, looking for signs and connecting the dots. You've only been on the case for a few days and already we have a pretty interesting lead,' said Anders, smiling at Ange and making her feel better. 'Keep your meeting with the accountant, but perhaps suggest that the chairman should be involved.'

Ange nodded her agreement before Anders spoke again. 'OK. Let's get on with it.' The meeting was now ended, no offence taken.

Ange looked out at the looming rain squall. There was no way she would make it back to her house before the squall passed through. Offers to hang out in the apartment were conspicuous in their absence, so another drenching was in order. At least she would walk with the wind this time.

She hadn't even made it back home before Billy had texted her.

That didn't take long! Anders has me following up on your leads. Looks like fun!

She quickly texted back a thumbs-up emoji as she shielded herself from the wind and driving rain. Sally Anders was no slouch in the action department.

Chapter 15

The Tempest

Ange didn't do boredom very well. After a day or so, she was itching to get more involved. The swell had arrived, but the relentless wind was showing no sign of letting up. Higgsy had sent a text, saying that the points should be excellent once the wind moderated. He and his crew were planning a surf down at Snapper Rocks on Sunday morning. Ange thought Snapper Rocks was south of the border and checked online, not wanting to run the gauntlet of the ongoing border restrictions.

It was a strange setup. Duranbah and the Tweed River were just south of the border, whereas Snapper Rocks was on the north side, sharing the same headland, Point Danger, the most easterly place in Queensland. Snapper Rocks and Greenmount merged into an iconic Queensland surf spot called SuperBank. Ange had heard lots of surfers raving on about epic days, but also crazy crowds that sometimes became violent. The prospect of hassling with intense crowds usually turned Ange off.

Though it sounded like just another surfers' nickname, an online search revealed that SuperBank was in fact its official name, a man-made surf spot of sorts, a type of augmented reality. Sand pumped from the Tweed River and over the headland formed consistent sandbanks that were manna from heaven for surfers. This seemed like a convenient way to dodge the headland bypassing event that had recently stolen Byron Bay's treasured sandy beach.

Higgsy and Ange traded texts on the prospect. He suggested it might be an excellent opportunity for Ange to score some nice, relatively uncrowded waves, as the border closure would prevent any surfers living on the Tweed Heads side from getting into the action. Ange agreed to meet them on Sunday at 8 a.m., just near the Greenmount Beach Surf Life Saving Club.

Looking at her surfer's weather app, she could see that an unusual winter low-pressure system had formed up north in the Coral Sea, just off Gladstone. Ange had always been confused about where the Coral Sea ended and whether it was separate, or part of, the Pacific Ocean. She amused herself for a while sorting out this confusion, surprised to learn that the Coral Sea extended north to Papua New Guinea and south to near Coffs Harbour, where it met the Tasman Sea, both seas part of the mighty South Pacific Ocean. She had always assumed that the Coral Sea was reserved for northern latitudes, tropical places like Vanuatu, Fiji, and the Solomon Islands. The Coral Sea sounded ever so glamorous and appealing, not to mention warmer, which was a pleasant midwinter thought. Ange resolved that she would forever more be surfing in the Coral Sea. Perhaps she might even win a few bets at the pub over that fun fact.

Anyhow, the low was slow-moving and not expected to pass by until later in the week. It might not even arrive; such was the uncertainty of tracking cyclones or low-pressure systems like this one. The wind and the rain were steady, keeping everyone off the beach. Ange spent Wednesday exploring the Gold Coast, driving around the mega-mansions of Sovereign Island in the north on her way to Sanctuary Cove and its manicured gated community. She grabbed lunch at the Sanctuary Cove Village and sat marvelling at the massive pleasure craft moored in the marina. Ostensibly, there was plenty of money swilling around on the Gold Coast. Ange played her usual mind game, imagining all the comings and goings, placing herself as one of the glamorous wives or mistresses sneaking on board. Money and time to kill were dangerous bedfellows.

By Thursday, she could bear it no longer and rang Billy to check on his progress.

'I wondered how long you could hold off,' was Billy's opening line, recognising Ange's number on his buzzing phone.

'Hi, Billy,' said Ange in her sweetest possible voice. 'I was just wondering how you're going. I thought I should check in to make sure that the job isn't too much for you.' Sugar wouldn't melt in her mouth.

'Yeah, sure,' came Billy's reply. 'I'll have a report ready for you by tomorrow. There are a lot of moving parts in this, and I think you should wait until I'm finished. I know you. If I send you something half-finished, you'll dive down too many empty rabbit holes.'

'Fair enough. Remember to put together a table of your media scans on the

Jack family.'

Billy sighed loudly for effect, as if in exasperation. He had great affection for his former colleague, now a boss of sorts. 'Leave it with me. I've been doing this for, what, almost a week now?'

The pair laughed at this before signing off. Ange knew when to pull back and leave Billy to do his thing. Now she really was bored.

She put on some exercise gear and headed to the Coral Sea, but it was even less inviting than the day before or the name suggested. She had heard about the Gold Coast hinterland and chose to take her exercise in that direction, targeting Mount Tamborine. The drive up to the hinterland was further than she had imagined, and much more rural than she would have believed, a stark contrast to the hustle and bustle of Surfers Paradise. Mercifully, the rain abated long enough for Ange to take a pleasant walking circuit through the rainforest, providing space for her mind to process the past few weeks.

The rain and wind slashed across her windscreen on the drive down the mountain, increasing in intensity as she got closer to the coast. By the time she arrived back at her house, darkness was setting in and Ange couldn't recall a night bleaker.

Ange was constantly woken up by vicious gusts of wind and sheets of driving rain, as they raced across the Nerang River. This was in contrast to her old apartment in the backstreets of Byron, where she had felt safe and sound, snug in bed and protected from the elements. As she lay awake listening to the tempest wage war on her house, she imagined how a real cyclone would feel, like the one that had ultimately resulted in the Gold Coast Meter Maids, neither of which she wanted to experience up close and personal.

If it was possible, the next day was worse. Ange paced aimlessly around the house, waiting for Billy to send through his report. A caged animal would have been happier, and she spared a thought for the thousands of Australians who had endured two weeks of hotel quarantine. She had grave doubts as to her ability to cope with two days, let alone two weeks. Finally, her phone buzzed with a text from Billy.

Just sent through a couple of reports. Interesting.

She almost ran to her laptop, anything to escape the boredom of her bedraggled day. Typical Billy—it was an extensive report, complete with a long list of media links. Settling in for a prolonged session in front of her laptop, she had barely started work when she suddenly remembered her meeting earlier in the week with Pat Crowley, and his own planned meeting with the chairman of Jack's Constructions.

She stopped reading and rang Crowley's office. The receptionist said that he was on another phone call, so Ange left her details and asked if he could ring her back before the close of business. She would sleep easier when their scheduled meeting on Monday morning was confirmed. She hoped that the chairman wouldn't close ranks and make her life difficult.

She pulled out her trusty notebook to take some notes. Ange always found that writing things down cemented them in her mind, and it was a habit she was loath to break. This practice had gotten worse, not better, over time. Perhaps this ailing of the mind was a symptom of the avalanche of information that came with her job. She had even recently taken to texting herself, often during walks, when light-bulb moments breezed through her consciousness. At times, she worried that old age may be setting in. For goodness' sake, she wasn't even middle-aged yet. Then again, perhaps she was and didn't realise it?

Pulling herself from those depressing thoughts, she started writing.

Jack's Constructions

- *The empire is extensive.*

- *Jack's Constructions: the mother ship.*
  - *Jeays Property Services: maintenance division, security services.*
  - *Jeays Building Products: business-to-business (B2B) supplier–both imported & locally sourced.*
  - *Jeays Labour Hire.*
  - *Jack's Civil Constructions: earthmoving, housing estates.*
  - *Jack's Investments No 1 thru 5: series of investment vehicles.*

- *No outstanding queries from the ATO.*

- *Plane crash–accident?*

- *The Jack family is private. Avoid media scrutiny where possible.*

- *Impact of Grenfell Tower fire and legislative crackdown. Caught on both sides of the fence, as a B2B supplier & installer of their own imported Aluminium Composite Panels (ACP).*

- *Family board of directors with independent chairman, Bob Turnbull, Tom Jack's former lawyer.*

- *CFO ex Ernst & Young out of Melbourne. Also acts as the company secretary.*

Once she had completed the report and clicked through each of the media links, Ange sat back in her chair and mulled it all over. She started a to-do list for the next day.

To Do

1. *Ask Crowley to explain the scale & scope of subsidiaries.*

2. *Are family aware of Crowley's investigation?*

3. *Extent of exposure w.r.t. ACP matter?*

4. *Client list.*

5. *Corporate or family enemies?*

Her phone rang. She recognised Pat Crowley's number and answered the call after a few rings. 'Hello, Pat. How did you go with the chairman today?'

'Frankly, it was a trying day. The extent of things quite alarmed the chairman. Even more so when I told him about my report to the police and that you were involved. He was furious with me at first, but I calmed him down in the end. I had to point out the trouble the company would get into if we covered up potential money laundering. Bob has a solid reputation as a straight shooter. However, it took him a while to understand the risks and come around.'

'That's good. I'm relieved. Are we still on for Monday at 11 a.m.? I'd like the chairman involved. Can you organise him to attend?' asked Ange, firing off the double-barrelled question that was concerning her.

'Yes. We can go over the details then. I'm sure Bob will want to be involved, seeing how serious this is. He's based in Sydney, but I'll organise a Zoom call. I must go now. I'm already late for a dinner party that my wife is hosting. She knows that if she doesn't organise these things, I'll likely stay here until midnight.'

Ange was relieved by this news. Things were moving forward at last.

'I hear you. Have a good weekend,' she said before hanging up and letting Pat head home to enjoy his dinner party.

Billy's report on his investigation into the two thugs was not similarly progressive and delivered no fresh information. Either they were good at covering their tracks, or there was no substantive connection between Jack's Constructions and their visit to the high-rise building site. Hopefully, the video surveillance would give them some more to go on.

Regarding his investigation into the owner of the Mitsubishi vehicle, Billy had written a single word.

Interesting.

Chapter 16

Super Sunday

By Saturday afternoon, the low had weakened and was travelling south along the coast. Ange had walked over to the beach at some point, now covered by a blanket of sea foam. Even though it was winter and snakes were less plentiful, she knew to stay out of the sea foam. Not so the group of teenagers who were frolicking in the stuff. Ange had to admit that it looked like fun.

One of her mum's favourite sayings leaped into her mind: 'It's all fun and games until someone gets bitten by a snake.' There were a squillion permutations and combinations of that little gem of a phrase. Her mother had used it often back on the farm when Ange and her siblings were playing some silly game or another.

Ange sat on the foreshore to watch the humongous swell roll in. The power of each single wave was spine-tingling, and she knew the swell would cause substantial damage to the beach. The news from the previous evening had shown footage of worried beachfront homeowners at Palm Beach, just south of Surfers Paradise. They were sandbagging the front yards of their valuable properties and berating the Council for not allowing them to install the more permanent protection offered by a large rock wall. It was a battleground of sorts, between those who wanted to let nature take its course, and a modern expectation that nature was just another thing to be controlled. Whilst Ange saw both sides of the argument, Mother Nature was powerful and unpredictable. It was dangerous and ignorant to believe that humans could ever best her—she would exact revenge in one form or another.

Late Saturday afternoon, she received a text from Higgsy.

Sea should calm down overnight. Tomorrow should be epic. See you at 8 a.m. as planned.

Ange immediately texted back.

Brilliant. Looking forward to it. Nervous...

Higgsy just replied with a thumbs-up emoji. Ange couldn't be certain whether that meant she should be nervous or calm. She went with nervous and made a poor effort of getting a good night's sleep, restless and antsy with anticipation. The analogy of her tossing and turning with what she might experience in the surf the next day was not lost. However, it was the movie she created and replayed in her mind that was the driving force behind insomnia. Cutting a stylish form, Ange imagined herself carving down a giant unblemished wave face, making a long elegant bottom turn and slotting into the pocket. How thrilling.

She was waiting near the Greenmount Surf Life Saving Club, well before 8 a.m. Watching the other surfers catch some incredibly long rides, she concluded that her midsize would handle the flat sections better. By the time Higgsy and the crew arrived, she had stretched, pulled on her wetsuit, and waxed her board.

This time around, they had another woman with them. Younger and shorter than Ange, her short hair and punchy figure matched an air of confidence. Clearly, she had done this before. Everyone was intent on getting into the waves, and Higgsy made a half-hearted attempt at an introduction. 'Jen, meet Ange, Ange, meet Jen,' he said, taking the minimalist approach given that this formality was taking up quality surfing time.

The crew were like seven-year-old kids on their birthdays, struggling to contain the excitement that was bubbling within. Higgsy, the oldest of the group, suggested that they surf until 11 a.m. and told his mates to get amongst it. They scooted off whilst he walked methodically with Ange along the beach to a jump-off point, explaining how the break worked and pointing out the flat sections where she would need to maintain some speed. Even within a Covid dystopia, the break was super busy and Ange was dubious about how many waves she might score.

The pair waded out into the surf, straining back against a sea that was intent on sweeping them off their feet. They waited for some semblance of a lull and then paddled like crazy. It turned out to be no lull at all and they found themselves slap-bang in the impact zone. In a flash, the pair were swept hundreds of metres down the beach. Being the weaker surfer, Ange was dragged further than Higgsy. She hauled her dripping self from the water and trudged around the bay to where he stood waiting.

'I didn't time that very well,' said Higgsy, sarcastic of his own team-leadership skills.

Ange laughed, showing Higgsy that she was up for the fight. 'Wow. There certainly is a lot of water moving around. I suppose there's no option than to take another crack.'

The pair walked back out along the headland in silence as Higgsy watched where the other surfers were paddling out, noting who was successful and who not. They picked their way around a small outcrop of rocks and weighed up the options. After a few moments of observation, Higgsy motioned to Ange and they charged into the fray once again. This time, after a mad scramble, with her heart in her mouth, Ange finally made it beyond the break and into clear water.

She was breathing heavily and took a moment to catch her breath. The waves that were streaming through were imposing, causing her to question whether she was up for this. Higgsy must have seen the look on her face and paddled over. 'Don't worry, once you get onto one of these waves, they break perfectly. The trick is waiting for a wave that isn't already occupied.' With that, the surfer on the approaching wave wiped out. Ange was in the take-off zone. Higgsy egged her to take it, yelling that he would keep any potential drop-ins at bay.

Ange turned her board and paddled in tune with the approaching monster, more afraid than she had ever been before. She would have loved to abandon ship, but her pride wouldn't allow such a capitulation in front of her new-found surfing buddies. Taking a deep breath, she stroked down the face, feeling the power of the wave as it picked her up. Given the tension and adrenaline coursing through her, Ange managed her take-off surprisingly well. The large wave face stretching below allowed plenty of time for her to make the jump and race diagonally down the wave face. The speed she quickly amassed was intense, and she tentatively fashioned the long, slow bottom turn envisaged the night before, taking care not to lose control and waste her opportunity.

Despite its size, the wave was more surfable than Ange could have imagined, offering an incredibly long ride. No wonder it was called the SuperBank. She finally pulled out just before a closeout section, quickly lying down on her board and paddling out wide to escape an approaching monster, a wave even bigger than she had just ridden. Once she was clear, she sat on her board and considered her options, ultimately deciding to make the long paddle rather than brave the beach again.

Her ride must have been hundreds of metres long; it would take her fifteen minutes or more to get back out, paddling against the sweep. Along the way, she saw Higgsy pick up a nice wave. An elegant surfer, he made it all look easy, as the best surfers always do. He even had time to notice Ange and smile as he zipped by. Brian and Gav were riding shorter boards and taking off further inside. While they picked up more waves, they also got pole-axed plenty of times. Jen was a firecracker, mixing it with the younger guys and hustling plenty of rides. So much for having another woman to surf with. Jen was a vastly superior and more experienced surfer than Ange.

Despite the imposing crowd, Ange caught plenty of waves, with the crew playing defence for the newbie and helping fend off drop-ins. Her smile, usually her best offence, made a scant impact on the younger crew that was in the water, wave warriors who treated surfing as a contest without rules. That smile always worked wonders at The Pass with the older Byron Bay guys. It was almost useless at SuperBank.

The paddle back out after each wave was a killer, but not half as bad as trying to get out from the beach again, something that was twice necessary after she copped a drubbing. When 11 a.m. came around, Ange was shot, her leaden arms refusing to behave on her last wave, where she crashed and burned badly, tumbled and tousled by the wave as it swept her along, the board tugging at her leg rope and keeping her squarely in the impact zone. By the time she had recovered herself to belly-board back to the beach and the assembled crew. Unfortunately, they had all seen her catastrophically bad wave and were grinning madly as she trudged up the beach to where they waited.

Ange laughed back. 'Man. I am beat. That was amazing.' Everyone agreed, reliving their highlights, both good and bad, as they wandered slowly back to their vehicles.

Gav suggested they grab a quick bite at a nearby cafe, walking distance along Marine Parade. After a quick rinse and change, they were all soon seated and enjoying some coffee. After they replayed some highlights from the morning's session, it wasn't long before Higgsy posed the question that Ange had been dreading. 'So, Ange, what do you do, workwise?'

As Ange heard her own reply, she knew it sounded evasive and mysterious. 'I work in investigations, corporate work mostly.' Sally Anders had made it sound so natural; Ange just sounded lame and unconvincing.

Higgsy had absolutely no idea where to go with that, particularly given that Ange was suddenly preoccupied with her feet. An awkward moment ensued before Ange looked up to break the silence and put everyone out of their misery. 'So, what about you guys?'

Gav gestured towards the other two men. 'We're tradies. I'm a sparky, Brian is a chippy, and the old man here works as a foreman on larger projects.'

Jen answered for herself, showing a big smile and a sense of humour that the challenging waves had hidden. 'I'm an engineer. I'm the brains of this outfit and the one who keeps these guys on the straight and narrow.'

'Our lives would be so much easier if it wasn't for engineers and architects always telling us what to do,' responded Higgsy.

'Until your next building collapses, that is. That's why you need to listen to me,' said Jen with a mischievous smile.

'Just like home,' commented Higgsy, over-exaggerating his look of resignation for effect. Ange felt that this concession was unlikely to be true.

Instinctively, Ange was back on the case again. 'So, tell me, Higgsy, have you had anything to do with those aluminium panels? You know, the type that caught fire and killed some people a few years back?'

'Sure have,' came Higgsy's quick-fire reply. 'I was on a big job in Coolangatta when the Melbourne fire happened. The project was half finished, and we'd already clad one-third of the building in the stuff. It was a complete mess. No one knew how the regulators would react or what to do.'

'So, what happened?' asked Ange, intrigued, and thinking herself lucky. Whether it was luck or being alert, the universe often spoke to her in this way, and she had learned to go along with her instincts.

'The developer stopped work for a week before ultimately getting us to take all the composite panelling down off the building and install a more traditional fibre cement product. It must have cost a bomb, but acting quickly like he did was the right move. The building probably wouldn't have gotten certified by the fire service if he hadn't been able to source another product, which was already flying off the shelves. He still had some trouble with the building's energy rating, but that was nothing compared to getting on the wrong side of the fireys.'

'Did many people get in trouble over the panels? I understand some had suspect fire ratings,' probed Ange, making the most of this good fortune.

Brian chimed in to answer. 'The government introduced some legislation that created lots of consultants' reports. To be honest, I'm not sure how this has all ended up, but it certainly cost the industry a truckload of money and made for some wealthy consultants.'

'What do you mean? Surely, it's all been sorted out by now. It seemed like such a big deal.'

Jen looked up from her bacon and egg roll to answer. 'Covid-19. Once that rolled in, the government became obsessed. Nothing else mattered. I suspect the next you'll hear about that type of cladding will be when another building goes up in flames. There are still lots of non-compliant panels out there. I wish I could be confident that all the creative solutions and workarounds the fire consultants have dreamed up will prevent another tragedy.'

Ange had no answer to that, her own experiences with bureaucratic decision-making telling her that Jen was probably spot on.

'Anyhow, I must go. The wife awaits. A BBQ with the in-laws. I can't wait,' said Higgsy with a broad and ironic smile.

With that, the crew dispersed to their cars. As Ange drove back to Surfers, she couldn't help but look up at the many high-rise buildings, wondering which were still afflicted with suspect panelling. She would definitely pay more attention to her choice of accommodation in the future.

Chapter 17

The Chairman

A nge had hoped to avoid the dreaded traffic and left early, aware that it was Monday morning after all. It didn't disappoint, and she crawled her way to the state capital. Luckily, her podcast series on financial crimes was riveting, which helped defray the boredom of her frustrating commute and whisked Ange away to another world of white-collar crime. The sums of money involved were spectacular.

Pleased that she had been ahead of the game, Ange managed time for coffee and a pastry in the foyer cafe before she made her way up to the twenty-seventh floor. After checking in, she had only to wait a short time before Pat Crowley came out to greet her. Ange suspected he had been waiting for her. After they had dispensed with the pleasantries, Crowley suggested they go to a much larger room than last time. 'This room is better for a video call. The chairman's ready to join in via Zoom. Anything we need to speak about beforehand?'

'No. Not really. I gather that you guys are just as motivated to keep our discussion confidential. How about you get the video call going and I can make that point at some stage?'

Crowley messed around with the technology until Bob Turnbull came on the screen. A shock of longish grey hair framed a weathered and handsome face. Black square-framed glasses combined to give Turnbull a distinguished air. Pat Crowley opened the batting. 'Hello, Bob. As you can see, I'm here with Detective Angela Watson, the investigator I spoke to you about.'

Bob Turnbull wasted no time. 'What are you doing in Brisbane, Detective Watson?'

'I'm with Major Crimes, a division of the New South Wales Police Force. We have a joint task force with the Queensland Police, so I'm based temporarily on the Gold Coast as part of that operation.'

'Your name is familiar. Weren't you in the papers recently? Part of a SACC investigation?' Bob Turnbull had obviously done his homework.

Pat Crowley looked sharply at Ange before she replied. 'Yes, you're well informed, Mr Turnbull. I was called to give evidence in a corruption enquiry involving an environmental activist and some councils in the Byron Bay region. It involved developers. You would understand that I can't go into the details, but much of this was in the paper.' Ange looked straight into the camera, pausing briefly before she tasered Bob Turnbull with her best *don't go there, buddy* look.

Turnbull seemed to enjoy her response and beamed at his own cleverness. He showed no discomfort over having been tasered. 'Call me Bob. How should we proceed?'

Ange opened her notebook before speaking. 'Perhaps we should start with some background on the company and the people involved, including how each of you fits into the picture.'

Turnbull was quick to take charge of that question. 'Thomas Jack founded the company some fifty years ago. His is a remarkable story, starting as a carpenter in Wollongong. His parents both worked in the steel mills. Tom began building the odd house, and the business grew from there. Within thirty years, Jack's Constructions became one of the largest privately owned building companies in the country. I acted as Tom's lawyer and we fell into a friendship, one that ultimately resulted in me becoming the only independent director on the board.'

He took a sip of water before continuing. 'Then the tragedy happened. Thomas Jack was a shrewd businessman and as tough as the concrete he used in his buildings. It was lucky that they had put me onto the board, as I could steady the ship and allow the family to step in gradually. Sam Jack is the CEO, and the company has flourished since he found his sea legs. The next eldest is Cam, an engineer who's the mad scientist of the group and looks after all the technical aspects of the company. The youngest of the boys is Bobby, who's always been a bit of a handful and probably the black sheep of the family. He is probably the smartest of the lot, but also the most difficult personality. He joined the company full-time a few years ago. I think the title we gave him was Director of Special Projects. Last, and by no means least, is Alison, who works in the finance sector in Hong Kong. She studied finance at MIT in Boston, where she met and married a lawyer. She's very successful and I doubt we'll ever see her back in Australia again.'

Ange probed the obvious. 'So, tell me about Bobby Jack. You said that he can be difficult. How so exactly?'

'Well, Bobby has no boundaries and says things when he should keep his mouth shut. He can also harp on about something well past its use-by date. Bobby was a nomad for almost a decade, travelling around the world. We only ever heard from him at dividend time or when he ran out of money. He can be abrasive and rub some of the staff up the wrong way. Like I said, he's super smart, so will be an asset if we can channel him on the right path. He has lots of good ideas, but also plenty that are hare-brained and a distraction from our core business.'

Ange would need to circle back on Bobby, but she kept moving on for the moment. 'Tell me about all the subsidiaries and how that all fits together?'

Bob Turnbull again. 'They're quite logical, and they develop from a need or gap in the market that we identify. An obvious one is the property services division. Once we finish a project, we figure that we're also best placed to maintain it. We were giving this work to third-party firms, who weren't doing a very good job, frankly. This would come back to bite us more often than not, so we cut out the middleman. As well as doing the maintenance, we also have a security arm and a property management arm. We often throw in maintenance and security for the first year as part of our construction contract. Clients usually leave these arrangements to roll over—sort of like the gym membership model. The property services division has been growing steadily.'

'What about Jeays Building Products? Didn't that get you into hot water over the ACP cladding debacle?' asked Ange.

Turnbull's face darkened minutely before he answered, enough for Ange to notice. 'Yes, that was a difficult time. The idea of importing panels was a good one. We had some Chinese developer clients who insisted that we use a certain supplier. We found it an excellent product, so becoming an importer seemed a logical step. Luckily, we did our homework on the product to make sure that it complied with the building regulations. It cost us dearly as it was, but it could have been far worse. Overall, we probably broke even on the panel disaster, but that market is starting back up. In fact, we sell a lot of cold room panelling—same stuff, just not in the news. Anyway, the division is more than just cladding, and it does well for us.'

'What other products do Jeays Building Products deal in, besides ACP cladding?'

'Insulation, fixings, hardware for solar panels, which are going gangbusters. We do complete furniture packages that we match to the apartments we're building. We also offer working modular buildings for rapid deployment of hotels and apartment projects. You know, like those created from shipping containers, but higher-spec and more professional. That product line is also great for mining camps and work in remote locations. Our main warehouse for the building products division is located out near the Port of Brisbane, and we also have satellite warehouses in Sydney and Melbourne,' replied Turnbull.

Turnbull's knowledge of the company's operations impressed Ange. 'Why the different names for most of your subsidiaries? Were you trying to hide something?'

'Not at all. It makes perfect sense to differentiate yourself when you're in the B2B business. We wanted our customers, who were often also our competitors, to be confident that we were operating the business at arm's length. I gather you read some articles about ACP cladding, so you know we didn't hide from the media over our issue.'

'OK. What alerted you to the fraud?'

'Sam Jack came to me, concerned about the Queensland division. It seemed to be busy enough, but the profits weren't there,' answered Bob Turnbull, less effusive than he had been in his previous answers.

Ange probed. 'Should the CFO have picked this up earlier?'

Turnbull and Crowley looked at each other, the question expected and evidently well discussed. Turnbull was hesitating, so Pat Crowley answered on their behalf. 'I agree, he probably should have. However, he had moved to a more hands-on role in the company, heading up Queensland operations. As I mentioned last week, there are thousands of invoices being processed each month. A few here and there would be easy to miss.'

Bob Turnbull, having regained his voice, took over from Crowley. 'Sam Jack was looking at the big picture and noticed something amiss, which is what a good CEO does. However, once we diverted John to a more operational focus, the board should have realised that we would need full-time executive-level management in the accounting department. That's John Williamson, our CFO. John felt he could handle both tasks, but it appears not.'

'OK, what about potential enemies of the firm? Disgruntled employees, business associates, or the like.'

'Pat and I have thought about this. It might be a competitor who wishes to see us struggling, but for someone in the industry to take this approach seems a stretch. In terms of current or former employees, the only person who springs to mind was one of the assistant CFOs.'

'Why do you say that?'

'Not long after Bobby Jack reengaged with the company, he had a blue with Sonia Nicol, one of John's direct reports. Bobby wanted her to allocate some money to one of his pet projects and she wouldn't do it without authorisation from John, who was in China at the time with some clients. Bobby was furious when he found out and sacked her on the spot. She was technically doing the right thing, as she reported directly to John. Frankly, both Sonia and Bobby could have handled themselves better. It cost us a pretty penny, that unfair dismissal claim,' answered Turnbull, somewhat ruefully.

'Is she a suspect, then?'

Pat Crowley chimed in. 'I suppose she must be. She's been out of the company for a couple of years now, but it's not out of the question that she set this up. She'd still need someone on the inside to help, but Sonia's clever and was also very popular with the other admin staff. It's not unreasonable to think that she'd have supporters after what happened.'

Ange checked her list, realising that she had a few remaining questions. 'You seem to dismiss competitors or other business associates. Can you elaborate on why?'

'It's possible, I suppose. As I said, I seriously doubt any of Jack's normal competitors would play in that space,' remarked Crowley. 'The company has quite a bit to do with China, both on the customer and supply side. There is always the possibility of a state-sponsored security breach. All the company's data is stored in the cloud. However, the funds are being systematically diverted to local companies, which doesn't support the idea of any state-sponsored cybercrime. Security breaches by hackers are normally discreet events, in and out. What we have here doesn't fit either profile.'

Ange thought through his logic, nodding in agreement before moving to her next question. 'Who in the company knows about the fraud?'

Bob Turnbull was quick to answer. 'Only myself, Pat here, and Sam Jack.'

Finally, Ange got to the last and most important question of all. 'So, do you want to pursue this, and are you willing to bring charges if we can? It might come with some reputational risk.'

'Yes, we do. We have weighed up the options and think that this is the only thing to do,' said Turnbull firmly, before shooting Pat Crowley a dark look. 'Anyway, we won't have an option if this turns out to be money laundering and you bring AUSTRAC into the picture, so best that we play off the front foot.'

Ange figured Turnbull might well have swept the matter under the carpet if that option had been offered. Now that she had their commitment, she saw no need to play her trump card about the potential link to the narcotics ring.

'OK. Here's what I suggest. You guys keep digging behind the scenes, tracing the money trail, and keeping me in the loop. We will use our resources to chase down the assistant CFO, Sonia Nicol, and see if there has been any similar hacker activity out there in cyberspace.' Ange looked them both squarely in the eyes. 'We need to keep this tight and confidential, at least until we have a thread that we can pull.'

Once she had extracted their commitments to confidentiality, Ange said good-bye to a grim-faced Bob Turnbull. Pat Crowley escorted her to the lift. She suddenly thought of one last question before the car arrived. 'One thing that's bothering me is that I still don't understand how someone could set up fake suppliers and process that many invoices, yet nobody noticed.'

'It is quite simple and clever. The dummy suppliers' names are all slight variations of existing legitimate suppliers. Everyone either didn't notice this minor inconsistency, or just assumed that they were different divisions. The crazy thing is, if they had just kept the amounts small, I doubt anyone would ever have noticed.'

Crowley's last phrase echoed what the narrator of her podcast series had been saying. Scale matters with financial fraud. The larger the sums of money, the higher the risk that somebody will notice the scam. Ange pondered whether greed or complacency had caused this step-too-far. Clues would be left for certain; they just needed to be found.

'You keep saying *they*. I gather you think that there must be multiple people in on this, as you alluded to with Sonia Nicol?' asked Ange as the lift arrived.

'Yes. I think there must be more than one person, just purely because of the scale of the theft. It's not pocket money that we're talking about,' replied Crowley as Ange entered the lift and waved her hand to keep the door open. Before saying goodbye, she extracted a commitment from Crowley to meet the following week at the same time.

While it had been a productive and interesting session, Crowley and Turnbull had provided her with more questions than answers. A hard slog loomed.

Chapter 18

Seaview

Sometime overnight, Billy had sent through a report on the mystery company, the one which owned the Mitsubishi Outlander that the two goons had been driving. It had been cc'd to Anders and Fredericks.

> *CVU Pty Ltd was first registered in September 2010. The registered office is out of an accountant in Blacktown, Sydney. The vehicle registration notice is sent to a post box in Nerang on the Gold Coast. I rang someone at the ATO, who told me that the company is fully registered for tax and has a steady stream of activity. The ownership is a blind trust. The directors are a bit all over the place and scattered around NSW. Interestingly, the company has never missed a lodgement deadline or tax payment. I contacted one of the credit agencies for a credit report on CVU, which directed me to a brand owned by the company called GlitterStrip Cosmetics, which seems a good name for a cosmetics company based on the Gold Coast. This all seems legitimate. They have a website and some products listed. It's easy to find and looks legit to me, but cosmetics aren't really my thing...*

As Billy had suggested, Ange found the website easily. It looked totally legitimate on the face of things. She added a small tin of tan-coloured zinc cream and a tube of sunscreen into her virtual shopping cart. Faced with entering a delivery address at the checkout, Ange drew a blank. After a quick walk up and down the street to check street signs and house numbers, she eventually completed the order form, adding in some coconut-flavoured lip balm at the last minute. As soon as she pressed the Go to Payment button, she paused, realising that she shouldn't use her own name. She kept her order page open before putting her laptop to sleep. She would discuss this with Sally Anders.

Ange got kitted up and walked to the weekly catch-up with her colleagues, picking up some coffee and a fruit bagel as she went. She wandered past the building site again, but there was nothing untoward and the site was in full swing, noisy, intrusive, and uninviting. Ange came across a young mother walking by on the other side of the street with her young son, who was obsessed with watching the crane as it lifted some large concrete panels from a flatbed truck. 'What is it with young boys and machinery?' she mused. When she was growing up on the farm, the boys were always obsessed with tractors and trail bikes, the girls more about the animals.

She smiled at the couple as she walked by and said hello to the young boy. He took absolutely no notice, eyes fixed skyward. His mother commented that it was like that every day, always ending in tears when her own patience for watching heavy machinery had worn thin. Ange laughed as they said goodbye, then became suddenly overcome by a feeling of loss, realising that this pleasure seemed destined to pass her by, holding a small child's hand and leading them through life.

She pressed on and arrived fifteen minutes early to the apart-ment-cum-nerve-centre. An uncharacteristically aggravated Sally Anders was on the phone. She made no effort to move out of earshot, glancing at Ange pointedly, signalling her exasperation with whatever or whoever was the subject of the call. Ange could hear a muffled male voice droning on and on. Finally, Anders found an opening to speak, loud enough that Ange and Fredericks could hear clearly. 'We've made strong progress, but we need them to make another move. I don't need to remind you that the supply chain has been disrupted. I know it sounds ironic, but we probably need this to start up again before we can pounce.'

Although she couldn't discern a single word he uttered, Ange imagined a grumpy balding man on the other side of the call, frowning and telling Sally Anders to 'get this case solved', then adding 'or else' for good measure. Ange would dearly have loved to learn the name behind this source of frustration, but her relationship with Sally Anders was not yet at that stage.

Anders was visibly annoyed and mumbled something about desk jockeys and their pencils. She turned to address her colleagues. 'I don't need to tell you that our superiors are questioning our lack of progress.' Ange thought this was a touch unfair, given that she had only been on the case for just over a week. 'We need to get a wriggle on. Have you got anything for us, Ange?'

'Well, you both received that email from Billy about CVU Pty Ltd. It looks opaque enough to be suspicious. I got onto their cosmetics website this morning. I thought I'd order some stuff to see if it was legitimate. However, I stopped short of finalising this when I needed to enter my name and payment details.'

Anders cut her short. 'We have a credit card for these types of things. Peter will email you the details.'

Ange was pleased to have listened to Billy's online safety rants. Save for him, she probably would already be one of those hapless people she saw on the current affairs shows, telling their tear-jerking story of how their life savings had stolen. 'I didn't realise that the email saying I had won a new car and one million dollars was a scam,' they would say with droopy eyes to a gravely nodding reporter.

'Moving on, I had a very productive meeting with the chairman and accountant for Jack's Constructions.'

Ange rustled around her small backpack to retrieve her trusty notebook, hidden amongst a 'just in case' combination of cosmetics, sunscreen, and backup surfboard wax. Finding the notes from her meeting, Ange spent the next twenty minutes filling the others in.

When Ange had finished, Anders popped the million-dollar question. 'So, do you think that they're legitimately wanting to help, or are they just paying lip service to us?'

'They're both serious guys, with big reputations to protect. So, yes, I would say that they're sincere—at this point, at least. They may close ranks if it turns ugly.'

'Where do you think we should go from here?' asked Anders.

'There's something very suspicious about the involvement of Lomax and Smith. I didn't go down that path, as I wanted to get your opinion first. I'd like to ask Pat Crowley to search the company's employment records for those guys. I'll fob him off if he wants to know why. Also, we should check the legitimacy of that accountant where CVU Pty Ltd has its registered address.'

'That makes sense. Peter, can you check the accountant out?' Anders said decisively to Fredericks. 'By the way, have Lomax and Smith shown up anywhere?'

Fredericks shook his head. 'Nowhere yet. Which is sort of strange, with all the face recognition surveillance out here now.'

Ange also thought this curious, particularly with all those new cameras looking at seat belts and mobile phone use on the roads.

Anders swung her gaze towards Ange. 'OK. Let's get on with it. Hopefully, we can keep the powers that be off my back,' she said, breaking off the meeting and making Ange feel weirdly responsible.

Ange repacked her backpack and trundled home, not exactly energised by this week's meeting. A brisk walk down the foreshore did wonders, the rhythm of her gait stimulating her problem-solving subconscious, ever-present but often elusive. By the time she was back at her house, she was raring to go, having worked out how to deal with Pat Crowley.

Opening her laptop, she saw that Peter Fredericks had emailed some credit card details in the name of 'G White'. Ange laughed at this, seeing the reference to her surfing bogeyman. She set about setting a Gmail address to match, something which proved more difficult than she had hoped, seeing that White was such a common surname. Finally, a mixture of Gloria White, some numbers and two exclamation marks was accepted. She then completed the formalities, using her backup mobile number Anders had provided. She imagined Gloria White as someone other than herself. Perhaps an actor in *The Real Housewives of Surfers Paradise*, complete with a fake tan and spectacular boob job.

Smiling at the image of her alter ego, Ange opened the GlitterStrip tab she had kept alive on her browser and completed her order using Ms White's money. When the delivery address came up, she paused. It was probably ill-advised to get anything sent to her house, so she selected a click-and-collect option at an Australia Post Office within Pacific Fair, over at Broadbeach. The process seemed no different to any of the other e-commerce sites that Ange had used. It all looked completely legitimate.

She rang Pat Crowley to get him on the case of Lomax and Smith, assuring Crowley that this was routine, a case of known fraudsters being chased down by Major Crimes following reports of them operating on the Gold Coast. Crowley seemed hesitant but agreed to Ange's request, plainly suspicious about her story. Ange ignored his lack of enthusiasm, staying nonchalant and promising to email some details and pictures to Crowley, insisting that he include all Jack's subsidiaries in his search. 'We're leaving no stoned unturned with these guys,' Ange clarified.

After dashing off her promised email to Pat Crowley, she then rang Billy. 'Hi,

Billy, how did you go with your research into Sonia Nicol, that accountant who used to work at Jack's Constructions?'

'She's a clean slate, boss. Never put a foot out of line, other than a couple of speeding fines. She's now working in Newcastle. I'll email you some details and her phone number,' replied Billy. Ange smiled at her new-found title of boss, something once reserved for their old sergeant at Byron Bay.

'OK. I'll call her. Anything interesting out there in cyberspace that could account for the embezzlement at Jack's?'

'Oh my God, boss, you will not believe what is going on out there. If the public knew, they would turn off their computers for good. However, I have found nothing that matches this sort of long-term scam. Most garden-variety hackers are in-and-out types. They hack their way in, take what they want and get out. Most times, nobody even knows they were there. Of course, there are always ransomware attacks happening, but they're the *everyone down on the ground—this is a stickup* type of cybercrime, and not particularly sophisticated. If one of the really talented cybercriminals out there had hacked Jack's, they would never have known about it.'

'OK, can you keep your ear to the ground on this?' asked Ange.

'Will do. We have access to some specialists, former hackers themselves. They know their way around, and I have one of them looking into it. By the way, your colleague up there, Peter Fredericks, asked me to check out some accountant's office in Blacktown. I'm planning to do that tomorrow.'

'Isn't there someone else who can do that, Billy?' asked Ange, thinking that Billy's skills were better deployed from behind the keyboard.

'We have lots of resources but seem to be light on the ground personnel-wise. There are loads of people tied up with the ATO over that Pandora Papers leak.'

Met with silence, Billy realised Ange didn't know what he was speaking about. 'You know, where all of those confidential banking records were leaked from a bunch of tax havens? I understand it totals some eleven million documents. There is an accountant in Australia who was organising affairs for his high-net-worth clients. The word around the office is that there are some serious names in those eleven million pieces of paper. It has everyone in a frenzy.'

'OK, let me know how you go tomorrow,' replied Ange before hanging up the call.

The tall poppy syndrome was another epidemic affecting Australia, and her law enforcement colleagues were not immune. A high-profile case such as the Panama Papers could be career-defining. However, tall poppies usually deployed top-notch legal firms when under attack, so it wasn't a job for trigger-happy or sloppy investigators. As the media magnate Kerry Packer had famously shown in his fight with the tax office, the definition of a tax cheat was a grey area in the court of public opinion.

Chapter 19

Odds and Ends

B illy must have been busy, as the email with contact details for Sonia Nicol didn't arrive until late the next day. She now worked at an outfit called Andrews Cabinet Makers. Ringing the number provided, Ange introduced herself as Angela from Carcharias, pre-emptively explaining that this was the Greek word for shark, as if this was a fun fact that everyone should know.

The receptionist was all business, asking about the purpose of Ange's call. Not long ago, she would have taken offence, wondering what they might be hiding. Not anymore. Your phone number was just one of the many avenues that cold-callers and scammers relied on to ply their trade. Ange took the receptionist's blocking move in her stride, explaining that her call was in relation to some reference checking, a little white lie designed to stifle idle office gossip.

When she had Sonia Nicol on the phone, Ange cut to the chase and revealed her full name and title. 'It's Detective Angela Watson here, Ms Nicol. I'm ringing to ask you some questions about your time at Jack's Constructions. Can you start by telling me what you do at Andrews Cabinets?'

'I'm the CFO. Call me Sonia, by the way. We're the largest cabinetmaker in the Central Coast area, probably one of the largest in the state, actually. I'm also the company secretary. It's a family enterprise, not unlike Jack's Constructions. I presume the question you're going to ask next is why I left Jack's?'

Ange thought this perceptive, and took note of Nicol's confident and no-nonsense approach. 'Go on, please,' was all she replied.

'I really enjoyed that job. We had a great team in finance, but I knew I would never make CFO. I enjoyed working with John Williamson, the CFO and my former boss, but he's close to the Jack family and I was never likely to take over from him. Notwithstanding the limited career path, I would have stayed there but for being sacked by one of the Jack brothers. Bobby was so inappropriate. It was the best thing really, as I bounced straight into this job with Andrews, one of their suppliers,' replied Sonia Nicol, coolly and with no apparent emotion.

'When you say inappropriate, what do you mean by that?' probed Ange.

'A confidentiality agreement prevents me from disclosing any details of my settlement with Jack's, but let me just say that it was enough to set me up nicely here on the Central Coast.'

'I understand. I knew you had a problem with Bobby Jack. Can you go into that? And by the way, I will treat whatever you say in confidence,' said Ange, putting on her most reassuring tone. She sometimes regretted saying this, as her cases and the law often required her to disclose information that she had promised to keep confidential. Genuine people became most uptight when their trust was breached, and Ange had upset a string of genuine people in her time as a detective.

'Bobby Jack was trouble for me the moment that he came back into the company. He knew full well that John, my boss, had the ear of the CEO and the chairman. So, he would wait until John was away or otherwise occupied before he would put the weights on me.'

'What, sexually?' implied Ange instinctively, sexual misconduct cases being another epidemic sweeping the country.

'No, nothing like that,' replied Nicol quickly. 'Bobby was always hatching some business scheme or another. He really does not know how companies the size of Jack's work. Bobby had the misguided impression that he could waltz in and spend money willy-nilly. Watching too many miniseries on Netflix, I expect.'

'What sort of business schemes?' replied Ange, checking herself that she was also prone to the occasional bout of miniseries misdirection.

'When he came back from his travels, Bobby was convinced about the investment potential of the climate change industry. He wanted me to sign off on unlisted investments into the sector. Grid-scale batteries being one. Then there was a large plantation in North Queensland that turned seed pods into aviation fuel. Then he became obsessed with growing saltbush for carbon credits. He put some of his own money into the saltbush venture. I must give Bobby his due. He had a finger on the pulse. Had we invested in the battery project, we would have made a fortune when it listed on the ASX.'

'I suppose he was angry about that?' pressed Ange, not entirely convinced that there was not more to her story.

'When we had our last fight, the battery company had just listed. I suppose he blamed me for the missed opportunity, but that wasn't the point. The board delegated certain financial authorities to us, ones that we needed to stick to. Anyhow, he came to me with another investment in CBD oil. When I said that he needed to run that by the board, he went mental. He dredged up every gripe he could and sacked me on the spot. He really didn't have the authority to sack me, but I had had enough and walked out there and then. As I mentioned, it was the best thing I ever did.'

Ange pushed harder. 'How would you describe Bobby's associates in the main?'

'I never knew him until he came back into the company, but John let slip that the family had bailed Bobby out of trouble on more than one occasion. I think Bobby spent some time on the wrong side of the tracks, but I never got that close. Nobody ever truly gets on with Bobby Jack.'

'What is your impression of the dynamics within the company? Family businesses like that must be challenging,' probed Ange, thinking that Nicol's perspective could be useful now that she was out of the company.

'John led the accounting division, and he reported directly to Sam and the board, which included the three brothers: Sam, Cam and Bobby. Sam seemed to do a good job, except with holding his brother Bobby in check. I've had very little to do with Cam. He's an engineer and everyone calls him the professor. He seemed a solid guy based on what I saw. Bobby's the youngest of the three brothers and could be a complete pain in the arse, as I mentioned. Then there's Alison, the youngest sibling, and a finance executive with Citigroup in Hong Kong. I understand she's smart and tough. She looked after the family's overseas investments, whatever they are. I often heard Alison referred to as *The Princess*, the apple of their departed father's eye, in fact. John only heard from her personally when the dividends were due to be disbursed, but I think she holds some real influence over her brothers and around the board table.'

'What about the chairman, Bob Turnbull?'

'I had little to do with him, but I heard John talk about him. Apparently, Turnbull's a shrewd operator, part of the Sydney business elite. Everyone speaks highly of him, and he seems to have done a good job chairing the company since Tom Jack died. I never met Tom Jack. The light plane accident was before my time.'

Sonia Nicol had easily answered Ange's questions, seemingly comfortable and relaxed, as if she had nothing to hide. Ange wasn't gaining any impression that she was a person with a deadly axe to grind. Greed was always a powerful motive, but Ange felt there were more likely suspects than Sonia Nicol. 'OK. Thanks, Sonia. This has been most helpful. I doubt that I'll need to be in touch, but if you think of anything, you can ring me on...' Ange paused, not knowing which number to provide. She finally gave out her old number, as she couldn't remember her new one. She would have to spend some time and memorise it.

Sonia had given Ange a strong lead. Her impressions of Bob Turnbull had been spot on, but he hadn't been entirely forthcoming about Bobby Jack. She would circle back on this at their weekly meeting. The difficulty of juggling family dynamics with a substantial business enterprise was not a totally foreign concept for Ange. Rural families regularly faced challenges when the farming and grazing holdings were passed down a generation, often with destructive consequences. That there would be tension between the brothers was entirely predictable.

Billy was having an absolute ball in his new job, diving down one rabbit hole or another and disappearing for hours on end. He had become fascinated with state-sponsored cybercrime. Whereas ransomware attacks were in-and-out raids, state-sponsored activity was more about stealing secret information or causing widespread disruption of services. These costly attacks were happening every minute of every day and on a huge scale. The hackers really knew their stuff.

Late Thursday afternoon, Billy finally pulled his head from his screens and focussed on his to-do list. Having located Sonia Nicol, he started on the job that Peter Fredericks had sent him. KC Partners Pty Ltd sounded more like a seventies rock band than an accountancy practice. Their address showed as Chapel Road in Bankstown, and Billy used Google Street View to wander virtually down the road. He quickly found the right building, an impressively named but unimpressively bland two-storey walk-up. The Bankstown Professional Centre was not exactly a dress circle address for corporate Australia.

There were lots of Vietnamese restaurants in the area, which made Billy's mouth water, seeing that dinner time was approaching. Ange had introduced him to Vietnamese food when they were working together in Byron and he was now a huge fan. Billy had been engrossed in the shadowy world of international cybercrime and had forgotten to have lunch—again. His stomach rumbled loudly, angry at having been ignored all day.

Using his IT box of tricks, Billy located a phone number, which went straight to voicemail. He didn't leave a message as it would achieve nothing other than potentially alerting anyone dodgy that the authorities were on their tail. Back at his computer screens, he found that there were quite a few business names listed at the same address. He started with the first on his screen, also finding no answer. The second was more productive. A heavily accented woman's voice answered, Middle Eastern perhaps. 'Hello.'

Billy put on his best boy-next-door voice. 'Hi. I'm trying to track down someone from KC Partners, but all I get is an answering service. Can you tell me if anyone still works there?'

'I rarely see anyone there, but a young woman comes to pick up the mail every day around 9 a.m. I suggest you try then.'

Billy realised he would need to visit the old-fashioned way. He remembered an old tennis mate from Bankstown, Joey Ma. One of the bad things emerging from Billy's new job was that he spent way too much time at his desk in front of his bank of computer screens. He had lost his rhythm since moving to Sydney, so he reached out to see if Joey Ma was around and up for a hit of tennis the next morning. Joey had taken a sporting scholarship in the US and Billy had run into him a few months ago at a tournament in Newcastle. Joey was back home working in his parents' successful dry-cleaning business, and the pair agreed to meet at the Bankstown Tennis Club at 7 a.m. the next morning.

Billy woke up before dawn, keen to get on the court. He was already stretching courtside when Joey turned up, so they got straight into it. Joey's time playing US college tennis had certainly sharpened his game. Billy consistently beat him when they were competing in age tournaments back in school, but he was no match that early winter's morning. By the time that they had towelled off and taken some water, it was 8:30 a.m. and time for Billy to scoot off. They made plans for a repeat game, although Billy felt the result would be the same. Still in his tennis gear, he was waiting outside the door to KC Partners when a twenty-something woman came and unlocked the door. 'Do you work for KC Partners?' asked Billy.

'Part-time. I just pick up the mail and check the messages,' replied the woman.

'Does anyone work here?'

'Occasionally. We're mostly just a registered office for lots of small shelf companies.'

'Is there someone I can speak to, then?' asked Billy.

The woman went on the defensive. 'Why do you ask, and who exactly am I speaking to?'

Billy fished around in his tracksuit pants for a moment, eventually retrieving his wallet and flashing his badge, something that he rarely did in his new job. The woman just shook her head and wrote a number on a direct mail catalogue that she picked up off the floor. 'Some of these companies get themselves into all sorts of trouble. You can ring my boss. Anton Mackellar. Look, I have another job to go to. Is that all?'

Billy peered into the office. Not only didn't anyone appear to work there, but Billy also doubted anyone would want to. A more drab-looking setup he hadn't seen. 'No, that's all. Thanks for your help.'

He was tempted to ring the number scrawled on the piece of junk mail during the drive back to the office, but he shot off a brief email with the details to Peter Fredericks instead, copying in Ange.

As pleased as Billy was with his detective work, his body was less than impressed with his tennis fitness. By the time he had driven the hour or more back to the office, he was stiffening up and knew that he would be very sore tomorrow. Even though he regularly worked out in the gym downstairs, it was nothing compared to how a good game of tennis would assault muscles and stretch tendons and ligaments. This was something he would need to work on. Roscoe, his doubles partner, was a fitness psycho. He would be unimpressed should Billy's fitness let the side down during this summer's tournament circuit.

Billy smiled at the thought of his good mate. Roscoe was a bit of a smart-arse in reality, but they were a formidable pairing. Billy's game revolved around a heavy serve, and Roscoe would invariably yell 'cop that' at their opponents as Billy thundered down another ace. Roscoe never tired of his own cleverness at this little play on words, and more than one pair of opponents had lost their cool and gifted the match over Roscoe's puerile chant. Losing one's cool rarely worked out, so Billy was happy to let Roscoe's cringeworthy antics continue. Keeping one's cool under pressure was one of the many things that sport had taught Billy.

Chapter 20

Brett Tompkins

By the time Friday afternoon arrived, Ange was feeling like she was going nowhere, treading water aimlessly. She was pleased when Higgsy sent a text at around 5:30 p.m.

> *Solid groundswell building through Saturday. Offshore winds predicted Sunday. Planning to hit South Straddie Sunday morning with the crew. Should be epic. R U keen?*

Ange wasted no time in texting back a big thumbs-up emoji. Her phone soon chirped Higgsy's reply.

> *Great. 8 a.m. at the Seaway. See you then.*

Confirmatory emoji sent, Ange felt much better, having a focal point for the weekend. Her phone chirped again.

> *PS. Don't bring your fancy board. Straddie can be heavy. Broke a board earlier in the year myself.*

She ditched the thumbs-up emoji this time, settling for an OK followed by a worried-looking face. 'Little Miss Scared,' she thought to herself.

Ange felt her stomach rumble, unsure whether that was hunger or fear calling. Whichever way, she needed to eat, so she jumped in the VW and headed towards

Broadbeach to find something nice to eat. She had been keen to try the surf club, a stylish modern building right on the beach that she often walked past when exercising. By the time she arrived, the car park was almost full. The Gold Coast seemed busy, but the locals kept telling Ange that things were quiet and business was slow. They were missing the regular Sydney and Melbourne tourists on account of the lingering lockdown and Covid border restrictions.

Vaccination rates in Queensland were glacially slow, which seemed oxymoronic to Ange, seeing as the only way out for everyone was for the population to get vaccinated. The press was full of nothing else, as other countries around the world opened up. Ange was due to get her second shot in two weeks, keen to get it over and done with.

The Gold Coast had experienced negligible cases and residents felt safe, lacking sufficient incentive to get vaccinated. It would be ironic if the only way out of this lethargy was a serious Covid outbreak itself. 'People are strange cattle,' Ange mused as she went through the check-in formalities. She wandered through the crowd, making her way to the bar, playing her usual game, imagining the personalities beneath the resort wear.

What a view. The dining room overlooked the wide sandy beach to the ocean, shimmering under floodlights mounted on the roof. When they weren't saving lives, surf clubs occupied some of the best real estate in the country, and Kurrawa Surf Club was no exception. The club would likely do well out of this facility, which seemed a fair reward for saving lives for free. She enjoyed a delightful meal of whiting and chips, lingering over a glass of wine and fending off a few hopeful stares. She was tired and simply not in the mood for being chatted up, happy to be fed and tucked into bed solo. A good night's sleep beckoned.

The surf was a mere ripple when Ange checked early on Saturday morning. She wondered if Higgsy might have been smoking something when he'd texted his prospective surf forecast. She took herself off for a walk, followed by her weekly shopping, perhaps even clean the house. Chores completed, Ange went over to the beach again at 3 p.m., shocked to see just how much the surf had jumped. Long consecutive swell lines stretched out to the horizon. It was still relatively small, but she could sense something in the air. Perhaps Higgsy had been on the money after all.

Excited that perhaps something was afoot, she settled in for an early evening to watch a couple of episodes of *Vigil*, a crime miniseries she was now hooked on.

A female detective was stuck on a submarine, trying to solve a series of murders. It was funny how detectives enjoyed watching detective shows. Ange was no exception.

Waking later than planned, Ange just had time for coffee and some muesli, getting some fuel in the tank, knowing that a surf session on South Straddie was a bit of a trek. She made it to the Seaway with only a few minutes to spare, quickly dragging on her wetsuit and getting her board ready. The guys were all waiting for her and were already in line. She hated queue-jumpers but nonchalantly joined the line beside them, ignoring the death stares from those behind.

The solid groundswell had continued to grow overnight, infusing the air with sea mist and a heavy smell of the ocean. The long interval swell was even making its way well into the Seaway, a hint of what lay around the breakwater.

There was a large line of surfers waiting patiently for their turn to climb aboard the surf taxi. Obviously Higgsy wasn't the only clairvoyant on the Goldie. A real buzz was running through the queue of wetsuited gladiators, sensing the challenge that waited around the corner. With only eight surfers per trip, Ange figured she would be standing in line for at least forty minutes. Every so often, impatience would bubble to the surface, and someone would break ranks to brave the long paddle—and the bull sharks.

As she jealously watched the next group of surfers climb on board, her heart stopped for a moment, finally shocked back into action with an enormous thump. 'Is that Brett Tompkins in the water? Surely not. Yes, it is. I recognise his board. It's the same one he used at Midway on that day I scored my first tube. His hair is longer, but it's definitely him.' These thoughts swirled around in her head as she watched the boat zoom off around the headland.

She was so preoccupied that she didn't hear Jen speaking to her, misinterpreting the look on her face as one of fear and apprehension. 'Don't worry, if it's too big for you, you should be able to hang in close to the breakwater and score some waves if you're patient.'

Jen's voice dragged Ange back into the real world. 'Sorry, Jen, what did you say? I was a million miles away.'

Jen repeated her advice, but Ange wasn't listening again; the shock of seeing Brett Tompkins was too confusing. She felt a tinge of anger flush through her. Jen could see that Ange was distracted and left her alone for the moment.

Ange stood in silence until it was their turn, the freezing water bringing her back to the present as she jumped into the Seaway and paddled over to the water taxi. As the boat sped around the northern rock wall of the Seaway, she gasped at the size and strength of the swell. Any thoughts of Brett Tompkins were well and truly relegated. There were literally hundreds of surfers scattered half a kilometre north along the beach. Jumping off the boat, Ange paddled directly towards the beach until she was just outside the take-off zone. She sat up on her board and scoped out the action to work out where she might surf.

It was on fire. When they weren't getting hammered, surfers were constantly scoring barrels. Looking north, there were several obvious peaks, marked by a concentration of waiting surfers. The waves to the north seemed bigger and more powerful. Brian, Gav and Jen quickly scooted off north, every man, and woman, for themselves. Higgsy paddled over, having seen the whites of Ange's eyes as she sat looking at the action.

'I'm not sure that I'm up for this, Higgsy,' offered Ange as he paddled over.

'Yeh. It's pretty heavy. More so than I expected. I suggest you paddle south and sit close to the rock wall.' Higgsy pointed out a spot near the rocks, where the swell wasn't penetrating as heavily. Ange just nodded, still not convinced.

Higgsy was keen to get into the action. 'Oh well, into the fray. Here for a good time, not a long time. I'm going to drift north until it's beyond my pay grade.'

They agreed to meet at the pickup spot at 11:30 a.m. before Higgsy paddled away and into the mix. Ange took his advice and slowly paddled south to the headland. As far as she could see, other than her and Jen, there was only one other woman in the water, something that didn't make her feel any more comfortable.

She paddled across towards the rock wall and caught a nice wave along the way. Finding the wave appropriate for her skill level, Ange kept her spot by lining up two markers, one on the beach and one along the rock wall. Provided she stayed patient and picked her waves carefully, she scored plenty of quality rides. When 11:30 a.m. came around, she paddled over to the pickup zone with leaden arms. There had been no tube rides racked up on her account, but it had certainly been a great session.

There was one guy waiting in the water with his board snapped clean in two, awkwardly trying to wrestle these two corks, now suddenly useless for anything other than a good story that night at the pub. The other four members of her crew paddled over in dribs and drabs until the five of them were sitting on their boards, talking through their successes and failures. Gav said that he'd seen Mick

Fanning in the water. 'He was ridiculous. I reckon every hot surfer on the coast was here today. Fanning seemed to have so much time and make every wave look easy. I suppose that's why he was world number one. I got hammered so many times, I don't think I'll ever get the water out of my sinuses, not to mention the sand in my ears.'

As the surfer with the broken board climbed on board ahead of them, Ange heard the skipper comment that his was the fifth casualty of the day, not quite a record, but certainly a solid performance by South Straddie standards. Ange had a good look at the snapped board, marvelling at how flimsy it seemed. Wafer-thin fibreglass bonded over a central core of foam, strengthened by a thin wooden stringer.

By the time they were back at their cars, it was much later than everyone had promised their partners, so they darted off quickly, leaving Ange to her thoughts on the day. She contemplated waiting around and confronting Brett Tompkins, but he might have already left. Anyway, Ange could smell that something wasn't right. She would take this up with Sally Anders on Tuesday.

Once she was dry and warm, Ange found a parking spot on Tedder Avenue and ordered some breakfast. The coffee got her thinking about the snapped board. There were lots of tales of surfers trying to smuggle drugs fibreglassed inside their surfboards. She had heard that most countries X-rayed boards to check, but undoubtedly plenty of drugs slipped through with the help of baggage handlers on the take. It got her thinking.

As soon as she was home, Ange jumped onto her laptop and started trying to find out how ACP cladding was manufactured. After all, they were just two sheets of metal bonded over a foam core, exactly like a surfboard. She eventually found some videos on YouTube that showed various manufacturing techniques, each one selling the production machinery, no doubt. She marvelled at how easy it was to learn even the most arcane subject on the internet, even scoring a free instruction video for good measure.

She spent the next few hours learning everything she could about ACP panels. The more she mulled this over in her mind, the more plausible her theory became. The dates when the supply of narcotics was interrupted roughly lined up with the ACP scandal. There were scads of unanswered questions, but Ange became convinced that the idea of ACP panels being used to smuggle narcotics was worth looking into.

This was what Ange did best, finding the thread and pulling it relentlessly. Sometimes the thread turned out to be just that, random and unconnected. Other times, it was crucial and opened a gap where she could discern a way through.

The matter with Brett Tompkins was more an itch, something that she dearly wanted to scratch, unsure if doing so would tingle pleasantly, or whether it was a mosquito bite that would fester and hurt. She opted to ignore that itch—for the moment, at least.

Chapter 21

Shadows

A nge was getting the hang of the Monday morning commute on the M1, but she hadn't factored in today's debacle. A concrete mixer had rear-ended a mattress delivery truck, its softish load failing to soften the blow. Putting the carnage of the trucks aside, there was concrete spilled over the road, something that needed to be cleared up. The traffic police had closed all but one lane and a massive traffic jam had resulted. It was death by queue, twice in two days. No spectacular waves awaited this queue, just more traffic and frustration.

Google Maps told her that the delay was looking at forty minutes. The M1 was the primary transport artery that hugged the entire East Coast of Australia, doubling as the sole commuter road linking Brisbane with the Gold Coast. There was no way around, and Ange rang Pat Crowley to slide their appointment back an hour. People normally made time for Major Crimes, but Crowley sounded annoyed.

She arrived stressed and frustrated. Once they had successfully connected with Bob Turnbull via Zoom, the first item of business was to reschedule next week's meeting for midday. Ange was not about to suffer that commuter's torture again.

Ange let Crowley open the batting—cricket metaphors seemed somehow appropriate for Pat Crowley and Bob Turnbull. 'First, those two guys you asked me to check on—Lomax and Smith. They've both worked for Jeays Property Services in the security division.' Crowley looked down at his notes to confirm he had the dates correct. 'From November 2016 until March 2019 and recently coming back onto the books on the nineteenth of June this year.'

Ange's hunch had been correct. 'Do you keep records of their movements? For example, do they need to log on and off building sites?' Ange asked as casually as she could.

'Well, they're supposed to,' came Turnbull's rapid-fire reply. 'Our safety auditor monitors these things.'

'What about the warehouses? Would comings and goings be logged to these facilities? Presumably they're secured by proximity card readers?' asked Ange, her series of rapid-fire questions courtesy of a runaway train of thought.

'I would hope so. Why do you ask?' said Turnbull, now looking Ange squarely in the eyes.

She dodged and weaved. 'Well, these are serious guys, and not someone I would trust with the family jewels. Just to be on the safe side, can you download their coming and goings and send it to me?' Ange said to Crowley.

He looked unimpressed with the prospect of that extra piece of work. Presumably he was being paid by the hour, so Ange was similarly unimpressed. Crowley agreed, albeit reluctantly. Ange wanted to keep her parallel investigation secret as long as possible, so she was relieved to secure Crowley's commitment.

That issue behind them, Ange pressed on. 'How is your forensic work panning out?'

'That depends on what side of the fence you're sitting. On one hand, I'm finding more and more evidence and a pattern is emerging. On the other, the amount of the fraud is growing every day. I'm up to five and a half million dollars already.'

'So, tell me about the companies where the money is being siphoned off to,' Ange said, keen to understand the ins and outs of embezzlement and fraud.

'As I explained the other day, the companies are all designed to mirror legitimate suppliers, with slight variations to the company names,' said Crowley.

'Give me an example,' queried Ange.

'Fred's Plumbing Pty Ltd might become Fred's Plumbing Services Pty Ltd. If nobody was looking, it would be reasonable for a processing clerk to assume that they were divisions of the same head supplier,' explained Crowley.

'Can't you trace these suspicious companies?' asked Ange.

Crowley and Turnbull exchanged a look before Crowley explained some facts of life in the world of white-collar crime. 'It should be easy, but it isn't. A registry search will supply the directors and shareholders, but a whole industry sits around avoiding scrutiny, mostly dodging the tax office. Whoever sets up the company often uses dummy names as directors. Builders are notorious, often convincing a young, green apprentice to sign on as director. The going rate is five thousand dollars in the building game. Another common trick is to use a maiden name, or perhaps a naïve family member's. However, in this case, the names look random, so I doubt that they're connected.'

'How does that happen?' asked Ange, highly engaged in her crash course on Embezzlement 101.

'Identity theft mostly. You must be a real person to act as a company director; however, you can buy a stolen identity from any number of black-market vendors. Then all you need to do is change the address and you're good to go.'

'That sounds ridiculously easy. How often does this happen?'

'All the time. It's a key link in money laundering. The government has finally woken up and is introducing a multistage verification process for directors, called a Director ID. This should help, but I give cybercriminals twelve months at the outside to find a work-around.'

'So, what about the shareholders?'

'That's another complication. The shareholder is usually a unit trust and there's no requirement to disclose the beneficiaries. Following the banking Royal Commission, the government has put the heat on the banks to verify trust deeds, but there's a lot of catch-up that needs to be done.'

Ange was a fast learner. 'I presume that each of the companies you have identified has been set up like this.'

'Yes, there's not all that many. I suspect three or four, five tops. It's been well thought through,' replied Crowley.

'How deep can you dig?'

'Not much further without police backing and some court orders,' replied Crowley, the ball now back in Ange's court.

Ange sat for a moment, considering her options. On one hand, she was now invested in finding out more about the embezzlement. On the other, she didn't want to risk alerting the syndicate that the authorities might be on to them. She needed to talk this over with Sally Anders.

'Can you guys give me a moment?' she said, standing up from her seat amidst their questioning gazes. Ange walked out of the room to a quiet corner in reception overlooking the Brisbane River, ensuring nobody was in earshot before she rang Sally Anders. Once Anders was on the line, Ange filled her in on what she had learned about Lomax and Smith and the extended period of their involvement.

Anders cut to the chase. 'What's your question, Ange?'

'Well, I feel I need to either pull them off the case or fill them in and keep Crowley working with us. I'm concerned that they might inadvertently poke the bear and the syndicate will go to ground again. We could take the matter out of their hands and use our own forensic team. What do you think?'

The call was silent for a moment while Anders thought all this through. 'I think we should keep Crowley on the case. I'm suspicious that we may have someone on our side feeding information to the syndicate. Also, if Crowley inadvertently digs too deep, it can be explained away as routine accounting work. If our team is involved, the syndicate will know that we're close. Fill them in and keep Crowley on the case. Let me know if you need any paperwork done.'

'I may need some court orders to allow Crowley to dig deeper into the fraudulent accounts. This all has to be connected. I just don't know how. Perhaps we can use Billy to help speed things up?'

'I agree. It's too much of a coincidence. We need to find the connection. Keep Billy on the job,' replied Anders before abruptly hanging up.

Ange didn't take offence, as she knew that Sally Anders was all business. Trivial niceties were simply a waste of time in Anders' eyes. Ange walked back into the meeting room. Turnbull and Crowley were talking, pausing as she entered the room.

'OK. I need to fill you in on some other factors. This must stay strictly confidential,' stated Ange as firmly as possible, sequentially deploying her best death stare to Crowley and Turnbull until she had secured their respective nods.

'We've been tracking Lomax and Smith for over six months now. They're part of a sophisticated drug syndicate and we suspect them of murder.' Ange looked up to see the shocked look in the eyes of the other two.

'Shivers,' replied Crowley. 'That's a big step from embezzlement.'

'Yes. It shocked us to find that those two characters were involved with Jack's. We found out by accident, if I'm honest. As you can imagine, we don't want to alert them. They probably think that they got away with their last misadventure, so they might become sloppy or careless at some point. I can secure court orders to get you behind the corporate veil, but that will all take some time. It's crucial that you keep a low profile in the meantime.'

Ange thought back to her lucky break at the building site. 'I saw them coming out of your building project at Broadbeach. The one on Britannia Avenue.

Somehow, we need to determine what they were doing there and who they were meeting. That's why I want those attendance logs. If we can establish who they're meeting, it might give us some direction.' She looked directly at Crowley. 'I've just spoken to my boss. We think it best that you continue digging. We need to find out how all this links up. Do you have any thoughts?'

Bob Turnbull had sat listening to all of this until now. 'This really concerns me. Pat is part of our team looking after the company's interests. Are you saying that this is effectively out of our hands now?'

'It would be better if we worked as a team. Pat digging around is easily explained as normal accounting stuff; not so if our guys get involved. Of course, I cannot guarantee where all this will go and the consequences of that,' replied Ange, letting it sink in for a moment. 'Provided you don't hide anything from us, your cooperation will look good.'

Crowley and Turnbull exchanged a glance before Turnbull spoke. 'Are you OK with this, Pat?'

Turnbull secured Crowley's nodded affirmation before speaking. 'OK. Let's do this.'

Ange squared them off again. 'Do not speak to anyone about this. It must stay strictly between us. And when I say nobody, I mean nobody. That includes wives, girlfriends, even Sam Jack.'

Turnbull gave a nervous chuckle, while Crowley's worried expression remained steadfast. Ange wondered if Turnbull had a wife and a girlfriend. Pillow talk was the ruin of many secret arrangements. Ange mulled over that thought as she said her goodbyes and accompanied a worried Crowley to the lift. Before the pair departed, Ange asked Crowley to send her any requests for court orders should he hit a brick wall in his forensic work.

As she drove back to the coast, Ange realised that Crowley normally dealt with white-collar crime, the sort who worked in offices. Perhaps they drove luxury cars and wore expensive suits. Now he found himself dealing with murder and a narcotics syndicate. No wonder he looked worried.

Chapter 22

In the Job

Because of her phone call with Anders the day before, Ange had a shorter list than usual prepared for her Tuesday catch-up. Anders didn't even give Ange a chance to open her trusty notebook before she cut to the chase.

'So, what do you think is going on here, Ange? I'd be surprised if you didn't have a theory or two by now.'

'I really don't know. I'm certain that Jack's Constructions is somehow involved, but I can't say how deep this goes,' Ange replied.

'Come on. I know you'll have some theories running around that imagination of yours,' probed Anders. Fredericks never seemed to look up from his computer during their meetings, but Ange knew full well that he was listening intently. She didn't yet have a bead on Fredericks.

Ange never liked to expose her theories too early. Her overactive imagination was prone to run off, fabricating fact from fiction if it galloped away unchecked. This trait often caught Ange by surprise, embarrassed when her hypotheses collapsed and turned to dust. Sometimes, her obsessive belief that she was onto something caused her to miss crucial clues, wasting valuable time in the process. Anders waited patiently for a reply whilst Ange put her misgivings aside.

'I have a feeling that the narcotics were concealed in building products and smuggled in through Jeays Building Products, one of Jack's subsidiaries,' replied Ange, somewhat tentatively.

'How so?' queried Anders.

'Do you remember the Grenfell Tower fire tragedy in London? The one that killed a bunch of people?'

Fredericks looked up from his laptop at last, giving Ange a puzzled look.

Ange pushed on. 'That fire was caused by a cladding product called Aluminium Composite Panels, or ACP for short. Essentially, they're two aluminium sheets bonded over a foam core, a sandwich of sorts. Not long after the Grenfell fire disaster, there was a similar incident in Melbourne. Luckily, there were no lives lost that time, but the government responded by opening an investigation into ACP panels. They found that there were lots of cheap imports flooding into the country and many had fraudulent or non-existent fire certification. You can imagine the confusion of building owners and builders. One person I spoke to was part way through a large apartment block when the proverbial hit the fan. The developer was forced to pull all the cladding down and replace it with a substitute. That all happened in 2019, about the same time when we suspect the syndicate started using trawlers.'

'How did you arrive at this idea? It seems a giant leap,' asked Fredericks, finally speaking up.

'I came across Sam Jack in a newspaper article when I was backgrounding the group. He was defending his company over their own imported panels. Jeays Building Products is a B2B supplier, so they got caught up in the ACP scandal. I did some research on the way the panels are manufactured. It's quite straight-forward and there are a few videos online. I came up with the idea when I was surfing and one of the other surfers had broken their board. As you probably know, surfboards are often used as a vehicle for smuggling drugs. Anyhow, I put two and two together. Actually, one of my surfing buddies was a foreman on that building project where the ACP panels were replaced mid-construction.'

Ange paused for a moment, waiting for any question before she launched into the topic that was really bugging her.

Anders looked interested. 'That Lomax and Smith are working security for Jeays would presumably give them unfettered access to any warehouse facili-ties.' She paused, as if double-checking Ange's logic. 'It seems worth running to ground, Ange.'

Anders looked at her phone, one of her habitual cues that their meeting was over. Ange wasn't so easily dismissed this time around.

'Speaking of surfing, you'll never guess who I ran across the other day,' said Ange, pausing for effect. The others just looked at her, not showing the least bit of interest in her apparent social life.

'Brett Tompkins,' she stated forcibly, looking Sally Anders directly in the eye.

'What the heck is going on? I don't for a minute believe that this was a lucky coincidence.'

'Did he see you?' asked Anders immediately.

Ange shook her head. 'No. I kept out of sight. It was very busy that day and we must have surfed in different spots.' She looked questioningly at Anders, waiting for an explanation.

Anders and Fredericks glanced at each other, both patently in the know.

'Brett Tompkins works for us,' answered Anders.

Ange cut her off sharply. 'You should have told me. I think I deserved to know what was going on.'

Anders went on the offensive, her voice sharp and decisive. 'I'm well aware of your indiscretion with Brett Tompkins. He got into some trouble about that. I wasn't happy. He could easily have jeopardised his cover.'

'What, you mean to tell me he was working undercover in Namba Heads?'

Anders sat down; clearly this was a long story. 'Yes and no. Not really, at least initially. Brett has been working with us for several years. He was in the job down on the south coast. It turned very ugly.'

Ange knew that *in the job* was police-speak for working undercover. She sat patiently for Anders to go on.

'Brett was suffering PTSD as a result of that terrible job, but he was hiding it from everyone. His marriage was torn apart before anyone realised how he was suffering. Brett was placed on indefinite stress leave. He was in Namba Heads, essentially recovering, when we got wind that Darren Billings had been compromised. We called Brett back into the job. It was all benign stuff, keeping an eye on that goose of a sergeant. Things fell into place nicely, as Brett had fortuitously created the perfect cover as a legitimate property developer. When Ted Kramer turned up in town, and then Joe Kramer tried to finger him over the townhouse development, we sensed that something was on foot. Then you turned up unannounced.'

Anders paused to look pointedly at Ange. 'We were concerned at first, but you were doing a great job poking around. When things heated up, we pulled Brett out of town to maintain the brilliant cover that he had created.'

'So that's how you knew when to step in and take over our investigation,' said Ange in a light-bulb moment.

'Exactly. Brett was very complimentary about your work, by the way. He was the main reason that I reached out after your little fracas with SACC.'

'What about his affair with Amy Lightfoot? Weren't you concerned about that?' asked Ange, unable to control her emotions, still smarting after being duped by Brett. It didn't help that Amy Lightfoot was willowy and attractive, also disturbingly younger than Ange.

'He wasn't having an affair,' stated Anders dismissively. 'She had reached out to the police, concerned about her own safety. She and Ted Kramer were listed on our case log as persons of interest, so we were alerted and stepped in to deal with it. The whole disappearance thing was Brett's idea. He figured she might be a valuable witness if, as we suspected, the Kramers were involved with the syndicate.'

'Why didn't you bring me in on it?' Ange snapped back.

'You were doing our job for us. The staged disappearance and subsequent reappearance achieved two things. It kept you on the case, poking and prodding as you did, but it also spooked Ted Kramer. Billings, on the other hand, had absolutely no idea what was going on. Still doesn't.'

A thought must have occurred to Anders, as she looked towards Ange out of the corner of her eye. 'How exactly did you *run into* Brett Tompkins, by the way? Have you been looking for him?'

'Of course not. I was waiting in a long queue for the water taxi that ferries surfers across the Seaway to South Stradbroke Island. I had completely forgotten about him until then,' lied Ange, conveniently failing to mention her predawn musings, reliving their steamy night together.

Ange pressed on. 'Is Brett working on this case as well?'

'Yes,' was Anders' monosyllabic reply, a blatant attempt to end this conversation.

Ange would not be sidestepped so easily. 'So... what is he doing here?'

'We're quite certain that the syndicate has links in the gambling industry, identifying compromised individuals that may be of benefit to them. Like Billings, for example. They must have seriously good intelligence systems. Think about how many gamblers are out there, most losing money. Very few would be of any help, so they must have sophisticated data analytics to pick the gems from the gravel. Brett is posing as a successful property developer with a slightly opaque history, which works well here. Lots of people on the Gold Coast appear wealthier and more successful than they really are. As well as keeping up his property persona,

Brett is posing as a partner of a start-up online betting agency called BeaBet. One of the co-founders owes us a few favours.'

'You said a startup. Isn't BBet a massive gambling outfit?' asked Ange. She also knew that repaying a favour meant staying out of court for that co-founder.

'It's spelt differently. Capital B, small e, small a, capital B, small e, small t. It's a bit cute and I'm surprised that they haven't received a cease-and-desist letter by now. Perhaps the founders set it up to be taken over at some stage. Anyhow, it all seems to be going quite well, and Brett is asking around about who might be the big fish in town. His ploy is that he wants them to join BeaBet, but the actual plan is to build a good database of people who might be compromised, either in the future or already. You need to check your feelings for Brett Tompkins, whatever they are,' stated Anders, obviously a wake-up to Ange's little white lie.

'No problem,' Ange replied nonchalantly. She knew deep down that this was going to be nigh impossible. Now aware that Brett hadn't had an affair with Amy Lightfoot, there would be no stopping those early-morning daydreams.

Anders stood up suddenly, signalling that this discussion was now over. She then surprised Ange with her next comment. 'I'm hungry. How about you order some takeaway, Ange? Vietnamese or Thai stir-fry? I'll need to make some calls in the meantime.'

Ange took this as an affirmation that she was across the threshold and now fully part of the team. She ordered Thai stir-fry from a ramshackle shopfront that she had spied on one of her walks, in a back street just around the corner from the apartment. Given how much development was going on, she knew that the days of that tawdry shopfront were numbered, soon to be swallowed up by a large skyscraper, any replacement restaurant forced to pay triple the rent. Ange gave the owner a nice tip when she picked up the food.

They had just tucked into their lunch and some small talk when Fredericks' laptop beeped. He went across to check what it was, intently studying his screen before looking up to fill in his colleagues. 'Lomax and Smith are on the move, picked up on a traffic cam. Looks like they're heading this way.'

Chapter 23

Triangles

Ange would have loved to stake out the construction site on Britannia Avenue herself but knew that this was not a risk worth taking. Even though they now had several data sources to triangulate, it would be helpful to somehow attach a GPS tracker onto the Mitsubishi. She was certain that Lomax and Smith were up to no good. Ange verbalised this thought over lunch as they waited for more camera alerts.

Anders turned to Fredericks. 'What do you reckon, Peter? Any chance we could pull that off at such short notice? If they are headed this way, I reckon we have fifteen minutes.'

Ange jumped in front of this train of thought. 'Wouldn't we need a warrant to do something like this?'

'Normally, yes, but we already have authority to do whatever is necessary concerning Lomax and Smith after Namba Heads. I think we'll be fine,' answered Anders. 'Peter?'

'Let me make a few calls. We would need them to park on the street to pull it off. I think it would be too dangerous to attempt it within the construction compound, particularly with such little planning,' suggested Fredericks as he made a move to his laptop, his lunch now forgotten.

Ange had a thought. 'Could we get the fire service to make a call and park across the driveway?'

'Great idea, Ange. Peter, you organise a team ready to install a tracker and I'll ring my counterpart here and see whether the fire service can oblige.'

With that, Anders and Fredericks leaped into action. Ange also had a thought and emailed Pat Crowley from her phone, asking him to include the visitor logs from today. She tagged the email as *Important—Confidential*.

Within five minutes, the three reconvened over their half-finished lunch. Fredericks had arranged for a couple of plain-clothes detectives from the Surfers Paradise branch to tag the vehicle. They planned to swing by in a few minutes and pick up a tracker that Fredericks had pulled from a cupboard. He scoffed down his lunch and headed downstairs to meet them on the street.

Sally Anders' task had been much more difficult. Apparently, the relationship between the Gold Coast fire and police services was at a low point. After some negotiation, the local police eventually agreed to ring their first responder colleagues with a concocted story of an anonymous report of a serious fire hazard on the site. Apparently, since the ACP cladding issue, the fire services weren't averse to leaning on builders and property developers. 'Interesting dynamics,' thought Ange to herself.

Fredericks was back soon enough and the three of them crowded around his desk to watch the action, courtesy of a feed to the security cameras set up previously. Fredericks' technological competency impressed Ange.

Seeing as their apartment was situated midway between the fire station and the construction site, they heard the blaring siren before the fire truck appeared on camera. It did exactly what they had hoped, parking squarely across the driveway, which was the only viable parking spot for their big truck. Ange watched the guys pile out and walk onto the building site, feeling somewhat guilty for imposing on their time in this way.

Within a few minutes, Lomax and Smith turned onto Britannia Avenue in their Mitsubishi Outlander. The SUV paused briefly outside the driveway before driving down the road to find a parking place, beyond the reach of the security camera. Soon enough, the two came into focus, walking east on Britannia Avenue and then entering the construction site.

Fredericks' phone pinged within seconds. He glanced at the message. 'Job done. Let's see if it's working.' With that, he pulled up a tracking app onto one of his auxiliary screens and logged in the tracker ID. Suddenly, a map of Britannia Avenue appeared, and they could now see where Lomax and Smith had parked their car. This was a major development and the three high-fived each other, thrilled to have been able to pivot like that and take advantage of this fortuitous opportunity.

Once they had stopped congratulating themselves, Fredericks was quickly back to his old self, punching something into his computer before looking and addressing his colleagues. 'By the way, I rang the owner of that accounting firm that Billy visited last week, Anton Mackellar. He was of no help. He swore he was essentially a postal service for notices, all of which he sends on to an accountancy firm called Finch & Chang in Sydney. I looked them up and they seem quite large, based originally in Hong Kong. I'm inclined to believe Mackellar. Apparently, his company specialises in creating shelf companies that customers can buy, fully set up and ready to go. The new owners often neglect to change the registered office. He charges a small annual fee, which he also sends to Finch & Chang in the case of CVU. He said that they always paid, but he had wondered why Finch & Chang hadn't changed the registered office. When I asked him for his thoughts on that, he presumed the directors of CVU wanted to keep Finch & Chang on their toes and retain flexibility to change tax accountants if they started charging too much.'

'Did you contact anyone at Finch & Chang?' said Anders, asking the obvious.

'I rang them in a general sense. That place is tight. They won't disclose any client information without a court order,' replied Fredericks.

'Should we get one organised?' asked Ange.

'No,' replied Anders decisively. 'That will alert whoever's behind this that we're on their tail. We can leave that ace up our sleeve when we have a better idea of what is going on.'

With that, Anders dived back into her phone and Fredericks into his laptop. 'Time to go,' thought Ange with a smile.

She strode back home, full of energy and revelling in feeling part of a team again, like she had enjoyed in Byron Bay with Billy and Jim Grady. That reminded her—she needed to ring Billy and check in on his progress. Once she was back at her house, looking out over the Nerang River, she made a note of things that she needed to discuss with Billy.

To Discuss

1. *Cybercrime possibility?*

2. *Activity logs from Jack's & Jeays*

3. *Video surveillance*

4. GPS tracker

5. CVU and other shelf companies

Her thoughts now in order, she rang Billy's number. She missed having Billy's smiling face around and settled for an imagined facsimile.

'Hi, boss. How are things going? Bit of a dead end here, I'm afraid.'

'It's about to get much busier, Billy,' she said, a huge grin on her face. 'How did you go poking around the world of cybercrime?'

'I have to say, boss, the more I get into this stuff, the more concerned I become. I now have so many online aliases that I sometimes worry I'll forget my real name. However, I can't find anything that resembles a long-term embezzlement scam—online, at least. I think we should cross that option off the list for the time being. The one upside of all this digging is that I'm building a nice list of potential suspects and a few informants. Hopefully, these will come in handy down the track.'

'OK. Agreed. Did you get anywhere with CVU Pty Ltd and GlitterStrip?'

'Well, GlitterStrip looks like a legitimate operation to me. They have an active social media presence and employ a few influencers to build their brand. CVU Pty Ltd is another matter. That is a black hole. I spoke to someone in ASIC, who told me as much as he could without a court order. The shareholder is a unit trust, as we know, but the beneficiary of that trust is itself a trust, something called a discretionary trust. I spoke to an accountant mate from uni, who told me that those types of trusts are relatively uncommon, but they allow a lot of flexibility where the money gets distributed. I think we'll need a series of court orders to understand what's going on behind the cover of those trust vehicles. Someone has gone to a lot of trouble to cover their tracks here.'

Ange thought through the practicalities of securing a court order based on the limited information that they had at present. They needed something more concrete than the mere fact that the corporate structure was opaque. There would be thousands upon thousands of companies who used a similar structure, all legal and legitimate. Unfortunately, overtly poking around in the financial affairs of CVU Pty Ltd would also increase the likelihood of alerting whoever was behind the operation, something that Ange wanted to avoid at this stage of proceedings.

'How about I ring my lifestyle influencer friend Kerrie and see what she can find out through the industry?'

'Sounds like a plan, boss.'

Ange filled Billy in on their progress to date regarding Pat Crowley and Jack's Constructions. 'Crowley is organising a download of all the access logs for their warehouse up in Brisbane, going back three or four years. He's also going to do the same for the construction site in Surfers Paradise, which will probably run to six months' worth of data in that case. We also have some video surveillance covering access to the construction site, but we caught a lucky break today and installed a GPS tracker onto the Mitsubishi SUV that Lomax and Smith are getting around in.'

'Wow, how did you manage that? Is that legal?'

'Part good luck and part good management. Sally Anders assures me it's all above board. We should get some interesting insights into their movements. Hopefully, the SUV is their primary form of transport. I'm convinced that these guys are in the thick of both the narcotics operation and the embezzlement from Jack's. We know the who but just don't know the how,' said Ange, her irrepressible sense of humour instantly recalling the classic *Get Smart* skit between Maxwell Smart and Harry Hoo, the famous Hawaiian detective. Her dad had loved that TV show when she was growing up, and she had seen every episode many times over.

Ange pulled herself from her impromptu *Get Smart* retrospective and back into the real world, where bumbling investigators rarely saved the day. 'What I need you to do, Billy, is see if you can discern any patterns from all this data.'

'What sort of patterns?' he asked. Billy thought that all this seemed a bit of a stretch, but he was happy to humour his boss. After the Namba Heads case, he appreciated what a good nose Ange had for things that moved out of sync. Some would call this a sixth sense, but Billy knew it was more a case of hard work overlaid with intelligence.

'Times when the same people were at the same Jack's facility, something out of the ordinary.'

'But what about exceptions? If I was involved in something dodgy, I probably would avoid registering whenever I was involved in a clandestine meeting. It would probably help if I had a full staff list and a list of all Jack's vehicles and who they're assigned to. That way I can cross-reference vehicle movements with site registrations. If a vehicle turns up but the driver didn't register on-site, then that tells us something.'

'Good idea. That shouldn't be too hard. I'll get that organised through Pat Crowley. However, that's going to be the painful part. Now that we have a GPS tracker on the Mitsubishi, you will have to manually trawl through the video feeds and cross-reference who turns up around the same time.'

Billy reminded Ange that she had sent him on a similar goose chase at Namba Heads with the drone footage, a highly successful goose chase in that case.

'Sorry, Billy, but I think this is going to be a hard slog for a bit. Today was a huge break, so hopefully we can find the needle in the haystack.'

'OK, boss. I know my place in this world,' said Billy, his voice taking on a browbeaten persona.

'Sure, Billy,' laughed Ange. 'You have such a tough life, sitting in your flash city office in your version of tech nirvana. Oh, I almost forgot. Crowley is going to send through a list of companies he suspects are involved in their embezzlement case. I'll need you to get court orders to investigate those entities.'

'What do you want me to focus on first, boss?'

'Definitely trying to link the movements of Lomax and Smith with someone at Jack's.'

'OK,' replied Billy. 'I'll look forward to receiving the data. I'll keep you posted.'

When Ange had hung up from the call, she quickly shot off another *Important—Confidential* email to Pat Crowley, asking for staff and vehicle records as Billy had suggested. That task completed, she figured that the day was done and so was she, barely finding enough energy to make dinner and settle in front of the TV for an hour. Watching the next episode of *Vigil* certainly didn't help settle her mind, which was still racing despite her bodily fatigue.

She had trouble sleeping that night, all the disparate pieces of her investigation tangling themselves around her frenetic mind. Inevitably, she turned to Brett Tompkins. It secretly thrilled Ange to learn that he wasn't a crook, and that she hadn't been duped, romantically, at least. She missed having a man in her life, someone who she found attractive and was also good company. Someone just like Brett Tompkins. She took that thought to sleep with her—when it finally came.

Chapter 24

GlitterStrip

A nge woke early to a delightfully sunny day. Winter in the northern half of Australia was her favourite: clear skies delivering warm days and cool nights. The seawater might be slightly on the cool side, but it was nothing that a good wetsuit couldn't fix.

She noticed that an email had arrived late overnight from Pat Crowley. Ange's extra pressure would not be helping Crowley's workaholic tendencies. Acknowledging her request from the day before, he hoped to have the information she was chasing to her by early afternoon. Other than that, the inbox to her new AWatson@carcharias.com.au address was clear. The spammers and junk mail bots were yet to catch up with her.

Not so her latest gmail.com account, the one that she had set up for her GlitterStrip purchase. Someone out there in cyberspace had already worked out that she should lose some weight and desperately needed a penis enlargement. She saw an automated email from GlitterStrip, informing that her recent order had been filled and explaining that they would send her another email when the parcel was ready for collection from her chosen click-and-collect venue at the Pacific Fair Shopping Centre.

She knew that this was all fully automated, but GlitterStrip was appearing more and more like a legitimate business. The order had taken longer to fill than she would have expected from an online vendor, but she passed that off as another inconvenience of the lingering pandemic. Perhaps Ange had become too fixated on the idea that everything touched by Lomax and Smith was dubious, and the reason that they were driving the Mitsubishi was simply because they were doing legitimate work for GlitterStrip? She also needed to consider the possibility that they were gainfully employed by Jeays Security. She quickly shook off any thoughts of virtue, aware of their involvement in the two deaths at Namba Heads.

She would ring her influencer friend Kerrie to see what she knew about GlitterStrip, cosmetics being a product category in which Kerrie excelled. It was Wednesday, and she knew Kerrie would be enjoying her Pilates class until mid-morning, followed by an obligatory coffee with the girls for good measure. Ange suffered momentary twinges of regret for what she was missing and the comfort of having some friends around. Not wanting to dwell on that depressing thought, she donned her exercise gear and threw her wetsuit and her boards into the car, just to cover all bases. She then drove over to the Spit to check out the action.

Some remnants of the weekend's swell persisted, but the sandbanks had copped a beating. She needed to make a series of stops along the foreshore before she found a suitable break. Ange was still not entirely comfortable surfing beach breaks. Like most surfers, she preferred the points, where the waves would break predictably, hitting the shallow water at an angle and usually offering longer rides. 'Beachies' were usually short and sharp, requiring a quick take-off, where one's choice of wave was critical. Closeouts and crash-and-burn take-offs were common. A decent ride could also result in an annoying paddle out again, directly across the impact zone. There were no such troubles today, as the swell was barely chest-high, but still loads of fun. Beach breaks generally offered little or no crowds as compensation for these shorter rides, and Ange was enjoying this side benefit.

She felt invigorated by her ninety-minute surf, catching plenty of waves in a decent workout. The walk could wait another day, so she stopped on Tedder Avenue for some coffee and toast. Looking down at the Casio G-shock that she reserved for surfing, she reasoned Kerrie should have finished her morning socialising.

'Hi, stranger,' came Kerrie's breezy reply, answering quickly. 'Where have you been hiding?'

Ange dealt with the elephant in the room straight up. 'I'm working on the Gold Coast. Sorry I haven't been in contact before now. I was a bit traumatised by that whole SACC thing.'

'Yeah. What happened there? What are you doing now?'

'Kerrie, you know better than anyone that it's never as bad or never as good as what you read in the media. It made life difficult at the station, so I took a job up here, working in corporate investigations.'

'When will we see you again?' asked Kerrie, her way of telling Ange that they were still friends.

'I miss you guys. I'll come down for a visit as soon as the border restrictions allow. This current closure looks like being the longest yet.'

'Tell me about it,' commented Kerrie with a long sigh. 'Byron is a ghost town. What with the Queensland–New South Wales border closed and Sydney in lockdown, I've never seen the place so quiet. That hasn't stopped the real estate boom. Have you seen the crazy prices that are being paid? It's a total feeding frenzy. It doesn't connect with what I'm seeing in the streets. Local businesses are really struggling down here.'

'Same on the Gold Coast. I guess it's a case of careful what you wish for. Perhaps locals might catch themselves next time before they gripe about southerners taking over.'

'I doubt that. Anyway, we need to get our lives back. I get my second jab in two weeks. Do you think the government will have the balls to restrict unvaccinated people from pubs and restaurants? It could get ugly in Byron if they decide to do that.'

'Hard to say. That will be a nightmare for the police. The whole thing is a shocker, really. Anyhow, I wanted your advice. Have you ever come across a brand of cosmetics called GlitterStrip?'

'I've seen them recently. They use one of my friends as an influencer. What do you want to know?'

'Well, what are their products like? How are they to deal with? How big is their customer base? Anything you can, really,' asked Ange. It was lucky that Kerrie knew someone, but then again, Kerrie knew everyone; that was her job, after all.

'I'll ask her. I know she's off on some paid gig on the Scenic Rim, some high-end multi-day hike. She posted some pictures on social. I'll make a note to ring her once she's back in Byron.'

'Great. Thanks. Nice to speak to you, Kerrie. Say hi to the gang for me,' said Ange before hanging up amid Kerrie's loud kissing sounds. That girl always made Ange laugh. What a firecracker.

She looked up to see a guy staring at her—older guy, wearing his sunglasses despite being seated inside. That was probably his Aston Martin parked ostentatiously out front. She wasn't that desperate, maybe not yet anyway. He offered to buy her coffee as she walked by. Ange politely declined. She wasn't up for dating men who wore more jewellery than she did.

Ange was soon showered and settled at her pyramid desk, the nickname she had given to her kitchen table. In Ange's new order, she rarely used the table for its intended purpose, favouring the coffee table and the TV as accompaniments to her solo evening meal. Her inbox revealed an email from Pat Crowley containing one of the reports she was waiting for. The attachment listed five company names and included their Australian Business (ABN) and Australian Company Numbers (ACN), a list of the directors and their addresses, and the bank accounts where Jack's had remitted payments. That was odd: the addresses were all post boxes at the same post office in Parramatta. As expected, the shareholders were all trusts, ones with innocuous names that revealed nothing about who or what might lie behind.

She opened Google and started working through the list of directors' names. She discerned no obvious hits on most, until she came to Glenda Jolene Wilkes, a somewhat unusual name. Glenda's name popped up in Wagga Wagga. A Glenda J Wilkes was listed in the annual report for the local tennis club, where she served on the committee. Ange dug deeper, looking through the tennis club's website until she had a mobile number for Glenda.

She sat back and thought through her strategy before she made the call.

'Glenda Wilkes here,' came the pleasant voice. Glenda had clearly failed to read the memo about avoiding blurting out one's name to an unknown caller.

'Oh, hi, Glenda. I was trying to chase down someone from A&B Plumbing Services. I made a mistake when I lodged my BAS, and I need to speak to someone to sort it out,' explained Ange.

'You must have the wrong number. I don't know anything about a plumbing business.' Glenda Wilkes was pleasant enough, but her reply was confident and straightforward.

Ange paused a moment, as if she was looking at her phone. 'Oh, sorry, my mistake. I punched in a three instead of a two. Sorry to have bothered you.'

'That's quite all right. I do it all the time myself. Buttons too small and eyes too old. Have a nice day,' said Glenda Wilkes before she hung up.

Ange continued her searching, finding a certain Sean Athol McAfee who lived in Liverpool. Sean must have read the memo, as he answered the call with a simple 'Hello'. However, he knew absolutely nothing about NorthSouth Roof

Fixings, the company he was supposedly a director of. McAfee was suspicious and provided one further clue when Ange pulled her little white lie about getting the number wrong.

'Are you legit? I'm sick of having my identity used to pull off scams.'

'What do you mean?' asked Ange, genuinely curious.

'Ever since I got robbed and my passport and wallet stolen, I've had to deal with all sorts of crap.'

'I can assure you, Mr McAfee, that I am no scammer. Sorry to have bothered you,' replied Ange, hanging up quickly lest she get in too deep a conversation.

Ange was confident that all the directors listed would be the same, totally unaware of their involvement. She forwarded the report on to Billy, instructing him to organise some court orders for the bank accounts listed in the report. He could add the contact details for Pat Crowley in case the magistrate needed any verification. Once he had secured the court orders, she instructed Billy to contact the banks in question and secure whatever details he could. They were all major banks, so hopefully the banking Royal Commission had done its trick and they would also hold copies of the respective trust deeds. As her old boss Jim Grady had told her, the key thing was to 'always follow the money'.

Billy's emailed reply came back immediately.

On it. Twiddling my thumbs here waiting for you—NOT!!

Chapter 25

Supply

Ange's phone rang early the next morning, just as she was considering whether her exercise would be based on water or land. It was Sally Anders. Ange answered with a simple but friendly hello, still not sure what to call her new boss. Was it Sally, Anders, boss, or Detective?

Anders was not similarly perplexed. 'Hi, Ange. Just letting you know that we have word from our informers on the street. The flow of narcotics into the market has started. It's good quality. We're trying to get a sample so that we can test it against the product that was coming through Namba Heads.'

'It might be a case of tunnel vision, but that Lomax and Smith are active in town seems way too much of a coincidence for my liking,' interrupted Ange.

'I agree. I suspect things might heat up. Just thought that you should know. Where are you at with security logs from your accounting friend? Crowley, isn't it?'

'Yes, Pat Crowley. I'll need to chase him up today,' replied Ange, making a note in her ever-present notebook.

'OK. Peter is keeping tabs on the Mitsubishi, but it's been parked at a property in Mount Nathan since we tagged it. Mount Nathan is west of Nerang, in case you didn't know. We'll keep you posted if anything changes.'

'Thanks, boss,' said Ange, falling easily into old habits, unconsciously resolving her dilemma over what to call Senior Detective Sally Anders.

'We seem to be knocking on a lot of doors in this investigation, none of them letting us in. Let's hope something opens up shortly,' commented Anders.

Ange hung up from the call with a guilty feeling that she was the one dragging the chain. Ange had always been conscientious, so those feelings didn't sit well.

She immediately rang Pat Crowley, even though it was still early. He answered straight away.

'I figured you might be an early riser. Have you had any luck with those security logs?' asked Ange.

'That's proven a bit of a challenge. We want to keep this on the down-low, not only for our own sake, but also not to alert Lomax and Smith. I'm not sure who knows who in the security division, so I didn't want to blunder in and ask for their names directly,' replied Crowley.

'I understand,' replied Ange, thinking that this was smart thinking by Crowley.

'Bob Turnbull and I came up with a ruse for Crowley's being engaged to undertake a deep-dive OH&S audit. That way, we can legitimise asking lots of hard questions, like the ones you want answers on. Bob still needs to get Sam Jack on board with the audit and put it into the business-as-usual basket. He plans to take advantage of the changing workplace health and safety laws, where directors are now criminally liable for the well-being of their employees. He feels that this should get Sam Jack focussed.'

'Good thinking. When do you think you'll have the info ready?'

'It's going to take longer than I hoped. Early next week, at best.'

Ange imagined Sally Anders shaking her head and scowling at this delay. 'OK, I understand your logic. We really need this information as quickly as possible. By the way, I hope to have some progress on your fraudulent suppliers by the time we meet. Speak Monday if not before.' said Ange, hanging up from the call.

Her morning's work had left Ange feeling antsy and dissatisfied. Her friend Kerrie rang. Ange was pleased to hear a friendly voice, telling Kerrie as much.

'I asked around about GlitterStrip,' said Kerrie.

'Anything interesting?'

'Well, my friend Lea said that they're bipolar in terms of their approach to marketing—her words. Very much hot and cold. She said that they're hot at the moment. Apparently, they're targeting the twenty-something market.'

'What does your friend Lea think of their products? I ordered some myself as a trial, but they haven't arrived yet.'

'Nothing special, mostly white-labelling and rebranding of third-party products, probably imported directly and then repackaged. Lea seems sure that they don't manufacture any products themselves. This actually makes sense, as they can sidestep all the TGA approval mess.'

'Thanks, Kerrie.'

'Let me know what you think of the stuff when it arrives. I'll pass on your thoughts to Lea. I think she hopes to grow her referral business with them, which is easier if the products are already being well received in the market.'

'Will do,' said Ange before she hung up the call.

All of Ange's doubts and insecurities were now in full bloom. GlitterStrip appeared more and more like the real deal. Then again, why would you go to so much trouble to hide behind the corporate veil? That Lomax and Smith were driving one of their cars was another issue. The registration search had shown that the vehicle wasn't stolen. She was getting nowhere fast on this twisted track.

Ange was suddenly finding this hard, being totally alone and not having someone to bounce ideas off, someone who could help clear up your doubts and workshop your concerns. Nostalgia for Byron Bay took hold. Billy and Jim Grady had been wonderful colleagues to work with. It's funny how often one doesn't appreciate the true value of something until it's gone.

Worse still was the prospect of twiddling her thumbs for a few days, waiting for the critical pieces of information that needed to come together. She was fast approaching the edge of self-despair when an incoming text pinged on her phone. It was Higgsy.

Free to talk?

It was as if Higgsy had heard Ange's brain fibrillation. She rang him, not in the mood for a long text exchange. 'Hi, Higgsy. It's Ange here.'

'Hi, Ange. The surf outlook is rubbish for this weekend. Have you had a look recently? It's a millpond. Even South Straddie won't have anything by the look of things.'

'I caught some small waves yesterday, and I was about to head over and check it out. I probably should pack my walking shoes instead of my wetsuit, based on that pitiful surf report,' she commented, finding her smile had returned to brighten her darkening demeanour.

'Anyway, if you're interested, we're planning to spend Sunday morning at the beach, followed by a BBQ. Gav blew your cover when he let slip how attractive you are. Brian and I gave him heaps about that. That guy has no filter. I suspect the wives got together and decided they needed to suss you out. The whole catastrophe will be there, kids and perhaps even the dogs.'

'Sounds like fun. Somewhat intimidating by the sounds of it. The word inquisition springs to mind,' replied Ange, laughing as she spoke.

'Great. Once I get a consensus, I'll text you the place and time. My guess is it'll be Main Beach or somewhere thereabouts. Depends on whether we decide to bring the dogs.'

'Brilliant. Thanks for thinking of me, Higgsy. That's very kind. I was feeling in need of some fun company.'

'Terrific. See you then. I'll make sure that the girls go easy on you. Anyhow, best get going,' concluded Higgsy before ending the call.

Ange's mood had brightened already. She thought that perhaps a walk would be in order. Somehow, getting out and about always helped lift her mood. Ever hopeful, she threw a surfboard in the car—just in case. As Higgsy had predicted, it lay abandoned in the VW while she completed her morning exercise and coffee ritual.

Feeling much better, she sat down at the pyramid desk and opened the GPS tracking app that Peter Fredericks had emailed her. She could see the blinking yellow tab that identified where the tagged Mitsubishi was standing. She found a timeline slider, which confirmed that the car hadn't moved in the past two days.

Searching for things to keep her occupied, Ange took a drive to Mount Nathan to check out the general area. Once she was west of Nerang, the country reminded her of Murwillumbah and Mullumbimby in the Byron Bay Hinterland. Mount Warren Road offered a lovely drive, with vistas back over to Surfers Paradise and the coast. It was also closer than she had imagined, taking only thirty-odd minutes from her house.

The semi-rural setting was populated by large home sites, all of them set some distance off the road. Going by the small roadside signs, home-based businesses were scattered in between the lifestyle residential blocks. Plant nurseries and intensive agriculture enterprises seemed the most common.

She wound her way along Mount Nathan Road, eventually coming to the address where the Mitsubishi was supposedly parked. Ange slowed down as much as she dared and peered down the driveway. She knew from the satellite image that there was a large house and two substantial sheds somewhere down amongst the gum trees, but she couldn't see anything from the road. It seemed a credible location for an online business like GlitterStrip. There was no glittering signpost to indicate that the brand lived there, which seemed incongruous with a business that employed social media influencers.

With no pressing duties, she kept driving on to Canungra, stopping at the Outpost Café for an early lunch, a meat pie no less. Honestly, sitting on the balcony at Canungra, Ange could have been at any number of regional country towns. The peaceful rural setting was totally at odds with the frenzied world that lay just a forty-five-minute drive east. It seemed a nice place to live—and a good place to hide if you were up to no good.

Chapter 26

Click & Collect

J ust after lunch on Friday, Ange received an email from GlitterStrip, informing her that her order was ready to be picked up at her chosen Australia Post parcel locker. The email provided her with a one-time PIN that would expire in forty-eight hours. Ange had chosen the post office within the Pacific Fair Shopping Centre, so she took a run over that way to do her weekly shopping at the same time.

She did the usual lap of the shops, opting to push around a shopping trolley. She didn't normally use trolleys, seeing that she was only shopping for one. A middle-aged woman kindly gave her the dollar coin that was needed to unlock a shopping trolley. Nobody carried actual money anymore. Lucky that friendly woman did.

Frustratingly, Ange was unlucky enough to choose a cart with a lazy wheel, one that had a life of its own, darting this way and that, a health and safety risk to anyone nearby. Her dismay turned to delight when she rammed a good-looking guy in the Aldi fruit and veg section. They traded sneaky glances for a bit as they wheeled around the store until she lost his attention to the weekly specials' aisle. 'Damn $199 arc welders. What hope does a girl have against that,' she thought, smiling at her own twisted view of reality.

She traded texts with Higgsy at one point.

> **Ange:** *What should I bring to the party?*
> **Higgsy:** *Just you and whatever you might like to drink*
> **Ange:** *Do the girls like champagne?*

Higgsy's thumbs-up emoji said it all, so Ange picked up a nice bottle of Piper-Heidsieck at the nearest bottle shop. She found shopping with a mask even more annoying than normal. Not only did she have trouble being understood by shop assistants, but her phone had become deeply suspicious about the masked bandit version of herself, a password required incessantly where once a smiling face would do. She had a most frustrating conversation with the young guy behind the counter, getting directions to the post office, which was miles away.

As best she could, Ange rolled her demolition derby in that general direction, wobbling and snaking her way through the massive shopping centre. Once the specified parcel locker was located and she had retrieved the email from Glitter-Strip from her mistrusting phone, Ange punched in the one-time PIN. Bingo, success. A small box awaited, emblazoned with stars and colour, unmistakably GlitterStrip.

As she was loading this into her poorly behaved shopping cart, she saw that a guy a few lockers along had the same packaging. It was hard to miss. He didn't look like a user of GlitterStrip products, certainly nowhere near the target market that Kerrie's friend had mentioned. 'Mid-forties, Gold Coast, click-and-collect—probably for his young mistress on the side,' she thought, playing her usual game of guessing his backstory. He caught Ange glancing his way and gave her a creepy look. She was unsettled and instantly annoyed. 'Lech. I think I'm too old for you, buddy,' was her immediate thought.

It wasn't until she arrived home and was unpacking her GlitterStrip package that the light bulb went off. Her mind started racing as she verbalised these thoughts. What if GlitterStrip was being used to distribute something other than twenty-something cosmetics? It was the perfect cover. Australia Post would be a perfect and innocuous courier for narcotics. Dealers could come and go as they pleased, under cover of legitimacy. That location at Pacific Fair would process hundreds of parcels every day.

She tried to put those fanciful theories behind her, but they just wouldn't go away. She would have to test that theory somehow; otherwise, it would drive her crazy. She rang Billy. 'Hi, Billy. I have a theory that I need your help to test.'

Billy was used to dealing with Ange's theories. She had sent him up a few dry gullies during their working relationship, but she often saw things that others missed. 'Sure, boss. I'm pretty much on top of things. Just waiting for the video feeds and the information that I've requested from the banks. What do you want?'

'See if you can track down any security video that covers the Australia Post parcel lockers within the Pacific Fair Shopping Centre? You might need to contact centre management. If that fails, perhaps Australia Post might have something. Let me know if you get any pushback and I'll get Sally Anders to sort it out.'

'OK, I'll make a few calls. What time period are you interested in?'

'Just the past week for the time being. If you need to, perhaps say something vague about anti-money laundering, maybe complain about all the extra work that the Banking Royal Commission is making you do. I'm sure you can sweet-talk your way through, Billy,' instructed Ange with her sweetest voice.

Billy rang back later that day. 'Pacific Fair centre management was helpful and looked into it for me. They have quite a few cameras. They sent me a map showing where these are located. I've just emailed it to you.'

'Thanks, Billy. Let me check it out. I'll get back to you.'

Ange sat and pondered how people would flow in and around the shopping centre, particularly someone visiting specifically to pick up a parcel. She needed to see how this might work on the ground, so she jumped in the VW and drove back to Pacific Fair, acting as if she was on a mission to collect a parcel and nothing else.

Being unfamiliar with Pacific Fair, she really struggled to find an efficient path. She wandered around looking at entrances to the car parks, identifying busy areas of the mall. The woman behind the Australia Post counter was most helpful. It was a common question, apparently, and gave Ange some good advice. Ange asked the woman who used the parcel lockers.

'They're really popular nowadays, what with so much online shopping going on. We get lots of tourists and people passing through who use them. It's also great for people who are working and not always home to accept deliveries,' the woman told Ange.

She rang Billy from the mall. 'See if you can get the feed from that one near Australia Post at the Melody Street entrance, and perhaps the one at the top of the aisle between Coles and Australia Post.'

'On it, boss,' said Billy.

He rang back around 5 p.m. 'I should have those feeds on Monday. It could prove like finding the proverbial needle in the haystack. Do you realise how many people visit that shopping centre each year? One hundred and fifty-eight million!'

'That's impossible,' replied Ange, rolling her eyes at this seemingly implausible number. 'That's over six times the population of the entire country.'

'Well, shoppers visit more than once per annum. It's a staggering number, isn't it? I'm going to contact one of my teachers from the cybercrime course. He works in this area. I'm hoping there might be some algorithm that can help. What are we looking for?'

Ange filled him in on her theory and told him about how she had taken delivery of her GlitterStrip package. She paused for a minute to text him a photo of the packaging and heard Billy's phone ping with her incoming photo.

'That's extreme packaging. Leave it with me,' said Billy, hanging up, evidently itching to tackle this fresh challenge.

Ange smiled, knowing that Billy was in his element.

She couldn't shake her proposition, thinking that it was quite brilliant for the syndicate to hide in plain sight, so to speak. She tossed and turned all night, having lots of dreams where GlitterStrip packages turned out to be all manner of crazy stuff—chemical weapons, nuclear bombs, a hairdryer that turned into a gun. This was typical of her absurd dreams when she was worked up over something.

As soon as she was up, Ange went to the GlitterStrip website and went through the motions of placing another order. When she came to delivery options, she took a note of some of the parcel post locations nearby before cancelling the transaction. With no surf to occupy her, she opted to take a long walk, over to Surfers and south along the beach. She put on some of the GlitterStrip sunscreen for good measure, finding it of good quality, non-greasy, annoyingly good, in fact. Her theory would be better served if the product itself was rubbish and an obvious scam.

It was a sparkling day, but her mind wasn't really taking in the magnificent show that the Coral Sea was putting on. By the time she had arrived back at her house, it was well past opening time for the shops.

Ange spent her Saturday visiting several of the nearby parcel locker locations, checking out how busy they were and observing the type of customers who used them. She vainly hoped to spy another GlitterStrip customer, but that notion proved far too optimistic. The only conclusion that she could come to was that there is a heck of a lot of online shopping going on and that parcel locker facilities were plentiful and convenient, certainly nothing that dispelled her theory.

Chapter 27

BBQ

Her mind was working overtime, preventing any prospect of a Sunday sleep-in. This was crazy, given that she didn't have all that much to worry about. When she was working in Byron, she would be constantly juggling many cases at once. Now she just had one.

One of Ange's Adages, something she was infamous for amongst her girl-friends, was that one's stress levels grew to meet one's level of responsibility. This explained how an itinerant surfer could feel stressed, perhaps as much as the CEO of a bank, even one under the spotlight of a royal commission. She really needed a break from her frenetic mind and was very much looking forward to her BBQ date.

Higgsy texted a Google Maps location early, just near the Southport Surf Life Saving Club. He was throwing in a surfboard, just in case the swell pulsed or the kids wanted to have a try. They should be there by 10 a.m., but he signed off with a hands-up emoji, suggesting that his actual arrival time would be a lucky dip.

Ange threw her shortboard and wetsuit into the VW, just in case, and assembled a backpack with the champagne and some nibbles that she had purchased. This was her first real social outing since arriving on the Gold Coast, and she was a tiny bit nervous about the prospect. She figured it would be safe to arrive fashionably late, particularly considering Higgsy's uncertainty as to his own ETA.

Ange had obviously underestimated Higgsy's organisation skills, as his troupe was already assembled by the time she arrived. She chided herself for doubting him—he was a construction foreman, after all. The kids were busy playing chase while their parents all sat around on camping chairs with drinks in hand. That was embarrassing; she could have easily picked up one from the Aldi specials aisle, even with the distraction of the arc welder guy.

The adults all stood up as Ange walked over. Higgsy made the introductions. 'I brought you a chair, just in case. Let me get it from the ute.'

Gav's wife, Zoey, wasted no time. 'So, you're the mysterious new surfer chick that we've been hearing about.'

Ange laughed easily, attempting to warm the air cooled by Zoey's somewhat frosty tone. 'Well, not so much mysterious and well past my use-by date to be a chick anymore. Actually, not even much of a surfer, as the guys can attest.'

Zoey was not so easily disarmed. 'Gav tells me you moved from Byron. That seems like a strange way to go. Byron is such a nice place. What brings you to the Gold Coast?'

'Well, I had some challenges at work down there. I was a detective at the Byron Bay station,' replied Ange. The word *detective* made everyone look up, something which often happened when her career came up in conversation.

'I read about you and SACC,' said Zoey, evidently well prepared for this encounter, something that must have been playing on her mind.

Ange met this issue head-on. 'I had a run-in with an environmental activist. I gather that you've read about it. He had a clever hustle on the side with developers and I got in the way. The activist milked the press and made life difficult around the station. He's an opportunist and threw mud around everywhere. Some of it stuck and here I am.'

'I used to live in Byron,' said Zoey. 'I actually met the guy at an information night, which was really nothing more than a poorly disguised fundraiser. He lost interest in me when he realised I was broke,' laughed Zoey.

'Same thing happened to me, but the word *detective* was my passion killer,' said Ange, smiling her way past Zoey's defences.

Jen cut to the chase of what was clearly bothering the three wives. 'Tell me, Ange. Anyone significant in your life?'

Ange knew exactly where she was going with that question. 'Not really, at least not currently. *Former detective* rarely translates to *great catch*. It was usually the older married guys who hit on me back in Byron, those on their second or third wife. I find being married to someone else is a bit of a passion killer for me.'

Ange was pleased to see smiles all around. The ice now broken, the BBQ was back on track. 'Oh, I forgot the bubbles,' she remarked, wanting to divert away from this conversation for good.

The girls were most impressed that she had brought French champagne. Higgsy, Gav and Brian opted to stick with their beers. The combination of champagne and the soft winter sunlight worked its magic, and the BBQ fell into a lovely rhythm. Ange felt herself slowly relaxing and split her attentions between the wives and the husbands. It was a typical Aussie BBQ, with the men and the woman occupying two camps, the children crashing through regularly. Ange expertly played her role as an enigma. At one point, she became annoyed at herself when work intruded, asking the girls if they had tried GlitterStrip products. Neither of them had.

After the meal, everyone went down to the beach. The sun was now behind and tilted to the north, casting a wonderful soft light across the gently undulating golden sand, tinting the ocean with a deep shade of rippled blue. Curious white ghost crabs scuttled over the soft sand, zipping back into a hole whenever danger beckoned. There were loads of people wandering along the beach, enjoying the serenity that the unusually flat sea offered. The bright colours of humanity dotted the soft blues and golds of nature, and this constant motion melded into a spectacular scene.

Now that the sun was well past its peak, the day was cooling off fast. Despite Higgsy's encouragement, none of the kids wanted to try their hand at surfing. 'I fear that I'm not going to find a surfing buddy out of my lot,' commented Higgsy at one point. 'It would be nice. I'll keep hoping that one of them might get the bug.'

Ange laughed at that. 'Well, that's one problem that I don't need to worry about.'

'Tell me about that,' said Jen, looking at her directly. 'I can't believe that there's not someone significant in your life.'

'Well, there was someone recently that I quite liked, but work got in the way again,' replied Ange.

'I guess that's a problem.'

'Yes and no. I sometimes think that the problem is all mine,' admitted Ange, the champagne and the setting sun stimulating more frankness than was usually her way.

'I'll put the girls on the case,' Jen offered kindly, a big smile on her face. 'Shouldn't be too hard. Look at you.'

Ange just smiled, a lovely feeling of being appreciated washed over her.

'Thanks, Jen. Warn them I'm a tough taskmaster.'

'Aren't we all?' replied Jen, more as an observation than a question.

With that, an avalanche of kids came rolling over, wanting their parents to join into a game of touch football. They scrambled around on the beach for half an hour, peeling off layers in defiance of the cooling afternoon, until the younger kids lost interest and the game dissolved.

Once the goodbyes were complete, Ange drove slowly back to her house, the type of comfortable driving you did after a holiday, as opposed to your frantic drive there. She didn't need any dinner after such a long and late lunch, so she settled in front of the TV to watch the last two episodes of *Vigil*. It had been a most delightful day, a welcome diversion from her complicated and perplexing case. Feeling more relaxed than she had in weeks, Ange could finally step aside from the shadow of her case, for the evening at least.

Chapter 28

Sprung

A nge was partway through her Monday commute to Brisbane. She hoped that Pat Crowley had got a wriggle on with obtaining the access logs for Jeays' warehouse and the Britannia Avenue construction site. Failing that, she feared that the meeting might be a waste of time for both of them, not to mention a long and exasperating drive for a meaningless chat.

She was just past Movie World, about one-third of the way to Brisbane, when Billy rang. She could tell that he was excited.

'Hi, boss. I finally got to the bottom of those companies. As you said, follow the money. Everything points to someone called J Williamson. Looks like he or she has a massive gambling habit. And a love of fast Audi motorcars. The accounts get cleaned out as soon as Jack's remit the funds. There are lots of legitimate-looking transfers, things like kitchen suppliers, furniture, and stuff. I found the name J Williamson on the purchase of a new Audi in November last year. However, most of the funds are going to gambling accounts. Williamson liked to spread his gambling business around a bit, but the largest beneficiary is a lesser-known mob called eZee Bet.'

'Great work, Billy. Roughly what sort of money was going to the gambling companies?'

'Millions and millions,' replied Billy. 'The data came in CSV files, so I created a macro to combine it all into a single spreadsheet. It might take me another hour to tidy it up and then I'll email it over.'

'Perfect timing, Billy. I'm about to head into a meeting about this. I might need to ring you from the meeting if I need any help.'

'At your command, boss,' Billy replied before hanging up the call.

Given that Ange was driving, she couldn't look at her notebook, as tempting as that was. She was almost certain that the CFO was a guy by the name of John Williamson. Her meeting today would definitely not be any waste of time, should that be the case.

As soon as she had parked, she pulled out her trusty notebook to check the name of the CFO. One and the same. She thought through the consequences of this news as she walked towards Pat Crowley's office. By the time she reached the lobby of his impressive building, she saw Billy had sent through the Excel spreadsheet, under the title *Giddyup_Summary_V1*.

The receptionist was getting to know Ange by now, so she simply indicated towards the conference room where Crowley and a virtual Turnbull were already waiting. The pair both seemed quite relaxed, making Ange suspicious that they were putting on the brakes. She hit them straight between the eyes.

'By the way, is there a J Williamson who works for you? I'm sure that I've seen his name somewhere or other.'

Bob Turnbull answered. 'John Williamson is our CFO. He's also the manager of our Queensland division. Why do you ask?'

'It appears your CFO has a massive gambling habit.' Ange waited for that bombshell to take effect.

'No way. John Williamson is highly trusted in this company. You must have made a mistake. Either that or someone has stolen his identity.'

'How well do you know Mr Williamson? Can you give me some background? How did he become involved with Jack's Constructions?' asked Ange.

'We all know John well. I guess he's been with the company for almost ten years now.' Turnbull paused, as if looking back in time. 'Yes, that would be about right. I had been serving on the board for almost four years when John joined us. He was working at Ernst and Young in Sydney and helping us implement a new integrated software package. Sam was CEO by then and liked what he saw, so he offered John the CFO position. I believe we appointed John to run our Queensland operation in 2017, four-odd years ago.'

'What about his personal life? Any problems at home that you know of?'

'Married with two children, twin girls. He wife, Jenny, is excellent company. I would describe her as attractive, vivacious, and highly socially adept. She's a great help to John in social situations. I'd heard John grumble about her expensive tastes during chit-chat around board meetings. Jenny comes from a moneyed background, part of the Melbourne establishment. I know her father. He's a heavy hitter. The Williamsons live in a lovely home in New Farm, close to the city. They hosted one of our Christmas functions there before Covid. I think Jenny was showing off her renovations. Part of the incentive for John's family to move to Brisbane from Sydney was a concessional deal on a holiday apartment at Broadbeach, one of our projects at the time. My guess is that both properties have leaped up in value these past few years. What with Jenny's family wealth and the substantial salary we pay John, I doubt they that have any money problems. That's why I think your accusation is misguided.'

'Does he or his wife drive a new Audi, purchased in November last year?' asked Ange, a simple enough question.

Bob Turnbull's face drained of colour for a moment before he recovered himself to go back on the offensive. 'This is absurd. What incentive would John have to defraud the company like this? Your theory makes no sense,' he said defiantly. That he chose not to answer Ange's question was damning. He stared blankly at the video camera. Ange could see his expression changing, a corrosion of confidence as he realised the truth of this gross betrayal of trust. 'Perhaps Jenny and her expensive tastes were putting pressure on John and he needed a little something to tide him over?'

'Let me assure you, this is not about any fetish for expensive shoes,' replied Ange. She would explain the quantum of things shortly.

The room remained silent for a while as the three of them contemplated the implications of this revelation. Bob Turnbull was the first to break the silence, speaking to Pat Crowley. 'This is now something that we need to take in-house and determine the best way to deal with John. If we can recover the money, then we may not need to press any charges. What are your thoughts, Pat?' Turnbull's face visibly hardened as he gave Pat Crowley a power stare, as if reminding Crowley who was paying the bill.

Ange needed to block that line of thought. 'Not so fast. How about I share what my colleague has put together before we make any conclusions about that?' she said, cutting him off abruptly. She sensed Turnbull was now firmly in damage-control mode, wanting to protect the company's reputation. He also had his own professional standing on the line.

'I'll just email this spreadsheet to you now, Pat. Can you share it on the screen with Bob?' Ange fiddled with her phone and forwarded Billy's earlier email to

Crowley.

Crowley positioned a wireless keyboard and mouse in front of him and pulled up his inbox. They waited in silence for Ange's email to arrive in Crowley's inbox. The avalanche of emails that scrolled incessantly into Crowley's inbox tempered the testy silence. 'Pat Crowley is one busy guy,' thought Ange.

Time dragged on. Ange imagined Crowley's email service and antivirus checker doing its thing. She suspected Bob Turnbull was wishing it would get lost in the ether, never to be seen again. Not so lucky, Mr Turnbull. Ping. There it was. Crowley opened Billy's complicated spreadsheet.

Ange turned to Crowley. 'While you share the screen with Bob, how about I get my colleague on the line and he can walk us through it?'

She didn't wait for an answer, pulling up her recent callers and stabbing on Billy's latest entry. Once he was on the line, she put her phone on speaker and made the introductions. 'Billy, I have Mr Pat Crowley from Crowley's Accountants here with me, and Mr Bob Turnbull by video call. Mr Turnbull is the chairman of Jack's Constructions. How about you run us through the spreadsheet that you put together?'

'Thanks, boss,' replied Billy. He was all business. 'We looked into the list of suspect companies you identified, Mr Crowley. Rather than try to get behind the corporate veil, we simply followed the money trail. The recipient accounts of the suspect transactions were mostly with the major banks, so I arranged for each of them to send across a CSV file containing all transactions pertaining to those accounts. If you click on the bank tabs along the bottom of the worksheet, you'll see what they sent me.'

Crowley clicked on one tab and pulled up a long list of transactions. 'OK, we see that now,' said Crowley.

'Basically, each row represents a transaction into or out of the subject accounts. I imported the CSV files the bank provided and arranged them by account number, which is the column titled *Source*. The next column shows the date of each transaction, then any credits going into that account, then debits going out, and then any reference or description.'

Crowley interjected. 'How far back does this go?'

'They only gave me five years' worth of data, which is the limit of how long financial records are normally kept, isn't it?'

'Correct. We can go further back if there is a serious crime involved,' answered

Crowley. This was his specialty, after all.

Billy continued. 'If you click on the first tab, titled *Summary*, you can see that I assembled the data into a sort of dashboard. Given that we know your account, a summary of payments from Jack's is in row two.'

'Holy crap,' said Crowley reflexively, seeing the number of $8,532,994 in black and white, so to speak. Billy had in fact added a nice touch, highlighting the box in bright yellow and presenting this massive number in bold red type.

'This is where it gets interesting,' said Billy, as if stealing over eight million dollars wasn't already riveting. 'You can see that several accounts have both debits and credits. It's the credits that brought him undone here. If you click the drop-down icon beside the credit in row seven, a list of transactions will appear.'

Billy paused whilst Crowley clicked on the cell Billy had suggested. A box popped up, showing a series of transactions. 'Got it,' said Crowley.

'You can see that the reference shows the name of the betting company and a betting account number. If you close that window, you can see the net position for each account. Despite the odd win, he was suffering some big losses,' commented Billy, stating the obvious.

'We need to contact the betting companies and recover this money. They're supposed to verify the source of funds as part of their responsible gambling obligations,' said Crowley, revealing that he had been in this situation before.

Ange jumped into the conversation. 'Hold up. I don't think it's quite that easy. The gambling companies are masters at playing this game. We've also had experience here. Let Billy finish and we can come back to that. Billy, where is the Audi transaction that we spoke of this morning?'

'There are several one-off transactions, all of them debits. If you click on the drop-down box for the debit amount in row forty-one, you can see that this references a single transaction of eighty-five thousand, three hundred and thirty-five dollars. The reference has an invoice number and the name J Williamson.'

Ange let this sink in for a moment before speaking. 'Are there any other interesting transactions, Billy?'

She could hear Billy clicking away on his keyboard before he spoke. 'If you click on the debit amount for row twenty-two, you can see a series of transactions for roughly the same amount. They refer to two females, both with the surname Williamson. I don't know what they relate to at this stage. We haven't had time to search each of the recipient accounts with the banks.'

Ange knew exactly what those amounts were for. Four payments per annum, regular as clockwork and relating to two female names. 'Those payments are for school fees. My father used to complain about paying my school fees each term. Jack's Constructions were paying the school fees for its CFO without you knowing.'

The look on the face of Crowley and Turnbull told her they were thinking the same thing. A sobering silence hung in the room for a good ten seconds.

Ange took control. 'Thanks, Billy. Are there any more questions before I let Billy get back to work?'

Crowley and Turnbull slowly shook their respective heads, stunned by what they had just learned.

Ange toggled her phone off speaker mode and lifted it to her ear. 'OK, Billy, how about I call you on my drive back to the coast so we can chat about how you're going with those video feeds?'

Billy couldn't help himself. 'It's going brilliantly, boss. I can't wait to tell you.'

Chapter 29

What Next?

Ange needed to put things into a holding pattern whilst she consulted with Anders and Fredericks on what their next move should be. She turned to Crowley. 'Pat, can you stop sharing the spreadsheet? We need to talk about what to do next.' She waited patiently as Crowley fiddled with his mouse and Bob Turnbull's face again dominated the TV screen on the wall.

Bob Turnbull's mind had been working overtime. 'I can't see that this changes anything. Whether we choose to press charges or simply write the money off is surely up to the board of directors.'

Ange looked directly at the camera mounted above the TV screen. 'I can see why you might think that, but there is much more to this.'

'Enlighten me, Detective.'

'We know that organised crime embeds stool pigeons in gambling companies where they can. Their aim is to seek out gamblers who they can compromise to help with some of their dirty work. We have a lot of resources invested in this area of criminal activity.'

'But you don't have any link between organised crime and Jack's Constructions. This looks to me like a CFO with a gambling problem, one that the company will need to suck up.'

Ange suspected what Turnbull's answer to her next question might be, but she asked it anyway. 'Did Mr Williamson have anything to do with importing ACP panels?'

Turnbull hesitated and Ange knew her hypothesis correct. A simple yes was all that Turnbull was prepared to concede for the moment. The whole ACP scandal clearly remained a significant sore point.

'How did that happen? Surely the board must have been all over such a move?'

'One of our large Chinese clients on the Gold Coast insisted on using a specific panel. We found them to be of high quality. Sam Jack checked the panels out and they passed every test with flying colours. The entire board even visited their factory in China as part of our due diligence. Given that we were using so much of the stuff on the Gold Coast, it made sense to base the warehouse and importing operation in Brisbane. John oversees that part of the business. How is this relevant?'

'We know that Lomax and Smith are involved with one of your subsidiaries, and we have strong suspicions that Jeays is unwittingly embroiled in a large and sophisticated narcotics importation operation. We also suspect that ACP panels were used to smuggle narcotics into the country.'

Bob Turnbull was not having a good morning. 'I gather you don't have any concrete evidence on any of this. Not yet anyway,' stated Turnbull forcefully, a veiled threat regarding the provision of security logs that Crowley was pursuing.

Ange was no pushover, having honed her skills on the streets of Western Sydney as a young constable. 'You could play that game, but that won't be a good look for you or the company. There is no doubt in my mind that all of this will come together. If you cooperate, you might come out looking like a good corporate citizen. If you don't, then it will probably look as if you guys were up to your neck in the operation.'

Ange knew full well that Mr Robert J. Turnbull would not risk his peachy reputation. A pregnant pause ensued whilst the three considered their respective positions. 'It's your call,' she said once the fruit had stewed sufficiently.

Finally, after some considerable time had elapsed, Bob Turnbull finally spoke. 'OK. You win. However, we'll cooperate on the condition that you have regard to the reputation of Jack's Constructions and our subsidiaries. Frankly, that's far more valuable than any money that we may or may not recover. I don't want the same thing happening to us as happened to you with SACC.'

Ange ignored Turnbull's jibe. 'I'll do what I can, provided that this is the work of a rogue CFO and not something that the wider company or the board is involved in. You can imagine that this assurance comes with qualifications, but I'm prepared to give my personal assurance to do what I can,' stated Ange, looking Turnbull squarely in the eye and giving him the video equivalent of a firm handshake.

Concerns about reputations made and lost duly aired, Crowley finally chimed into the discussion. 'How do we move forward?'

'We need to keep this quiet for the next week, at least. I don't want Williamson to know that we're on his tail, or alert Lomax and Smith. There's a risk that the syndicate may collapse the operation and cover its tracks once they know we're closing in,' commented Ange, thinking out loud.

'How do I hold off payment of any suspicious invoices? Like the one from last week that's coming due for payment. If we do that, we probably need to hold up all invoices, not just the dodgy ones. John is the CFO after all,' asked Crowley.

'Yes. That's a problem,' observed Ange.

Bob Turnbull's corporate credentials showed through. 'If that happens, then how about we blame the new Payment Times Reporting Act that we need to comply with now? We've discussed this around the board table, and the penalties are quite significant. At the appropriate time, I can send a note to the CEO and CFO that I'm concerned about the new Act and suggest that we need to undertake some independent audit of our existing practices. Anyway, I've always suspected that we pay some of our suppliers too quickly.'

'That's a good idea, Bob. You could commission us to undertake the audit and put a hold on any payments for seven days. That way, it would appear legitimate. I could put one of my more junior accountants on it. You probably need it anyway if truth be known,' said Crowley, his expression giving no clue that he was pleased about the additional revenue coming his way.

'That sounds like a good plan,' said Ange, never having heard of a thing called the Payment Times Reporting Act.

'I'll prepare a fee proposal for you, Bob. I'll do it straight away. Given that we already have an invoice in the system awaiting payment, you should quickly run the idea past your board. I'll add in some stuff about the Act and the penalties. That should put the willies up them,' concluded Crowley.

Turnbull grimaced at the mention of yet another fee from Crowley. Ange briefly wondered if any of Crowley's other clients were suffering delays at her hand. The latest fee proposal coming Turnbull's way would probably not help things.

'Great. I still need that video footage as soon as possible,' she said to wrap up, issuing the last demand to ensure that Crowley and Turnbull knew who was in charge.

Despite the testy start to the meeting, it had ended well, each of the three galvanised by the immediate jobs at hand and not so focussed on the potential outcome. Ange walked back to her car, feeling quite chuffed about how she had handled Crowley and Thornton. She rang Billy as soon as she was whizzing along the highway back to the Gold Coast.

'Hi, Billy. That was great. I've secured their cooperation. I was quite worried that they would close ranks and make life difficult for us. I think the clincher was the payment of those school fees.'

'No problems,' replied Billy, hastening on to what was really on his mind, obvious excitement showing in his voice. 'You won't believe what I've been doing. I contacted my old lecturer from the cybercrime course. He put me in touch with the company that provides our facial and number plate recognition software. It's a company called Pixelate, and they kindly provided me with a beta version of a new piece of software. I checked with Sally Anders and she was OK with this, given that we already use their products. What you can do is to train the software to recognise certain objects, even faces. Basically, each time you run the video feed through, it comes up with likely images that you can accept or reject, teaching an AI algorithm as you go. The software gets progressively more accurate with each pass.'

'How accurate is it?' enquired Ange.

'It's as accurate as the quality of the source images. I could identify you in the video feed—you know, when you visited to pick your own parcel from Glitter-Strip. Once I had you carrying the parcel, I could isolate the packaging from lots of different angles and under different lighting conditions—when you walked back past Coles, for instance. Your shopping trolley sure had a mind of its own.'

'Nearly took out a few shoppers with that. Have you identified anyone else yet?'

'Yes, but I'm nowhere near finished. My computer is just not powerful enough, so each pass is very slow. I'm going to put a request in for a new computer. I've been researching what type of processors I need this morning. This software will be a game changer for me. I only wish that I had known about it earlier, particularly when I sat through a week's worth of drone footage looking for the swimmer we thought had drowned in Namba Heads. That's three days of my life that I won't get back,' Billy wryly observed.

'When do you think that you'll have your analysis completed? It would be good to have something before my meeting with Sally Anders and Peter Fredericks tomorrow morning.'

'I'll stay back until it's done. It's so cool watching the software do its thing. It shows a live dashboard as it zips through the video. When it finds something that resembles the library of images that the AI engine has assembled, it slows down and gives me time to override the process. That also helps train the AI engine more quickly. I'll get something back to you overnight when I'm happy with the results.'

Ange imagined Billy sitting in front of his screens, picturing him as Tom Cruise in *Minority Report*. She smiled at the prospect. 'Thanks, Billy. You are a wonder.'

The rest of the drive was a blur, deep in thought the whole way, amazed that she could still drive safely, almost unconsciously. She imagined the AI engine as a real person, whizzing through the video feed looking for patterns, just like she did during an investigation, particularly one as complicated as this.

Ange often thought that an investigation was like a jigsaw puzzle. This puzzle was a five-thousand-piece monster, like the type that Ange and her family would tackle on their annual summer holiday at the beach. To expose the image that lay scattered in pieces, one worked first on the edges, establishing the boundary conditions. Then one moved into the picture itself, identifying any obvious vein of colour or imagery, mined until exhausted. Then one would move to another, perhaps on the other side of the puzzle. Gradually, the image would form out of these disparate fascinations. Progress at the start would be painfully slow, accelerating progressively until the crescendo of the ultimate piece. If one tried to cut corners and jam a piece in the wrong slot, then one would pay dearly at the end.

Chapter 30

Dealing

A nge opened her inbox early the next morning and saw that Billy's report had arrived. She had failed to resist the temptation to check her emails before going to bed, something she hated doing. More than once, she had been quite relaxed before making the fateful move on her way to bed, one that resulted in a terrible night's sleep and a thoroughly messed-up body clock. Billy's would be a complete disaster, as the timestamp on his email was 2:13 a.m.

He had identified eleven people, all of which had collected a GlitterStrip parcel from a Pacific Fair parcel locker. All but one had collected a single parcel. Billy had attached a document that showed images of each person, along with a date and timestamp to show when they had collected their parcel. There was even one of Ange and her modest package, sitting on the top shelf of her recalcitrant shopping trolley. The accuracy of the software impressed her, picking up something so small.

One guy had two entries against his name, five days apart. Late-forties male, medium-length blond hair, fashionable stubble and of unremarkable height. He was wearing sunglasses on each occasion and Ange briefly wondered if this was de rigueur on the Gold Coast. Underneath her own image, she saw the man who had looked at her weirdly when she was collecting her parcel. He had only visited once during the seven-day period covered by the video footage.

She contemplated emailing this to Anders and Fredericks, instead opting to keep this little gem under wraps until she could explain how it had transpired in person. This was a significant development and Ange felt it deserved some backgrounding. Unable to stay still, she donned her exercise gear and headed towards Broadbeach and her Tuesday meeting.

She arrived early. Anders buzzed her into the foyer and left the door ajar so Ange could enter the apartment. Both Anders and Fredericks were on the phone. Anders was sounding quite defensive, mentioning Brett Tompkins on more than one occasion. Ange could hear a dominant male voice booming through Anders' phone, despite it being pushed hard up against her ear. After a long period where Anders just listened, she lifted the phone from her ear and looked down, as if to check that the call had ended, mumbling something or other beneath her breath. It did not sound complimentary.

Anders looked up at Ange, her face shaded with a dark cloud. 'Hello, Detective. What have you got for us today? I hope it's more than your friend Brett Tompkins. The powers that be are losing patience with the idea of owning shares in a gambling company.'

'There are two matters that I need to discuss with you both. First, remember that company CVU Pty Ltd, the one that owns the vehicle driven by Lomax and Smith? Well, that same company operates GlitterStrip, the cosmetics company,' said Ange.

'Why is this relevant?' interjected a testy Sally Anders.

'I discreetly checked out the address where the Mitsubishi is parked. It's a semi-rural location in the hinterland, which also seems plausible. As you know, I ordered some GlitterStrip products online and used the G White credit card you provided me. I didn't want them sent to my house address, so I had them delivered to an Australia Post parcel locker. It's a brilliant service. When your package arrives, they send you a one-time PIN and you have forty-eight hours to collect it.'

Fredericks looked up out of his screen, multitasking as usual. 'What happens if you don't collect it in time?'

'You then need to collect your parcel in person over the counter, during normal business hours and with ID. Anyhow, whilst I was collecting my parcel, there was another guy, also picking up a GlitterStrip parcel. He looked totally out of character for someone buying women's cosmetics. It occurred to me later that day that this would be a perfect way to distribute narcotics to dealers, legitimised through GlitterStrip and sanitised through Australia Post. Pacific Fair is a very busy location with around one hundred and sixty million visitations every year. It would be easy to lose a few visits by dealers in amongst all of that.'

Anders looked sceptical. Ange wasn't sure if she was sceptical about her theory or her statement about the number of visitations to Pacific Fair. It was both, as it turned out.

'That's a lot of people, but where exactly are you going with this, Detective? I have a feeling that it has something to do with your colleague's very recent request for a new computer.'

'Spot on. We obtained a week's worth of video feed from two camera locations at Pacific Fair near the parcel lockers, which Billy analysed using the software that he's trialling. Let me email over the findings of that analysis now. He just sent it through to me.' Ange fiddled with her phone as she spoke, forwarding Billy's email to Anders and Fredericks. She took the opportunity to plug her colleague. 'Billy was up all night working on this. It would have been much quicker with a more powerful PC.'

Within seconds, Fredericks' laptop pinged with the sound of incoming mail. He pulled up the attachment onto one of his auxiliary screens and swung it around so that Ange and Anders could clearly see.

'If you scroll down, you can see that Billy has identified eleven people who collected GlitterStrip parcels in that week. It helps that the packaging is very distinctive,' explained Ange.

She asked Fredericks to scroll down further, telling him to stop at the image of the guy with two dates and timestamps. 'This gentleman picked up two parcels, five days apart. Not sure about you guys, but he does not look like a heavy user of mascara and lipstick to me. He might well be a heavy user, but not of cosmetics.' Ange looked across at her two colleagues. Both had intrigued looks on their faces. 'I wonder if you could run these faces by our Queensland colleagues. I have a hunch that they might recognise at least one.'

Anders seemed convinced, at least enough to issue an instruction to Peter Fredericks. 'Peter, how about you ring our contact and see if any of these characters ring a bell? Can we trust them?'

'That's a good question. It is the Gold Coast after all, but there's one guy that I feel I can trust. I'll reach out and ask him to be discreet. It's still a risk, but we need to go down this route to test if Ange's theory holds up,' replied Fredericks.

Ange had a sudden thought. 'How about I get Billy to edit out the GlitterStrip packaging and any imagery that might identify the location, just to be on the safe side?'

'Good idea,' replied Fredericks.

Anders looked back at Ange. 'What else have you got for us?'

'This one might help you with your earlier conversation, the one about gambling companies. Billy traced a series of companies that Pat Crowley had provided us.' Met with puzzled looks, Ange elaborated. 'You know, the fraudulent companies that seem associated with the embezzlement from Jack's Constructions.' Ange looked at her colleagues to check that they were now following this change of topic. 'Rather than try to tear open the corporate veil that covered each company, Billy followed the money through the banks. He analysed five years' worth of transactions and uncovered who looks like the culprit.' Ange paused for effect.

'Well, are you going to tell us who?' said Anders. She was not one for small talk. Ange wondered what her conversations with her partner would be like—if she had one. Ange suddenly realised that she had no idea about the personal stories behind the professional facades of her two new colleagues. This was in stark contrast to her time in Byron Bay, where she had become quite close to Billy and her boss.

'It seems like their CFO has a gambling habit. His name is John Williamson. Yesterday, I met with Bob Turnbull, the chairman of Jack's Constructions, and Pat Crowley, the forensic accountant, to give them the good news. It seems the CFO became either sloppy or overconfident. He made a couple of transfers that he should have disguised more carefully. The first was to purchase a new Audi, which had his name in the reference, and the second was a series of payments for his daughters' school fees. He must have set up a direct debit for those.

Anders cut her off. 'How did Turnbull and Crowley react to the news?'

'Their first thought was to close ranks, but I convinced them that this was not a good idea. I had the feeling that Crowley and Turnbull were dragging their heels on the security logs, but they seem on board now,' replied Ange. 'We came up with a plan to use some new financial legislation and put a temporary hold on making payments. They don't wish to donate any more money to Williamson.'

'How is this related to my earlier conversation, the one you overheard?'

Ange was learning not to underestimate Sally Anders and her powers of observation. 'Williamson was spreading his gambling money around. Let me send you the worksheet that Billy put together.' Ange repeated her clumsy email dance of thumbs before Fredericks' laptop pinged delivery. He opened the Excel worksheet attachment.

Ange continued speaking. 'All the transactions are arranged by bank account, and contained in the tabs along the bottom of the worksheet, but most of the information we need is on the *Summary* tab.' She paused for a moment while her colleagues studied what was showing on the monitor. There was a lot of information. 'You can see that Billy has collated the transactions to show where the money was going.'

Fredericks scrolled down to the bottom, where a total was displayed. 'Whoa! That's a lot of money,' he observed.

'I know. It blows me away that someone could even spend that amount of money, let alone siphon it out of the company unnoticed. If you go up to the top, you can see the destinations that have the most transactions. Billy identified some of these destinations by the transaction reference text. If you click on any amount, all the relevant transactions will be displayed in a pop-up box.'

Fredericks seemed impressed. 'This is a cool worksheet. Billy must know his way around Microsoft Excel.'

'Billy was in IT before he joined the police service,' Ange replied. Fredericks looked up at her; this was obviously fresh news to him.

Ange continued. 'You can see that the amounts transferred to most of the gambling companies are relatively small.'

'I wouldn't call some of those amounts small,' interjected Anders.

'Remember that these transactions span five years. Let's say he gambled one hundred thousand dollars per annum through a gambling company—then I imagine they would consider this a manageable loss for a person in Williamson's position and salary. They could probably feel justified in accepting his money each year without running afoul of the responsible gambling regulations.'

'OK. I see your point.'

'The one that's super interesting is at the top. You can see that Williamson transferred over three million dollars to a company called eZee Bet. Peter, click on the amount and you can see that Williamson was a regular. Frankly, I cannot imagine how he found time to do his job. He was almost a professional gambler.'

Anders turned to Peter Fredericks. 'Have you come across eZee Bet?' Fredericks shook his head, showing that he had not.

'Can we get Brett Tompkins to look into eZee Bet for us? Maybe he can ask about acquiring them, or perhaps vice versa?' suggested Ange.

Anders looked intently at Ange. 'You've evidently given that idea some thought, Detective?'

Ange blushed perceptibly, wondering if Anders could read her mind and the full extent of her recent early-morning thoughts on Brett Tompkins.

'That could justify Brett's operation. You've got to admit, this all seems dodgy, particularly when eZee Bet hasn't reported Williamson for suspicious gambling activity,' said Ange, quickly recovering her composure.

'OK. You've won me over, Detective,' replied Anders. 'Peter, can you put together a brief for Brett Tompkins? Perhaps get someone back in Sydney to prepare a basic summary on each of the smaller betting companies, the ones that might be potential takeover targets. Brett would need to convince his partners to go down this route, and it would need to look as if he had done his research. It will be best if this looks legitimate and very business as usual. How long do you think that should take?'

'Not long. We already have a lot of background information. I'll make sure it's ready by the end of the day,' replied Fredericks. He promptly picked up his phone and rang someone at the head office in Sydney, issuing instructions.

'How about I set up a meeting with Brett and us two?' said Anders, looking at Ange. 'Let's do it at your house, say 8 p.m. I'll suggest that Brett use his boat, but I'll walk over so that we aren't all seen together. I need the exercise anyway. Oh, by the way, that call I was on when you walked in earlier. Ted Kramer has skipped town. The dumb ones always break cover eventually. Apparently, we are to blame for that as well. I think Kramer had outlived his usefulness.'

The prospect of seeing Brett Tompkins again plunged Ange deep into thought, and she wandered back to her house in a daze. It made little sense to her how she felt about Brett. After all, they'd only had a brief encounter, not much more than a one-night stand. She reasoned that these things rarely made sense. In fact, nothing ever seemed to make sense regarding her own male relationships.

Chapter 31

Reunion

The prospect of meeting up with Brett Tompkins was causing Ange some angst. She paced around the house like a cat on a hot tin roof, waiting for 8 p.m. and their planned meeting to come around. She wandered down to the jetty and peered up the river, looking for speedboats, then hurried back to the house, not wishing to appear pathetically keen, waiting for her man on the dock like a post–WW2 reunion romance.

Pat Crowley had finally provided Ange with the security logs she had been waiting on. She had glanced at them briefly before sending them to Billy. She was far too preoccupied with her upcoming reunion to trawl through security logs.

Sally Anders arrived first, looking fit and casual in her exercise gear. Ange was most impressed with her new boss. She seemed to always stay level-headed and exuded an aura of relaxed competence. The pair chatted aimlessly about the Gold Coast until they heard a speedboat slowing down. Ange walked outside and raised her arm so that Brett knew he was in the right place. She hastened back inside once Brett had securely moored the boat, not wanting to appear overeager.

'Hello, Brett,' said Sally Anders as Brett Tompkins walked through the patio door. 'I believe you two know each other?' Anders was obviously enjoying herself, the discomfort of her colleagues palpable.

Ange looked Brett in the eyes. 'Hello, Brett. Fancy meeting you here.'

Brett Tompkins seemed to feel none of the apprehension that Ange was experiencing. 'Hi, Ange. Nice to see you. I had a bit of trouble identifying your house. It's amazing how different the houses look from the water at night.'

Anders was straight down to business. 'I've filled Brett in on our progress to date, but how about you explain your theory, Ange?'

Ange was relieved to skip any small talk. 'It's clear from the information we've gathered to date that John Williamson, the CFO, has a massive gambling problem. We know that organised crime is on the lookout for problem gamblers like Williamson and it seems plausible that they may have their hooks into him, perhaps even threatening his family. My theory is that the syndicate squeezed him when they figured he could assist with importing narcotics. We're still trying to join the dots, but I think we'll find that Williamson has been turning a blind eye to importing drugs, transported within building materials.'

'What type of building materials?' asked Tompkins.

'I think it started with aluminium cladding, but that came to a halt after those dreadful fires—you know, like the Grenfell Tower tragedy in the UK.'

'That whole sorry saga was a disaster for everyone. ACP is such a great product in so many ways,' observed Tompkins. 'It would be a perfect way to conceal narcotics now that you suggest it. Ideally, the drugs could be sealed in as part of the manufacture process. I guess that wouldn't be too difficult to organise.'

Ange remembered Brett had experience as a property developer and was pleased that she didn't need to explain ACP panels or justify her theory any further. 'Not long after the crackdown on ACP panels, the trawler operation started up. As you know, this was shut down only months ago.'

Anders inserted herself into the discussion. 'The word on the street is that the flow of cocaine has increased markedly in recent weeks. We're trying to get a sample to compare with what we identified in Namba Heads. The two thugs who were involved with the deaths in Namba Heads have also shown up on the Gold Coast, associated with Jack's Constructions. There's another piece to the puzzle that Ange is working on, but that doesn't really concern you at this point.'

'OK. Where do I fit into this?' asked Brett Tompkins.

It pleased Ange that Brett had blown no gaping holes in her theory. She had no actual evidence of the ACP panel idea yet. 'Williamson gambled with all the major companies, but they mostly seem to have exercised some restraint. However, there's one company that's been taking him to the cleaners. An outfit called eZee Bet. Have you heard of them at BeaBet?'

'I have,' replied Tompkins. 'Gambling companies lay off their exposure where they can, usually with their competition. If everyone plays the game, then we all make money. It's like a club, one where you can't lose. I know eZee Bet lays off some large positions, suggesting that their client base comprises some big punters and heavy hitters. Our outfit targets smaller and more regular punters. Tradies make up a big part of our client base. I think eZee Bet is a better name than ours.'

No gambler herself, Ange found herself confused by Brett's gambling lingo. 'What do you mean about eZee Bet laying off bets? How does that work?'

'Laying off is the term used to describe how gambling companies spread risk. It's a type of insurance. Think of a horse race. If eZee Bet takes a big bet on horse number five, they might wish to limit their exposure by placing some level of a corresponding bet with BeaBet. BeaBet will have a different profile of stakes on the same race and might offer eZee Bet some good odds, which might help BeaBet balance their own book. If horse five wins, then eZee Bet pays out to their punters but collects some winnings from BeaBet. There's some serous math behind all of this, which happens in real time as bets are placed and the gambling companies build their books. By the way, a book is the spread of bets on any given gambling event. In the perfect world, the bookmaker cannot lose, no matter which horse wins. It doesn't always work like that, particularly when a sting is involved and there isn't time or opportunity to properly lay-off their exposure with other bookmakers,' explained Tompkins.

Lesson about the ins and outs of bookmaking over, Anders cut to the chase. 'We want to know more about eZee Bet. Our idea is that you make enquiries to see if they're for sale. Perhaps spin a consolation story. You should find out more about them during that process, perhaps even identify who sits behind the company. '

'I'll have to run this by my partners, but we've been having conversations about the number of new entrants coming to the game and whether it makes sense to either expand or get out. I think I can swing them around,' said Brett, appearing confident that he could pull this off.

'Peter is preparing you a brief, which includes some background information on other possible consolidation targets. It's better that your partners believe that you have done some homework and they don't suspect your motives concerning eZee Bet. We need to move quickly on this, Brett. The chairman of Jack's will not allow Williamson to continue to skim money forever. Sooner or later, the syndicate will sense we're circling them. They won't have suspected that we've gotten this far so quickly, but I guess we have a week or two at the most,' concluded Anders.

'OK. I'll get onto it tomorrow,' replied Brett.

'Great. I'll leave you two to it,' said Anders with a knowing smile before excusing herself and heading to the door.

Anders' glacial exit made for a pregnant pause. Ange broke the silence first. 'How have you been going, Brett? Sally told me about what had transpired at Namba Heads.'

'Pretty well in the main. Sally told me you thought I was having an affair with Amy Lightfoot. I felt terrible that you had that impression. She's not my type anyway,' he said as a tentative smile crept across his face. 'I hope you understand about why I left so quickly. It was really hard, but I was still a bit gun-shy after my previous undercover job. I understand Sally told you about that and the circumstance about me being in Namba Heads.'

Ange looked away, pondering how she should handle this, whether to let any emotion show or remain all businesslike and reserved. She chose the latter. 'It's all good, Brett. I understand. I enjoyed our time together, and I was upset when you skipped town, but that's all water under the bridge now.' Brett took this news with a somewhat pinched look on his face. Ange wasn't sure whether he looked relieved or disappointed.

Suddenly, Brett's face brightened. 'Did you get any barrels at South Straddie the other day? That place was going off.'

'You saw me? I thought I'd stayed incognito,' replied Ange, surprised.

'I couldn't mistake your figure, decked out in neoprene as it was. Anyhow, I can't see how you thought you could stay hidden with so few women surfing at South Straddie that day. I need to give you a lesson about staying under the radar sometime.'

The pair laughed together easily over this truth, then moved on to share a spectacular memory of their time together, when Brett had helped Ange score her first tube ride. The ice seemed sufficiently broken, perhaps even enough to start over. As Brett walked down to his boat, Ange couldn't help but glance at his broad shoulders and remember.

Chapter 32

Patterns

Two files of security logs had arrived in Billy's inbox, one for the construction site on Britannia Avenue, and the other for the Jeays warehouse in Brisbane. Fortunately, the logs came in CSV format, which Billy loaded into an Excel spreadsheet. He focused first on the Britannia Avenue site, which received lots of visitors, not surprising for a project of that size. Ange had told him to concentrate on the two dates and times where they knew for sure that Lomax and Smith had been on-site.

He ran a quick search for their names. Nothing. That their visit hadn't been logged was potentially telling in itself, so Billy painstakingly went through the logs manually. Still nothing. He would need to cross-reference the video feeds from the two street cameras that Fredericks had provided. Pulling up the video for the first date in question, he quickly found the Mitsubishi. Despite the sleeting rain, he could isolate a clear image of the number plate as it came to the intersection of Britannia Avenue and the Gold Coast Highway. He set the video analysis software and his underpowered computer in motion.

Billy knew that they would have been meeting someone, probably someone associated with the company, most likely John Williamson. A search for Williamson's name revealed that he was an irregular visitor to the site. However, he had signed in on both days when Lomax and Smith had been spied. Patently, Williamson was no criminal mastermind.

Billy felt annoyed that the video analysis would take so long. It was funny, but until last week, he'd felt his computer was amply fast enough. Suddenly, it felt like the equivalent of a Model T Ford. Billy was totally obsessed with getting his hands on the new computer that Anders had promised. 'Just like a haircut,' thought

Billy to himself. 'One day it's fine, the next it's long and unwieldy and you obsess about visiting the barber.'

Billy tried to turn his attention towards the warehouse security logs, but the video analysis was tying up CPU resources on his computer. He switched to his personal laptop and downloaded the file from Jeays' warehouse, setting up an Excel worksheet and undertaking a similar search. There were nowhere near as many movements through the warehouse, but Pat Crowley had provided a full five years' worth of activity. It was a large file and hard to handle, so Billy wrote a quick macro to copy matched entries into a separate tab, sequenced by date order. Once the macro was working, the complete list of visits by Lomax and Smith was ready in a flash.

The pair made regular entries between November 2017 and March 2019, then a sizeable gap until recently. They had made a handful of visits in the past month. His desktop beeped to say that the video analysis was complete, so he saved the warehouse file to the cloud before looking into the video results.

There were only two visits to Britannia Avenue in total. Billy tagged a few of the number plate images, teaching the software from different angles before running the scan again, just in case. When his computer beeped an hour later, it revealed nothing new.

He compiled a summary report for Ange and Fredericks, suggesting that it would be helpful to obtain video surveillance footage of the warehouse on the dates Lomax and Smith had visited. If Ange could arrange that, he would deploy his new software and perhaps see what they had been doing.

CVU Pty Ltd and GlitterStrip had been bothering Billy. Being unable to get behind the corporate veil annoyed him. Ange's theory that GlitterStrip was the courier front for narcotics distribution was appealing. He needed to find some way to get more information on this corporate structure.

Billy took a break to do a workout at the gym. During those exertions, he recalled a colleague from uni days who worked at the tax office. Nelson Li had been one of the smartest guys in the class, and it had surprised Billy when Nelson had taken that job. He had assumed that his former colleague would join a flash IT start-up, just like Billy had lusted after. He suspected Nelson would be already well up the ranks in the tax office, such was his intellect.

The tax office was a fortress, even despite Billy being a police officer with Major Crimes, and he spent a good half hour tracking Nelson down. The two traded small talk about what they had been doing since uni. Both were intrigued with the work of the other, and they agreed their paths might cross more often. Billy asked if Nelson could have a look at CVU for him. 'Whatever you can dig up, Nelson. I'm sure you see lots of companies, so perhaps you can run it through some of your data-matching software and let me know if anything out of the ordinary shows up.'

'Will do, Billy. Is tomorrow OK?'

'Absolutely. Whatever you can do is much appreciated,' replied Billy before hanging up.

It surprised Billy when Nelson rang back later that same afternoon. 'Not much to see here, Billy, I'm afraid. They're up to date with their BAS and GST payments. They also lodge their annual tax returns on time. CVU turned over just over six million dollars last year and it's been growing steadily since they started in 2014. They still don't make any real money, but that seems to be the way nowadays—growth trumps profits. They look legit to me.'

'Thanks, Nelson, you've been no help whatsoever,' replied Billy, laughing. 'We should keep in touch. How about we have a drink in the next couple of weeks? I've only just moved to Sydney, so I don't have much of a social life. Text me a couple of dates that suit you and we can catch up.'

Billy was just about ready to hang up when he had a thought. 'Nelson, by the way, if you had a flow of money that you wanted to keep under the radar, perhaps a lot of actual cash you needed to launder, how would you go about it?'

Nelson did not hesitate in his reply. 'Spread betting online. Definitely spread betting.'

'Why do you say that?'

'It's just maths. You could take contrary positions and simply lose the house margin every time. If I was the numbers man on the team, it would be as simple as doing the maths and placing the positions that were guaranteed to only lose the house margin. Provided you spread the money around, maybe use a few beards, and never bet too much at any one time, nobody would really notice. Actually, I would develop a betting bot, one that placed all the bets automatically.'

'Thanks, Nelson. Very interesting. What's a beard, by the way?'

'Oh, that's someone who places bets on behalf of someone else. I do a bit of a punting myself, and we all love the slang.'

This revelation surprised Billy. The image of Nelson-the-punter seemed somehow incongruous with the image of Nelson-the-tax-collector that he had imagined. 'Interesting word choice, that one. I thought it was more often used in a dating sense, when a woman pretends to date a gay man, or something like that. Anyhow, thanks for the info and see you soon for that catch-up.'

After he had hung up, Billy reasoned he should make a concerted effort to connect with Nelson. He felt sure his boss would be most interested in learning of Nelson's theory. Speak of the devil, he saw Ange had tried to ring him whilst he was speaking to Nelson.

After obtaining the consent of his partners in BeaBet, Brett Tompkins looked at the eZee Bet website, hoping to find a phone number he could call. As with many online outfits these days, there was no telephone number shown. He figured they would register the company in the Northern Territory, just like BeaBet. The Northern Territory applied a lower tax rate and had become a mecca for online gambling operations. Brett asked around the office for a contact and was given the name of a guy called Tim Rathy.

'Hi, Tim. My name is Brett Tompkins. I'm a director of BeaBet. I wondered if you could help me.' Rathy didn't speak straight away, but Brett distinctly heard a tapping keyboard as Rathy pulled up the BeaBet profile. He then asked a couple of direct questions to verify Brett's identity.

'Sorry about the inquisition, but we get lots of reporters and people digging for information. I make a habit of checking who exactly I'm speaking to,' explained Rathy.

'Sure, understand. Actually, it makes me feel better that you're so careful,' observed Tompkins.

'What can I do for you?'

'I need to contact someone at eZee Bet. Their website doesn't show any contact phone numbers. I wondered if you could point me in the right direction?'

'What do you need to speak to them about, if you don't mind me asking?'

The question surprised Brett. He needed to gain Rathy's confidence, so stuck close to his acquisition story. 'eZee Bet often lay off with us, and we wondered if there might be some synergy moving forward. The market is becoming crowded with all the new entrants and we wondered if we should get ahead of the game.'

'Understand. I agree with that comment about a crowded marketplace, even more so when you add in all the illegal overseas outfits. Those mobs are causing a lot of grief, particularly when they brazenly portray themselves as Australian operations. You won't believe the flack we cop over outfits that we have absolutely no control over. It drives us crazy. I have the number here,' said Rathy, reading out a Northern Territory telephone number.

'Thanks a lot. Good luck with closing down those overseas operations. It hurts me to think how much money is flowing out of the country, unregulated and untaxed. I suppose we all pay the price for that at the end of the day.'

Without breaking stride, Brett rang the number that Rathy had provided. A woman answered in a very matter-of-fact way, as if the call was distracting her from a busy day. It was easy to assume that she was sitting in Darwin or Alice Springs, but Brett knew that the call could be diverted to anywhere in the country—even overseas. The call rang five or six times before being answered.

'eZee Bet,' came the reply, delivered as a statement of fact rather than any invitation to engage.

'Hi. I was wondering if I could speak to the managing director or someone from the board, please.'

'Sorry, it doesn't work like that. Who may I ask is calling?'

By the sound of her voice, Brett imagined a strict fifty-something-year-old woman, the type that would easily keep nuisance callers at bay and run interference for her boss with consummate ease. 'My name is Brett Tompkins. I'm a director of a company called BeaBet, and eZee Bet regularly lays off with us.'

This news seemed to soften the woman's impenetrable defences, and a small opening appeared. 'I see. What exactly do you want to speak to someone about?'

'Seeing as we seem to trade in the same circles, I wanted to explore if there was any opportunity to deepen the relationship in some way.'

The woman was no fool. She knew who would lead those types of discussions. Perhaps she had fielded this type of call before. 'You'll have to speak to our chairman.'

'Great, can you put me through to him?'

'It doesn't work like that,' replied the woman, using her favourite move to once more block Brett's approach, as any good personal assistant should. 'How about you give me your phone number, and I'll pass that on to the chairman?'

Brett dictated his number, after which the woman broke off the call. Evidently, she had no time for pleasantries. Brett realised she hadn't offered her name or given him even the smallest clue who the chairman was. He didn't even know whether any call was to be expected. Brett wished he could convince her to come and work for them at BeaBet.

Chapter 33

Imports

Now that Ange had a list of dates when Lomax and Smith had visited the warehouse, she needed some more information from Pat Crowley. She rang him first thing. 'Hello, Pat, thanks for the security logs. Our friends Lomax and Smith have been busy visiting the warehouse in Brisbane. They never registered their trips to the Britannia Avenue project, but we know from surveillance video that they visited twice. From the way the logs and the video line up, it looks like they were visiting Williamson. He's toast already on the embezzlement, but this could also implicate him in the narcotics operation.'

A credit to his profession, Crowley had money on his mind. The narcotics matter was a distraction. 'What about the gambling companies? Do you think we'll have a case to recover any money under the responsible gambling regulations?'

'There's only one that stands out for sheer volume, and we have someone checking them out. I think you'll struggle with the others. The amounts are relatively modest when you think of Williamson's job and salary.'

'Damn. Anyhow, how can I help?'

'If I send you a list of dates, can you obtain any corresponding security footage from the warehouse?'

Crowley fell silent for a moment as he thought this through. 'Probably, but it's a risk. My guess is that the breach isn't confined to just Lomax and Smith. There could be others involved. Actually, someone had to put them on the payroll initially. Maybe it was Williamson himself? I'm not sure. Getting answers to those questions will take a lot of work.'

'You never sent me that list of vehicles, Pat. Things have moved on, and we probably don't need to cross-reference every little thing. Any chance you can send me the number plates of the vehicles used by the security division?'

'I'm pretty sure I can manage that. I'll make that an end-of-year accounting enquiry. Let me think about the security video.'

'OK. We definitely don't want to ring any alarm bells. My theory is that Lomax and Smith are picking up narcotics from the warehouse on their visits. This must coincide with products coming into the warehouse from overseas. I wouldn't expect that happens all that often?'

'Not daily, for sure, but it's more regular than you might think. Where are you going with this?'

'Can you look through your manifests to see if any patterns emerge?' asked Ange.

'I'm under the pump right now. The more people that I involve in this job, the harder it will be to stay under the radar.'

Ange knew just the guy. 'Understand. Can you send me a dump of your import manifests? If you could give me that in spreadsheet format, I'll put Billy on it. You remember Billy, the guy who assembled the spreadsheet we looked at the other day?'

'OK. That was impressive, by the way. I'm thinking of offering him a job,' said Crowley in a mischievous tone.

'Over my dead body,' said Ange with a menacing laugh, hoping to scare Crowley off from that disturbing line of thought.

An email from Crowley arrived later that day containing two attachments. The first was a list of vehicles allocated to the security division, and the second was a huge file of manifests. She loaded up the manifest file and saw that the list went on and on, making Ange realise just how significant the building products division was. She tried Billy, but his phone was engaged. Hopefully, he would see the missed call and get back to her.

As expected, Billy rang back shortly. 'Hi, boss, I see a missed call from you.'

'Thanks for ringing back. I'm about to send you two files. The first is a list of registration numbers for the vehicles that the security division uses. Lomax and Smith must be using a car other than the Mitsubishi. I just checked, and it hasn't moved out of the Mount Nathan area. See if you can find a surveillance camera near to the warehouse and triangulate the dates. I'll include the address for the warehouse in my email. Ring Peter Fredericks if you need help to gain access to the video cams. He seems to know his way around the local scene.'

'No problem. Maybe my new software will come in handy again.'

'The second file should be easier for you to analyse. It contains a list of products that have been imported and passed through the Jeays warehouse. Have a look to see if you can discern any pattern with the visits made by Lomax and Smith,' explained Ange.

'No sweat. I'll write a macro that looks at the dates and strips out any significant data,' said Billy, his tech-addled mind racing ahead. 'How far back should I go for each visit?'

'Good question. I'm not sure. I guess they would want to pick up the narcotics shipments as quickly as possible to minimise the risks of anyone sniffing around. Couple of days, perhaps?'

'OK. I might build in a variable that lets me vary the gap between the visits and the product movements.'

'Sounds good. I knew you'd have a plan, Billy.' She imagined the cogs whirring in Billy's brain and sent the promised email as soon as she had hung up.

Ange needed to grab some lunch. She had been so preoccupied that she'd forgotten about her beloved surf. It took no time before she was sitting on the sand dunes eating a sandwich. The wind was still offshore, but there were definite lines creasing the ocean. Something was afoot. Ange would check back later that day, if not tomorrow morning. Her phone buzzed with an incoming email. It was from Billy and contained a file and instructions to call him. Finishing her sandwich, Ange jumped back in the VW and headed home, plopping down in front of her laptop before calling him.

'Have you got the file open?' asked Billy, not bothering to say hello when he saw who was calling.

'Let me do that,' said Ange. She scratched around on her touchpad to open the email and then clicked on the attachment. 'Got it.'

'Your theory was spot on, boss. Every time they visited between 2017 and 2019 coincided with a shipment of ACP panels from China.'

Ange scrolled down the list. She was excited to have her somewhat-out-there theory validated. 'That's a lot of panels, Billy. It's scary to think of the volume of drugs that probably came in during that period.'

'Now go to the 2021 tab, the second one along.'

Ange clicked as directed. A much smaller list came up. 'Got it.'

'They must be concealing the narcotics within the prefabricated units. There's a perfect correlation between the product arriving and visits by Lomax and Smith, two to three days later.'

'Good work, Billy. I think you're right. Let me think about what to do next.'

'Fredericks is hunting down some surveillance video, so I'm not sure when I can get the other stuff done. I'll let you know.'

Ange sat back in her chair and spent a moment revelling in the thrill of making such a leap forward, all from a wacky idea hatched whilst surfing at South Straddie. The pieces were falling into place.

Chapter 34

High Profile

It was Friday before Brett's phone rang, one of those annoying *Unidentified Callers*. Brett didn't normally answer those types of calls, or calls from numbers he didn't recognise, as they were usually scammers or time-wasters. Given that he was hoping for the chairman of eZee Bet to make contact, he put those concerns aside and accepted the call, hedging his bets with a simple hello, ready to end the call quickly.

'Brett Tompkins?' said the voice, unmistakably a real person and not some Russian computer bot ready to pounce.

'Yes,' answered Brett, still hedging his bets on the risks of identity theft.

'It's Eddie Falconi here. You rang yesterday, wanting to talk about eZee Bet?'

This revelation took Brett by surprise. Everyone knew who Eddie Falconi was; friend and advisor to premiers and prime ministers, prominent racehorse owner, celebrity magnet, general big man about town. This was not what Brett had expected.

'Yes. I did. I'm a director and shareholder of an outfit called BeaBet. eZee Bet has been laying off quite a few positions with us, and I wondered if you would consider an offer to sell. The market is becoming crowded with all these new entrants, and we're on the acquisition trail.'

Falconi's reply was quick and decisive. 'Not a seller. I could be a buyer if you're interested.'

'Everything's for sale if the price is right, Mr Falconi.'

'Call me Eddie. I see that you're based on the Gold Coast. I didn't want to miss the Magic Millions again this year, so I've set up digs on the Gold Coast until this Covid-19 border nonsense is all sorted out. We should get together and chat. I'm having a small function at my house this Saturday night. Why don't you come along? Bring a friend.'

'Sounds like fun,' replied Brett. He knew just the friend to bring.

'Great. Any time after 7 p.m. The house is on Cronin Drive, just after the road splits. You won't miss it. The lights will be on.'

'See you then, Eddie,' said Brett. He knew Cronin Island, one of Surfers Paradise's most prestigious addresses, particularly if it sported a north-easterly aspect. Brett felt quite certain that Eddie's pad would be dress circle.

As soon as he had hung up, Brett sat down and googled the man. The guy was everywhere. Social pages, gossip columns, articles in the business section, on the board of the Golden Sands Casino here on the Gold Coast. There were photos of him, looking very suave in black tie, shaking hands with the Prime Minister. Others looking relaxed and affable in the company of glittering celebrities and sports stars.

Falconi's reputation as a serious racehorse owner meant his name was associated with almost every big race in the country. Handsome, tanned, distinguished, grey hair, there were plenty of glamorous women around. Brett searched up 'wife of Eddie Falconi', only to learn of his messy divorce some years ago. 'There's a lot of that going around,' observed Brett sarcastically, discovering that he at least had one thing in common with the man.

He closed the door to his office and texted Sally Anders.

We need to talk.

His phone rang almost immediately, another Unidentified Caller. Even though he was 99.99 percent sure who this caller would be, he still fell into habits and answered nothing more than a simple hello.

'It's Sally here.'

'Hi. I've made contact. The owner of that company might be a bit of a problem. It would be good if we met again for a drink, same people as last time,' Brett said, falling into engrained habits of never disclosing more than was absolutely necessary. One could never be sure who exactly might be listening.

'I've got a better idea. I'll grab our mutual friend for a walk from Main Beach to Surfers. I'm sure you need some exercise, so how about you walk in the opposite direction? We'll leave at 4 p.m.'

'OK. See you then.'

Anders and Ange met on the beach in front of the Southport Surf Lifesavers, both in their exercise gear, caps pulled down over sunglasses, looking like any number of locals on their daily jaunt.

'I'm glad you called,' said Ange. 'I was planning to contact you this evening, anyway.' With that, Ange gave Anders an update on their current developments and the apparent link between ACP panels and visits by Lomax and Smith to the Jeays warehouse.

'So, it seems like you were right,' conceded Anders. 'I thought that your idea sounded fanciful at first. Have you got any proof of what they were doing in the warehouse?'

'No. I've asked Pat Crowley to access the security video for me, but he's trying to do it discreetly and not raise any alarm bells that might alert Lomax and Smith.'

'Surely those two won't be dumb enough to get caught on video camera extracting drugs?' observed Anders.

'I know. Criminals are always dumber than we think, so fingers crossed that Lomax and Smith are true to their species,' replied Ange, recalling a favourite saying of her former boss at Byron.

'The logical thing would be to pick up the panels they needed and extract the drugs elsewhere. If my theory is correct, they would need power tools to cut up the panels.'

'How would they know which panels to take?'

Ange had already given this some thought. 'If they inserted an RFID chip in within the drugs, then they could easily narrow in on the panels they were looking for. Either that, or they used some defining mark, which would be more obvious. Perhaps even some combination of the two. It would need to be foolproof to prevent the narcotics being fixed to the outside of a building, five stories in the air.'

Then Ange gave Anders the somewhat disappointing news that nothing untoward had shown up in the tax returns for CVU Pty Ltd. 'If it wasn't for the involvement of Lomax and Smith, then I would pass right by the GlitterStrip business.'

'I hadn't gotten around to telling you, but Peter had the list of parcel recipients vetted, the ones Billy identified on security footage at Pacific Fair. Two raised alarm bells,' said Anders.

Despite only having worked together for a month, Ange knew that information needed to be prised from Anders. She wasn't evasive or difficult but just operated on a strictly need-to-know basis. Ange looked at her expectantly. 'Tell me—which ones? The guy who picked up twice?'

'Yes, he's someone of interest. There was also a woman known to our Queensland colleagues. Late twenties, stud in her nose and distinctive tattoo on her neck. I think we need to assume that there's more to GlitterStrip than appears on the surface of their tax affairs. Keep digging around GlitterStrip's operations. We know the syndicate is highly organised and sophisticated, so we need to assume that they will be expert at covering their tracks. If anything, finding something obvious would be out of character.'

Ange had expected the guy who had given her the strange look when she'd collected her own parcel to be on the hit list. He must be just your average garden-variety lech, not the drug dealer Ange had assumed. 'OK, that's interesting. The Mitsubishi being driven by Lomax and Smith hasn't moved from their Mount Nathan address, but we should assume that they've remained mobile and active. Billy is cross-checking vehicles used by Jeays' security division, but I'm pretty sure we'll find that the pair have access to one of their vehicles. That would also provide them an excellent cover. By the way, have we determined if the narcotics hitting the street is a match for Namba Heads?'

'Oh yes. Two of our Gold Coast colleagues apprehended a small-time pusher who was carrying a modest stash of cocaine. The lab suggested an eighty-two percent match with what we came across in Namba Heads. That's not conclusive, but when you add in Lomax and Smith, I think we can be confident that we're dealing with another incarnation of the same narcotics operation.'

Ange wondered if Anders' left hand even knew what her right was doing. She stewed on that thought for a few moments until she saw Brett Tompkins striding towards them, looking every bit the part of a local surfer, tall and fit, his fashionably longish hair held in place with a Rip Curl cap. When he saw them, he stopped, ostensibly to check out the increasing swell. The three gathered near the water's edge, like any walkers might when they ran into a fellow surfer, pointing and gesturing towards the ocean.

'The swell is on the rise, Ange. We might get a wave by the weekend by the look of it,' commented Brett, fully into his cameo as an ever-hopeful waterman.

'What have you got for us, Brett?' said Sally Anders, not remotely interested in the prospects of good waves on the weekend.

'You'll never guess who is behind eZee Bet,' he replied, pausing for effect. 'Mr Eddie Falconi, friend of premiers and prime ministers, not to mention loads of celebrities.'

'Bloody hell. Cool name. I assume Falconi is derived from the bird of prey that swoops down on small rodents,' replied Ange reflectively. Whatever his name might mean, her run-in with Joe Kramer had made her gun-shy to high-profile targets.

'Yes, I know. He's invited me to a party at his house on Cronin Island on Saturday night. Would you like to meet him? I'm looking for a date,' said Brett with a wide smile.

'Is that really necessary, Brett?' asked Anders, a reserved expression on her face.

'I did some research on Eddie Falconi. He's a serial womaniser. I reckon he'll be most impressed with you, Ange.'

'Are you pimping me out now, Brett?' asked Ange with a mischievous smile.

Brett had clearly been enjoying this banter before his face turned serious. 'I assume that some of Falconi's more salubrious friends and associates will be there. Birds of a feather flock together. I'm hoping that you might slip under their guard.'

Anders was convinced. 'OK, Brett. Let's do it.'

Whilst Ange didn't feel comfortable playing Mata Hari, the prospect of a role as Brett's glamour date was appealing. 'I may need some new clothes. Could I pass that off as expenses?'

'Not after the Cartier watch scandal at Australia Post,' replied Anders with a smile, referring to the luxury watches that were gifted by the CEO to high-performing executives as a bonus for securing a major contract. 'The knives will be out if we expose Australia Post as an unwitting drug courier. Not to mention Eddie Falconi's political mates.'

'OK. I'll send you the details, Ange,' said Brett as he turned and walked back towards Surfers. Ange and Anders traded small talk whilst they wandered back to their respective cars. Ange thought that the weekend really was looking prospective, not just in terms of surf potential.

On the drive home, she rang Billy. 'Hi, Billy. Don't stop on GlitterStrip. We've identified two people of interest after your work on the security video, so I think we continue with the assumption that cosmetics aren't the only things GlitterStrip deals in. Can you get back to your mate in the tax office and ask him to do a deeper dive into their affairs?'

'Roger that, boss. Nelson is a good guy. I'll ring him now.'

Chapter 35

Party Time

A nge's social life had been a drought following the SACC train wreck. Even though her salary at Major Crimes had made a significant turn for the better, she had spent nothing on herself for ages. Worse still, her wardrobe was a remnant from her former life in Byron Bay, not really suited to the glitzy Gold Coast party scene.

Ange had absolutely no clue what would be appropriate for Falconi's party, so she opted to head to Pacific Fair, where she could explore some options. Her police service salary wouldn't stretch to the uber-high-end shops, but that didn't stop her drooling as she searched for inspiration.

She wasted a few hours trying on this and that, ultimately settling on a slinky jumpsuit from Silk Laundry, teamed with a smart denim jacket from Outland Denim. The challenge was that Ange needed to look the part for Saturday night. The more affordable mainstream brands wouldn't pass the scrutiny of the glamour set on Cronin Island. She would take that point up with Sally Anders at their next Tuesday meeting. Surely there was a row in the expenses sheet titled *Unexpected Necessities*.

Higgsy and Ange had a text conversation mid-afternoon.

> **Higgsy:** *South Straddie looks good for Sunday. 8 a.m. at the Seaway if UR interested.*
>
> **Ange:** *Big party on Saturday night. Will try, but don't wait for me.*
>
> **Higgsy:** *Party no excuse! CU there!*

By the time Saturday came around, Ange was feeling excited. She had never been a party animal, but the last month had her feeling like an old maid, left to darn socks on Friday nights whilst everyone else was out having fun, the Gold Coast reincarnation of Eleanor Rigby. She was looking forward to getting back amongst real people, even if they might be mostly plastic.

Ange wasted a few hours in the surf at Main Beach, catching some chest-height beach breaks. The water remained hostage to winter, but the sun was shining and the water was crystal clear. The swell was from the north and hitting the sandbanks at a slight angle, perfect for practicing her backhand take-offs. Most of Ange's surfing had been at the right-hand point breaks of Byron Bay and Namba Heads, so backhand wasn't her strong suit. South Straddie produced both right and left-handers, and she needed to lift her game on the latter.

Sometimes, as Ange dozed off to sleep at night, she fantasised about slipping backhand into a steep left-hander, clutching her outside rail and slotting into a classy tube ride. She knew that this was way beyond her skill level, but a girl can only dream. In those last moments of lucidity before slumber arrived, she would sometimes chide herself. 'This is why I'm still single. What sort of girl dreams of wicked backhand tube rides in bed at night?'

She checked her inbox late Saturday afternoon before getting ready for the party. Billy had sent her an email.

> *Hi Ange. My friend Nelson at the ATO found something interest-*
> *ing. Even though GlitterStrip has a healthy turnover, their cost of*
> *goods sold is completely out of whack with their peers. Nelson thinks*
> *they may be shifting profits offshore, something that the ATO is*
> *cracking down on. He has no idea that we're looking into narcotics*
> *importation and supply. Hope this helps. Billy*

Ange dashed off a quick reply.

> *Thanks Billy. Let me think about that. Can you ask your friend*
> *Nelson to stay clear of GlitterStrip for the time being? We don't need*
> *the ATO stirring up the dust, at least until we understand what*
> *exactly is going on here. Ange*

Billy emailed straight back.

Roger that. Will let him know to stay clear until we give him the go-ahead. Nelson's no fool. I think he understands that our interest is serious.

Ange struggled to put aside thoughts on GlitterStrip. The products were OK, but not high-end and certainly no better than other mainstream cosmetics brands one might buy at the local pharmacy or department store.

After Ange had showered, she put on her best underwear, the set that she had been saving for a special occasion. The new silk jumpsuit felt amazing over her skin, still alive and tingling after her long surf. She twirled in front of the mirror, feeling good about how she looked in her new outfit. The warm new denim jacket was the perfect accompaniment to the slinky suit on a late winter's evening, but the shoes posed a problem. After trying on every pair of shoes she owned, Ange ultimately settled on some pink Tiger leather sneakers that she juxtaposed with some oversized jewellery and some glitzy earrings that a former 'male fail' had gifted her. She would have felt guilty about keeping those earrings had she not found him hitting on one of her girlfriends at the same time they were dating.

Brett turned up just before 7 p.m. 'You look amazing, as always,' he said as she met him at the door.

This sent a shiver of appreciation down Ange's spine. 'You scrub up well yourself, Brett,' Ange replied, trying to keep some modicum of distance, for the moment at least. Brett was wearing a floral shirt under a navy sports jacket and dress denim jeans. He certainly did look good.

'The party is on Cronin Island. Do you want to walk or drive?' asked Brett.

'Let's walk. It's quite mild for this time of year. That way, we don't need to worry about a car should we have a few drinks. I'm sure our Gold Coast colleagues would just love to catch us drink driving.'

Ange closed the door behind her, and the pair walked north towards Cronin Island. Along the way, she came across her new friend Ada, out walking Frank. He came straight up to Ange, wagging his tail like an out-of-control metronome. Ange rewarded him with a vigorous head scratch, much to his delight.

'Hello. Ange, isn't it?' said Ada.

'Very good, Ada. This is my friend Brett.'

'You two are all dressed up. Are you heading to the party on Cronin Island?'

'Yes, in fact we are,' replied Ange, her suspicion about Ada's neighbourhood watch skills proven correct.

'Be careful. That's a pretty sharp crowd that hangs around Falconi. His house is on my regular walking loop with Franky, and I see all the comings and goings. Not my cup of tea,' said Ada, her penetrating expression showing that she might be worried that Ange and Brett were part of Falconi's inner circle.

Brett quickly got the gist of what was going on. 'I've never met the guy. I've been invited as part of a work thing. Ange is my plus-one.'

'Well, she sure is a good-looking plus-one. Enjoy yourselves and make sure you don't get slimed,' Ada said as she walked away. She called back to Frank, who was still hanging around Ange and Brett, hoping for some more attention.

'She seems to be in the know?' enquired Brett after they had left Ada and Frank.

'Long-time resident who I met out walking one day. I get the feeling that nothing passes by Ada unnoticed.' Ange stopped and turned, pointing to Ada's house in the distance. 'She lives in the classic fifties house you can just see on the corner. Her husband has passed away, but she can't bear to move.'

'You have a way of disarming people, Detective Watson. Fingers crossed those skills come in handy and we find out something interesting tonight. I suppose we should stick to the truth about our relationship and how we met.'

'Except for the bit about narcotics trafficking and murder,' Ange remarked with a big smile.

The walk across to Cronin Island took longer than they had thought, and the party was already in full swing. The pair had chatted comfortably on the longish walk, moving easily from one topic to the next, and Ange had been sorry when they finally arrived at Falconi's house. It was hard to miss; bright lights, expensive cars parked out front, the babble of lively conversation spilling out onto the street, straining to be heard over loud music. An imposing gentleman stopped them at the door and checked that Brett's name was on the invitation list. Black shirt, bolo tie, cowboy boots—the doorman looked like he had stepped straight out of an episode of *Yellowstone*.

The pair moved through the house and Ange couldn't help but notice the impressive artwork scattered throughout, conspicuous trophies to signal Falconi's apparent wealth. She paused briefly to admire a large landscape featuring a lounge chair plonked in the middle of the desert. It was one of many striking paintings on display. Moving through the house, the pair spilled onto a sprawling riverside garden. Over a hundred guests were mingling around on the synthetic grass lawn, their champagne flutes constantly topped up by attentive waiters. Brett went off to find Eddie Falconi, leaving Ange to wander among the crowd of beautiful people, more glitz than glamour perhaps, but enough for Ange to feel self-conscious about her appearance. A few guys and more than one girl surreptitiously checked out Ange's form as she mingled. Ever the optimist, she took that as a sign of approval, knowing all too well that it could mean the opposite.

The music was coming from a large cabana situated right on the riverbank, courtesy of a disco, manned by a stunningly beautiful guy. Ange didn't normally refer to men as beautiful, but that was the only word to describe the guy who was dishing up the music. Headphones on, he seemed lost in the music and oblivious to the crowd, ensconced in his own little world. Ange could see that he had collected an ardent following, women who seemed obsessed by more than the music.

Ange was standing there sipping her champagne and enjoying the show, playing her game of building stories behind the groupies, when a voice spoke up behind her, close and confident.

'I see you've found Jay. All the girls like Jay,' said the velvety voice.

Ange turned to find a handsome fifty-something man, well-dressed, tall, tanned, self-assured and oozing confidence. 'He's not my type. I don't like to date men who are more beautiful than me.'

'That's leaves you with ample choice,' said the man, holding out his hand, smooth as the silk Ange was wearing. 'Eddie Falconi.'

She smiled, secretly imagining Falconi as his namesake, swooping down to pick her out of the crowd. She shook his hand like a good country girl should, firm, direct and without guile. Falconi, for his part, managed a two-handed version, one that edged suggestively up her arm and left Ange feeling somewhat unsettled. 'Angela Watson, but most people call me Ange.'

'I haven't seen you around before. Who are you with?'

'Why would you think I needed to be here with anyone, Mr Falconi? However, you are correct—I'm here with my friend Brett Tompkins. I believe you invited him. I'm his plus-one.'

'Call me Eddie. I see. Brett Tompkins from BeaBet. I must say, I like his style.

Where is he, by the way?'

'He's off looking for you, actually.' She spied Brett coming their way. 'Here he is.'

'Quite a party, Eddie. Nice to finally meet you,' said Brett, all relaxed and affable, his undercover experience showing through.

'Let's find a quiet corner for a quick chat before the party gets into full swing,' said Falconi, a serious undertone suddenly upon his ever-present smile. 'Will you be OK on your own, Ange?'

'Do I look like a girl who needs to have my hand held, Eddie?' said Ange with a playful grin before turning and wandering closer to beautiful Jay, leaving the two men to chat.

Jay either was not interested in women or had learned to keep his eyes to himself. Some of the fawning women who had gathered around Jay's shrine were escorted by serious-looking men, jealous types, men who made no effort to hide wandering eyes as Ange walked by. She guessed Jay would be a marked man in a crowd like this, so his strategy of disinterest seemed sound.

Ange wandered around the property, checking out the guests and hoping she might recognise a face. She walked past the cabana to admire the river view. A large launch was moored to an extensive industrial-strength jetty, like one might see in a marina. She gasped when she spied Lomax and Smith. The thick tropical vegetation surrounding the cabana gave her excellent cover. She watched them for a moment. It looked as if they were guarding the jetty. This changed everything. She would need to be careful.

She saw Brett had finished his chat with Falconi, so she moved over to join him, straining to remain calm and casual.

'Guess who I saw guarding the jetty? Lomax and Smith,' revealed Ange. Brett looked confused, as if he was missing something. Ange realised he was in a different loop of the investigation. She also knew the silos in which Sally Anders operated. 'Lomax and Smith, the thugs who we suspect are responsible for the Namba Heads murder.'

Brett's eyes widened. 'Did they see you? Would they recognise you if they did?'

'They didn't see me and I'm not sure if they would know who I am. Maybe they would. Remember, I'm wearing the shoes of a dodgy cop nowadays, but we still don't need to take the risk.'

'I don't want to leave straight away—that would be weird,' said Brett. He looked around for a discreet spot to hide. The place was now heaving, so it was a case of the crowd being the best place to hide. Brett looked towards a group dancing to the right of the cabana, on the opposite side to the jetty entrance. 'How about a dance?'

Ange smiled and took his hand, leading him towards the makeshift dance floor. She could feel Brett's eyes on her back, and she revelled in the feel of the silk jumpsuit as it slinked across her body. When they were settled amid the crowd, Ange moved naturally against him, draping her arms over his broad shoulders, relishing the feel of his arms as they fell around her, tentatively at first before nestling comfortably on her lower back.

Ange had almost forgotten how good a man's body felt against her. They danced for a good hour and left fashionably early. Others would report that the couple appeared oversexed, all over each other and obviously skulking off to somewhere more private. 'All part of the cover,' Ange would report to Anders should she raise the subject.

Considering their relaxed walk over to Falconi's house, their journey back to the house bordered on awkward, the tension between them palpable. She barely had the presence of mind to deal with the front door before she collapsed into Brett's arms and lost herself in a long, passionate kiss, abandoning any pretence of restraint and reserve.

Ange wouldn't admit to being desperate, but her late-night doubts and early-morning musings had created a pent-up desire that exploded in a mad rush of passion. She had worried that the passage of time had embellished the memory of their previous night together in Namba Heads, after a spectacular day spent surfing together. She was not disappointed.

Chapter 36

Morning After

A nge woke early. She hadn't slept particularly well, but that was a small price to pay for the night before. She admired Brett's form, sprawled across the bed and still sleeping soundly. Instinctively reliving their lovemaking, a contented smile spread across her face. It had been a long hiatus and having a man in her bed again was very much to her liking.

The early-morning light had found its way into the bedroom, hesitant and flinty, still low to the north as was winter's way. She lay there still and silent, trying vainly to keep any thoughts of work at bay, needing to fully appreciate this rare pleasure. It didn't work. The presence of Lomax and Smith at Falconi's party was gnawing at her, unsettling her peace. Although those two goons could conceivably moonlight as freelance bouncers, she reasoned that this would be one coincidence too far.

Brett stirred, disturbing her train of thought. He smiled when he saw her looking at him. A moment of post-coital discomfort flickered between them before Ange smiled back and asked how he had slept.

'Pretty well considering that I'm not used to sharing a bed with someone,' he replied, much to Ange's delight. She was no Jezebel.

'You never told me about what happened when you spoke with Falconi last night.'

'I didn't have time. You were too busy seducing me,' said Brett, his natural manly smile continuing to blossom.

'Well, someone had to show some initiative.'

'He isn't interested in selling. I also asked him if a merger was an option. His only interest was in purchasing BeaBet,' explained Brett.

'Where did you leave things with him?'

'I said that we were open to an offer at the right price. We didn't get into specifics, but his accountancy firm is going to contact our CEO next week and *get the ball rolling*—his words,' said Brett, forming air quotes for effect.

'Let me guess? Finch & Chang. Sydney office.'

'How did you know that?' asked Brett, curious how Ange had made that connection so quickly.

'Lucky guess. All roads seemingly lead to Rome and Eddie Falconi. Are your partners happy to go through the notions and consider an offer from Falconi?'

'I think so. If Falconi is involved with the syndicate, then the whole thing will collapse. If he's in the clear, then he might make an attractive offer. At the very least, it will help us establish a price for the company. It seems time for me to exit anyway,' replied Brett, taking on his persona as a pragmatic entrepreneur.

Ange looked down at her watch. It was just after 7:15 a.m. 'Do you have time to grab your board and meet me at the Seaway in forty-five minutes?'

'I'm sure that I can make that. What's cooking?'

'After you ditched me, I had to make some new surfing buddies. Higgsy is a bit of a savant with surf forecasts. He reckons South Straddie is the go today. We're supposed to meet at 8 a.m., so let's get cracking. I'll pick up some coffees.'

This proved an easy way to avoid any awkward moments, and the pair were soon in the line-up for the South Straddie surfer's express, bang on 8 a.m., extra-large takeaway coffees in hand. Ange introduced Brett as 'a surfing friend from Byron Bay'.

This little white lie was no match for Jen, who whispered in her ear as they scrambled onto the boat. 'I think Brett is a bit more than just a surfing friend, going by the body language between you both.'

'If only she knew the entire story of our relationship,' Ange thought to herself. The reality of having two detectives around would probably put a dampener on the boatful of surfers, if not her relationship with her new surfing buddies.

The waves were small and punchy, and the gang of five surfed together in the main. The lefts seemed to hold up the best, so Ange was pleased to have done some practise and not make a fool of herself. Brett was surfing well, impressing the guys with his fluid and relaxed style. Higgsy called the session after a good two and a half hours, and the group paddled their way to the pickup zone.

As Ange was sitting on her board, bobbing up and down in the swell, watching the surfers who were first in line to clamber onto the taxi, she concluded that the system with the taxi was certainly efficient. You only paid once, the return trip included in the fare. She guessed that some would try to scam a free ride after paddling over to Straddie across the Seaway. This would be a risk, as the owner seemed to know the ins and outs of his cargo, recognising both surfers and their boards. As Ange handed her board to the skipper on the way over, he had commented on her striking board, recognising it after her previous visit. 'Ah, nice to see we have some culture back with us this morning,' he said, admiring the muralled board and waving it around to show the other surfers.

This got her thinking about GlitterStrip, and Billy's news that the company was potentially shifting profits. As the boat sped its way back around the headland and turned into the Seaway, her mind meandered similarly. Perhaps GlitterStrip was the vehicle for the syndicate to shift some money overseas and pay their own suppliers of narcotics, something that would pass casual scrutiny and avoid alerting AUSTRAC. The more she thought about this scheme, the more plausible it became.

And then, the street dealers needed to pay their dues once they had taken delivery of their fake GlitterStrip packages. Perhaps this was where eZee Bet fitted into the picture, a forum for the street vendors to settle their debts. Finding sufficient evidence to prove these theories would need some thought, but it was the only idea that fitted into the jigsaw puzzle Ange was forming in her head.

Now was not the time to discuss these ideas out loud, so Ange pushed them aside as the boat slowed into the Seaway and glided to the jump-off point and the end of their ride. Higgsy snapped Ange back to the moment. 'Where did you just go? You looked like you were a million miles away.'

'Girl stuff, Higgsy,' she laughed—if one could call an international drug importation operation *girl stuff*.

The group separately made their way to Tedder Avenue, hungry for a scrambled egg and bacon wrap at their regular cafe. The guys didn't cut Brett any breaks, grilling him about work before trading surfing stories and tales of magical waves. When the conversation turned to epic wipeouts, Brett put Ange under the bus. 'You guys should have seen the dusting Ange suffered when she caught her first tube ride,' he said with a wicked smile, which softened to affection. 'Tough cookie, our Ange.'

After breakfast, Brett followed Ange to her car. Their job inserted itself rudely, obvious and ever-present.

'We need to fill in Sally Anders on Tuesday. Let's see if Finch & Chang contact you tomorrow. I must brave the morning commute to Brisbane for a meeting. There are a few things I need to lock down before Tuesday. How about I dial you in once I'm with Anders and Fredericks? I guess my name coming up on your phone won't raise too many eyebrows after our little show this weekend,' said Ange.

'That was my sort of show,' said Brett with a smile. 'Speak then, if not before.'

Ange watched Brett walk towards his own car, admiring his manliness. While she had no regrets for last night, she wondered how Sally Anders might feel about their reunion. The revelation of this development would make for an interesting meeting on Tuesday.

Chapter 37

Surveillance

P at Crowley had been conspicuous in being unable, or unwilling, to supply surveillance video from Jeays' warehouse in Brisbane. During her Monday morning commute to Brisbane, Ange worked through the implications of this, thinking through multiple permutations and combinations ahead of their regular meeting. The painfully slow traffic gave her ample time to firm up her strategy, and she was feeling well prepared by the time she sat with Crowley in his conference room. She waited patiently whilst he joined Bob Turnbull by video call and they dispensed with greetings.

'Pat. How are you going with the video footage from the warehouse?' asked Ange, getting straight to the point. 'I need to keep this investigation moving, and that footage is pivotal.'

Crowley looked sheepish. 'We have a slight problem with that.'

'What sort of problem?' shot back Ange in reply.

'There is none,' replied Crowley simply. He felt compelled to elaborate under Ange's incredulous look. 'You know I was trying to keep this under the radar, so I contacted the service provider who archives our video footage into the cloud. They told me that the auto-archive feature was disabled.'

'How could that happen?' enquired Ange.

'I'm as surprised as you are. The provider told me that clients can toggle the auto-archive option on and off themselves. Someone must have toggled it off—someone with administration privileges at Jeays.'

Ange had suspected trouble with this footage, so she was prepared for this eventuality. 'OK. I need to make a call. Give me five minutes.'

She stepped out of the conference room and found a quiet corner of the reception area to ring Sally Anders. The strategy that she had in mind needed authority. They chatted for a good five minutes, Ange pacing around in circles while she explained her rationale. Once she had secured the approval of her boss, she re-entered the conference room.

'Here's what I propose. We need to bring in Williamson. We have sufficient evidence about his embezzlement to lay charges, but nothing concrete regarding his involvement in narcotics importation. With all due respect to your matter, shutting down the narcotics syndicate must take priority. Therefore, we need to bring him in without raising any alarm bells, and then keep him off-grid until we can move on the syndicate.'

Bob Turnbull spoke up. 'Makes sense, but how on earth do you suppose we achieve that? Presumably we need to keep his wife and family in the dark as well?'

Ange had thought all of this through during her commute. 'What I propose is that you call him to say that he's needed to travel to Adelaide on Wednesday and negotiate a contract. Perhaps an acquisition or alliance of some sort? I'll leave those details up to you. Tell him to secure his travel permit as per normal and pack enough clothes for a couple of days. He then needs to come here, ostensibly to be briefed by Pat, before the two of you head straight to the airport and travel to Adelaide. My boss and I will be here to greet him.'

'How will you keep him off-grid?' enquired Crowley.

'We say that he's a close contact of a Covid-19 case in Adelaide, and that he's been ordered into hotel quarantine for fourteen days. If he sticks to that story, then we should have enough time to do what we need to do. We can cover that when we interview him on Wednesday. His family should be safe from any repercussions. I'll organise a suitable hotel here in Brisbane.'

'That is very clever,' said Bob Turnbull, a look of respect coming over his face. 'What sort of repercussions?'

'We know this mob's not above murder, so I suppose the safety of Williamson and his family is a consideration. If we become concerned, I will increase surveillance. However, if we all stick to our story, then they should be fine. I'm hoping that the well-being of his family will be sufficient motivation for Williamson to play his part. Are you both on board with this?'

Both Turnbull and Crowley nodded gravely. Playing a part in bringing down a sophisticated narcotics syndicate and a couple of hitmen had not been in the brief that they had signed up to.

Ange turned towards Pat Crowley. 'Pat, in the meantime, you need to assemble a brief of evidence on Williamson's embezzlement that could stand up if we need to go to a magistrate. I presume you've been down this road before. Perhaps you can send me a copy tomorrow so that I can get Billy to add in the stuff that he has uncovered. I want us both on the same page on this. Can you get that report to me by lunchtime tomorrow?'

'OK. I had a few other things on my plate, but I guess I can shove those off to one of my staff. I'll get onto it straight away.' Crowley turned to Turnbull. 'Bob, we need to discuss my bill. I checked the WIP this morning. It's getting up there.'

'I'll leave you two to discuss that. Bob, can you arrange for Williamson to be here at 11 a.m. on Wednesday? My boss and I will be here by 10:30 so we can get set up.' With that, Ange stood up and said her goodbyes. Crowley evidently had other things on his mind, so he didn't escort her to the lift this time around.

During the drive home, she confirmed the arrangements with her boss, asking Anders to arrange a suitable hotel in which to hide Williamson, somewhere nondescript, where comings and goings wouldn't be obvious.

She then rang Billy to tell him to clear his Tuesday afternoon schedule and be ready to quickly turn around the brief against Williamson. By the time she had arrived back at her house on the Gold Coast, she was itching to get some thoughts assembled and written in her notepad. She spent the rest of the afternoon preparing for her meeting with Sally Anders and Peter Fredericks, cogitating on the various angles that they would need to run once John Williamson had been reeled in. She concluded that the next week was going to be very tricky.

Chapter 38

Easy

Despite spring being some way off, Tuesday morning was a cracker. By the time Ange was walking towards her meeting with Sally Anders, the cool, crisp morning had conceded defeat to a dreamy, warm day. Sunday's swell pulse was hanging on and Ange wished she had time for a surf, but short winter days played havoc with any attempts to balance work with her surf habit.

Sally Anders was deep in conversation when she entered the apartment. Whereas Ange paced when she was on the phone, Anders had a habit of staring out across the ocean, standing perfectly still, as if concentrating on a ship far off on the horizon. Peter Fredericks gave Ange a cursory greeting before refocussing his attention back to his computer screen, leaving Ange to fidget. As seemed to be the modern way, she raised her phone to read the latest news. Like most people, she was now sick and tired of news about Covid-19, yet she was easily hooked by the latest infection statistics and news of duelling politicians, scrapping over borders and votes. She was pleased to find that Williamson's fake trip to South Australia hadn't been ruled implausible by any fresh state border closures. Football, in all its guises, dominated an otherwise dull news day.

Anders looked unhappy when she turned to speak with Ange. 'I'm copping some serious heat over our investigation. Most unusual and more than a touch disproportionate, given what we're dealing with. I suppose that's why we get paid the big bucks,' she said in a sarcastic tone, referring to their relatively modest salaries. 'Where are we at, Ange?'

Ange gave her a summary of the arrangements for Wednesday, suggesting that they leave by 9 a.m. at the latest to account for any traffic. 'I think we need to scare Williamson first up. Before we get bogged down with lawyers getting involved, we should explain the type of people he's involved with and what they're capable of.'

'I agree. How about we discuss our plan of attack on the drive to Brisbane? I'm happy for you to take the lead on the interview. You've been thinking about this more than I have,' commented Anders.

Ange nodded her agreement. 'OK. Once we pull the trigger with Williamson, the clock is ticking. I think we need to move on as many angles as possible. Hopefully, we can entice Williamson to spill the beans on how the narcotics were being smuggled into the country. Some video evidence would be nice, but I'm at a loss to see how we can piece that together in two weeks, particularly when we have no real guarantees of any shipments arriving within that time span. We could waste a lot of time going down that route.'

Sally Anders nodded her approval of that logic. Peter Fredericks looked up from his screen. 'Why can't we get access to archives of the security video at the warehouse?'

Ange realised that Peter Fredericks was out of the loop on this development and gave him an explanation of what had happened with the failed upload to cloud storage. 'I'm suspicious about all that, but I feel that trying to either fix the video upload issue or install another camera isn't worth the risk. That assumes we can get Williamson to reveal what was going on. We may need to revisit that problem subject to how tomorrow goes.'

Once Ange had secured the nods of agreement from Anders and Fredericks, she went into stage two of her plan. 'We should do some more work on Glitter-Strip. Given how well the syndicate compartmentalises its operations, I think it's reasonable to assume that Williamson doesn't know how the narcotics reach the street. I think we should try to apprehend someone picking up a delivery.'

'Makes sense. How do you plan to achieve that?' said Anders.

'Well, we now know the identity of two dealers who use the Pacific Fair parcel drop facility. We could ask Australia Post to alert us if any parcels get logged for either of those two. They only have forty-eight hours to collect their delivery; otherwise, it gets taken back inside the main office. I feel sure that they'll turn up and collect their parcel within twenty-four hours of being notified to avoid showing up in person and presenting ID. We can set up some surveillance, which shouldn't be too big a drain on resources. Once we catch one of the dealers red-handed, I'm sure we can persuade them to spill the beans on GlitterStrip.'

Ange looked at each of her colleagues, who both remained silent, unwilling to commit. 'I think that the crux of the operation rests with eZee Bet. How about I get Brett on the phone so we can get his input?' she asked, more a statement of intent than any question. She rang Brett, putting her phone on speaker and placing it on the coffee table. It only rang twice before Brett picked up.

'Hello, Ange. I presume you're with Sally and Peter?'

Sally Anders answered on their behalf. 'Hi, Brett. Ange is updating us. She wanted you in the conversation about eZee Bet. How was the party?'

'The party was flash and lavish. Eddie Falconi is a smooth customer. We've already had a call from one of the merger and acquisition partners at Finch & Chang about potentially acquiring BeaBet. I've provided some preliminary numbers and by the sounds of things, we can expect an indicative offer in the next day or so. If I didn't know any better, Falconi and eZee Bet would seem totally legit.'

'Brett, it's Ange here.' Perhaps an unnecessary qualification, seeing as they had spent the weekend together. 'We suspect eZee Bet put the squeeze on someone who was heavily indebted to them, co-opting their support to smuggle the narcotics into the country. Sally and I are planning to bring some heat on that person tomorrow.'

'How will you do that without compromising our investigation?' asked Brett.

Sally Anders answered on Ange's behalf. 'Ange had a brilliant idea to use Covid-19 to keep him squirrelled away. Once we do that, we should have fourteen days before anyone gets suspicious.'

'The guy had been embezzling money to fund his gambling addiction, which is how we stumbled across all of this. We have plenty of evidence against him on that front and should be able to cut some sort of deal to secure his cooperation,' explained Ange.

'What sort of money are we talking about? He might just agree to pay it back and cop a minor penalty,' enquired Brett.

'Billy ran the numbers and came up with over eight million dollars.'

Brett whistled before verbalising what they all thought. 'How on earth does someone steal that much money?'

Ange declined to answer that question, as she still found it astonishing herself. 'Brett, if you were using BeaBet to launder debts owed by drug dealers, how would you go about it?'

'Easy,' he replied instantly. 'I would make any dealers set up a betting account, deposit money into their account each week, and then gamble it away.'

'I'm no gambler, Brett,' piped in Sally Anders. 'Elaborate.'

'Well, if you so desire, losing money via online betting is super easy. If I was involved, I would tell the dealers-cum-punters to deposit money in their account on Friday and keep gambling all weekend until there was nothing left in their account on Monday morning. Who knows, seeing how addictive online betting is, the dealers might also gamble some of their own money on the side.'

'That's brilliant,' said Sally Anders, amazed at how simple it all was.

'If Falconi is involved, it will explain why he isn't interested in selling or merging. He wouldn't want anyone looking through his books. Acquiring BeaBet would give him another platform and another way to spread his exposure. Also, BeaBet would give Falconi access to another set of potential punters to squeeze for more of his dirty work.'

That raised something which was gnawing at Ange. How had Falconi known that Williamson would be useful to him for smuggling narcotics? It seemed a lot of work to find a needle in a haystack. There must be hundreds of problem gamblers, none of which would be much use to Falconi. An image of the wannabe cowboy minding the door at Falconi's party flickered past, and Ange realised the likely source of his muscle—perhaps even Lomax and Smith had fallen prey to this ruse.

There was a pause in the conversation whilst everyone went down their own thought foxholes before Brett asked the obvious question. 'If Falconi is behind the drug importation operation and using eZee Bet to collect money from the dealers, then how do the drugs make it onto the street?'

Ange afforded Brett a summary of her theory about GlitterStrip, explaining her plan to entrap one of the dealers Billy had helped identify. 'We can't say for sure that Falconi is involved with GlitterStrip, but that Lomax and Smith are showing up everywhere is far too coincidental for my liking. Also, GlitterStrip and eZee Bet use the same firm of accountants in Sydney. All circumstantial, I know, but suspicious nonetheless.'

The experience of Sally Anders showed through. 'The challenge will be to pin any of this on Falconi. He seems way too clever by half. I'll bet Finch & Chang will have all the financial tracks covered and Falconi will have fall guys lined up from here to kingdom come. We need to keep looking into Falconi. Keep us posted, Brett.'

Anders signalled for Ange to hang up the call before going any further, every bit as good as Falconi in compartmentalising. 'Peter, can you get onto Australia Post and get them on board? I'll arrange for some surveillance to be on call. Ange, do you think we will need to install any cameras?'

'No, I think we should be able to use a mobile setup. The parcel lockers are open twenty-four hours and accessed from the side street. We should be able to monitor the site from a mobile van.'

'OK, let's get on with it. Can you pick me up here tomorrow morning, Ange? Text me when you are leaving your place.'

With that, the meeting was over. Ange used the time walking back through Surfers to probe a gap in her theory that had been gnawing at her. She would need to do some more digging into Falconi.

Chapter 39

Wet Wednesday

Ange spent the rest of the afternoon trying to find out everything she could about Eddie Falconi, what circles he ran in and who he hung out with. She rang Billy for some pointers on how to search social media. 'Eddie Falconi and Racing' brought up a plethora of photos, as did 'Eddie Falconi and Cricket' doing the corporate hospitality thing. However, it was 'Eddie Falconi and Golf' that proved the biggest surprise. Ange was shocked to find the smiling face of Bob Turnbull, arm in arm with Falconi at several impressive-looking golf courses around the country, looking like peacocks in their brightly coloured golfing kit. The two golfing buddies were club members of The Australian, no less.

This raised more questions than it answered. Was Turnbull in on the whole show, or was he an unwitting pawn in Falconi's scheme? Perhaps Falconi had used their time on the golf course to hatch his import scheme and lean on Williamson? It made little sense that Turnbull would be involved and then play an active part in the investigation. Maybe Turnbull was feeding Falconi information so that they could shut up shop and cover their tracks at the last moment? Her head was spinning with all the potential implications of this development, making for a restless evening that provided no answers.

She picked up Sally Anders bang on 9 a.m. Drizzling rain had developed overnight and Anders was waiting patiently in the lobby of her apartment block, hiding from the rain and on the phone as per usual. Ange figured that Sally Anders would be a good test case to debunk the conspiracy concerning brain tumours and mobile phone use.

As soon as Anders was in the car, Ange filled her in on the link she had discovered between Falconi and Turnbull. After a lengthy debate, the two detectives decided that, on balance, Bob Turnbull was most likely an unwitting pawn. However, there were risks of disclosing their investigations into Falconi, so they concluded it was best to distance themselves from Turnbull, at least for the time being.

Before they discussed any strategy for their interview with Williamson, Ange broached another subject that had come to her in the night. 'Once we bring in Williamson, we have fourteen days to bring this to a conclusion. I don't want to mess around waiting for lawyers. Williamson is unlikely to have a criminal lawyer on speed dial. We should be ready to offer him someone suitable.'

'I agree,' said Anders. 'If we were in Sydney, then I could give you a dozen names. I don't know the local DPP well enough to broach the subject, and I don't know who to trust up here in Queensland. What about your forensic accountant, Pat Crowley? He deals in lots of fraud cases and must come across plenty of criminal lawyers. Perhaps he can put a few names together? Let's ring him now and get him thinking.'

Ange used Siri to help dial Crowley's mobile number. For once Siri got it right, dialling Crowley's number instead of Bev's Pet Grooming, or something similarly absurd, as was often the case. The phone almost rang out before Crowley answered.

'Sorry, Detective. I was on the phone over another matter that's going totally pear-shaped. How can I help?'

'I have my boss, Senior Detective Sally Anders, in the car with me. We wondered if you knew of a competent criminal lawyer, someone nearby who might come around at short notice today. We figure Williamson may be at a loss in that regard.'

Crowley responded quickly. 'I know a couple who I've worked with. Let me make a few calls and I'll have someone on standby. I'll see if I can get two on the hook so that Williamson doesn't feel that he's being set up. Well, anymore set up than he is already.'

'Thanks, Pat. See you soon.'

The two workshopped their impending interview for the rest of the drive, thinking through all the potential twists and turns that they might need to navigate, beating windscreen wipers and the odd idiot driver the only intrusions to their thoughts. Ange would take the lead, and Sally Anders would stamp some authority when needed. Pretty soon, they were seated in Crowley's meeting room, anxiously waiting for Williamson to arrive.

Crowley eventually brought in Williamson, dressed in a stylish navy suit, ready for his phantom business trip to Adelaide. Crowley made the introductions.

'John, this is Detective Angela Watson and Senior Detective Sally Anders. They would like to speak with you.'

Williamson's face crumbled as he sat down slowly, buying time to collect himself. His smart suit didn't look nearly as well cut anymore; somehow it now seemed as crumpled and worry-worn as its wearer. Ange observed his disintegration and marvelled at the impact of confidence and bearing on one's outward appearance.

'I knew that this day would come,' said Williamson, eventually looking up to face the two detectives in front of him. 'It's almost a relief, actually.'

Pat Crowley turned to leave, but Ange cut him short. 'Pat, since you've been looking into this matter, can you stay while we work through some details?' Ange then looked over at Williamson. 'Mr Williamson, you can request a lawyer to be present. As you can gather, your trip to Adelaide was a ploy to get you here, but the clock will be ticking from now on. Apart from the money that you've embezzled from your employer, it's your involvement with a major narcotics importation and distribution syndicate that has us most concerned. You've gotten yourself mixed up with some bad people. Once they realise you've been compromised, we have concerns for the safety of you and your family.'

Ange let that revelation sink in for a moment. 'Do you have a lawyer that you could call? One that can come here immediately. May I suggest that a criminal lawyer will serve you best?'

Williamson put his head in his hands, mumbling something about putting his family at risk. 'No, I don't. All the lawyers I know up here are commercial and construction lawyers. Anyway, they all work for Jack's and would therefore be conflicted.'

'We suspected that this might be the case. Mr Crowley deals in this area and has put together some names for you.'

Crowley rattled off three names, impressing the detectives given the short notice. The names meant absolutely nothing to Ange and Anders. By the look on Williamson's face, they also meant nothing to him.

'Who would you choose?' asked Williamson, looking up dejectedly at Crowley, his glum eyes signalling defeat.

'If I was in your shoes, John, I would choose Luke Maddison. He's expensive, but I guess it's all relative when jail is the only alternative.'

'OK. I'll trust your judgement. Not that I really have any option. Can you get him to come around to represent me?'

Crowley went to his phone, pulled up his recent calls and rang Maddison. 'Hi, Luke. It's Pat here. Can you come around to the office on that matter I spoke to you about? I'll let reception know to expect you.' He turned to the others. 'He should be here any minute. Luke works in the same building.'

Crowley organised some coffee for everyone while they waited. Small talk didn't seem appropriate given the gravity of the situation, and the room was silent save for the sounds of coffee being sipped. If there had been a clock in the room, it would have ticked loudly. For a full ten minutes, the room morphed into a Wes Anderson movie set, where the protagonists took turns to glance self-consciously around the room from time to time. It was excruciatingly uncomfortable, which served some purpose in itself, dissolving any residual fight response that Williamson might have possessed.

Eventually, the receptionist brought in Luke Maddison, besting his new client in the impressive suit department, resplendent with a bright pocket kerchief and pink paisley tie. Maddison was younger than Ange had expected. He couldn't have been much older than her, but he exuded a distinct air of competence. Ange was unsure whether this would be a good or a bad thing for their investigation.

Once the introductions were complete and everyone had taken their seats again, Ange gave Maddison a briefing, explaining the evidence that they had on Williamson's habitual embezzlement and his involvement in narcotics trafficking. As she heard herself speak, she realised how little direct evidence they had against Williamson regarding the latter allegation.

'The case against Mr Williamson on embezzlement is significant, but it will ultimately be a matter for the company whether or not they press charges. Providing Mr Williamson assists us with the narcotics case, then we are prepared to strike some sort of deal that downgrades his involvement. As you would know, Mr Maddison, stealing from your employer is one thing, but being at the centre of large-scale narcotics trafficking operation is a whole other problem for your client. We also believe Mr Williamson and his family may be in danger once elements from the narcotics syndicate realise that Mr Williamson has been compromised. We have a scheme to keep him squirrelled away, but that can only hold water for fourteen days, so time is of the essence here.'

Maddison was as cool as a cucumber, giving absolutely nothing away. 'Can I have some time with my client? I suspect that I'll need an hour at least. Perhaps you could take the opportunity to have some lunch. So that we can keep this moving, I'll get my assistant to bring up some sandwiches for me and my client.'

The others stood and exited the conference room, leaving the lawyer alone with his client to do his thing. Crowley excused himself and went back to his desk, leaving the two detectives to wander downstairs and find a spot for lunch. Ange suggested Korean, and they soon found a funky yet discreet upstairs restaurant, one street back from the pedestrian mall. Barely forty-five minutes had elapsed since leaving Crowley's office when a text from Pat Crowley pinged into Ange's phone.

'They're ready for us,' said Ange as she shovelled up the last few scraps of kimchi fried rice. Sally Anders was already finished her meal and watched with apparent amusement.

'That was quick,' said Anders. 'Hopefully, this means they've reached a firm agreement on the way forward. Let's hope this goes the way we hope.'

With that, the two detectives paid the bill and scurried back to Crowley's office, leapfrogging from building to building to avoid getting soaked by the rain squall that had developed. Ange hoped the waterworks didn't herald a bad omen.

Chapter 40

Quarantine

Maddison seized control as soon as the detectives were back and seated in the conference room. 'My client wishes to cooperate. Whilst he appreciates his situation regarding the embezzlement from Jack's, any involvement in narcotics trafficking was through blackmail and his genuine concerns over the safety of himself and his family. We're willing to cut a deal for cooperation on two provisos. First, that my client will not face any charges in relation to narcotics trafficking, and second, that you will ensure his safety and that of his family. Do either of you have the authority to cut a deal on that basis?'

'I do,' stated Sally Anders confidently. 'Are you happy with a verbal commitment at this stage, with the others here as witness, or do we need to hash out something in writing first?'

Maddison sized up the detectives before glancing at Crowley. Crowley nodded discreetly and Maddison turned back towards Sally Anders. 'We can move forward today while I prepare an agreement for us to execute.'

'It doesn't work that way. We need to draft any plea bargain,' said Anders.

'I've done hundreds of these. I'm sure that whatever I draft will be in a format you're happy with. Plus, I'm certain that it will expedite the process,' replied Maddison. 'In any event, it's only a draft to get the ball rolling.'

Anders exchanged a glance with Ange before agreeing to Maddison's proposal. 'OK. I presume that the drafting is already underway? Isn't that the golden rule? Always be the one to prepare the first draft?' she said with a steely stare, wresting some control back away from Maddison. 'Let's get started, shall we?'

As agreed, Ange turned on a portable recording device she had brought along and started the interrogation. 'Let's start at the beginning. I presume this all started with your gambling habit, so fill us in on that, please.'

'I had never gambled before, save for a small punt each year as part of the Melbourne Cup celebrations. It never really connected with me, but that was before I could bet on my phone. They hook you in and make betting so engaging. You feel in control, but nothing could be further from the truth.'

'When did you first embezzle money from Jack's?' probed Ange.

'I'm not really sure anymore. I suppose it was three or four months after the Macau trip—2016, I guess. Before I moved to Brisbane.'

Crowley looked up sharply at this news, obviously surprised that Williamson's embezzlement went back that far. He jotted something down on his notepad.

'Can you elaborate, please?' asked Ange.

'Well, business was booming and one of our Chinese clients shouted me a trip to Macau. It was an all-expenses-paid extravaganza, complete with luxury hotels, magnificent restaurants, golf, massages. I'd never experienced such opulence. One night, my hosts took me to one of the flash casinos, The Venetian. They gave me a thousand dollars in cash and told me to have some fun. When I won three thousand on the roulette wheel, it was as if a lightning bolt had hit, electrifying beyond my wildest imagination. Whenever I suffered a minor loss, I would pony up and win it all back. I convinced himself that I'd discovered a sure-fire strategy, but soon tired of the roulette wheel and turned towards the card tables. One of my hosts showed me the ropes and the etiquette of playing blackjack.'

Williamson poured himself a glass of water and took a moment to drink half. 'By the time everyone was ready to leave, I'd won eighteen thousand dollars. I tried to give back the thousand dollars to my host, but he simply laughed at me. He said that I was a very good gambler, a lucky man, in fact. I purchased an expensive Burberry handbag at one of the luxury shops on the way out, one that Jenny had been lusting after one for ages. It was intoxicating. I felt like James Bond. Unfortunately, I gave most of it back the next night, save for two thousand dollars that I'd left back at my hotel room. In hindsight, it would have been better if I'd just lost the thousand dollars quickly. I might not have become addicted if that had happened.'

'Tell me about that. How did you get in so deep?'

'Things escalated quickly from there. Using the two-thousand-dollar stake I'd won in Macau, I started gambling online. In no time, I was lying awake playing roulette on my phone while Jenny slept. At work sometimes, I would wander down to the river and gamble some more money away on my phone. My losses were modest at first, but soon spiralled out of control. Those gambling apps are insidious. They keep egging you on,' implored Williamson, looking to explain away his weakness, hoping to find some sympathy. None showed.

'How did you hide this problem from your wife?' asked Sally Anders.

'Like any addict, I guess. I became an expert at making plausible excuses, explaining away overdue school fees and other missed payments. My credit cards were all maxed out, and it made me sick in the stomach. For a while, I reasoned that my best way out was to score a big win, but this only made my losses and my indebtedness worse. That's when I skimmed a little money off Jack's.'

Ange fixed him with a penetrating stare. It was a stretch to explain away stealing over eight million dollars as skimming a little pocket money. 'How did you work out how to go about it? Stealing the money, that is.'

'It wasn't hard. I had seen something similar before when I was at EY. Once the first couple of transactions went through, my gambling became progressively worse. The money I was losing somehow didn't seem real anymore. I had no reference point. If I suffered a big loss, then I would simply take some more money and place an even bigger bet to make up for it.'

'Where did you learn how to set up companies with dummy directors?' asked Ange, something that she had wondered about ever since her conversation with Glenda J Wilkes from the Wagga Wagga tennis club.

'That part was easy. Through the Dark Web. Reasonable prices and surprisingly good service. They even told me how to change addresses. I suppose this will be harder with the Director ID system being introduced, for a time at least,' responded Williamson casually, as if explaining where he had purchased his new Audi.

As Williamson explained the intricacies of his scam, Ange marvelled at how normal everyday people could sometimes fall onto the wrong side of the tracks. The ability of the human spirit to adapt and survive, quickly normalising previously unconscionable behaviours, was simply astonishing. Early episodes of *Breaking Bad* sprang to mind.

Anders interrupted Ange's wandering mind. 'How did you get involved in smuggling narcotics?'

Williamson looked positively distraught. 'I didn't know it was narcotics. All they asked me to do was arrange for certain products to be brought from China and Vietnam from time to time.'

'You're clearly a smart guy, Mr Williamson. Surely you suspected that something illegal was going on?' shot back Anders, her voice finding a sharp edge.

Williamson regained some of his spine, looking Anders in the eyes. 'I was just relieved to have them off my back. Frankly, I didn't want to know.'

Ange was getting annoyed with these interruptions by Anders, which were contrary to what they had agreed. She gave Anders a pointed look before taking back control of the interrogation, pointed looks and death stares being Ange's specialties. 'Get who off your back?'

'Lomax and Smith.'

'Tell us about that. How did they approach you?'

'I was walking down to the markets with my wife and family one Saturday morning when they approached me while I was buying coffee. They forced me to meet them in the park later that day, down by the river,' replied Williamson. He looked up at Ange as if imploring her to understand. 'They knew where I lived and they must have been watching our house. I was scared.'

'What was the deal they offered?'

'I couldn't settle my gambling debts. They had gotten out of hand and there was a limit to how much I could take from Jack's in one hit. Lomax and Smith offered a solution for my debts to be forgiven. In return, all I had to do was order some building products from time to time. Oh, the other thing I needed to do first up was to arrange for Lomax and Smith to be employed in Jeays' security division. It was all quite easy.'

'How deeply indebted were you?' asked Ange.

Williamson looked embarrassed, lowering his head before mumbling his reply. 'eZee Bet was the only mob that would take my bets anymore. I guess I was in the tin for well over five hundred thousand dollars with them.'

This was news to Maddison, whose reflexive whistle betrayed his thoughts about the extent of things. How the numbers tallied up confused Ange. 'How did this work? Did they pay off all your debts at once?'

'No, they paid off a hundred thousand each time I arranged for a shipment of products. They also agreed to put a hold on collecting the rest.'

'What sort of products were you ordering?'

'The products were all ACP panels initially.'

Ange smiled inwardly, as Williamson confirmed the theory that she had hatched in the surf. She attempted to trade a smug glance with an impassive Anders, which hung suspended, embarrassing Ange with her own vanity.

'What's an ACP panel?' asked Maddison.

Williamson answered his lawyer. 'Aluminium Composite Panels. Terrific product that was put under the spotlight after those fires. You know, like the Grenfell Tower fire that killed all those people. We had to stop importing them while the authorities worked out what to do.'

'Who's they? Are you referring to Lomax and Smith?' asked Sally Anders, impatience getting the better of her.

'I always figured that Lomax and Smith were just the muscle and that they had some link with eZee Bet. Otherwise, how would they know I was so heavily indebted? Whether it was people at eZee Bet itself, or whether they were feeding information to someone else that Lomax and Smith worked for, I'm not sure.'

'How many times did you make these transactions?' asked Ange.

'I lost count. At least six or seven times. The whole thing was a shock, one that made me take stock and stop gambling. I've been clean for a while now. Anyhow, the global pandemic hit, and they stopped calling—well, until six months ago.'

'So why the recent fake invoices that you've put through Jack's?' asked Pat Crowley, as intrigued as anyone about all of this.

'I wanted out of the whole thing. I was going to pay out the rest of my debts and hopefully get on with my life,' replied Williamson.

'You know they wouldn't have let you off that easily,' said Sally Anders, pausing for that observation to sink in. 'What products have they been interested in this time around? Presumably not ACP panels.'

'I probably knew deep down that they wouldn't let me off the hook that easily, but I had to try something. They asked me to import some specific flat-pack housing accommodation, like the type that gets used in remote locations. I really don't know what they did and how they organised things at the other end. It must be a very slick operation. Placing the orders was straightforward, and the paperwork was always impeccable. Plus, the products were top-notch. We had no troubles with any of those products.'

'Let me get this straight. Your only contacts were Lomax and Smith, and you had no contact with anyone at eZee Bet over these arrangements?' asked Ange.

She waited for Williamson's nod of agreement before continuing. Ange was now very concerned that the trail was going cold. This was not the outcome that she had hoped for, perhaps naively hoping that Falconi's name would have come up by now. Anders was busy texting someone, annoying Ange with this distraction. 'Does the name Eddie Falconi ring a bell?'

'The racehorse owner? Never met him. Lomax and Smith were my only contacts. Those guys give me the willies.'

The two detectives looked at each other, recognising the brick wall that they had just run into. Sally Anders quickly changed gear. 'Thanks, Mr Williamson. We will have more questions for you in due course, and perhaps we can move to settle your plea bargain quickly. From here, you will be taken to a secret hotel, ostensibly away on your business trip. You should ring your family tonight, if that's what you normally do when you're away on business. The weather in Adelaide is freezing and wet, by the way. Tomorrow afternoon, you will ring your wife again to say that you're a close contact of a confirmed case of Covid-19, someone you met in Adelaide, and that you've been ordered into hotel quarantine for fourteen days. You also need to contact your personal assistant and perhaps your superior at work. Tell them the same story and stick to it. Given that you will be in a form of hotel quarantine, you should have no trouble playing out that charade. However, it's essential for your safety and that of your family that they believe your story and you do not disclose any of this conversation. Can you do this?'

Williamson just nodded, the parallels with jail time obvious to everyone.

'I think that's as far as we can go today,' said Sally Anders, standing up and handing Maddison a business card. 'I look forward to receiving your draft plea bargain.' She beckoned towards a large and imposing man who was walking towards the officer, obviously the subject of Anders' recent texting affair. 'This gentleman will escort you to your accommodation. We'll post someone to watch over you at all times. No funny business, Mr Williamson. Is that clear?'

Williamson just continued nodding reflexively, reminding Ange of one of the chintzy happy drinking birds. This particular bird was not the happy kind.

Chapter 41

Compartments

The two detectives drove in silence for the first part of their trip back to the Gold Coast, realising that Williamson would be of no further use to them in piecing things together.

'Even if we can pin something on eZee Bet, Falconi will have a plan for diverting any attention away from himself. I can hear him now, blaming an unnamed former rogue staff member. The only thing to come out of that meeting was further proof of Lomax and Smith. Perhaps we should bring them in now? If we do that, then the syndicate will close ranks and disappear into the ether,' asked Ange, more a statement than a question as she verbalised the thoughts that were whizzing around in her brain.

'We need to keep Lomax and Smith on an extra tight leash. I don't want to be the one responsible for letting those guys off the hook. However, I agree with you about Williamson. We'll need him to testify in due course, but he won't help us in the short term,' responded Sally Anders.

'I'm dubious that Brett will uncover anything by going through the front door at eZee Bet, other than keep Falconi engaged. I reckon our best bet is to collar someone through the GlitterStrip connection.'

'I agree. The surveillance of the parcel lockers at Pacific Fair takes on a whole new level of importance. If we close in on Lomax and Smith, then presumably deliveries through GlitterStrip will stop and we run into another dead end,' stated Anders, staring straight ahead through the slapping windscreen wipers in deep thought. 'We currently have nothing on GlitterStrip, other than a couple of video images that prove absolutely nothing.'

The pair sat in abject silence for the balance of the trip. Thankfully, the rain had stopped by the time they arrived at the apartment block. As Anders exited the car, she turned and spoke to Ange. 'I'm going to look over the arrangements for the surveillance operation at Pacific Fair and strengthen them if necessary. We have a lot riding on this. Peter will be in touch as soon as we get an alert from Australia Post.' With that, Anders promptly shut the car door and marched towards the foyer, leaving Ange alone with her disappointing day.

Feeling flat, she decided to blow some cobwebs off. Packing her boards and wetsuit, she drove south, first checking out The Alley at Currumbin. The overcast beach was closed because of a large shark having been spotted, a perfect event for the day she was having. Burleigh was far too crowded for her liking, so she continued driving south to Greenmount and SuperBank. It was nothing like her previous encounter, but the odd small wave appeared to push around the point, so she ventured out for a paddle. Her earlier visit to Currumbin gave cause for some anxious glances below. Greenmount had suffered a horrific shark attack last year in clean, clear, and sunny conditions. This was an image that she failed to dispel, dampening the mood of her session.

As was often the way, when the waves were inconsistent, Ange drifted off into a trancelike state as her subconscious mind took over, stimulated by the steady ripples that rolled by and lifted her gently up and down. The syndicate seemed incredibly well organised and resourced. How could Falconi achieve all of this under everyone's gaze? He was no shrinking violet, and he certainly wasn't hiding under a rock in some obscure location. Her wacky imagination created a low-budget *James Bond* movie, with Eddie Falconi taking the role of the nefarious Ernst Stavro Blofeld as he strove for world domination. Certainly, Lomax and Smith looked the part, but the real Blofeld would have a veritable army of henchmen to do his bidding, not just those two goons. Something just didn't stack up.

She stayed in that meditative state as she showered and changed. Her surf, normally a mind cleanser, had worked none of its usual magic. As she rolled the case over and over, she barely remembered driving home. She even reimagined the events of Namba Heads, the first case where Lomax and Smith had come into her life. She arrived back home, confused and clueless.

The rest of the day collapsed into the next morning, which morphed into a thoroughly depressing weekend. It was excruciating. She rang Billy for a chat. He was busy doing someone else's bidding, something about the old Luna Park fire disaster. She wasn't really listening and Billy didn't need the burden of playing the role of therapist, so she left him to it.

She tried Brett, hoping that they could catch up. Unfortunately, he was going to be busy all weekend compiling information that Finch & Chang had requested on behalf of eZee Bet. The surf had turned to a messy easterly slop. Even Higgsy had no clues. She spent the weekend wandering the Gold Coast, alone with her thoughts and many doubts.

She had a brief respite when she rang her friend Kerrie, the lifestyle influencer from Byron Bay. Kerrie put Ange onto a new artist that she had recently become enamoured with, the quirkily named Juice Wrld. Ange was instantly hooked on this sublime hip-hop music that flowed like quicksilver. Kerrie was not someone who dug deep, a trait well suited to a social media influencer who stayed on the shiny surface of things. She also told Ange that she had ordered some products from GlitterStrip to try. Ange didn't have the heart to tell her that she had probably blown her money. Lucky Kerrie had plenty.

As per usual, Kerrie had a full book of engagements that weekend and needed to get on with her busy life, leaving Ange alone again. She amused herself for a while, researching the world of Juice Wrld. With hundreds of original songs to his name, she was thoroughly depressed to find that he had sadly died of a drug-induced seizure, at the ripe old age of twenty-one. Who knew what masterpieces he would have gifted the world given a few more years? If nothing else, this news helped build her rage against those who trafficked in such tragedy.

It was just before midday on Monday when her heart finally kicked back into action, the jangle of her conspicuously silent phone barging its way into her consciousness. It was Peter Fredericks. 'Hi, Ange. A GlitterStrip parcel has been logged for collection at the parcel locker. Zack Briggs, the guy we identified previously. The crew is in place and they'll take him to the Southport station. I can let you know when that happens. You're quite welcome to come up to the apartment and watch. Australia Post told us he normally takes less than four hours to collect. The perfect customer, in their words. He has a prior conviction for supply, by the way.'

Ange jumped at the chance to escape her own company. She didn't want to risk missing anything, so she drove over to Fredericks' apartment for a change of scenery. Finding a parking spot nearby was normally a challenge, but at least the gloomy weather proved good for something.

'I hear you had a disappointing day with Williamson,' said Peter Fredericks.

'Sally was not a happy camper. She should be here any minute to watch the fun.'

Almost as if she had heard her own name, Sally Anders wandered through the front door, phone pressed up against her ear. The call did not seem to be going well. She walked over to Ange and held the phone away from her head. Ange could hear a man speaking loudly and authoritatively. Ange imagined him smoking a big fat cigar.

Phrases like 'massive bureaucratic overreach' and 'this will be on your head, Detective' drifted to her ear, in obvious reference to Anders and their investigation. 'A great Australian' and 'connected at the highest levels' followed. Ange bristled when she heard 'why do you have a corrupt cop working for you, anyway'. She presumed that meant her. Anders rolled her eyes and took both barrels for a good five more minutes. This barrage ended when the caller loudly told her, 'you're barking up the wrong tree on this', and then 'I won't take the fall for you when it all goes pear-shaped'. Sally Anders calmly thanked the caller for the heads-up and ended the call.

'I gather that I'm the corrupt cop, and that Eddie Falconi is the great Australian with connections at the highest levels. What are you going to do?' asked Ange.

Anders was fuming. 'How did Falconi know that we're bearing down on him? How dare they? This confirms that we're onto something. Any action at Pacific Fair, Peter?'

'Yep, Briggs just turned up. That software that Billy has organised is bloody useful. It picked him up well before our guys saw him. Come and watch.' Fredericks turned his monitor so that his colleagues could observe the pantomime. Briggs was at the locker, entering his pin number. No sooner had he pulled the parcel out of the locker than a large police officer tapped him on the shoulder. Briggs turned and tried to run the other way, not even making half a step before slamming into the chest of another. He quickly dropped the parcel, hoping to distance himself from it and its contents. The officers were having none of it, forcing Briggs to pick up the parcel before escorting him to a waiting unmarked police car, shoulders slumped, not hiding the fact that his was not a happy place.

Ange was itching to question Briggs and confirm theory number two, that GlitterStrip was a front for narcotics distribution and that Australia Post was being used as an unwitting courier. A modern incarnation of the train station and airport lockers deployed in old spy movies. 'How soon do you think we can question him? I'm concerned that our case will fall to pieces now that Falconi knows we're circling nearby.'

Anders simply made a call on her phone, insisting that she needed to interrogate Briggs. She asked whoever was on the other end of the call to quickly deal with the formalities. 'If Briggs wants a lawyer present, then you need to get that sorted as a matter of urgency. I'm coming straight over to the station with my colleague.'

Anders turned to Ange. 'Ready? Let's go.' She didn't wait for Ange's reply before grabbing her stuff and walking towards the door. Ange followed obediently. Given what was riding on it, she guessed Anders would take the lead on this interview.

Chapter 42

Briggs

O nly thirty minutes had elapsed before they arrived at the Southport police station and were seated in the reception area, one where bland and
uninviting must have been the interior decorators' only brief. The duty officer
told the detectives that Briggs was being processed and that they had found him
a lawyer—not a very good one, but a lawyer at least. The pair sat patiently, Ange
reading the news on her phone, Anders sitting impassively and deep in thought.

'How on earth could Falconi have known? We must have a mole in our midst,'
she mumbled to no one in particular, snatching Ange's attention away from her
phone.

'I've got an idea about that,' commented Ange. She texted Crowley.

> *Hi, Pat. Can you text me Bob Turnbull's number? I need to speak to
> him.*

The phone buzzed with a reply.

> *Who is this?*

Ange tapped a quick-fire reply.

> *Detective Angela Watson.*

The phone buzzed again with a contact card for Bob Turnbull. Ange rang his number.

'Hello, Mr Turnbull. It's Angela Watson here. Have you been speaking with Eddie Falconi by any chance? I know that you guys are golfing buddies at The Australian golf club.'

Turnbull was suddenly defensive. 'Why your sudden interest in my golfing companions?'

Ange noted Turnbull referred to Falconi as a companion rather than a buddy. 'I can't tell you that. Just answer the question, please.'

There was a lengthy silence before Turnbull replied. 'Eddie rang me over the weekend. He wanted to know if I was coming up to the Gold Coast for the Magic Millions thoroughbred sale. He plans to organise some golf at Sanctuary Cove. They've just redone their greens.'

'Is that all you spoke of?'

'Well, we spoke about business, of course,' replied Turnbull.

'What sort of business?' probed Ange.

'Eddie wanted to know the state of the building industry, what with all the crazy price escalation of building products that's going on. He's planning to develop some townhouses in Robina. Eddie knows we import products from overseas. We've spoken about that before on the course. He's always interested in how business is going.'

'Did you mention anything about your CFO and the embezzlement?'

'Maybe.'

'Define *maybe* for me, please,' shot back Ange. She already knew the trajectory that Turnbull's answer would take, but she wanted to hear him say it.

'I might have mentioned that I was dealing with a problem with our CFO, and that the police were involved. Did I do something wrong?'

'Of course you did,' snapped Ange. 'I thought we had an agreement on confidentiality. You may have put our investigation at risk, not to mention lives. Confidentiality can be a two-way street, Mr Turnbull.' The threat of leaking something about Turnbull, Jack's, and their involvement with Falconi was a hollow one, but some journalist would make the connection—perhaps with a bit of help if Ange was of a mind.

'Is Eddie involved? He's a top bloke. Knows everyone.'

'If I were you, Mr Turnbull, I would start distancing yourself from your golfing buddy. That's all I can say. Keep your mouth shut from now on. Oh, and don't waste your time booking tickets to the Gold Coast,' said Ange before abruptly hanging up the call. She was angry that Turnbull had jeopardised their case, and angrier still that the Sydney old boys' network seemed to work against her.

She suddenly had a light-bulb moment. 'That's how Falconi conceived the importation scheme. He must have worked it out during their friendly golf games,' she said to no one in particular, even though Anders was sitting right alongside. 'Be careful of the company you keep.'

'Explains a lot, but it doesn't help us with the freight train we're on right now,' remarked Anders, evidently having followed this exposé.

A spivvy-looking guy sauntered in. Shiny suit, sunglasses sitting on top of his head, excessively pointed light brown shoes, trying to look sharp but failing badly. Ange guessed he might be Briggs' lawyer, so she quickly stopped speaking and flashed a look at Anders. She was right, overhearing his conversation with the duty officer. He took a seat nearby, and the three sat in the reception area. It was yet another Wes Anderson movie moment.

After a few minutes, the duty officer escorted the lawyer through a door, presumably to meet with his client. An obviously more senior officer returned to greet the two detectives. 'Eric Pearson. That was Briggs' lawyer. Give them a few minutes and they should be ready for you. Do you want me to join?'

'That might be useful. Could you sit to the side and observe? We've been working on this case for over a year now, so we should be able to cut to the chase. You'll need to take on any local actions that might be necessary. Going by the amount of stuff this guy was receiving, I'm guessing there might be an entire network of local dealers that will sit underneath.'

They discussed shop for a bit, chatting about the drug scene on the coast and the latest trends. Methamphetamine was a big problem, not just with addicts but everyday people like lawyers, teachers, even doctors and nurses. The duty officer interrupted this depressing little chat, informing them that Briggs and Pearson were ready for them.

Briggs and his lawyer were no match for Sally Anders. 'Before we get started, Mr Briggs, you're in serious trouble. Given your prior record, you're looking at some major jail time.'

'My client did not know what was in the parcel. It was sent to him by mistake,' said Pearson, puffing himself up like one of those bearded dragons that sunned themselves on the walking tracks that Ange pounded.

'Nobody is going to believe that. We have ample evidence to show that this was not a one-off affair. It's up to you. Either you cooperate, or we throw the book and the bookshelf at you,' said Anders in full flight. Ange thought her colleague was playing a big game and walking a tightrope with her approach. A lengthy whispered conversation between lawyer and client ensued, the only interruption to an otherwise silent room.

'What sort of guarantees does my client have that you'll take his cooperation into account?' said the lawyer, looking totally ridiculous with his sunglasses still perched on his head, hopelessly failing Body Language 101. Whatever authority he might have possessed was not in play today.

'Absolutely none. Other than the assurance of me and my colleagues. What's it going to be?' demanded Anders.

Another whispering event took place, staccato style and shorter this time. The lawyer turned from his client and spoke. 'OK, but I'll hold you to those assurances, Detective,' said the lawyer, vainly trying to inject some authority back into his performance. Anders gave him that minor triumph, nodding her reply.

Now that Anders had done a masterful job at getting their cooperation, Ange played some good cop. 'Tell us how you placed the orders at GlitterStrip. How did they know you didn't want lipstick?'

Briggs spoke for the first time. 'That was easy. I simply select anything in their catalogue but then enter a special promo code just before completing the order. The promo code changes each time.'

'How did they do that? Change the promo code, that is?'

'There's a code hidden in the packing slip inside each package. It's pretty smart, actually.'

Ange secretly agreed with him on that point. 'How did you pay for your purchases?'

'I didn't. They were free.'

This statement met with confused looks on the part of the police officers before Ange realised what was going on, almost smiling at this absurdity. 'Not the cosmetics. I meant the drugs.'

'Oh. Yeah. I had to deposit chunks of money into a betting account and then gamble like crazy until it was all gone. It was pretty fun. It almost makes up for paying their exorbitant prices and hooked me in, for sure. I also gambled some of my own money away. Same result. Lost the lot.'

'What's the name of the gambling company you dealt with?' asked Anders.

'eZee Bet. Good platform. Did it all on my phone.'

Armed with the information that they needed, Ange and Sally Anders excused themselves. Outside the room, they explained the urgency of the matter and asked that Briggs be detained until they could return. They had bigger fish to fry.

Chapter 43

Cronin

The two detectives walked briskly out of the station. Anders threw over her car keys, asking if Ange could drive. Anders was on her phone in no time.

'Peter, it's Sally here. We need a warrant to search the GlitterStrip address up on Mount Nathan. Can you get the ball rolling on that?'

'Sure. I was waiting to call you, as I knew that you were busy with Briggs. The Mitsubishi has been on the move—you know, the one that Lomax and Smith were using. I first thought that it was heading to Ange's place. I was a bit concerned, but it drove straight past her house before stopping on Cronin Island. It's been stationary for a good hour now.'

Anders turned to Ange. 'Isn't Cronin Island where Eddie Falconi lives?'

Ange nodded a distracted over-the-shoulder affirmative, struggling with the unfamiliar car as she attempted to extract them from the narrow police station car park. She hadn't even made the street before Anders barked an urgent order. 'Stop. Turn around. We need to go back to the station.'

Ange stopped the car and glanced at her colleague strangely, one eye watching the JUCY backpacker van that had just backed out straight in front of her.

'You can wait here,' demanded Sally Anders as she jumped from the car, still waiting for the beaten-up JUCY van to finish its gyrations. Ange waited patiently, then executed an awkward three-point turn and raced back to the space they had only just vacated. She remained seated in the car, twiddling her thumbs, eager to get going. She presumed they would pay Falconi a visit, but she had been so focussed on getting out of the tightly packed car park unscathed that she had registered none of the conversation between Anders and Fredericks.

Anders was back five minutes later, opening the passenger door but remaining standing, as if not yet ready to leave. 'I've organised some backup. If we're lucky, we might even nab Lomax, Smith, and Falconi in one fell swoop. It looks like they're all at Falconi's house.' Anders glanced back towards the rear of the car park, causing Ange's eyes to follow the direction of her gaze.

Two marked police cars edged out of the secure compound at the rear of the parking lot, looking their way. Anders jumped into the car and slammed the passenger door shut with a loud clunk. 'There they are. Quickly. Let's go. I presume you know the way to Falconi's house.'

The three cars raced back down the Gold Coast Highway before turning into Thomas Drive, then taking a right towards Cronin Island. Sure enough, the convoy arrived to find a white Mitsubishi Outlander parked directly outside Falconi's mansion. The police cars parked quickly and haphazardly, slamming their doors loudly as they exited, all pretext of discretion totally abandoned. Ange reflected that her hazy cover was blown for good, and their impromptu visit would be the talk of the town at Ada's next bridge morning.

The two detectives joined the other four uniformed police officers assembled on the grassy verge. The front gate was slightly ajar. Sally Anders took charge and gestured towards the officers. 'OK. Two of you stay here and watch the roads. Once we enter the property, I want one of you to check the jetty and make sure nobody gets away by water.' She looked at the third officer. 'Given that my colleague and I are unarmed, I want you to stay with us and give us support if needed. I need to warn you—we're certain that the two drivers of the Mitsubishi over there are guilty of murder, so we all need to take care. I'm not sure what they might be capable of.'

With that, Anders nuzzled the front gate fully open and the raiding party entered the property. Ange checked that the front door was locked before peering in through the narrow glass panels on either side. She couldn't see any activity in the entrance or in the other areas of the house. 'I can't see anyone from here—let's go around the side and look in through the back. By memory, the back of the house opens onto the courtyard.'

One officer looked sharply up at Ange. 'Have you been here before?'

'A party two weekends ago,' said Ange. 'I was undercover.' Ange knew she was gilding the lily, but she was sick and tired of being portrayed as a rogue cop. A modicum of respect crept into the eyes of the police officer. Undercover work was one of the toughest assignments one could have in the force.

The others quietly followed Ange along a cobblestone path which circumnavigated the house. They passed through another gate, flimsy and creaking loudly. Ange cringed at the noise, holding the gate open to prevent it from clanging shut. Her three colleagues filed through.

One of the uniformed officers had his gun out and peered cautiously around the corner of the house. When he saw the coast was clear, he replaced the weapon in its holster and walked into the deserted courtyard. Anders motioned for the other officer to secure the jetty while Ange helped her to check out the house.

Nothing.

The house was secure and there was nothing untoward to see. Disappointment welled in the pit of Ange's stomach as they wandered around the courtyard. The scene painted a very different story from the glitzy night-time party spectacle of her last visit. Under the harsh light of day, the place looked tawdry, tired, and badly in need of a facelift. She reflected the same was probably true for many of Falconi's partygoers.

A voice yelled from the jetty. 'Over here!'

Ange led the way around the cabana toward the ramp that led down to the jetty, the place where she had spied Lomax and Smith at the party. They tramped single file down the noisy aluminium walkway and stood beside the other officer. He simply pointed into the back of the boat.

There, suspended by a thick rope, dangled a lifeless Eddie Falconi. Ange was furious. This was the calling card of Lomax and Smith, for sure. The discomfort in her stomach exploded.

'What the hell?' yelled Ange, her voice raised in anger.

Anders motioned to their two uniformed colleagues. 'Nobody goes onto the boat until we can get a team over. You two keep searching,' she said, gesturing at the two police officers before whipping out her trusty phone. 'Hi, Peter. Can you search for any vehicles registered in Falconi's name? Oh, and check boat registrations. Besides the big boat, he might have had a speedboat or a tinnie.' Anders read out the registration of the large motor yacht.

As soon as she had finished the call with Fredericks, Anders pulled a business card out of her back pocket and punched in a number listed on the card. 'Hi, Sergeant. It's Detective Sally Anders here. I'm at an address on Cronin Island. We have a body. Mr Eddie Falconi.'

Ange overheard the sergeant's reply. 'Eddie Falconi? The racehorse owner?'

'One and the same. Can you organise a crew? It looks like a suicide, but we need to treat this as a murder site. I'm almost certain that Mr Falconi did not kill himself. They won't have any trouble finding us. There's only one road in and out of Cronin Island, and I stationed two of your officers outside. As soon as you can, please Sergeant,' asked Anders, before ending the call.

Ange was stunned. Sally Anders appeared equally floored. In an instant, their case had been turned on its head. The sounds of the river took prominence as a depressed silence hung between them. Ange stared blankly at a passing tourist barge filled with snap-happy holidaymakers, taking advantage of this moment, soon to be shared with their Instagram friends. The wake from the barge disturbed the scene, jolting Ange out of her reverie.

'You know this means that they'll already have covered their tracks. They seem one step ahead all the time. I'll bet we find diddly-squat when we raid GlitterStrip up at Mount Nathan,' observed Ange.

After a few seconds confronting the obvious, a grim faced Sally Anders replied. 'It would seem that Falconi is not the boss of this operation, as we first thought. He must have presented a liability to someone.'

Ange mused that Eddie Falconi was not the top predator after all and this bird of prey had fallen victim to something bigger and more dangerous. Something suddenly dawned on her. 'Lomax and Smith have been playing us for fools. They knew full well that we were tracking the Mitsubishi. I'll bet they led us here to show us up, maybe even to divert us from Mount Nathan while they cleaned the place up.'

Anders' phone rang. Ange saw Peter Fredericks' name come up on the screen. She trailed along as Sally Anders walked down to the jetty and surveyed the area. 'The speedboat is not here. Can you put out an urgent alert for the vessel? We need to act quickly if we have any hope of tracking these guys down. How are you going with the search warrant for Mount Nathan?'

Anders spoke to Ange after she was done with Fredericks. 'Lomax and Smith might have used Falconi's speedboat to exit the property. We need to see if Falconi's Range Rover is still here. My guess is that the boat will be abandoned somewhere handy to the main road and those guys will have already disappeared. Peter expects to have the search warrant any minute. Once the forensic team arrives, I don't think there's much more we can do here, at least for now.' She pulled up her recent call log.

'Hi, it's Sally Anders again. Can I have these police officers for the rest of the day? We need to check out an address at Mount Nathan. I'm just waiting for a search warrant to come through, but I'd like them to accompany us.'

An impatient Sally Anders abruptly concluded the call and redirected her attention to Ange. 'Can you tell the police officers to stay here while we pick up the search warrant from Peter at the apartment? They can then accompany us to Mount Nathan. Hopefully, the forensic crew should be here by then. Quick, let's go. Can you drive? I've got a few calls to make.'

Whilst Ange had no sympathy for Falconi, a peddler of misery and addiction, she was upset over his death and the crucial information which had died along with him. 'And that's the end of Eddie Falconi,' mumbled Ange as she jogged back to pass on her boss's orders. 'Probably also our case—if my hunch is correct.'

Chapter 44

Mount Nathan

S earch warrant in hand, the two detectives raced down to Anders' car and looped back towards Cronin Island to pick up the uniformed officers. A forensic van was there, so Ange quickly ran into the property whilst Anders briefed the officers on the task at hand. She jogged down the ramp, her thumping steps causing the jetty to spasm in response, a battle of rhythms that caused Ange to lose hers. Her last crashing asynchronous step at least won the attention of the forensic team, who glanced up sharply, annoyed at this noisy intrusion. Forensics could be precious once they had control of a site.

'Hi, guys. We have good reason to suspect that this is a murder disguised as a suicide, so can you treat the site as such? Also, when you get into the house, can you let me know if there's a black Range Rover in the garage?' They exchanged phone numbers. It annoyed Ange that she still didn't possess a business card like Sally Anders, operating off-grid as she was. That was yet another thing on her growing list of things to speak with Anders about.

By the time she had jogged back to the car, Anders was at the wheel and the team was ready to roll. The three cars zoomed off sharply as soon as Ange's door slammed shut. Once they were off Cronin Island, one of the marked police cars took the lead, and the convoy ran to a siren. Ange didn't normally like a siren but she was angry and annoyed. The flashing lights and blaring siren were strangely satisfying to this rage, building rather than relieving, focussing her energy on the impending task.

The drive up to Mount Nathan was frustrating and endless, a stark contrast to the pleasant and leisurely jaunt that she had enjoyed on her last visit. The three cars crashed into the driveway and scud to a halt on the gravel courtyard connecting the house with a large Colorbond shed. These histrionics somehow seemed childish to the abject silence that greeted the raiding party. A crow called, its watchful cry a perfect melody to the sequence of swear words that instinctively formed in Ange's mind.

In total contrast to their arrival, the officers tiptoed around the house, checking doors and windows, finding nobody at home. Anders and Ange moved towards the shed and pulled at the large barn door. It slid open, screeching disobediently and breaking the solitude of the bushland setting. The crow objected to this disturbance and launched into a series of baleful cries, casting a depressing spell over the show beneath.

The shed, like the house, was depressingly empty, save for the detritus of a rapid exit that littered the pockmarked concrete floor. Taking advantage of the open door, the zephyr that entered caused a few brown paper remnants to flutter, but the place was otherwise deserted and abandoned.

Ange was so angry that she couldn't trust herself to speak. Sally Anders seemed resigned and more accepting of the situation. 'Let's close up and leave the buildings to forensics. I doubt we'll find anything that will help us in the short term. I think we should take a walk over the property, just in case.'

With that, the team scattered and walked through the trees. Ange came across a small, poorly maintained rotunda, positioned on the edge of a cluster of eucalypt trees and boasting an impressive view down to the coast. Ange stood there for a moment, staring blankly, the sinking feeling in the pit of her stomach stealing any appreciation for the vista below. The watchful resident crow gave its best velociraptor impression, jump-starting Ange's resolve. 'I will not let these guys win,' she said out loud, clenching her jaw as she hastened back to the cars.

Sally Anders was waiting. 'I just had a call from Peter. They found the speedboat beached at Southport on the Broadwater.'

'That's beside the Gold Coast Highway,' observed Ange, dejection obvious in the tone of her voice. 'Lomax and Smith set all of this up. They'll be long gone by now.'

Anders asked two of the police officers to secure the site until forensics arrived. She then instructed the remaining two officers to doorknock adjoining properties and see if they could determine when the place had been cleaned out. She handed her business card to the most senior-looking officer. 'Can you ring me if you find out anything useful? We need to work out roughly when they skipped town. It might give us a clue how they were tipped off.'

This jogged Ange's memory. She dialled the number that she had recently stored on her phone. 'It's Detective Watson here. Did you find a black Range Rover on the property?'

'Yes, it's in the garage.'

This answer did not impress Ange. 'I asked you to ring me. It's important. We need to find who did this.'

'Anyway, it looks like a vanilla-style suicide to me. I didn't see that it was important.'

That response further enraged Ange. Now even their own team was working against her. 'This is a murder. Keep looking.' The words were spat out with venom.

She abruptly hung up without awaiting a reply, unable to trust herself to say anything further—at least anything that might help the situation. She turned to her boss. 'Falconi's Range Rover is in the garage. We really have no idea what car they might be driving.'

Anders threw over her car keys, asking Ange to drive back to Southport whilst she called Peter Fredericks. 'Hi, Peter, we need another forensics crew at the Mouth Nathan address. Also, put an alert out for Lomax and Smith. Perhaps one of the motorway cameras might have picked them up, but I doubt it. These guys are better than we've given them credit for. It's too late in the day to get an alert into the news, but we should think about that for tomorrow. Also, can you search for any cars registered at the Mount Nathan address? Include the company that owns GlitterStrip.'

She turned to Ange with a questioning look. 'What's the name of the company that owns GlitterStrip?'

'CVU Pty Ltd,' replied Ange, loud enough so that Peter Fredericks could hear.

'Got that, Peter?' said Anders. 'If you find any potential getaway vehicles, put an immediate alert out for them as well.'

Fredericks must have passed comment on the hopeless position that they were now in, as an uncharacteristically bleak look came over Anders' face. 'Yes, I know that we're grasping at straws. These guys have done a number on us.'

With that hapless sign-off, Ange realised her boss was spot on. She had completely underestimated Lomax and Smith, passing them off as nothing more than hired muscle. Perhaps they were still that, but the way they had made her look silly was testament to a certain intellect and capability. They took turns to remonstrate themselves on the drive back down the mountain.

When they arrived at the Southport Broadwater and the address where the speedboat had been found, Ange immediately realised why Lomax and Smith had chosen this spot. Not only was it a convenient place to beach a boat quickly, but it was also only a short walk to a large car park and the Gold Coast Highway. The pair could have been out of the boat and on their way in a matter of minutes.

There were several boats similarly beached, insured against a rising tide with their snaking anchor ropes, probably locals making a waterborne trip to the Australia Fair Shopping Centre opposite. Ange reasoned that the arrival and departure of Lomax and Smith would have looked commonplace. She doubted anyone would notice anything out of the ordinary that would help them track the pair down.

After a brief reconnoitre, Ange rejoined her boss on the grassy verge. 'I suppose we should get forensics to go over the boat, but it won't help us. We know it was them, and it's obvious why they chose this spot.'

Anders looked thoughtfully out across the Broadwater, unable to appreciate the spectacular expanse of water. 'These guys will have disappeared. This couldn't have been arranged at a moment's notice. They've been onto us for days. They were sending us a message by using the Mitsubishi. This changes everything.'

The pair sat down on a park bench overlooking the Broadwater as the sun set behind, thinking through the implications of their depressing afternoon. Peter Fredericks rang at one point, telling Sally Anders that he had put out an alert on four vehicles that Lomax and Smith might have used to make their exit. Of course, there could be many more that they had no clue about.

The outlook was indeed bleak.

Chapter 45

Collapse

The next few days were the most frustrating of Ange's career as a detective. Not only had they lost the trail, but Lomax and Smith were still on the loose. She desperately wanted to bring them to account. What would she tell the families who had their lives ruined by Lomax and Smith in Namba Heads—that she accidentally lost them? With no one to give witness, Sergeant Darren Billings would likely get off and continue along his inept way, tormenting the unsuspecting residents of Namba Heads with incompetence.

Worse still, it had become increasingly obvious that the syndicate was well informed of the investigation's progress. Brett had come around one evening and was surprised to hear of Falconi's demise. News of his death was being suppressed while the team worked through the consequences of that unexpected event. That Brett did not know of this development made Ange conclude that the left and right hand of Sally Anders might never even share a meal.

'Why would Finch & Chang still be chasing me for information about BeaBet?' Brett asked.

The pair assembled several theories on this. Perhaps they were in the dark about Eddie Falconi's death? Perhaps they were working for someone further up the chain of command? Perhaps they were simply racking up as many fees as they could until someone told them to stop? It all seemed illogical.

Those questions remained unanswered until Ange's next meeting with her boss on the following Tuesday. She arrived at the apartment to find Peter Fredericks packing files into an archive box. 'What's going on?' she asked.

'We've been told to shut up shop and get back to Sydney. We're done here,' said Fredericks with a resigned look.

'What, all of us?' asked Ange.

Sally Anders looked up to join the conversation. 'You can stay here for a while longer, but Peter and I have been told to get back to Sydney ASAP.'

Anders was one cool cookie, not betraying any hint of the frustration she must have been feeling. After all, Sally Anders had been working on the case far longer than Ange.

Ange showed no such restraint. 'That's a joke. Is Operation Carcharias still afoot? We need to stop these guys.'

'The Carcharias operation is on hold, for now at least,' replied Anders before she showed the smallest of insights into what she was feeling. 'We've been diverted onto other, more pressing cases,' she said, forming air quotes with her fingers around the last three words.

'What about Brett and BeaBet?'

'Well, that's really interesting. Finch & Chang have told Brett that they have another client who is interested in acquiring BeaBet. Upstairs has instructed me to exit our position in BeaBet. I'm still not sure what I think about all of that. What are your thoughts?'

Ange took a moment to think through the implications, making a brief lap of the apartment as stimulation to those machinations. 'My first thought is that they want to get Brett off the scene and out of the picture entirely.'

'Mine too,' said Anders. 'However, it could be legitimate, and Finch & Chang have simply worked up a plan to ensure they get a lucrative M&A job. I'm suspicious but I can't take it any further.'

Ange looked crestfallen and defeated, a fact that was not lost on her boss.

'You did nothing wrong, Ange. At least we shut down this latest operation and helped stem the flow of drugs into the coast for a while. There's something much bigger going on here. None of us saw this coming.'

Ange knew the drugs would soon start flowing again. Where there was demand and cash, then supply would surely follow. 'Temporarily, perhaps. We both know what will happen within weeks,' she said, referring to the river of drugs that constantly found its way into the country. 'What about Lomax and Smith?'

Her heart sank as Anders and Fredericks exchanged a look. Anders confirmed Ange's worst suspicions. 'Yesterday, a worker found a suspicious car parked in a container up at the Port of Brisbane. It wasn't even any of the vehicles that we were looking for, but we suspect it was the escape vehicle used by Lomax and

Smith. We found sand in the footwell that matches the sand on the Broadwater. I'm not sure exactly how they did that, but the forensic report seems quite certain. Something about a specific trace element that they identified.'

Ange stated the obvious. 'They could be on any ship heading anywhere. There must have been hundreds of vessels that left port over the last week. We know from the Namba Head operation that the syndicate has contacts in the shipping game.'

Anders and Fredericks exchanged another look. 'There's another thing. When they discovered the car, there was a sheet of paper on the dash. It was a photo of you, with a set of coordinates and the words TREAD CAREFULLY printed underneath in bold type. We have someone checking it out. Do those words mean anything to you?' asked Anders.

Ange's eyes widened at this news. She looked at the image that Fredericks had pulled up on his computer screen. It was her all right, coming out of the surf at Greenmount. Who knew how long they had been watching her?

'Nothing other than a warning of some sort,' said Ange, the only comment that she could muster.

That foreboding sentence hung in the air for a moment before Ange pulled herself together and tackled the elephant in the room. 'How were they onto us? We need to investigate how the syndicate got wind of our progress. Aren't we going to look into that?'

'Officially, that's a big no. Unofficially, the whole thing stinks. Let's keep this off the record, but we all need to think through who we spoke to and when. I have my suspicions, and they're not good ones, but I can't raise them until we have some proof.'

The implications of this were not lost on Ange. 'So basically, everyone's a suspect and we can't trust them until they're crossed off the list.'

'Exactly, and this all must be kept on the quiet. I want you and Brett to work through your respective local connections for the next couple of weeks. I've told upstairs that you two need to wrap up some loose ends. This is not something that we are going to solve quickly. You can use the house and car for as long as you need to. In fact, I'll get the car assigned to you for a while longer. Seeing as you came here straight from Byron, why don't you take some time off before heading back to Sydney? We all need a break to let us process what has gone on. I'm going to take some time off myself as soon as I've dealt with the politics. How about I see you back in Sydney in a month's time?'

These were not questions, more statements of direction for Ange to follow.

That disconcerting discussion was now over, and Anders changed the topic. 'What's happened with Jack's Constructions?'

'Oh, that. The chairman rang me and they've decided not to press charges. They realise they won't recover any of the money from the betting companies, so they did a deal with Williamson over his house and whatever other assets he can liquidate. It probably makes sense and avoids any negative publicity and loss of reputation. I don't see that Williamson was any more use to us. Do you think he might have blabbed?'

'I doubt it. The officer that we assigned to watch him at the hotel told me that Williamson was frantically worried about his family. It doesn't rule him out, so you'll need to interview him again. Also, write up your investigation and send it to me when you can. Just stick to the basics on the embezzlement. Since Jack's aren't pressing charges and our narcotics importation case is toast, the plea bargain we negotiated is probably superfluous.'

Ange made a mental note that she would need to include Bob Turnbull and Pat Crowley on her suspect list. She was suddenly deeply fatigued. The adrenaline and pressure of the past few weeks rudely crash-tackled her. She muttered a pathetic response, still in a daze about what had just transpired. 'OK. I'll speak to you if I find anything. Otherwise, I'll see you in the office in a month.'

With that, Ange left the apartment to seek refuge in her beloved sea.

Epilogue

S eeing as Ange had only been on the Gold Coast for a short time, the list of contacts she needed to scrutinise was small. She felt bad about probing Higgsy and his mates. During one of their post-surf breakfasts, Ange fessed up that she was, in fact, still a detective and had been working on an active case.

Evidently, Jen had been on to her. 'We never really thought that you were working in corporate investigations. What does that even mean, anyway?'

Higgsy had been vehement on the topic of drugs. 'One of my best mates died of a drug overdose. If the average Joe knew the pain and heartache drugs caused, I suspect they might take a different view of the way we have normalised drug use in our community. Whatever we're doing now is clearly not working. All the money that we spend on policing seems to make little or no impact, at least as far as I see.'

Ange knew Higgsy was correct. Her job was not to question government policy, only to enforce it. Chasing the trail of illegal narcotics was likely to remain in her position description for some time yet. Despite the odd victory or two, the flow of drugs was endless. The profile of drug usage was also changing. A brief high and a short escape from life's pressure could be picked up for a meagre ten dollars. Ice or crystal meth were being manufactured locally and had poisoned every part of the country. Even small rural towns had fallen prey to this epidemic. Cheap manufacture and local distribution had the effect of crowding out traditional and more expensive drugs, making new and smaller markets viable.

Perhaps sophisticated mobs like the syndicate would be priced out of the market? Ange mused the syndicate was like one of those arcade games she used to love playing at the Tamworth Show, the game where you smashed down buttons that popped up randomly. No matter how successful you were in dispatching buttons back into their holes, another one would pop up in a different spot, in endless defiance of whatever skills you brought to the table. She suspected the syndicate would not lie down so easily just because little old Angela Watson had tapped them on the head a few times.

While Pat Crowley had convinced her he was not involved, Ange was not at all persuaded by Bob Turnbull. He ignored or avoided several calls, proving evasive and unconvincing when they ultimately spoke. There was something weird about Turnbull and Jack's Constructions, something that she couldn't put a finger on. It made little sense that Turnbull would have commissioned Pat Crowley to do some forensic investigation if he was in on the gig. Perhaps an old favour owed, or a new favour gifted? Ange was not of a mind to cross Turnbull off her naughty list just yet. She rang Billy with a plan to run that to ground.

'Hi, Billy. It's Ange here. How are you going?'

'Things are going brilliantly. The work that I'm doing is fantastic. Sorry to hear about your case.'

Ange realised Billy was nowhere near as heavily invested in the case as she was. Like all in his generation, he had leaped on to greener pastures without so much as a backward glance. 'You know your friend at the ATO? Nelson, wasn't it?'

'Yes, Nelson. We catch up often now that we've reconnected.'

'Do you think Nelson could check out Bob Turnbull and Jack's Constructions for me? Something doesn't stack up for me. Not immediately—I don't want to be too overt about it just for the moment. Perhaps as part of a wider look into the construction industry?'

'Sure. I'll speak to him. I'm certain that it doesn't work like that, but perhaps he can keep an ear out for an opportunity.'

Ange concluded her backup interview with John Williamson, which proved of no further use. She felt for the former CFO, having fallen victim to the insidious charms of online gambling. She left Williamson with his life in pieces.

Sally Anders rang one morning with some disturbing news. 'I just received word that a search of the coordinates left by Lomax and Smith had revealed the buried body of Ted Kramer. Someone had stabbed him in the left kidney and cut his throat before burying him in a shallow grave in the scrub. It had been an expert kill by someone who knew their stuff.'

A momentary flicker of guilt passed over Ange, seeing as her investigation had brought his world crashing down. She quickly shook off those thoughts, knowing that Ted Kramer's choices had been his own.

'That note was clearly a warning for you, Ange. You need to be extra vigilant. I wouldn't panic, as killing another drug dealer is one thing—killing a detective is quite another. Just be careful, that's all. Lomax and Smith are serious guys. Hopefully, now that we've been officially shut down, they'll lose interest in us. When you get back to Sydney, perhaps you should brush up on your firearms training.'

That conversation had not made Ange feel any better.

Before she packed up and left town, she went to the effort of baking a cake for Ada—an old-fashioned lemon syrup cake, the type that her grandmother had taught Ange to make back on the farm. Ange liked Ada instinctively. She reminded her of many women she had met in the country. Capable, independent, insightful, kind—a general force to be reckoned with.

Her own mother had often come home late after her Country Women's Association meetings, fuming about some clash of personality that she had endured. It was usually water under the bridge by the time the group next convened, besties again. However, heaven help the person who betrayed or belittled—that wrath was welded on and not easily removed.

When Ange visited to tell Ada that she was leaving town, Ada was delighted with her gift. 'I haven't had lemon syrup cake for years. I used to make it all the time. It's amazing how small things like this come in and out of your life. It will impress my bridge group no end to hear the story of how I came by their morning tea.' Ada fixed Ange in the eye. 'I presume you had something to do with that nasty business on Cronin Island. I have no time for those types.'

Ange stayed silent. While she had already abandoned any pretence of being a rogue or undercover cop, she was no blabbermouth. Ada was not so easily fooled. 'You know that someone or other will drift in on the breeze to take his place. We are on the Gold Coast, after all. Anyhow, you needn't look so surprised. I presumed you were a police officer from the outset. Something important, like an undercover detective, I suspect. Where's your next case?'

Ange didn't know where to go with that. She dodged and weaved, checking out her shoes as if they desperately needed attention. Ada just gave Ange a knowing smile. She was no fool, that woman. Ada joined Higgsy atop Ange's nice list.

Brett had a larger job ahead. Finch & Chang had pivoted beautifully, and an overseas gambling organization was on the verge of acquiring BeaBet. The transaction was due to settle in sixty days, and he would need to be on hand for that.

Ange had already abandoned any pretext of being a rogue or undercover cop. After her last meeting with Ada, she realised she wasn't particularly skilled at this dark art. She and Brett had fallen into a comfortable and relaxed relationship. Brett stayed over a couple of nights a week, at least. He seemed to sense that Ange needed breathing space. Perhaps he did as well. Ange appreciated him not moving in on her life as had sometimes happened in the past. He was also not a gushy type, which also suited her. Ange could think of nothing worse. She would get a puppy before another gushy man.

Higgsy had told Ange about a terrific surf spot up north called Agnes Waters, enabled by a gap in the Great Barrier Reef that allowed the swell emanating from the Coral Sea to reach the coastline. North of that, the Barrier Reef protected the coast from any swell. Southern reef shoals and K'Gari Island, formerly Fraser Island, shaded the mainland to the south. Ange unearthed a delightful-looking bungalow at Springs Beach, booking it impulsively and then convincing Brett to take a break and accompany her.

After a long and somewhat disinteresting drive, the pair felt that they might have discovered paradise. They surfed by day and made love each evening, choosing to eat in each night. Brett was quite a fisherman and caught some flathead from the beach or the rocks every other day. An unusual-looking fish, flathead seemed to like the coastline every bit as much as Ange. Using just a short fishing rod and something called a soft plastic, basically a bit of silicon on a hook, Brett amazed her with his skill. She nicknamed him the Flathead Whisperer. Ange tried her luck at his arcane art but failed dismally. It was still her favourite fish to eat, despite their elusiveness at her hand.

In between surfing and fishing, they explored the myriad of headlands and secluded sandy coves, stopping for a skinny dip when the sun became too intense and the coast was clear. They felt like hermit castaways on a desert coast. It was delightful. The surf was small in the main, but similarly deserted and thoroughly enjoyable, perfect for a relaxing break from their intense careers. While Ange found the waves well matched to her standard, Brett waxed lyrically about thundering surf experiences on past expeditions to Indonesia and places like the Mentawai Islands. Ange wondered if her skill would ever match such power.

They also spoke about their careers and what they wanted out of life from here on. Ange expressed excitement about her new job, even in the face of her recent failure. Brett confessed how much he had enjoyed rolling up his sleeves and building a business, as he had with BeaBet and dabbling with property development in Namba Heads. He was not about to quit his job immediately, but he planned to keep his eyes open and stay alert to any opportunities that may come his way.

As the week rolled by, Ange mulled over the sensation of having a man in her life once again. It had been quite a while since she could say that, and it was something that both thrilled and scared her. She worried sometimes that her life might have reached a point where she was incapable of having a relationship and sharing her life. Brett seemed to come from the same place, scars from his messy divorce still showing.

One afternoon, as they sat on a rocky headland looking out over the vast expanse of the Coral Sea, Ange realised she was happier and more contented than at almost any time in her life. Like the swell and current below, she resolved to let that feeling ride to see where it took her.

There remained, of course, the small matter of a bright red target on her back. Whoever was pulling the strings was in for a giant surprise if they thought Ange would turn a blind eye to this scandal. There was work to be done.

Read Snaked—The final instalment of
The Saltwater Crimes trilogy

Does Ange have what it takes to bring the shadowy criminal syndicate to justice?
What price will she be forced to pay?

Scan or click here to purchase Snaked on Amazon:
https://www.pg-robertson.com/snaked

Scan or click here to join the author's mailing list and stay alert to new
releases and the latest news:
www.pg-robertson.com

 facebook.com/profile.php?id=100090607141784

 instagram.com/petergrobertson/

 amazon.com/stores/P-G-Robertson/author/B0BY4B55VP?ref=ap_rdr&store_re
f=ap_rdr&isDramIntegrated=true&shoppingPortalEnabled=true

Now read the beginning of Snaked...

As far as assignments went, this was one of the easiest ever—also one of the most pleasurable. Previous jobs had caused some difficult moments, but he had no option but to take those calls and complete his tasks, no matter how distasteful. Today was an exception. What could be better than a trip to Bondi Beach, enjoying the sights of a sparkling Sunday morning?

Between transit cards and phone pings, it had been childishly easy to follow the woman. For those that had the means and knew where to look, privacy was a delusion of yesteryear. He spied her walking from the surf and zoomed in for a better look. She wrapped a bright yellow leg rope around the tail of her board before walking slowly up the beach with the confidence of someone comfortable with herself. Even from this distance, she cut an impressive figure, the type of figure that came with care and constant activity. He watched voyeuristically as she struggled to change, using a large multicoloured beach towel as cover, a tough move, as Australian as a day at the beach itself.

The man tore his eyes away from the woman to check on his beautiful iridescent riviera-blue BMW coupe, blatantly parked in a loading zone. He was unsure which of the two was more beautiful. His boss, or bosses—he was never entirely sure of that point—would probably not be happy about his expensive glistening phallic symbol. He was supposed to blend in and stay under the radar, although he would take care to indulge himself only on weekends. However, this was the perfect situation to explain away his extravagance. Such machines as his were a dime a dozen in the rarefied sea air of Sydney's Eastern Suburbs. If called to task, he would argue that he *was* blending in—at least today.

He noticed a parking inspector a hundred metres away and walking purposefully towards his illegally parked car. The man was not worried, and he amused himself for a few minutes as the inspector punched his number plate into her handheld revenue earner. She looked up sharply and frowned before she moved on empty-handed, as he had known she would. The man had made sure of that. The casual observer would assume that the car was owned by some VIP with the council in his pocket. After the recent series of highly publicised exposés into council corruption, each shamelessly leaked by the state's anti-corruption watchdog, no other conclusion made sense.

The man looked back towards the object of this Sunday excursion, now collecting her things and making her leisurely way off the beach and up onto the grassy foreshore. It was time for him to go as well. He had what he'd come for. Glancing from the corner of his eye to see if anyone was watching, he popped the engine of his beauty into action. The crackle and rasp of the sports exhaust made his neck tingle. A few heads snapped around for an instant, mostly men, unfortunately, before they turned back to sipping their lattes.

Back in his apartment, the man put on some latex gloves and printed out the series of photographs he had taken. He soon picked out a favourite, a closeup of impressive clarity. She was one fine-looking woman, that was for sure, the type of women he had imagined sitting in the passenger seat of his BMW as they wove through the hills on their way to his weekend getaway, the one with impressive views over vineyards and golf courses. His groin stirred impulsively as he thought about what they might do each evening, winding down after their days of indulgence.

In his heart of hearts, the man knew that these fantasies would never happen. Tomorrow, after his task was complete, he would stash his flash new car and crawl back under his cover, dissolving back into an otherwise bland and unremarkable existence. It was a genuine pity, but mostly for the woman. In his experience, once his boss, or bosses, had someone in their sights, they rarely turned away.

 If you would like to continue reading Snaked, scan the QR Code, or visit:

https://www.pg-robertson.com/snaked

Also By...

Head back to where the story started and read **Tombstoning**, the first installment of The Saltwater Crimes trilogy.

Scan or click here to learn more about Tombstoning:

https://www.pg-robertson.com/tombstoning

facebook.com/profile.php?id=100090607141784

instagram.com/petergrobertson/

amazon.com/stores/P-G-Robertson/author/B0BY4B55VP?ref=ap_rdr&store_re
f=ap_rdr&isDramIntegrated=true&shoppingPortalEnabled=true

Author's Note

The characters in this book are entirely fictional. I have created them from good friends, work colleagues, acquaintances, strangers I've encountered, some people that I've met in the surf, and others that are purely imaginary. Even though the storyline is purely fictional, personal experiences and events have influenced many of the situations and ideas that support the plot. Likewise, except for any household names, the companies and enterprises that underpin the plot are figments of my imagination and similarly fictitious.

My heroine, Detective Ange Watson, is a mixture of friends, some who surf and some who do not. I hope you like Ange as much as I like my friends.

The Gold Coast, Surfers Paradise, Byron Bay and Brisbane are real places, as are the fabled Gold Coast surf spots that form the backdrop to GlitterStrip. Namba Heads is an imaginary town that is based on the many small coastal villages of the Northern Rivers region in New South Wales, Australia. I hope my writing has done justice to these spectacular places.

Much of the story is set on the traditional lands of the Bundjalung Nation, which extend from Yamba in northern New South Wales up into southern Queensland, a region much loved by most Australians. I acknowledge the Bundjalung people, who are the traditional custodians of this magnificent place, and pay respects to the Elders, past, present and emerging of the Bundjalung Nation.

So Many to Thank

Massive thanks are due to you, the reader, for having read GlitterStrip. I hope you are immersed in the story and ready for Snaked, the final installment of The Saltwater Crimes trilogy. The fact that you have persevered to read my books is incredibly gratifying.

Of utmost importance, is the need to thank all those who gave me the encouragement to push on with the series and write GlitterStrip. I probably should list you all individually, but the list is long and I risk missing someone important! Hopefully, I have already told you in person how much your input has meant to me. I cannot thank you all enough.

The Island Book Club deserves a special mention. I will forever remember the scene of our inaugural book club meeting, sitting in our camp chairs on the beach one glorious afternoon, champagne in hand and laughter in our hearts.

I am also grateful for my 'media team', Annabel Robertson, Sophie Robertson, and Ben Hall, whose skills and comfort with new media amaze me. I must also thank my editor, Eliza Dee, and my cover designer, Karri Klawiter, for their dedication and forbearance in enduring my many rookie errors.

Finally, if you have a spare minute, I would appreciate you posting a review of GlitterStrip on Amazon via your purchase history.

Surfing Terminology

A brief description of some of the surfing terminology that I have used throughout The Saltwater Crimes series follows:

'Tombstoning' occurs when a surfer is held under the water by a wave following a heavy wipeout. Whilst the surfer is being dragged deep beneath the water, their surfboard is straining on the surface, connected as they are by a fully stretched leg rope. An obvious metaphor for a perilous situation, tombstoning is never a good sign and rarely fun for the surfer, although bystanders or fellow surfers will invariably find it all most amusing after the fact.

A **'left-hander'** is a wave that breaks to the surfer's left. That is, as the surfer catches the wave, he or she will turn to the left. Obviously, a **'right-hander'** breaks to the surfer's right.

A **'goofy-footer'** is someone who surfs with the right foot forward, and a **'natural'** is someone who leads with their left foot. The decision to choose one side or another is instinctual and set for life.

Surfing **'forehand'** indicates that a surfer is facing the wave face, **'backhand'** is the reverse. Most surfers find surfing forehand easier, particularly in steep demanding waves. Hence, a 'right-hander' favours a 'natural', and a 'left-hander' best suits their 'goofy-footed' cousins.

The **'line-up'** is the term used for the queuing area where the waves start breaking.

The **'peak'** of a wave is a term commonly used for beach breaks. It defines the apex of the wave face. Once perfectly positioned at the 'peak' of a wave, a surfer can choose to go left or right. The other descriptor for perfect beach breaks is 'A-frames', but these dreamy situations are disappointingly rare.

A **'rip'** is where seawater, carried in by the crashing waves, combines into a channel and rushes back out to sea. Dangerous for swimmers, they can be a godsend for surfers to help ease a long and tiring paddle.

Being **'inside'** means the surfer is the one closest to the breaking point of the wave, which is the surfer who is farthest inside on the line-up. On a headland or reef break, this would be closest to the rocks or reef, and inevitably the most ambitious take-off point. The surfer sitting farthest 'inside' technically has a right of way, a case of fortune favouring the brave. It does not always work that way, with **'drop-ins'** being the scourge of surfers around the world, usually spoiling the wave and often dangerous to all concerned.

Jostling for the premier position at the take-off zone is part strategy, part bravado, and part aggression. Called **'hassling'**, this can easily spiral out of control, and fights in and out of the surf are not uncommon in crowded surf breaks, and where localism is rife. **'Dropping in'** on an aggressive local will usually end badly. The old way to surf was to take turns. As the 'inside' surfer departed on their wave, the next would slide across and assume the vacated spot in the line-up, gaining rights to the next wave, and so on. This type of surf etiquette is now relegated to isolated or sparsely populated breaks.

A **'grommet'** is surfer slang for a young school-aged surfer, a term usually reserved for those with talent, their lightness, speed, and flexibility sometimes grating on the older surfers around them.

The **'rail'** on a surfboard is the outside edge, the shape and taper of which are critical in how a board performs.

The **'rocker'** of a surfboard describes how the nose turns up. Boards made with a pronounced rocker are more forgiving when tackling powerful, steep waves. Boards fashioned with minimal rocker make catching smaller and fuller waves easier, but are prone to nosedives during steep or late take-offs—but this might be my age talking.

'Longboards' and **'shortboards'** create quite different surfing styles and favour different wave formations. Longboards typically range from eight to eleven feet, or 2.5 to 3.3 metres. Shortboards are under seven feet, or 2.1 metres. The weight of a surfer will often dictate the type of board they choose, and the division between a longboard and a shortboard has blurred over time.

The number of fins on a board varies depending on the style of board. **'Single fins'** are mostly reserved for longboards or surfers wanting a traditional style. The original surfboards were all single fins. **'Twin fins'** are highly manoeuvrable, usually earmarked for small wave boards. A **'thruster'** sports three fins and is the most popular and versatile configuration for shortboards. **'Quads'** have four fins and sit somewhere between a twin fin and a thruster in terms of functionality.

A **'quiver'** is simply a collection of surfboards used by a surfer, as in a 'quiver of arrows' used by an archer.

Finally, a **'tube ride'** is when the surfer positions themselves within the curl of the wave, precariously covered over by the breaking lip, but remaining relatively untouched within the eye of the storm—so to speak. It's the most exhilarating of all surf manoeuvres, and waves that are 'tubing' are highly prized, yet relatively rare. Surf spots that regularly produce tube rides are usually very popular, difficult to travel to, or jealously guarded secrets.

Australian-isms

For the benefit of non-Australian readers, below is a short explanation of some idioms that I have used on occasion.

'Back of Woop Woop'. Far away from everywhere and anywhere. Beyond the black stump is another synonym.

'Bad egg'. Someone who is rotten to the core.

'Berko'. Going crazy mad, angry and out of control. The Tasmanian devil goes berko if cornered while eating their dinner.

'Buggered, stuffed, screwed, rooted'—you get the drift.

'Bushie'. Someone who lives in the country, most commonly on a rural farm/property/station, and well away from any major towns or cities. In general terms, one's degree of 'bushie-ness' is also directly proportional to the distance one lives from the coast.

'Curly request or question'. Refers to a difficult request or loaded question.

'Deckie'. A shortened name given to the deckhand working on a fishing trawler.

'Feeling crook'. Feeling sick or unwell.

'Firey'. Slang for firefighter.

'Larrikin'. Part rogue, part joker. The sort of person to enjoy a beer at the pub with, but not someone to risk with the family jewels. Larrikin is often used to describe the affable kookaburra, one of the coolest and most personable birds in Australia, also a ruthless killer of small birds and animals.

'Nong'. An idiot or fool, a term used endearingly and in jest toward a friend or loved one.

'A park'. A park can refer to either a park with grass and trees, or a single parking place for a car. Go figure!

'Roached'. Has its roots from the word cockroach. Being roached normally refers to the situation where someone has scuttled behind your back to do no good.

'Rort'. Another word for scam or con.

'Seachange & Greenchange'. Seachangers leave their lives in the city and move to the coast. Greenchangers move to the country.

'Spit the dummy'. A dummy, in Australian vernacular, is also known as a pacifier. When a baby is about to throw a tantrum, their face with turn sour, before they spit out their dummy and go berko. It's a wonderfully descriptive phrase—part facial expression, part change of mood, part warning for the carnage about to be unleashed.

'Stunned mullet'. Refers to someone who is in a form of temporary shock. An actual stunned mullet will be floating helplessly on the surface and unable to swim away.